Beyond The Veil

Beyond The Veil

Ronald Bagliere

To the ancient indigenous tribes of the Amazon. May they live long and prosper, unabated and undefiled.

Prologue

June 6th, 2012 – 3° 59' 57" S Latitude, 67° 11' 33" W Longitude, 100 kilometers southeast of Santo Antonio do Içá, Amazonas, Brazil

MORNING SUNLIGHT trickled down through the forest canopy, spraying golden beams on the thick dappled mats of silver fern. At length, Mahl came to a grinding halt and breathed deeply of the humid, damp air. He would be home soon. Already, he could smell the scent of water. Capuchin monkeys chattered in the spidery branches above. Reaching out, he broke off a slender branch and ripped the outer bark away with his teeth. As he chewed the sweet inner cambium amid the incessant whine of insects, he surveyed the dense forest.

A minute later, he tossed the branch aside, re-slung his bow over his dark shoulder and struck off into the waving sea of green with the black tail of his talisman head dressing flapping in the wind. From here on, the trail ran under the thick green vegetation and he would need to rely on his memory on where to place each step. One wrong placement could mean a broken leg or worse yet, death, in one of the many gaping holes strewn out over the ragged landscape.

After several hundred meters, the landscape leveled out, and in the distance a stream could be heard trickling around rocky outcroppings. Once he came across it, the trail would veer downward toward his village. He hurried toward the stream, and just as he was about step into it, heard strange voices. His heart thudded, and he crept silently into the dense thicket of heliconia with arrow drawn. Whoever they were, they were not Manaqüi, from whom his people had hid unseen since the days of old.

Anxiously he waited, peering through the veil of sword shaped broad-leafs at the forest ahead. As the voices grew louder, he considered his next move. The path leading to his village had to be protected at all costs, but he was only one man against how many? He didn't know. The sound of thumping feet on the soft brown earth drew nearer until at last he saw three men dressed in strange white skins. Who they were and why they were here, he didn't know, only that they were threatening his home. The arrow strung on his bow twitched. Slowly, he lifted the weapon, aimed it at the lead man, and let the arrow fly.

An instant later, a grunt was followed by cries. He quickly fitted another arrow to his bow and aimed it, then stopped when he saw a man draw out long, menacing blade from behind his back. But he stayed where he was, and after much chattering between the other men, he dragged their fallen leader off.

Once Mahl was satisfied they weren't coming back, he slipped his bow back over his shoulder and fled down the steep, sloping path toward home. But deep inside, he was scared. The world was changing beyond his tribe's shrouded borders.

June 6th, 2012 – University of California, Berkley, Kroeber Hall

Claire El-Badawy scrolled down her computer calendar. She had a Lyceum lecture at 1:00 PM, her A330 class at 3:00 PM, and an interview to conduct in twenty minutes, not to mention dinner with Jason. Turning around in her swivel office chair, she peered through the window of her second-floor office, thinking about the grant for the expedition to Brazil. After the huge disaster in Guatemala, she was taking an enormous career risk searching for a lost bushman of the Amazon. The department would only suffer one mistake before showing you the door. But if this lost man turned out to be what she hoped he was, her prestige would skyrocket. As she considered her future, a knock on her open door startled her. She spun around and found herself looking into the bluest eyes she'd ever seen.

"Hi, I'm Owen," the man said, walking in. He extended his hand, and as they shook, went on, "We talked a couple weeks ago 'bout my showing ya 'round da forest. Am I too early?"

Claire took in the rugged Aucklander's long booted legs, faded jeans, and crisp, white button-down shirt; its top two buttons were undone.

"No, have a seat," Claire said, collecting her thoughts. "Can I get you something to drink?"

He crammed his long, lean body into the chair in front of her desk. "Nah, I'm good as gold. Quite da campus ya got here. I almost got lost."

Claire took her seat behind her desk and tried to relax. "Should I be worrying?" she said.

"Bout what?"

"You getting lost," Claire said, noticing the faded scar above Owen's brow.

"Nah. Da forest an' I do fine. It's da 'big smokes' that get me turned around. Too many roads."

"Yes, me too," Claire said, not quite understanding the term, "big smokes". She guessed he meant cities. "So, how'd an Aucklander end up in Peru?"

"Westhaven, actually, north of da big town, out in the wops." Owen handed her an envelope and sat back looking her over. "My pop studied fish on da river when I was a tyke, so I grew up on it, so ta speak, yeah."

"Wops?" Claire said, opening the envelope and glancing down at his credentials.

"Yeah, ya know, boonies," he said. "I think ya find everything in order there."

Claire nodded as she read down the list of past treks he led. The resume wasn't exactly what she was expecting, but then, she wasn't looking for flash. "Must have been interesting growing up on the river."

Owen shrugged. "It was alright. Not all it's cracked up ta be. Lots a nasty critters down there – say nothing bout yella fever."

"And malaria," Claire added. I'm not a tourist, Mr. Macleod. "I take it you were sick?"

Owen's expression tightened at the mention of the malaria. "Nah. Just a run-in with an aranhas armadeiras."

Oh, we are trying to impress. I'll give you the benefit of a doubt. "A banana spider? You should be dead."

"Yeah, yeah. For a while, I wished I was. So, why ya wanna find this Lost Man?"

"To learn about his people before it's too late," she said folding up his resume and tucking it back into the envelope.

"What if he don't wanna be found? Big forest down there."

"Are you saying you can't find him?"

"Nah, not at all," Owen replied. He crossed his legs and shifted awkwardly in his chair. "Might take time. T'aint easy finding someone don't wanna be found; that and where we're going ain't a walk in da park. Manaqüi don't take kindly ta people tramping in their back yard."

"Well, we have four months, Mr. Macleod, so either you can or you can't," Claire said, handing him back the envelope.

"Ah now, no need ta be so formal. Call me Owen, and no worries. We'll find 'im."

Claire smiled. *You're smooth. Too smooth maybe. I bet you'd tell me you could find Nessie if you thought it'd get you the job. Except, you come highly recommended.* "Where you staying?"

"Cross town."

Claire looked at her watch. It was almost noon. "You hungry?"

Owen shrugged. "Wouldn't mind a round of shark and taters."

"Right ... I don't know if we have shark."

Owen laughed. "Not shark. Fish."

"Oh, like fish and chips."

"Yeah, yeah."

Claire tried to think if the cafeteria offered fish. It was Friday. "Let's see if we have shark and taters then. Unfortunately, I have a lecture at one, but if you want, I can have my RA give you the nickel tour."

Owen smiled. "Sure, why not? Got no place ta be."

One

Amazonas
December 10th, 2012, Lima, Peru

OWEN OPENED the door to the company apartment and dropped his backpack beside the couch. Exhausted from the trans-Pacific flight, he rubbed his neck and shuffled to the sliding glass door. Pulling back the screen, he let the sound of rush hour traffic six floors below filter into the room. After a minute of looking out over the hazy coastline, he headed to the bathroom and splashed water on his face.

The mirror over the vanity reflected eyes in need of sleep. But it'd have to wait until he checked email: that, and removing his large banana spider from the shower's soap shelf. The furry critter had escaped his terrarium again and taken up residence there. He snatched the arachnid between finger and thumb, sending its long legs into a wriggling frenzy.

"Calm down, Shelob," He muttered. "We'll have ya home 'fore ya know it," He walked to the kitchen and popped him back into his glass home.

"Now, hopefully," he said to Shelob, "Robbie left me some coca tea." He felt around cans of vegetables and boxes of dry goods until he found a canister. Shaking it next to his ear, he smiled as the spider pawed the pane of its terrarium. "Good boy, Rob," he said, and set a kettle of water on to boil. Fifteen minutes later, he sat on the deck overlooking the street below sipping tea with the laptop open on his lap.

Booting it up, he saw a dozen emails. Clicking the one named, Claire El-Badawy Itinerary, he scrolled down the page.

As he read the flight information, the memory of his conversation with the cultural anthropologist popped into his head. He smiled, thinking of the tall, silky brunette with flashing blue eyes. She had a killer smile and a pair of legs that wouldn't quit. His body stirred as the memory of her flashed before him. But, what really grabbed him was her sharp, challenging and feisty mind. He liked intelligence in a woman.

A taxi below blew its horn, and the memory ran away. Cracking his knuckles, he pulled a candy bar out of his shirt pocket and peeled the wrapper back. As he bit into it, he opened a file he'd downloaded a while back. The screen page opened to a photo of a stepped pyramid. "That's one wild theory, Luv," he muttered, tilting his head. He stretched and scrolled down the page to her picture. "You sure are one put-together package, I'll give ya that. Just keep ya pretty little nose outta my business and we'll get along just fine."

December 10th, 2012, San Francisco, California

Hot showers always refocused Claire when bad shit happened. She turned the hot water up another notch and gritted her teeth. Since her fiancé, Jason, decided his career was more important than hers three weeks ago she had been trying to forget him. But it wasn't easy. She scrubbed her hair as his ultimatum played over in her head. Of all the times to draw the line in the sand, he had to pick twenty days before the Project started. She felt her throat tighten. Screw it! CBS and New York can have him. I need to call Thad.

She stepped out of the shower, toweled off, and marched into the closet. In the corner, sat a new tan duffle bag. Next to it, stood her Zamber boots and a dozen pair of 150 thread ultra-light hiking socks. She eyed them as she pulled a pair of nylons on, wondering if the duffle bag was big enough for all the gear she'd need for the expedition.

Twenty minutes later, she pulled her Volvo out onto the arterial, and after stopping at Double D's to get her regular morning bagel, turned the radio on to listen to the morning news. As she settled in for the hour-long commute, her blackberry buzzed. Setting her breakfast bagel on the passenger seat, she dug into her purse and pulled out her PDA. Thad's number showed on the screen.

Thaddeus Popalothis, or Poppy as he was known on campus, was her research assistant.

"Hey, what's up?" she said.

"You on the 880?"

"Just getting on."

"Well, you might want to get off at Artesia and hook up with the 680. Tractor-trailer jackknifed at Exit 120. It's a mess."

"Shit. Okay." She tapped her finger on the steering wheel as five lanes of traffic began slowing down. "You hear anything more from this guy, Owen?"

"Yeah, he emailed back. We're all set. He'll meet us at the airport," Thad said. He cleared his throat and his voice dropped down. "There's something else."

"What?" Claire said, bracing herself. When Thad's voice dropped, trouble lurked.

"Noah's rethinking my going to Brazil with you."

Claire blinked. *What is it with fucking Noah? He just can't let go of shit.* She collected her nerve, and with a level controlled tone, said, "Don't worry, Poppy. I'll take care of Noah."

"But he's department chair."

"Yeah, I know. Don't worry about it, okay?"

A long pause ensued on the other end. Finally, Thad said, "Okay. And if he doesn't change his mind?"

"He'll change it," Claire said exiting onto the 680. Oh, shit, a cop. She glanced at the needle touching 80. Wonderful. "Got to go. Bye."

Claire threw her office door open and set her purse on her credenza. Her desk was in disarray. Files piled up four and five deep. Post-its with phone numbers and to-dos were stuck all over her computer. Beside the screen, stood a framed photo of her parents. Tucked in the corner of it was a small, faded wallet shot of her grandmother. She cleared a stack of mail from her chair, sat, and checked email. As usual, a long list stared back. She triaged a few, shot off some replies, then quickly reviewed her day's schedule while debating if she should phone Noah. *No. Better to deal with him face to face. Problem is, I have class in thirty minutes.* Tapping her nails on the desk, she heard a knock on her open door.

Looking up, she saw Thad leaning against the frame with his arms folded across his chest. Tall, with jet-black curly hair that framed a Mediterranean olive complexion, Poppy was quite popular with the young ladies on campus.

"Oh, there you are. I need to see Noah, but I have class in–" she looked down at her watch, "–twenty minutes." She dug the lesson folder out of her bag. "Would you mind filling in for me?"

He stepped up to her desk and took it from her. "Well, I'm not really prepared, but okay."

"Thanks."

Thad nodded. Then cleared his throat. "Hey, just so you know, don't go nuts trying to change his mind. I'll be all right. Really. I mean, don't take me wrong, I wanna go–who wouldn't? But I don't want to be shoved down his throat. He can really fuck with me, Claire."

Claire studied Thad's long, angular face, feeling his guarded concern. She knew he was right. Noah could really do a number on Thad come dissertation time. "Don't worry. I know how to handle Noah."

The walk from her office in Kroeber Hall to the other end where the Department Chair ran things gave Claire some time to plan how she might twist the silver-haired Scotsman around her finger. She saw Noah no differently than she saw the rest of the men in the department. He was self-centered, arrogant, and stubborn. Unlike the rest of the men in the department, Noah was her ex-husband, and therein lay her advantage or disadvantage. She took a deep breath as she came to his office suite and opened the door.

"Hi, Claire. Can I help you?" the admin assistant said, looking up from her typing.

"Noah busy, Maggie? I need to see him."

"He's on the phone. Anything I can do for you?"

"Don't think so," Claire said, eyeing Noah through his open door. "I'll wait."

"Coffee?"

Claire shook her head.

Maggie got up and joined Claire. "You hear about that horrible accident on 880 this morning?"

"Yeah, tractor trailer and a bus? Oh, he's off," Claire said. "Sorry, I need to catch him before he skates."

As Claire stepped into Noah's office, he swiveled around in his chair.

"Well, hullo, Claire," he said, pushing his wire-rimmed glasses up over his forehead. "I wondered how long it'd take before I saw your face in here."

Claire crossed her arms and eyed him. "What are you doing?"

"Doing?"

"Yes. My project? You're screwing with it. Why?"

Noah leaned forward. "No class today?"

Claire smiled. "Thad's filling in."

"I see. Well, to answer your question, I'm looking out for the college's interests. Thad's an excellent grad student, but you need someone who knows his way around down there, don't you think?"

"Thad can hold his own," Claire said.

"I'm sure he can," Noah replied as he met her challenging gaze with one of his own.

"So, I suppose you have someone in mind?" Claire said.

"As a matter of fact, I do."

"And that would be?" Claire said as Noah's gaze slipped over her blouse and down her skirt.

"Name's, Jorge, Micheal's boy."

"Jorge? Are you kidding me? He knows nothing about my project!"

"He is, however, a native Brazilian who knows how things work down there. Need I remind you, the only reason you got funding for this folly of yours is because I put my ass on the line for it."

"I'm well aware of that," Claire growled.

"And make sure if you find this lost man, which you have as much chance of doing as finding canopic jars in a stepped pyramid, that you remember you're there to observe only. No contact."

Claire forced a smile. "Why is it you can't find it in your tiny little pea brain to question why they found cocaine in the Pyramid of Giza?"

"That's all anecdotal, but hey it's your career. If you want to flush it down the toilet, be my guest. Anyway, it seems a moot point. You have your grant."

"Yes, I do," Claire replied.

"However," Noah said, "It's my job to see it doesn't end up in a waste basket."

Claire leaned forward. "Then leave it alone. Look, we both know what this is all about. You're still trying to control me."

Noah laughed. "Oh please, what makes you think I'd spend one second of my precious time with screwing you? Believe me, I have better things to do."

"Right, but you certainly liked screwing me a few years ago, didn't you? Better be careful with Maggie. I've seen how she looks at you. The newest Mrs. Henderson might not like it."

"What are you talking about?" Noah snapped back. His face reddened as he furrowed his brow.

"You know exactly what I'm talking about." Claire let him sit with that a moment then went on. "Noah, dear, if there's one thing you're not very good at, it's keeping your pecker in your pants."

"Are you threatening me?"

Claire almost burst out laughing. "Honey, I don't have to make threats, you self-implode without any help from me."

Noah studied her with talon-like eyes. "Might I remind you, I'm Department Chair here, so unless you want to be standing in front of glassy eyed freshmen all day for the foreseeable future, mind your manners. By the way, how's Jason these days?"

Claire's eyes widened, and she fought to keep from blowing up. Through tight lips, she hissed, "Jason has taken a job in New York."

"I heard. Long commute, don't you think?"

"It's what they make planes for," Claire said, with her best fuck-you grin. "So, back to Thad."

"Yes, back to Thad," Noah said averting his gaze out the window. "Smart kid, but I'm not sure he's your best choice. Did you know Jorge speaks several tribal languages? Can Thad say the same?"

Claire considered her ex-husband's loaded question. This was the one area Poppy did not excel in, and to be truthful, it bothered her. But his involvement with her work trumped that deficiency. She said, "He holds his own."

Noah steepled his fingers. "Really? In what, besides a dalliance in ancient Egyptian, unless you plan on running into some pharaoh?"

"He speaks Quechua, and some Ayaya," Claire fired back, ignoring Noah's sarcasm.

Noah cocked an eye. "Fluently?"

Claire paused and thought about her answer. She wanted to be careful not to say the wrong thing. Noah grinned, and obviously taking her silence as a 'no', said, "What I thought. Tell me, what is it about this RA you're so hot on bringing with you. Are you fucking him?"

Claire closed her eyes and balled her fists. "You asshole! Why am I wasting my time here?"

"I don't know, why are you? Unless perhaps, you thought you could manipulate me. You were good at that once, you know. Sit down."

"Fuck you!"

"Sit down!" Noah snapped. He locked his eyes on her like a tomcat sizing up a mouse. Finally, he said, "Let's cut the crap. This is more than just a goddamned grant here. A niece I'm very fond of is involved and I'm going to make damned sure she comes back in one piece."

He pushed his glasses back down onto his Romanesque nose and looked off through his window. "You need more experience down there."

"I've run expeditions before."

"Yes, yes, I know – Togo," he said, looking back at her. He shook his head. "Look, this isn't some little dirt village on the west coast of Africa. It's the damned Amazon!"

"I know that," she spat back.

Noah shook his head. "No, you don't!"

"And you do? I wasn't aware you'd ever been there."

"A long time ago, yes."

Claire was taken aback. "You never told me that."

Noah stared at her, and for a moment she saw a pained expression on his face. "It's hard to talk about."

Now it was Claire's turn to lean forward. "We were married for five years, and I'm just finding this out now?"

"It was personal and if you'll shut up a minute I'll tell you why." He paused. "Twenty-five years ago, my brother and I received a NSF grant to research some of the indigenous tribes."

"Really?" Claire said.

Noah cleared his throat and frowned. "As I was saying, my brother led a small team of men into the forest one morning while I stayed back to mind camp. It was just a short day trip, reconnaissance and collecting data. He was supposed to be back by dinner, but he and his team never returned. A week later, we found him and his boys. They were skewered alive and left on long bamboo poles: a warning to stay out of where they didn't belong. They'd crossed some hidden boundary. We got them down and ran the hell out of there. Am I making myself understood?"

Claire was dumbstruck. She knew Noah had lost a brother, but never knew how. Though she'd asked about it many times, he wouldn't speak of it, nor would his sister. Noah went on, "You have no idea what you're going into Claire and I've tried to keep my mitts out of it.

But you need someone who knows his shit down there. And who's this guide, Owen Macleod? I hear he leads tourist treks? Christ, woman!"

"True, but he's spent a good deal of his life right in the backyard of where we're going," Claire said, still trying to wrap her head around Noah's revelation.

"Yes, I looked into it once I found out. But you need a guide. Living there might have only taken him a few kilometers into the forest. You're going deep into that world. And can I ask you why you're going through Peru to get there?"

You never stop! "Because that's where his company operates out of. And his references are excellent."

Noah sat with that a moment then said, "Well, I do see your point about his living there being worthy. But a tourist guide? Really?"

"He's multi-lingual and fluent in most of them, not to mention a naturalist with a BA in Forestry and Land Management. He knows the river. He knows the people," Claire said. She looked at her ex-husband with fresh eyes. "Noah, we'll be okay."

"Hmmm ... And Molly?"

"I'll guard her with my life."

"See to it and you better bring her back alive." He took his glasses off and looked at her hard. "I know you don't like me after what happened between us. Few people do now-a-days it seems. Tell you the truth: I don't really care. What I do care about is people getting hurt or worse yet, killed, on my watch – especially family and talented professors."

Claire looked at him agape and against her will, felt a twinge in her heart for the man. "Thanks," and added, "And like I said, I'll look out for Molly, don't you worry."

"You do that. We done?"

Claire got up, fighting the urge to thank the man she had come to despise over the last five years. "I expect so."

Two

OWEN TOWELED the scattered daubs of shaving cream from his face. He had slept dreamlessly for a change and that he prized. The nightmares of his past rarely left him alone since his son died years ago. He stared at the man in the mirror. A faded scar across his hip peeked over his boxers. It was a gift from a jaguar three years ago during one of his tramps to supply one of the many Manaqüi splinter tribes with weapons against a Brazilian copper conglomerate. Even now, the ragged wound still pained him. The Jadatani medicine man said the great cat had marked him for its own. The recurring visions of the black hunter of the forest only confirmed it.

He ran a tooth brush over his teeth, then stepped into his closet and pulled a pair of khakis from the hanger.

An hour later, he walked up Circuito de Playas under a bright blue sky. He liked walking, the feeling of melting into his surroundings. The smoky aroma of La Patarashca wafted in the air. Salsa melodies floated out from the upper windows.

He grabbed a butifarras from the café and found a bench across the street. As he ate, he listened to the thwapping waves of the shrouded ocean and the cries of sea birds. He thought about the expedition, the long haul up the river into uncertain waters. It had been a long time since he had gone so deep into the bush.

Ten minutes later, he sat in the back seat of a cranky yellow taxi sipping yacón tea from a Styrofoam cup as the driver wove in and around traffic. It had started to rain and tiny drops were pelting his window. The taxi turned left, then right, and motored through the maze of cobblestone streets until at last it came to an old brick building. A sign read, 'Amazon River Tours' over the door. The driver pulled through an open gate and crossed a rutted gravel lot dotted with puddles.

As the taxi splashed along, Owen eyed the ratty, chain-link fence battling cacti and pink cinchona, wondering where all the money the tour company took in went. He drained the last of his tea and directed the cabbie toward an open overhead door leading into a large corrugated metal-sided warehouse. As the taxi pulled up in front and stopped, Owen dug into his pocket for the agreed-upon fare, handed it to the driver, and got out.

Ducking inside, he was met by his long time tramping partner, Manny Ortava. "Você está atrasado," he said in Portuguese, wrinkling his leathered, bronzed face. He pulled his work gloves off and dragged a small hand-made cigar from his gaucho's pocket.

Owen shrugged. "Overslept."

Manny cocked an eyebrow and struck a match. "Good flight?" he said, breaking into English.

Owen tossed his empty cup in the garbage can. "Sucked. How's Loretta?"

"Very good," Manny said.

"I was plenty worried 'bout her, yeah. What with her pneumonia and all."

Manny wedged the cigar into the corner of his mouth. "Ah, si, she was very sick, but now is all better. And you?"

"I'm all right. And da crianças?"

Manny smiled. "They are very well."

"An' Ernesto?"

Manny sighed and put his work gloves back on. "Same. He still has his head in the clouds. All he see is the big money he make at the mine. I keep telling him, go to school; learn something. But he does not hear me. He is more interested in meninas. Oh, well, what can I do?"

Owen shrugged. "Not much, I expect. Lads 'ill be lads. They like their chicas fast an' furious."

"Like a certain Kiwi I know," Manny said, then shut his mouth when he saw Jack Burgess coming toward them. He shot Owen a knowing glance, furrowed his brow and walked away as the boss walked up.

"Hey, you ready for this?" Jack said, nodding toward the pile of gear on the warehouse floor. Translated: 'Don't fuck this gig up'.

Owen pulled a chocolate bar from his shirt pocket, tore the wrapper off. Biting into it, he narrowed his gaze on the man. "Morning, Jack. How's tricks?" Translated back: 'Kiss my ass'.

"Cut the shite," Jack snarled.

They faced off like a pair of tomcats: Owen in his tan khakis, a faded T-shirt and frumpy jandals against the wiry Kiwi's three-piece suit and leather loafers. Jack pointed to the pile of canvas bags on the pallet. "You really need all this shite?"

Owen took another bite of his candy bar, looked off into the shadowed warehouse. "Yeah, I think I do."

Jack didn't say anything for a moment but Owen knew the man resented him. Most likely, it was because of the respect and camaraderie he enjoyed with co-workers and patrons alike. Finally, Jack said, "You know, I don't see what my pop ever saw in you."

"Well, ya not your pop, are ya?" Owen said. He stared back at the man, waiting for him to pick a fight - not that Jack would against a man head and shoulders taller than himself.

"No, I'm not," Jack growled and tightened his jaw. "But I run this show, if you follow me,"

"Yeah, I think I do," Owen replied in a level tone. "'Cept I bring da business in, mate."

Jack bristled. "Is that what you think?"

"It's what I know," Owen said, and after he said it, realized how angry he really felt. But the anger went beyond Jack to something he couldn't put his finger on. He took a deep breath. "Look, just leave it alone, okay?"

Jack reached into his pocket and pulled a pack of cigarettes out. "You know what your problem is?"

"No, what's that?" Owen said, looking toward the rear of the warehouse. Owen heard the lighter click, then the sound of a long exhale.

"You're an arrogant son-of-a-bitch who probably hasn't been banged in a month of Sundays."

Owen almost broke out laughing. "Yeah, yeah, Jack. I'm sure a nice piece would straighten me right out. Now if ya don't mind, I've got work ta do, eh?"

"Yeah. And, mate…"

"What's that?" Owen said.

Jack butted his cigarette under his shoe. "Try to keep your paws off that pretty college professor. Your wit falls flat on its arse with the highly educated." He turned and as he walked away, Owen flipped him the middle finger.

December 12th, 2012, San Francisco

Claire threw the rest of her salad together for dinner, thinking about what Noah had said. Why had he divulged the secret of his brother's death now, unless he still cared about her? She shook her head, turned up Alanis Morissette's, You Ought'a Know on the CD player and took a sip of her wine.

Since Jason left, Alanis's hard driving lyrics had become Claire's mantra. But things were looking up now. Soon, she would be heading down to the Amazon, and if everything worked out the way she hoped, she would be on top of the world. She eyed the framed photo of the gray wolf her aunt her given her upon completing her thesis defense and danced into the dining room with plate in hand.

Sitting down at the table, she nibbled at her salad while sifting through her mail. "What's this?" she muttered, picking up a small, white envelope. Her eyes zeroed in on the return address. "Jason?"

Her heart pounded as she looked at it. Easy Claire. Remember, he's the one who walked out, not you. She took a deep breath and ran a fingernail under the flap, prying it away. When she saw her townhouse key, she was furious.

"You son-of-a-bitch! You asshole!" she shouted. She poked inside to see if there was a note and found nothing: no good-bye, no 'sorry things didn't work out'. The end of their five-year relationship reduced to nothing but a returned key.

She held it up in front of her, and felt her throat tighten. "Fucker!" she muttered, feeling like a deleted paragraph in one of his shitty editorials. She clenched her jaw and ripped the envelope in half, then again and again until it was in tiny pieces on the floor.

Three

C LAIRE PEERED out the passenger-side window as a long peninsula jutting out into the ocean crept into view below. Wisps of thin clouds were casting faint shadows on its muted hills. In the seat beside her, Thad was busy with his thesis research. Behind them, sat Jorge and Molly, both second year grad students. Jorge was going for his doctorate in social anthropology and Molly in evolutionary anthropology with a second understudy in computer sciences. Just now, Molly was preaching to Jorge about her upgraded search engine for the department. But Claire wasn't listening. For the last three hours, she had been fighting persistent background nausea, and it was getting stronger.

Thad turned a friendly smile toward Claire, nodded over his shoulder and pursed his lips.

Claire took a deep breath and leaned over and peeked at the open document on his laptop. "How's it going?"

"All right I guess," he muttered. "Just can't find a lot of data to draw conclusions from."

"Perhaps your subject matter is a little too obscure." she said. As his advisor, she had warned him about tackling the migrations of the South Pacific peoples during their Neolithic period. "Why don't you shift your argument away from why they left and focus on their arrival and cultural myths?"

Thad shook his head. "It's been done to death."

"Yeah, but there's always something new to discover," she suggested.

Thad sighed. "That's what Molly said."

"She's right," Claire pointed out. "So you're working with her then?"

Thad shrugged. "Yeah. Ms. Tech-Head offered to help me dig through the web, so I took her up on it."

Claire shook her head. Though Thad wouldn't ever admit it, she knew he liked Molly, but seeing how she was Noah's niece, knew better than to spit into the wind. "I'll leave you to your torture then," she said, opening to the first page of an article she had been working on over the last two weeks for Anthropology Today.

They landed at Chavez International Airport four hours later, and after playing twenty questions with the customs agent, Claire and her team pushed through the terminal's front doors into the oppressive heat of Lima's afternoon sun. Claire looked right, then left before seeing Owen standing next to a red mini-van that was ready to fall apart at any moment. Behind the mini-van, sat a bus boasting painted trees and plants on its side panel. Two smiling bronzed men in pressed tan shorts and button-down shirts stood in front of it.

"Ya made it!" Owen said walking toward her with an outstretched hand.

"That we did," Claire said, shaking hands with him while glancing toward the van. "Those our taxis?"

Owen pushed his wide-brimmed canvas hat back off his forehead and took her pack. Handing it to a middle aged man coming up beside him, he said, "At your service. This is Manny here, yeah. He'll be looking after ya gear and such."

Clair took in Manny's rugged brown complexion and toothy smile. But behind the beaming grin, she felt an air of suspicion. "Hi, Manny."

She put her hand out, and as he shook it, his dark, brown eyes burrowed into her.

"Welcome to Lima," he said, turning toward Molly, who had quietly drifted beside them. "And who is this pretty moça?"

Claire put her arm around her feisty grad student. "This is my queen of tech, Molly."

"Uma rainha," Manny said taking Molly's hand. He bowed with such graciousness, Claire couldn't decide whether he was playing along or truly meant it. Molly blushed and Thad rolled his eyes.

Claire aimed a down-boy stare at her RA. "And this is Thad. Thad, come around and say hi to Manny."

Manny turned and gave Thad a long, measured gaze. "O meu Deus. Owen, look at him! He and my Ernesto could be irmãos."

Molly tapped Claire, and motioned her out of earshot of the men. "You okay?"

"Yeah, just a little upset stomach is all. I'll be fine."

Molly frowned. "You're not a very good liar, but you're the boss. Anyway, my Spanish isn't very good and my Portuguese is worse. So help me out here, I get the reference to Uma rainha, but what is irmãos?" She said, murdering the pronunciation.

"Brothers," Claire said.

"Hey, Claire," Owen called over. "Where's da rest of ya gear?"

"Inside. The rest of our equipment's coming in on a cargo plane later tonight."

Owen looked back at the porters and nodded at the terminal doors. "Rammy, Hector, would ya go fetch their gear for me?"

The men left and ten minutes later the gear was loaded into the bus. Claire climbed into the mini and sat in the midsection beside Owen with Thad and Jorge behind her. Molly sat up front, riding shotgun with Manny. Claire thought of asking about air conditioning but dismissed it because she doubted the rust bucket had it. Besides, they needed to start getting used to the heat if they were going to get through the next few months in the forest.

"Sweet as, Manny," Owen said, pulling the mini door shut. "Let's get a leg on."

"Excuse me?" Claire said.

"What?"

"Sweet ass?" Claire said. *Foreign men, they're all the same, doesn't matter where they come from!*

Owen shook his head. "Yeah, what about it?"

"You might refer to women like that in your country, but I'd appreciate it if you didn't do it with us."

For a moment the man looked at her as if she just stepped off another planet, then laughed. "Oh … I said, 'sweet as'. Means everything's under control; real good."

Claire cocked an eye. "Under control?"

"Yeah, yeah."

"Slang," Manny put in.

"Right," Claire said, eyeing them dubiously.

The city of Lima sprawled out before them like a quilted tapestry. White-washed stucco and cinderblock buildings hugged an endless maze of cobbled and semi-paved macadam streets. Here and there, open-air markets sprang up, and with them echoed the staccato come-ons of shopkeepers hawking goods and produce to the meandering masses. They drove for what felt like an hour, and Claire wondered if they'd ever get out of the city. "What's that smell?" she said, fighting the persisting nausea.

Owen chuckled. "Cuy. Roasted Guinea Pig. I assume you'll be passing on that one, eh?"

Claire nodded her head as the mini bounced over a bone-jarring pothole. *Very funny, mister, but I've eaten stranger things.*

"Easy, Manny. I'd like ta keep my teeth in my head," Owen said. He turned back to Claire as she took a deep breath. "Queasy?"

She swallowed hard and tried to smile, but failed miserably.

Owen reached into the pocket on the back of the driver's seat and pulled out a crumpled paper-bag. "Here," he said, flattening it out and handing it to her. "Sit tight. Almost there."

"You said that a half-hour ago," Claire grumbled, loosening the collar of her shirt. *What is going on with me? I've flown a thousand times. The heat? And there's no way I'm blowing lunch in front of you.*

"What ya need is a spot of coca tea. Straighten ya right out."

Claire looked at him as if he'd lost his mind. "I'm not drinking anything."

"Ya funeral," he said, and tapped Manny on the shoulder. "Hang a right."

The mini turned, and a minute later came to a large open space where ancient, brown adobe buildings stood in decay.

"That's the Pachacamac Ruins!" Molly gushed, looking out the passenger window.

"Yeah, yeah," Owen said.

"Oh my God, I can't believe it," Molly said, and proceeded to grill Owen and Manny about everything they knew about the ruins and whether they could arrange a visit to it after the expedition.

Despite how Claire felt, she couldn't help craning her neck as well. The mini passed around the ruins and turned down a long four-lane street leading toward a poor excuse of a highway. But at least they were no longer in stop-and-go traffic.

The highway veered toward the ocean, following a long curving coastline dotted with grassy bluffs that were bursting with red flax. Here and there, clusters of palm trees swayed in the breezes. A deep blue ocean piled waves upon a long crescent beach as a rambling stucco villa with terracotta-tiled roofs came into view.

Owen pointed toward it. "Ya digs for da night."

Manny pulled off the highway and drove down a cobbled road bordered with pink and red lupines. At the end of it was a broad loop that slid under a vaulted Porte Cochere that was supported by polished wood timbers. Owen jumped out, opened the back of the van, and set their bags on an empty luggage cart.

Behind him, Thad, Jorge, and Molly piled out, leaving Claire alone. She watched them stretch their backs, then pried herself off the seat and stepped out. As she eyed the ocean between the tall grasses, Owen came up behind her.

"Pretty nice, eh?"

"Yeah, real nice," Claire muttered, and she could just imagine the look on Noah's face if he knew they were booked in a five-star villa.

Four

December 18th 2012, Lima

THE FOLLOWING morning, Claire felt better. Grudgingly, she admitted Owen had been right. The coca tea did the trick. She went out onto the veranda and took in the distant shoreline. A faint, pink glow painted the world and warm zephyrs swirled around the hotel, playing with her hair. It was just after five AM, and in an hour she and her team would meet Owen in the lobby.

She sipped her tea, made drinkable by a healthy dose of cream and sugar, and pondered for the hundredth time the chain of events that brought her here. It started with the sighting of an Indian of unknown origin in a remote part of the Amazon forest. Then soon after, word of a 'Lost Man' followed, which ultimately led to a disastrous first encounter.

But it was Thad who brought the 'Lost Man' to her attention, and it was a friend of a friend of Thad's who recommended an unlikely guide named Owen Macleod, who as it happened, once lived almost in the 'Lost Man's' back yard. It all seemed so pre-ordained, and if she were a religious person, she could almost believe there was a higher power at work here.

She imagined meeting the 'Lost Man'. If his DNA could be linked to African roots, her theory would gain irrefutable proof of the existence of a trans-Atlantic connection, and thus erase years of grief from her peers, who laughed at her. Called her theory, 'Chariots of Fire' garbage. Except, no one had a good explanation for cocaine found in ancient Egypt or the uncanny resemblance the stepped pyramids in Central and South America had with the Ziggurats across the ocean.

The defining test, of course, would be in the DNA, if she could get any. His mitochondrial DNA would go a long way in confirming her belief of early contact with the Egyptian peoples or it could wipe out fifteen years of work and set her career spiraling into a black abyss of community colleges.

Claire tried to shoo away that terrifying notion as Molly burst into a string of four-letter epithets in the room next door. She drew the sash of her terry towel bathrobe around her and stepped off the veranda into her room. The lamp next to her bed that had been on a minute ago was off and the digital display on her alarm clock was gone. Puzzled, she opened her door and gazed down the darkened hall. People milled around outside their doors, talking in hushed tones. Claire slipped out of her room, walked down to Molly's door, and knocked.

Her young redheaded RA answered in her university gray sweats, looking like a feral cat who'd just been stuffed into a box.

"You all right?" Claire said, eyeing the blackened surge protector in Molly's hand.

"No! My fecking laptop just got fried!" She threw her arms up and fired the surge protector at her unmade bed. "We have other lap-tops," Claire soothed, but as she said it, her stomach flipped. The Sat-Lynk transponder lay on the bed with its screen lifted open. "Tell me that wasn't plugged in?"

Molly shook her head. "No, thank God." Looking back at her computer, she let out a loud sigh. "I just bought this fecking thing."

Claire breathed a sigh of relief. They could live without a laptop. A Sat Lynk, they couldn't. "It's okay, we'll get you another one when we get back."

"You don't understand. It took me all day to transfer all my data onto that. Arghhhh!"

"I'm sorry, Mol, I really am," Claire said, trying to calm her ex-niece down. As apt and able as Molly was, she had a nasty temper when things went wrong. A shortcoming Claire had been fully aware of when selecting her for the team, as well as the fact she was Noah's niece. But she needed Molly's technical strength, and it didn't hurt that Molly had a keen interest in the Amazon peoples.

She went to Molly and looked her straight in the eye. "Go take your shower. It's the last good one you get for some time."

Owen stood in the stairwell of the transport, looking out the windshield at a clear morning without a cloud in the sky. He smiled. Soon, he'd be in his element – out in the forest with no one looking over his shoulder. He tossed the wrapper of his morning candy bar in the trash bag hanging off the dashboard as Manny brought the transport in front of Claire's hotel.

Out in front stood Molly, Thad, and Jorge with their bags. Claire hadn't come down yet. Owen looked at his watch. *Probably putting her face on.* He hopped out as the other transport pulled up and slipped alongside his vehicle.

"Gidday mates, lady. Sleep well?" Owen said over his shoulder as he checked the web of ropes crisscrossing the supplies on the roof-rack.

"Like a baby," Molly said with a hint of sarcasm.

Glancing back, Owen saw her grab her duffle bag and head toward the transport. *We're in a mood, aren't we?* He pulled the slack out of one of the ropes. As he retied it, he said, "Molly, is it?"

"Yes."

"Best be slathering on sun-block. Sun'll fry ya down here."

He heard Molly huff as Jorge and Thad strode up beside him. Thad said, "Don't mind her. She's had a bad morning." He gave the thumbs down and added, "Computer."

Owen nodded. "Any idea when da boss might show up? Daylight's wasting, an' we gotta long slog ahead of us, yeah."

Just then, Claire's voice rose up behind them. "Morning."

Owen turned to see her walking toward him with a full pack slung over her shoulder. The toned and curvy brunette filled out her crisp tan blouse very nicely. As she strode toward him with a leggy gait, she added, "Looks like we have a good day for traveling."

Owen nodded. "That we do. Nice pair of Zambers."

"Yeah. They've seen a lot of mileage over the years," Claire said, admiring her boots.

Owen shrugged and looked down at his. Their once dark brown leather had faded to a milky gray and a couple of the steel eyelets were missing around the laces. "Yeah, mine, too. How ya feeling?"

She flashed him a quick smile. "Good, thank you. We all set?"

"Sweet as," Owen said, and shot her a devilish smile.

Claire frowned. "You know, that down-under slang is going to get you in trouble if you keep it up."

"What, me?"

"Yeah, you." She smiled and headed for the front door of the transport.

Six hours later, the transport descended from a grassy hillside into Tingo Maria. The small colonial village of brick and adobe buildings snuggled into the sprawling hillsides like a kitten into a pile of laundry. Manny brought the bus to a stop at a small, vibrant square dotted with stout palms. After he opened the transport door, the team spilled out into the warm, humid air.

"We'll take morning tea 'fore heading ta our next stop," Owen said. "If you're hungry, I suggest ya follow me ta that there café down da road, yeah." He slipped his hat on and started toward a small, crumbling adobe building hemmed in by a low sandstone wall.

As they tramped along the narrow dirt road under the frowning brown hills, Owen pointed out places of interest until he came at last to a small opening in the wall. Turning through it, he shuffled up the path to a crude slate terrace. On it sat four round tables draped with red tablecloths.

They all pulled out chairs and sat as the side door of the café opened. Out of it scurried a tiny brown woman with a wrinkled face. She was dressed in a deep pink pollera skirt embroidered with colorful orange, blue, and green flowers. "Buenas tardes. ¿Les apetece un refresco?" she said, coming to their table with a broad, toothy grin.

"Usted tiene té helado?" Claire replied, as the woman handed her a paper menu.

The woman nodded. "Si."

"Entonces quiero uno," Claire said, ordering a tall glass of iced tea. As the woman moved on, Claire leaned toward Owen and quietly said, "Any recommendations?"

"That depends on how adventurous ya are," Owen said, eyeing her sidelong. "If I were ya, I'd stick with da Tacu Tacu or da Pollo a la Brasa 'til you get your legs under ya."

Claire shot him an exasperated look and gazed down the menu. "Right. I think I'll try this."

"Papa Rellena," Owen said, and felt a smile come to his face.

"What's in it?" Molly said.

Manny spoke up. "Potato and meat cooked in herbs. Local dish, everyone eats it. It is good."

"What kind of meat?" Molly said.

Jorge shrugged. "Could be beef or chicken-"

"Or bush meat," Owen interjected with a playful wink.

Molly's face screwed up into a crooked frown. Owen felt Claire's elbow digging into his ribs. She shook her head as Jorge and Thad broke out laughing.

Thad set his menu down and turned to Owen. "So, how long have you been doing this?"

"Guiding?" Owen said, as the little dark woman moved up beside him. He looked up at her. A tall mug of beer was definitely in order. To her, he said, "Sólo una cerveza." After the woman left, he leaned back in his chair. "Don't know, twenty years maybe. Anyway, I like it. Ya always know where ya stand out here."

"What's that mean?" Molly said.

He turned an eye toward the RA. "Means, somewhere near da bottom rung." Smiles broke out on Manny and Jorge's faces.

Claire sipped her drink, and said, "You have a way of putting things, Mr. Macleod."

"C'mon now," Owen said, shooting her a hurt look. "No need ta be formal. It's Owen." He stretched his legs out in front of him and pushed his hat off his brow. "Anyway, just trying ta keep things real. That forest out yonder is unforgiving an' ya better respect it 'cause it sure won't respect ya. That's what my Pop used ta say, yeah."

"So where's our next stop?" Molly said.

"Tarapoto," Manny said.

"We'll spend the night there before picking up our water transportation in Yurimagus," Owen added. "From there it's three days down da river ta Iquitos an' another three ta Santo Antonio do Içá. Hope ya brought plenty of reading material an' bug juice. Skeeters on da river don't take prisoners." He eyed Molly who sported a pair of capris. "Might wanna think twice 'bout wearing them on da water."

"Eight days," Molly said. "How far away is this Santo Antonio do Içá?"

"Once we are on the river, it is about 1,500 kilometers," Manny said, "providing we do not have any detours."

Claire frowned. "Detours?"

Owen glanced at Manny. *Not a good time for bringing that up, mate.* Turning to Claire, he shrugged and said, "Sometimes da river level drops an' we have ta take alternate routes. No big deal. We'll get there in plenty of time." *That is, as long as da FARC stays off da river.*

Five

O WEN STARED out the transport window as the narrow road climbed into the mountain pass. Here and there, the tires sent streams of gravel into the dark ravines as they wound around the twisting route hemmed in by towering kapok and strangler figs. In the understory, ferns, and philodendrons fled into the dark gloom. Sometimes, when the canopy relented, the Andean range could be seen peering down at them with snow-covered faces. Owen tapped Manny on the shoulder.

"Time ta stretch our legs, mate." He got up and faced the team. "There's a turn-off up ahead. We'll hang there for fifteen," he said, then pointed toward a gap within the trees to their left. "There's a loo down that path over there if ya need it. I'd advise using it. We've a shag ta go 'fore we stop again. Believe me, you don't wanna be tramping around in da forest. Lots of nasty critters out there, yeah."

Thirty minutes later, they were back on the road heading toward the city of Tarapoto. In the mirror above Manny, Owen saw Molly inspecting mosquito bites on her legs. As he turned to get his bag and dig out some salve for her, he noticed Claire eyeing the steep drop outside her window. Her fingers were fiercely clutching the seat back in front of her. "Hey, no worries. Manny knows this road better than his own wife."

Claire let go of the seat and shot him a smile, but he knew it was forced. "I'm not worried," she said. "Just can't get comfortable, is all."

"Right," Owen said, not believing her.

She turned back toward the window. "It's breath-taking."

"Yeah, it is," he said, pulling a tube of aloe out of his med-kit. "Say, I'm thinking someone needs ta tell Miss Molly back there ta ease up digging a hole in her legs. She's gonna be raw by da time we get ta Tarapoto." He held the tube up, and went on, "Got some salve here. Might be better if ya gave it ta her, I think."

Suddenly the tires slid on the narrow road, sending a pinging shower of gravel down the sheer slope beside them. Claire drew a sharp breath and her hands leapt for the seat in front of her. It had caught Owen off-guard, too, and sent him forward. He regained his balance and glanced over at Manny, whose attention was fixed firmly on the road. Taking a deep, controlled breath, Owen muttered, "Easy mate!" Then chuckled, and said, "He does that every once in a while ta give people a thrill. Thinks he's a Kiwi, you know, bungee jumping an' all."

Claire relaxed her grip from the back of the seat and rolled her eyes. As Owen looked at her, he felt something more than just a passing attraction stir inside him. He sat with that a minute, trying to decide whether he liked it or not, then said, "Say, mind if I ask ya a question?"

"No. What do you wanna know?"

Owen peeked down at her left hand. She had a charm bracelet, with of all things, a wolf pendant on it. Her ring finger was bare, save for a faint impression. "Ya travel a lot for ya job?"

"Some. Mostly lectures. In the beginning, it was a lot."

"Yeah, I saw ya went ta Togo. Spent time in Guatemala an' Honduras, too. How'd ya like it down there?"

"It was good," Claire said. "I don't get out in the field much anymore. Too busy writing grants, papers, and teaching. What about you? You like what you do?"

Owen shrugged. "It's okay. Pays da rent."

Claire looked at him dubiously. "Bullshit. You have a degree in forestry. Running tours is not what you had in mind when you graduated. I'm sure of it."

Owen rubbed his chin and nodded. "Guess ya found me out."

"Is that why you contacted me?"

"Actually, ya contacted me," Owen said. "Although I suppose I had something ta do with it."

"How's that?"

Owen shrugged. "When I heard from ya mate's friend in da states about da tramp, I made it known ta him I was interested."

"I thought so," Claire said. "So, any children?"

Where did that come from? Suddenly, his son's face flashed before his eyes, stealing his breath. He blinked and composed himself. "No, none I can speak ta anyway. You?"

Claire shook her head. "Never seemed to have the time."

"Right," Owen said.

They sat in their own thoughts for awhile, watching the passing landscape. The road had leveled out and the dense forest had pulled back, leaving vast meadows of swaying grass and thick brambles. To the left, the Andes ran as far as they could see under a deep, blue sky. Puffy white clouds gathered at their peeks.

"You ever get lonely?" Claire said. "I mean, you get to meet a lot of people, but you never get close to anyone. At least that's what a friend of mine who guides in Hawaii says."

Owen took his time before answering. He didn't want anyone probing too deeply into his life; her, least of all. "Ya get used ta it. No different than yourself, I'm sure."

Now it was Claire's turn to be quiet. She sat looking out the window a moment, then sighed. "Yeah, I guess."

When she looked back at him, Owen saw the same haunted expression that stared back at him every morning. He resisted the urge to go into more detail, and said, "Hey, I read ya paper, da one about da trans-Atlantic trade connection."

Claire brightened. "Did you?"

"Yeah, I thought it interesting, an' well written for da most part."
Claire's face broke into a crooked smile. "For the most part?"

"Yeah." He shot her one of his classic bad-boy grins. "Just a few typos
an' some minor factual errors. Nothing earth shattering."

Claire furrowed her brow. "Is that so? And just what errors are you
referring to?"

Time ta escape, 'fore she skewers me alive. "Hold on," he said, getting
up. "I think Manny needs me. Be right back."

"You make sure you are. We're not done here," Claire snapped back
with a smile.

Night had fallen over the city of Tarapoto when the team pulled in.
Claire stretched and looked around the darkened transport. Thad and
Jorge were quietly discussing some minor point regarding Polynesian
culture while Molly listened to her IPOD in back. As Manny pulled
the vehicle in front of an old stucco building, a broad wrap-around
porch came into view. Lit by handsome wrought iron lanterns hanging
on chains, the porch gave the inn a welcoming presence among the
broken clapboard buildings of the surrounding neighborhood.

"All right folks, we're here," Owen said as the front door of the transport opened. "Just grab ya gear an' leave da rest on-board."

One by one then, they lumbered off and stood in the humid night
air. As they looked up at the spattered stars, Owen went in, and a few
minutes later returned with their room keys. Handing them out, he
said, "The kitchen's open 'til midnight if ya hungry. I recommend da
polla a la brasa or the butifarras. Both are excellent." To Manny, he
said, "Have da lads see to da bags. I'll be back in a bit."

As Owen turned and headed down the street, Claire looked at her
watch. Huh … where's he going?

"Something the matter, senora?" Manny said, suddenly beside her.
She started. "Where's he going?"

"To take care of travel business," Manny said, but his smile wasn't
convincing.

"At ten-thirty?"

"Si. No time tomorrow," Manny said. "We need to meet the boat very early." He waved her toward the inn. "Come. The cozinha is going to close soon. You must be hungry, no?"

Reluctantly, Claire picked her duffle bag up. Whatever Owen was up to, travel business wasn't it. However, she was tired, so she followed Thad, Molly, and Jorge into the lobby. But as she went, her glance strayed down the gloomy lamp-lit street.

Once inside, a tap on her arm interrupted her musing. "What's up?" She turned and found Thad looking at her with a puzzled expression.

"Nothing, just thinking," she said. As she pondered Owen's sudden departure, a gold-painted glass mirror across the lobby caught her eye. "Wow, wonder what that's doing in here?"

"What'd'ya mean?" Thad said.

"That isn't just a piece of folk art. See that," she said, heading toward the mirror. "The frame's rendered with painted villages around its perimeter and they're detailed right down to the individual houses. And look there, a barn. And there, a herd of cattle." She stepped back. "The artisan was likely a local who traveled a bit. Likely twentieth century."

"How can you tell?" Thad said.

"The architecture," Claire answered. "There, see the detail of the stucco? It's smooth. Early stucco was scored."

Just then, Molly joined them. Setting her duffle bag on the floor, she bit into a cookie and said, "Sweet."

Thad furrowed his brow. "Hey, where'd you get that?"

"Over there on the table, by the coffee urn," Molly said. She popped the rest of the cookie into her mouth and wiped her hands.

Thad glanced over at the long, wooden table standing opposite the registration counter. On it was an empty silver tray. "They're all gone."

"I know," Molly said, giving him a toothy grin.

Thad wrinkled his long face. "Cute. You've got crumbs in your teeth."

The comment drew a stuck-out tongue from Molly.

"Ah, a painted mirror," Jorge said, joining them.

"Claire thinks it's twentieth century," Thad said.

"It is," Jorge said, matter-of-factly.

Thad rolled his eyes. "Oh really? And you know this how?"

"The style, it's –"

Thad put his hand up. "God save me, I'm in the midst of art critics. Never mind, I get it. Well, you guys can stand here gawking at it. I'm going for chow," he said, and strutted away.

Claire laughed as she watched him retreat across the subdued lobby furnished with lacquered teak tables and chairs. "I better get settled. Make sure he doesn't wolf down everything in sight, would ya?"

"Don't worry, if Poppy goes for thirds, I'll stick a boot in his mouth," Molly said, bending down and lifting her duffle bag over her shoulder. She donned one of her evil grins, then struck off down the hall.

Claire rolled her eyes and headed for her room on the second floor. Shunning the elevator, she climbed a sweeping staircase, turned right, and went down a narrow corridor to the last door. Opening it, she hit the light and dropped her gear to the floor. Although the furnishings were old and a bit tattered, they were passable. The linens were white; the red, green, and blue bedspread bright and cheery. She treaded over to the sliding glass door that offered a view of the darkened hills. Sliding it back, she stepped out onto the tiny wood-framed terrace. Bathed in the still night air, she drank in the sounds of Tarapoto's nightlife.

As she was about to go back in, she heard a familiar voice below . She moved closer and listened to Manny's furtive words spoken in Portuguese.

"Si, they are all in and getting settled. Although I think she saw you go into Migel's. When will you be back?" He paused, and Claire realized Manny was talking on a cell phone. "Yes, I will have everything ready. How many are you getting? You think that is enough? Okay. I am going in to eat and then off to bed. You have your key to the bus? Okay, see you in the morning."

Claire heard him flip his cell phone shut then saw a tiny yellow flame erupt beneath the terrace floor. A moment later, a strong pungent smoke wafted up over the railing and into the night air.

Six

WEN WALKED into the dining room as Claire, Thad, and Molly finished eating. Claire looked up as he shuffled over to their table with his hat pushed back off his brow. Pulling a chair up, he sat beside Thad, and let out a gaping yawn. Claire searched his expression. As an anthropologist, she prided herself on reading people's faces and actions. Since she heard what Manny had said, she knew if he were up to no good, his expression would betray him. But his face, which was sporting the beginnings of a dark, gold beard, showed only exhaustion.

"So, all settled in?" he said to the group.

Draining the rest of his soda, Thad nodded, leaned back in his chair and stretched. "I'm heading up," he announced, and dug a twenty note out of his pants pocket. Tossing it on the table, he added, "What time we push off tomorrow?"

Owen shoved the money back at him. "It's all taken care of, mate. We leave at six ... sharp."

"Six?" Molly said, her eyes widening.

"Sharp," Owen repeated, taking off his hat and setting it on the table. "How's da skeeter bites?"

"They were doing fine 'til you just mentioned them," Molly snapped. "Thanks."

"No problem," Owen said, shooting Claire a wink. "Make sure ya wear ya long pants tomorrow, eh."

Molly groaned. "You are a tool!" She bade the rest of the group good-night and slogged out of the room.

"Think I'm off, too," Jorge said, getting up. "Where are we meeting in the morning?"

"In da lobby," Owen said. He cast a boyish grin at Claire. "Seems like I'm scaring 'em off. What 'bout ya? Ya deserting me, too?"

Claire waved to Jorge and Thad as they headed toward their rooms, then turned back toward Owen. "No, I'll keep you company," she said, wondering how to bring up his mysterious disappearing act. Although Owen was easy-going, and she had to admit she liked him, she couldn't tolerate secret dealings that could put her expedition in jeopardy.

Owen called the waiter over and ordered a butifarras and a bottle of beer. They sat awhile afterward discussing Tarapoto and the day's events, until the waiter came back with Owen's supper. He bit into the sandwich, and with his mouth half-full, said, "Well, it's onta da river tomorrow. Ya ready?"

"Ready as I'll ever be. Too bad you couldn't have joined us earlier. We had an interesting discussion," Claire said.

"That so? 'Bout what?"

"Art, the river, the forest … you."

Owen grinned. "Me, eh?"

Claire smiled, downed the last of her beer and said, "Yeah, like … where were you?"

Without a blink, he said, "Rounding up goodies for my mates, why?"

Very funny, Mr. Macleod. Goodies indeed! "Fine, have your little secret, but this is my expedition, and the last thing I need to worry about is you doing something illegal and landing us all in jail."

"I'm touched," he said as the waiter came back to ask if they needed anything more. After the man left, Owen took a long pull of his beer and smacked his lips. "Damn, but that hits da spot." He paused, and as he eyed her, his smile dimmed. After a moment, he leaned forward and said, "Okay, you're da boss-lady, but there's something ya need ta understand. We're not on holiday here. We're going deep into da Amazon, an' people don't play by da rules there, yeah. So, when it comes ta getting ya there an' back, my rules trump yours. An' for that matter, Manny's too. Understand?"

Claire stiffened. "As long as you keep things on the up-and-up, we'll be fine."

Sitting back, Owen snatched his beer bottle and found his smile. "Of course we will. You wanna'nother drink? I'm buying."

She looked at him dumbfounded. In the span of moments he went from a laid back bad boy to a no-nonsense take-charge commando and back again. Suddenly, she didn't know whether to resent or respect him. "No, I'm good."

Owen yawned. "That Molly's a real pistol."

Despite her mixed feeling at the moment, Claire couldn't help from grinning. "That, she is. You like twitting her don't you?"

"Keeps her on her toes. Though, I have a good feeling, she's on 'em most da time," he said. When the waiter returned with his beer, he said, "Say, didn't mean ta get surly back there. Just wanna make sure I bring everyone back, is all."

"Well, I would expect nothing less for what I'm paying you," Claire said, watching him gobble down the last of his sandwich. "Say, my eyes are starting to get heavy, so I guess I'm going to have to desert you after all. See you in the morning."

"I'll be there. Oh, one thing 'fore ya head up."

"What's that?" Claire said getting up.

"Make sure ya all have ya visas and immunization docs handy to-morrow."

"Why? We've got a ways to go before we hit the border."

"Yeah, I know, 'cept we're on da water. Rules are a bit different there. Ya have a good night. Cheers."

The team arrived around eleven at the tiny village of Yurimagus on the headwaters of the great river. It was now past noon and most of the gear had been transported onto the large twin prop diesel-powered boat that would be their home for the next seven or eight days. Owen walked up to the bow of the seventy-five foot vessel and stood behind a steel rail sorely in need of paint. As he looked out over the muddy waters of the Amazon, he felt like he'd come home after a long trip. He took a deep breath of the pungent diesel and fish scented air swirling over the waters and smiled. *There ya are, yeah. My Lady, Amassona. I wonder what surprises ya have for me this time.*

"Penny for your thoughts," Claire said, coming up beside him. She had two cans of beer and offered him one.

"What's this? For me?" Owen said, taking it. He tipped his hat to her and drank in her faded blue jeans and thin, white gauze shirt with its sleeves rolled up to the elbows. A thick hank of hair was loosely tied behind her graceful neck and the top two buttons of her shirt were open, offering him a hint of cleavage. A gentle breeze skipping across the water played with her upturned collar.

"You worked hard," she said.

"Ahhh, it's nothing, but thank ya all da same," Owen said. As the last few items he had picked up the night before were loaded onto the Lírio do Rio, he took a long drink of his beer and nodded toward the river. "In this country, it's called Amassona by some and Apurimac by others. Looks tame, but don't let it fool ya. People 'cross da border, call it da Boat Destroyer, an' for good reason."

"Rapids?"

"Yeah that, but mostly 'cause it can change in a heartbeat. One minute, deep as can be, then 'round da next bend, just a few meters, say nothing of flash floods an' stumps hiding 'neath da surface."

"Sounds like we're in for quite a ride," she said, gazing out over the water. Behind them, the Lírio do Rio's main engine revved, sending out a large puff of gray smoke.

"Sure are," he said, admiring her profile. For a moment he felt like he could talk to her about anything, but the thought quickly evaporated. He drained his beer and turned back toward the river. "She an' I go back a long ways, yeah. She's like family. Some people say she has mystical powers. Don't know 'bout that, but I know she's in my blood."

Claire smiled. "It is mesmerizing." She turned toward him. "Can I ask you a question?"

"Yeah, sure."

"How come you don't live here? Isn't traveling back and forth a pain? It's not like you're commuting across town."

Owen bit his lip as the image of his dead son flashed before his eyes. "Sometimes, I ask myself da same question. Guess I don't like da idea of abandoning home an' family."

Claire nodded. "You have a large one?"

"Not really. My Mum; she's living in one of da fancy care facilities. Pop passed several years ago from a medical complication; embolism from a prior injury. My brother raises deer an' sheep on da south island."

"Deer?" Claire said, cocking her brow. The wooden deck under their feet lurched as the Lírio do Rio pushed away from the dock.

"Yeah, what about it?" Owen said, glad to steer her away from the subject of family.

"Never heard of raising deer. I take it, kiwi's are big on venison."

"Some of us are. I can take or leave it," Owen said. He crushed the empty beer can in his hand with ease and tossed in a barrel nearby. "Ya like venison, do ya?"

"It's alright." She fell quiet a minute as the boat motored out into the main current.

Content to leave her to her thoughts, Owen watched a group of young boys playing football on a grassy field near the passing shoreline. His thoughts shifted back to his son. Calen would've been fifteen next month. The greenstone that hung around his neck beneath his shirt had belonged to Calen. It was the only thing left he had of his son except haunting memories and dreams that taunted him from time to time.

Seven

Nauta, Peru

A PALE DAWN light crept into Claire's stuffy cabin through a dirty round window. Sitting on her cot, she looked out the portal at the ever-brightening sky, tracing wisps of umber clouds as the Lírio do Rio's diesel engine droned in her ears. For the second day in a row, she had awoken, nauseous and soaked in sweat. Seasickness, perhaps, but she doubted it.

Closing her eyes, she fought the growing terror in her heart. *I can't be pregnant, I just can't be!* Taking a deep breath, she counted backwards to her last period. Ninety-five days. She had missed periods before, but it had never bothered her because the odds against her getting pregnant were in the stratosphere. The removal of an ovary and part of the other at thirty-three had seen to that. Or so, her GYN had said.

Suddenly, her stomach flipped and her eyes watered. She lurched for the wastebasket beside her and grabbed it in the nick of time. After several uncomfortable minutes, her body's revolt ended and she sat up, catching her breath. Oh God. Now is not a good time for this bullshit. She swallowed, composed herself, and got up. I need some air.

Pulling on a pair of jeans and a sweatshirt, she opened the door to her cabin and treaded out onto the foredeck. Through the hot, damp mist rising off the river, she saw a ragged shoreline peppered with rustic wood and whitewashed buildings.

"Bom dia," said a deep, melodic voice behind her.

She turned to find Manny sitting in the shadows on a skid of supplies under the upper deck. "Morning. Looks like nice day."

"Si. You up early."

She rubbed her hands together and wrapped her arms around her chest. "Couldn't sleep." She went to the rail and eyed the old wooden boats, skiffs, and canoes pulled up onto the banks of the river. The smell of fish hung in the air.

Manny joined her at the rail. As he bit the end of his cigar off, he pointed toward shore. "Nauta. It's where we start our tours most of the time. Soon, this beach will be very busy."

An image of laughing brown-skinned children playing around their working fathers flashed before Claire. She knew it was a romantic notion; most of the men and women on the river gutted out tough lives. Still, for all of their troubles, people in villages like these were ofttimes happy and close-knit. As the thought swirled in her head, she wrestled with the fear of being pregnant, of Jason's walking out of her life. Suddenly, her fancy condo, the Volvo, the closet full of clothes, and all the things she had believed she needed didn't seem so important. She felt her throat tighten. *How can I be pregnant?*

Manny broke into her musing, jarring her into the present. "So, what do you think of Peru so far?"

Claire gathered her thoughts. "It's a beautiful country." She cast a long sweeping gaze over the muddy waters, steeling her heart against rising anguish. She would not break down in front of this man. At last, she said, "Owen told me the Amazon is in his blood. Called it family."

Manny nodded and lit his cigar. "It is true for him. He grew up on this river and in the forest. There, life is much simpler than the complicated world we live in. To understand Owen, is to understand he is a simple man. He takes you at your word. A handshake is good enough for him. It is a pity we live in a world where no one trusts anyone, I think."

"Yes. It is sad."

Manny gazed out over the water, letting the words hang between them, then turned and said, "Tell me, why do you want to find this 'Lost Man'? What can he tell you, hmmm?"

"His blood can tell me if there was once a connection between Africa and South America." She paused, realizing how clinical it sounded, and shook her head. "That sounded awful, didn't it?"

Manny shrugged.

Claire sighed. "Let me back up. Yes, getting a blood sample is a big part of it, but there's more. I want to know his story. What happened to his people, and why?" Then to her surprise, she added, "I want to let him know he's not alone, that there's someone in the world that cares about him."

"But you will go home and write your paper, and he will be left here, no?" Manny said. "I do not mean to sound harsh, but your words are empty promises. In your heart, you want to believe you care deeply, but in reality you cannot live up to them, because if you do it would mean you would never leave, and we both know you will."

She blinked as Manny's words hammered home. He was wrong. She really did care! Didn't she? She paused, and in the silence between them, looked inward and knew he was right. She couldn't make a difference in the bushman's life any more than she could flap her wings and fly. No, her best intentions were just dust in the wind, and she felt like a sham in front of the insightful director. She cleared her throat and said, "Yeah, I guess you're right. It was a stupid thing to say."

"Oh, I know you meant well," Manny said. "I was just making sure you did not think you could change the way things are."

Claire felt a smile come to her face. *How did Owen ever hook up with you?* Aloud, she said, "You're a wise man, Manny. Can I ask you a question?"

"Si."

"How long have you known Owen?"

Manny blew a ring of smoke and tapped the growing head of ash off his cigar into the passing water. "About twenty years. Why?"

Claire shrugged. "Just curious."

Manny glanced at her from the corner of his eye. "I think it is more than that, senhora. I think that science brain of yours is trying to figure him out, no?"

Claire grinned. "I do wonder sometimes. It's the anthropologist in me."

A large gray fish jumped out of the water ahead of the boat. "Characin," Manny said, pointing toward it. "Very good eating." He watched it surface a couple of times, then turned to Claire. "Owen is a very private man. Much has happened in his life that has, how do you say, made him hard."

"That's what they all say," Claire said off-handedly.

Manny narrowed his gaze and wrinkled his brow. "No, senhora. Someone died that he loved very much many years ago. He blames himself."

Claire's grin left her face, and before her brain could censor her mouth, she said, "Who?"

Manny shook his head and held her in a penetrating gaze. "If he wants to tell you, he will. I have said too much already."

Claire blinked. Owen was divorced, but that didn't mean it couldn't be an ex-wife. Did he lie about having children? Seemed unlikely.

Manny went on. "I see how he looks at you. Different than other women."

Startled, Claire drew breath. *Which means what?* She studied Manny's enigmatic expression then looked off over the river. The muddy, brown waterway had widened considerably since they left Yurimagus two days ago. The land on their right had leveled off into dense ragged fields of tall, waving grasses. To her left, two and three story clapboard storefronts replaced the rag-tag wooden hovels she'd seen minutes ago. Three men carrying heavy loads of bananas over their backs trudged along the street bordering the shoreline. A short distance ahead of them stood several women brightly clothed in reds, whites, and yellows. She watched them busying themselves displaying fruit and vegetables on makeshift wood tables until she heard Manny stir beside her.

Crushing his cigar on the rail, he said, "I am going in for café now. You want me to bring you some?"

"No, thank-you." As he stepped away from the rail, Claire turned around and reached out, touching the director's arm. "Manny?"

He stopped and met her searching gaze. "Si."

She opened her mouth to ask him what he meant about Owen looking at her differently, but changed her mind because she didn't like the ramifications of the possible answer. Shaking her head, she smiled. "Never mind."

The director winked and patted her arm. "Do not worry about Owen. He will find this 'Lost Man' for you, okay?"

"Yeah."

Just then, Thad walked out onto the deck. He yawned and stretched his long arms upward. A pair of faded jeans hugged his bare waist and a tiny, gold cross-hung on a thin gold chain around his neck. Clearing his throat, he snuffed and said, "Morning."

Claire made room for him beside her. "Sleep well?"

He shrugged. "All right, I guess. You?"

She swatted a mosquito on her arm. "Not really. I'll be glad to get off this boat. You better put a shirt on. You'll get eaten up."

"I think they're more interested in you," he said, plucking one off her shoulder. "And I hear ya, I'll be glad to get off this thing, too. We got a long ways to go, though."

"Yeah. Don't remind me. And stop yawning."

He looked at her sidelong and grinned. "You know, in this light, you remind me of Katherine Hepburn in The African Queen."

Claire rolled her eyes. "Down, boy! Are the others up?"

"Yep. Miss cranky Tech-head was bitching about no hot water again." He spat into the water and wedged a fingernail between his front teeth. "She ought to be a real delight once we get in the forest."

"She'll be wanting cold showers soon enough: trust me," Claire said.

"I believe ya, don't worry about that," he replied, nudging her with a friendly elbow. "So, where's the boss-man? Figured he'd be up by now."

"Oh, I'm sure he's around somewhere," Claire said.

"Yeah, probably below decks checking cargo." Thad knotted his brow, erasing the boyish expression that lived on his face most of his waking hours. "You have any idea what's in those two large crates he brought on board in Yurimagus?"

"What crates?" Claire said, surprised.

Thad's brow rose. "You didn't see 'em?"

"No! Where are they?"

"Up front in the cargo hold."

Claire mulled over Thad's comment, remembering Owen's disappearing act back in Tarapoto. She felt her gut tighten as her suspicious instinct kicked in. *They're probably for one of the villages – holding parts for a generator or something like that. Better check it out though all the same.*

Eight

Iquitos, Peru

OWEN PULLED back the sliding steel door and entered the claustrophobic bridge of the Lírio do Rio. "Bom trabalho, Lino," Owen said, patting the captain on the shoulder.

The middle-aged, dark-skinned man smiled. "O seu nada. We'll dock here for a couple days to take on supplies and fuel. So, my passengers, they are comfortable?" He added, looking over the ragged shoreline cloaked in evening shadows. He turned the large wooden steering wheel of the boat two and a quarter turns.

"Good as gold," Owen said, looking out at the overcast sky that was darkening over the main channel. In the distance, he saw a bank of tiny yellow lights. The city of Iquitos was not far away.

Although the first 500 kilometers had been easy, Owen knew that guiding the large boat on the moody Amazon was never a small feat.

"I'll be needing your fare before we dock," Lino said.

Owen reached into the inside pocket of his bomber jacket. "How much?"

Lino leveled a narrow gaze at him. "Don't give me that crap. You know how much."

Owen laughed. "Just checking. I never know when ya gonna raise my rent. Fifteen hundred, right?"

Lino stared back.

"All right, eighteen-hundred," Owen said, peeling off a handful of notes and handing them to him. Unexpectedly, he heard a tap on the window outside on the gangway. He turned and saw Manny motioning for him to come out. Owen gave Lino a friendly jab in the arm. "Looks like I'm needed."

When Owen opened the bridge door, Manny furtively nodded toward the back of the boat. "You have a problem."

Owen slipped past him and came to the rail over-looking the stern. Down below, Claire came marching toward the ship's ladder with one of his modified compound bows in hand. When she saw him, she thrust the weapon upward and yelled to him. "Care to clue me in?"

Manny, who had followed him, quietly said, "She went below decks."

Owen sighed and started down the ladder. "I believe it's a compound bow," he said, hopping off the last rung.

"Don't patronize me," she snapped back. "I know what it is. There are two crates of them down there. What're you trying to pull?"

Owen marched forward, taking in her fierce gaze, flared nose and rigid jaw. Angry as she was, she still took his breath away. He took the weapon from her, smiled and said, "Nothing, Luv." But the minute he said it, he regretted it.

She drew a thin breath and through clenched teeth, said, "Just … don't!"

Oh-oh. I put my foot in it now. He braced himself for what he called the 'princess tantrum', which he had been on the wrong end of more often than he liked over the years. "Now don't get ya nickers all in a lather. I didn't mean anything by it. Just trying ta be friendly's all."

"Stop the bullshit, Mr. Macleod. I'm not in the mood. What are these things doing here? I want to know right now!"

There was no way he was going to tell her the truth; that the bows were for the Manaqüi. That was none of her business. His responsibilities were to guide and keep her team out of harm's way.

He stared back at her and said, "Tell me, what business ya have snooping in my gear, eh?"

Claire's expression iced over. "It's my expedition!"

"Yeah? Well, it's my charter here, Luv, an' out here an' in da bush, I'm da boss," Owen said. He held the bow up. "An' if you'll excuse me, I'll be putting this back where it belongs now."

Claire looked off over the water. Turning back, she said, "You think I'm stupid, Mr. Macleod? You think I don't know what you're up to? You can't arm primitive cultures with advanced technology."

"What'd'ya know about 'em, eh? You don't live here," Owen said, jabbing a finger at her. "Everything ya know, ya read in some rag up in da states. Spend time down here, get ta know 'em; then come talk ta me. 'Till then, keep ya preaching ta yourself."

Claire shook her head. "If you think they're going to use them for just hunting, you're quite mistaken."

Owen couldn't help but chuckle at her allegation.

"Go ahead, laugh," Claire growled. She opened her mouth to say more, but stopped and shook her head. "Why am I wasting my time?"

"I don't know. Why are ya?"

She narrowed her eyes at him, but beneath her fierce expression, Owen sensed something else. What was it? She looked back off over the water. Quietly, she said, "I took you for someone who gave a shit. Apparently, I was wrong." Her gaze drifted back to him, and it was exactly the same gaze Monica had given him the day she walked out of his life. "You're not interested in anything except yourself. So, what are you getting in return? No, never mind, I don't wanna know," she said. She shook her head and stalked off.

"Yeah, that's right, cast ya verdict an' walk away. God, save me from a righteous woman!"

Claire spun around. "And me from a Neanderthal."

From under the upper deck canopy, Owen heard Manny chuckle. "Yeah, that's right. I'm a Neanderthal, but when it comes ta bringing ya back in one piece, I'm da best ya got."

"I'm sure that's what you think, Mr. Macleod," she said over her shoulder.

"It's what I know," Owen shot back defiantly. He gave her long, retreating legs a last look and took a deep breath. This woman had gotten under his skin unlike any he had met in a long time. He stood there at a loss for words for a couple of minutes before heading for the galley door where Manny stood watching the whole thing. As he pulled the door open, Manny gave him a knowing smile.

"Naff off," Owen said, giving him a sidelong glance. He marched down the corridor and pushed through his cabin door into the tiny dim lit room. Eyeing his nightstand, he went over and picked up the silver hairpin he'd bought for Claire the morning they'd left Tarapoto. He'd been planning to give it to her tonight, but that was out of the question now. He stuffed it into his backpack, the jerked his hand back and sucked his finger. The pin had stuck him, drawing a bead of blood.

Later that night, Claire followed Thad, Jorge, and Molly down the wooden gangplank onto the long timber pier jutting out into the river. The sun had fled over the mountains an hour ago and in its wake left a black sky glittering with stars. From the distance, came the sound of mandolins. But Claire was not in a festive mood. *Compound bows! As if they'd use them for just hunting. Stupid Kiwi.*

A string of tiny green lights winked at her from somewhere out in the middle of the river. She watched them slowly move upstream as the smell of diesel and rotting bananas wrinkled her nose. What was Owen up to? Was her expedition a means to an end for him? She felt like that boat in the middle of the river, groping in the dark to find its way. Since she and Owen had parted, she had tried to make sense of things. But at this point, there were more questions than answers.

Twenty minutes later, she sat at a table in front of a little adobe restaurant. Beside her sat Molly and across from her were Thad and Jorge. Lively salsa notes flowed out through the open doors of a cantina down the street. Milling around outside of it was a group of leggy young women in colorful cotton skirts. As the sounds of laughter dribbled in the warm spring air, Claire felt Molly shift beside her.

"Look at Poppy with his fecking tongue lolling out of his mouth. He's like a bloodhound," Molly said leaning toward Claire.

Thad shot Molly a sneer and nudged Jorge with his elbow. "Look at the one in the short green dress. Man, is she sweet!"

"Not bad," Jorge answered picking at the label on his beer bottle.

"Oh, really?" Thad said, eyeing him.

Jorge took a long pull on the bottle. Wiping his lips with the back of his hand, he turned a furtive eye to Molly.

Claire cocked a brow. *Seems like Molly has another admirer.*

Thad said, "Think I'll buy them a drink. You coming, Jorge?"

Jorge shook his head. "I'm good."

"Suit yourself," Thad said, and downed the last of his beer. Getting up, he winked at Molly. "Don't wait up, kid."

Molly saluted him with a middle finger.

Claire polished off the last of her drink. As the tangy cocktail passed her lips, her tongue shriveled. Jorge wasn't kidding when he said pisco packed a punch. She set her glass down and gave her troubled thoughts over to Molly's pained expression. She aimed a thumb towards Thad's retreating back. "Don't let him get to you."

Molly pulled back and looked at her quizzically. "I don't."

Claire shook her head. *Oh, yes you do. It's written all over your face. He'll come around eventually, unless a certain somebody beats him to it.*

Molly was quiet a minute, then got up. "I'm going to the lady's room." She pointed towards Claire's empty glass. "You want another?"

Claire looked up. "Sure, why not."

"What about you, Jorge?" Molly said, as Claire dug a twenty note out of her pocket.

"Yes, but I will escort you," he said, then quickly added, "to the bar that is."

Claire smiled, handed her money over to Molly and watched them weave through the chattering crowd into the restaurant. Alone now, she sat back and closed her eyes, and as she did, her thoughts returned to Owen. Sure, he's a friend of a friend of Thad's, but that's no excuse, girl. You know you should've have researched him more. Now you're stuck with a ... what? A mercenary? Jesus!

She was sitting, fingers drumming on the table waiting for Molly to get back with their drinks when she heard the Kiwi's lilting voice ring out down the block.

Owen!

Her breath caught in her throat. *Great! Just what I need.* She crossed her arms, wanting to get up and leave when Molly and Jorge came back to the table.

Molly handed Claire her drink. "Uh-oh, don't look now, but the tool from down-under's here."

Oh, he's a tool all right, Claire mused picking up her glass.

"Hey, there ya are! Figured ya guys would find Hilario's. Having a good time?"

Claire took a deep breath and caught a whiff of his sandalwood cologne. It was a favorite of Jason's. She tried to ignore the effect it was having on her and stared ahead.

Molly said, "Marvy."

Which was Claire's sentiment exactly, although for different reasons. Out of the corner of her eye, she saw Owen pull a chair up. Felt his eyes on her back. *So, we're mister friendly all of a sudden. Hide behind a smile and dare me to strike first. Well, I'm not biting.*

"So, what'd'ya all think of Iquitos?" Owen said.

"It's okay," Molly said.

"Yeah, it is," Owen answered. He was quiet a moment, then tapped Claire on the arm. "Nice shirt. Red suits ya."

Claire eyed him sidelong. "Thank you." Suddenly, she had to get away from him before she ended up throwing her drink in his face. She stood. "Can I get you a beer?"

He leaned back in his chair, gauging her with a wry expression. "Why not?"

"What's your pleasure?" Claire said.

"Whatever's on tap, Luv. An' thanks. Mighty generous of ya." He turned, looking in Thad's direction. "I think da lad's in over his head with those pretty young chicas."

"He'd be in over his head with a moron," Molly snapped.

Owen raised a brow and shot Claire a sidelong grin. "Seems there's a bit trouble in da ranks here, Boss."

Molly scowled. "What?"

Claire shook her head. "Let it go, Jungle Boy."

Owen laughed, "Jungle Boy, is it? Well, I've been called worse. Actually, I kind'a like it. Rings of Tarzan!"

Claire gritted her teeth and rolled her eyes. "I'm off to the bar."

Claire fumed as she made her way through the crowded restaurant. *Tarzan, my ass! Well, Tarzan would never give advanced weapons to people who aren't ready for them. I ought to dump those things overboard! Hmmm ... what's stopping me?*

She thought about it a moment as she waited for the bar maid to fill her order. What she needed was an excuse to get back to the boat un-noticed. But nothing came to mind. She collected Owen's beer and headed back to the table. When she saw Thad still struggling to impress the young ladies, she smiled. Composing herself, she said, "I'm gonna round up the boy. Be right back."

With a curt smile, she turned heel and headed toward the cantina down the block, and when she was sure no one was looking, snuck off. But the cobbled street she had walked up hours ago was now hidden under a drape of sullen gloom. In the houses up in the hills, she heard the sounds of barking dogs and muttered voices.

A hundred yard down the road, she veered under the arms of a sprawling banyan tree, and in its drooping branches heard the skittering of some small animal. Her heart jumped. Taking a deep breath, she pushed on. But with every step, the feeling of being followed weighed in her mind.

Suddenly, the leaves of the banyan shivered, and out of the shadows walked a stout silhouette. Claire took a deep breath and gripped her Mace as the man stopped in the middle of the street. She gauged her options. Slipping out of her hiking boots was out of the question.

The man's arm went to his pants pocket. *Shit!* Her muscles tightened and her heart thumped. The space around her was wide open.

That was good. Five years of Tae-kwon-do arts had taught her not to get hemmed in. She fingered the pressure valve on the little canister in her purse. *Keep it hidden 'til he's just within reach.*

"Claire, is that you?"

She squinted into the gloom. "Manny?"

"Si."

Claire let out a sigh and pulled her finger away from the nozzle. "You scared the begeezus outta me!"

He drew a cigar out of his pocket, put it to his mouth, and started toward her. "What are you doing out here? Not safe for senhora to be walking the street alone so late at night."

"I'm heading back to the boat," she said. *To take care of some business I should've taken care of earlier.* She cleared her throat. "Long day, and I'm tired."

Manny struck a match, lit his cigar, and looked hard at her. "Hmmm ... You know, Manny is many things, but he is not mudo," he said tapping his head. "You are a smart senhora. You would not come back alone unless something has happened."

"Nothing happened, Manny. Really. I just want to get back to my cabin," Claire said, but couldn't hide the edge in her voice.

Manny cocked his brow and took a long thoughtful pull on his cigar. "Hmmm ... Okay. I will walk you back, though."

Claire gauged his staunch expression, trying to decide if he believed her. Knowing he'd seen her argue with Owen over the bows, she wondered what he might be thinking about her returning to the ship alone and unsupervised. She liked Manny, but he worked for Owen, and therefore looked to Owen's interests first. Finally, she said, "Thanks, I'd like that."

They strolled down the street together toward the docks, and as they walked, their conversation turned to family and friends. Manny asked her if she had brothers and sisters, and what her father did, and she was more than glad to keep things light. Anything to keep him away from asking probing questions she didn't want to answer. A liar she wasn't, and she was fairly certain he'd know if she were telling one.

"So, your padre; you and him, you weren't close?" Manny said.

Claire eyed him fleetingly. "We were until I left for college. My father was a military man. Navy. Old school. I love him, but he's a bit of a chauvinist. He sees women one way; married and raising children. I saw things different."

"Hmmm … he must be proud of your accomplishments, no?"

Claire stopped and looked at Manny. She had told him more than she had intended. In a matter of minutes, he had disarmed her. *Clever man.* She smiled and went on, "Yes, but he still hasn't forgiven me for abandoning him and Mom. Tell me, do you like guiding, or would you rather be doing something else?"

Manny blew a ring of smoke into the night air. "I like what I do. Senhor Burgess, Deus de maio rest his soul, started the company a long time ago. Hired me when I was just married."

"Oh, I thought the company was started by Owen." Claire said, surprised, as they started walking again.

"Nah," Manny said, tapping the ash from his cigar. "He came to work for Senhor Burgess fifteen years ago and they become very good friends … Say, did you see him in town?"

Claire groaned. "We passed."

Out of the corner of her eye, Claire saw him studying her again. He said, "Hmmm … you two got into things again, huh?"

"Not really. He knows how I feel."

"Si, but do not judge him. There is much you do not know."

Claire snorted. "Really, care to share?"

Manny swatted a mosquito. "That is not for me to say. I will tell you this; he loves the people of the forest more than you know. He gives them arcos for good reason. Pray you never have to see why."

Claire looked at him hard. *What did that mean?*

Nine

**The Valderón Compound – Rio Momon – eight kilometers
north of Iquitos, Peru**

J UAN MENDALINO opened the patio doors of Senhor Valderón's
sprawling mission revival mansion and stepped out onto the
stone patio. He had been pouring over details of the cartel's ex-
pansion into the rainforest for the last twelve hours and he was
tired and irritable. Drifting over to a stone knee-wall sweeping around
the patio, he wondered what Valderón was thinking.
*A coca plantation in the middle of the fucking forest? Is he crazy?
They're all crazy!* He drew a cigarette from behind his ear, put it to
his lips, and lit up. A ring of smoke drifted up into the warm, muggy
night teeming with mosquitoes. He eyed the path leading to the docks
at length. At the end of them were two fifteen meter custom jet boats
bobbing up and down in the water.

Suddenly, Valderón's deep, gritty laugh boomed from the open windows behind him. Juan glanced back then turned and panned the
prodigious forest as the sunset gave itself up to the ensuing darkness.
In the distance, a colony of bats spewed out over the trees, their erratic
flight peppering the fading sky.

Watching them, Juan thought of Valderón's plan and shook his head. He knew the farmland south of Iquitos was rich, easily monitored and maintained, and that Valderón had the locals under his thumb. Except, Valderón was running things. Not for long though. Soon, he would make his move. But first he had to made sure of the loyalty of his lieutenants.

The patio door opened behind him, spewing the voice of Latin America's famed tenor, José Cura, out into the night air. Juan turned as the barrel-chested Valderón headed toward him with a glass of bourbon in hand. "What are you doing out here? Come in. Have some food and drink."

"I'm not hungry," Juan muttered.

Valderón sipped his bourbon. "What is wrong? You are very moody these days. Something on your mind I should know about?"

Juan took a drag of his cigarette, hoping the evening shadows were hiding his scowl. "Just thinking, is all."

"Good. That is why you are here with me and not standing up there with your thumb up your ass," Valderón said, nodding toward the sentry on the upper deck behind them. "Just don't think too much. It could be unhealthy for you. Even though you are engaged to my Reyna, business is business. Comprende?"

Juan felt sudden heat come to his face. "Comprendo."

Valderón was quiet a minute, then fell into an easy conversational tone, talking about classical Latin music, which he loved, and baseball, which was a close second. Juan just listened. A complex man, Valderón had risen to the top because he was ruthless, willing to do whatever it took. And those who underestimated him quickly found themselves swimming face down in the river.

At length, Valderón halted his musings on music and took a long look at Juan. Even in the gloom, Juan could feel the man's coal-black eyes measuring him, gauging his mood. Valderón leaned in close, and in a soft, menacing tone, said, "I know your aspirations. Do not fuck with me. You will regret it."

Juan didn't say anything. He knew better than to argue the point.

Valderón went on. "Yes, it is good to be hungry. Just remember not to take more than you can eat."

Juan felt Valderón's powerful hand on his shoulder. "Si," Juan said, tightening his jaw.

"See you keep it that way," Valderón said. "I don't want to spoil my daughter's big day after all the money I spent on it." He drank down the rest of his bourbon and went back inside.

Iquitos, Peru

Owen stormed back to the boat with Thad, Jorge, and Molly on his heels. Of all the stupid, idiotic things Claire could possibly do, walking alone on the darkened streets of Iquitos was the worst, especially down to the docks. Even he respected that area. With every step he took, his anger rose. Thankfully, Manny had been on his way to see him and had run into her or who knows what could've happened. And why did his heart skip when he found she'd headed back alone? Sure, she was a client, but it was more than that.

He squashed the uncomfortable thought and stomped up the gangplank. Stepping on board the Lírio do Rio, he removed his hat, and surveying the stern, found her at the aft bulwark rail looking out over the water and chatting with Inacio. When the young porter saw him marching toward them, he made a hasty retreat and joined his brother Paulo across deck.

"Just what in da hell were ya doing?" Owen said.

Claire turned. "Excuse me?"

"I said; what in da hell were ya doing?"

"I'm sorry, I don't believe I understand your question," Claire said, her voice calm and reserved. "In fact, it's a question I keep asking myself, too. What was I thinking when I hired you? And you know what? For the life of me, I can't answer it. You've been nothing but evasive and cavalier since we left Lima." Her gaze turned toward her team, who were looking on a few meters away, then swung back onto him. "What aren't you telling me? I want to know the truth, and I want to know it now."

"Say what?" Owen said, wondering how she had turned the tables on him so quickly.

Claire leaned back against the rail and crossed her arms. "There's something coming up ahead that you're hiding, and I want to know what it is."

Manny! I need ta have a chat with 'im. He looked up into the night, gathering his wits.

"I'm waiting, Mr. Macleod."

Only one person could ever back him into a corner like this, and that was Monica. The memory of her ultimatum echoed in his mind, and his body stiffened. He set his gaze on Claire like a firebrand. "The only danger ahead, is if ya pull another stunt like that. You have any idea what ya could've walked inta?"

"Don't go caveman on me. I can take care of myself just fine."

Owen snorted, his hand crushing the brim of his hat. Turning to the uninvited audience, he said, "Isn't there someplace ya all need ta be?"

There were frowns all around. Claire said, "It's all right guys, I'm fine."

"That right?" Owen said.

"Yes, quite," Claire said, and shooed her entourage off.

When they were alone, Owen lowered his voice. "Tell me, what would ya have done if Manny had been a skin trader? Huh? Point that can of Mace at 'em an' scare 'em away?"

Claire's defiant expression thawed.

"Yeah, I saw it your bag in Tarapoto." He looked off over the dark waters, collected himself and continued, "Look here, da cartels pay big money for foreign women down here. American women, especially! Use 'em as collateral when things get sticky ... among other things. These wharf rats know that, an' where there's one, there's always more waiting nearby."

Claire drew herself up. "If you're trying to scare me, save it."

"Just trying ta keep ya alive."

"Right. How is it men like you always think we women are into the strong-and-silent types? Not all of us are bimbo's, Mr. Macleod. If you think I don't know what you're trying to do, you're sadly mistaken."

"Yeah, and what might that be?"

"Deflecting my questions about what's going on. You're hiding something, and I want to know what it is. Does it have anything to do with the cargo below?"

Owen looked at her hard. "I'm not deflecting anything. An' if ya pull something like that again, I'll end this tramp."

"Is that so?" Claire said in an icy tone.

"Yeah, contract be damned, I'll turn this whole thing around," Owen said, meeting her gaze.

As they squared off, he saw her mind working. Finally, she said, "I wonder … how does that work with your overall plan, hmmm? Seems to me, that puts a crimp in it. You have a good night, Mr. Macleod. I'm going to bed." She turned and walked away.

Owen remained on deck after Claire left, mulling over how to deal with her. He stood at the bulwark rail where she had left him with his hat in hand, watching the waxing moon wade through the murky clouds. As he did so, he realized Claire's uncanny resemblance to Monica. Leave it alone, he mused shaking his head.

But it was too late. His attraction to her had already taken root. He pulled the leather cord hanging around his neck out from under his shirt. Lifting the pear-shaped stone on it to his lips, he thought of Calen. He didn't have room in his life for a woman. He listened to the steady lapping of the water against the hull of the boat. Looking down onto its dark reflective surface, he imagined himself and Claire together. He grunted. *I don't need this shite, not now, not ever.*

"Hey, Boss," Manny said, coming up from behind. Owen slipped the stone back under his shirt and turned around. Manny had a can of beer in each hand. He handed one to Owen and pulled the tab on his own. After taking a gulp, he said, "Senhora is very feisty."

"Yeah, an' it doesn't help ya giving her fuel for da fire, mate," Owen said, popping his beer tab open. He took a long pull and eyed his friend. "Ya know why she came back, right? She had mischief on her mind. Make sure ta keep my bows under wraps, okay? Our friends need 'em."

Manny nodded, "Si. But Senhora is clever. It is only a matter of time before she does something you do not want her to. Why not tell her why you are giving bows to the forest people? She will understand."

Owen chuckled.

Manny shook his head. "Do not judge her too quickly. She has told me some things."

"Such as?"

"Her time in Africa with the people there. She told me how she got them medicine for the sleeping sickness that overtook their village, and when famine came the following year, she bartered for food with the local militia. She cares about people. I see it in her eyes – hear it in her voice. There are many things people can hide behind their tough exteriors, but compaixão, no."

Owen sighed. "Nah, she's too headstrong and full of herself."

"Hmmm … just like a certain senhor I know," Manny said. He took a sip of his beer and yawned.

"What's that supposed ta mean?"

Manny eyed him sidelong. "You know exactly what it means." He bent his neck, stretching thick muscles, then cast a knowing glance at Owen. "You know, she like you."

Owen raised a brow. "Yeah, like a praying mantis loves her mate. Don't look at me like that. I saw ya lurking in da shadows, watching her bite my head off."

Manny shrugged. "For one who knows so much, there is a lot that passes you by, my friend."

"Is that so?"

"Si."

Owen always enjoyed Manny's 'insights' about him. Not that Manny didn't know a lot about his past; he did. It was the assumptions Manny made about him that amused him most. "Go on."

Manny eyed him pointedly. "She talks about you, asks questions." He put his finger up in a halting motion. "It is not what you think. She asks about who you are when you are not guiding. Why you are so distant? Trust me, this woman would not waste her time talking about you if she did not like you."

"Really?"

"Si. She care about you."

Owen snorted. "Yeah, right."

"You laugh, but there is much you do not see," Manny said. He paused then continued. "We go back a long way, no?"

"Yeah, we do," Owen said, wondering where this was heading.

Manny paused. "You know me, I never mess around in other people's business. But I need to tell you something ... You live in the past too much."

"You're right, never a good idea messing in people's business," Owen said.

Manny ignored him. "I see how you look at her. Not like the others. She does something to you down inside," he said, thumping his chest. He put his hand on Owen's shoulder. "It is okay to love again. Monica walked out on you for something that was not your fault. Calen got bit by a mosquito. Malária took his life, not you."

"Yeah, well, tell that ta Monica," Owen snapped back.

Manny went silent for a moment then quietly said, "You still care about her. I can see it?"

"That's where you're wrong," Owen retorted. But in truth, he couldn't be sure. Part of him hated her for condemning him, part him needed her forgiveness, and another part wanted ... what? He gritted his teeth and eyed Manny defiantly. "I don't want ta talk about this. Understand?"

Manny drained his beer and looked away. "Si, but you cannot hide forever from the truth."

"What truth, Manny?" Owen cried. "It was me who insisted on taking Calen inta da forest against her wishes. It was me who didn't make sure he took his meds." He crushed the can in his hand. A raindrop hit his arm. "Don't lecture me on da truth. I live with that shite every day of my life!"

"Is that so?" Manny said, raising his voice. "I think it is guilt, and it will eat you out from the inside until you are old and alone. Is that what you want?"

Owen was dumbfounded. Manny had never raised his voice at him. More than that, Manny had trod on sacred ground. He balled his hand around the crumpled can. "What I want is another can of beer, an' for this conversation ta end," Owen growled. A flash of lightning lit the black sky far off and another raindrop hit his face.

They stared at each other under the dim yellow halo of the ship's running lights as the drops turned into rain. Of all the people in the world, Manny was the one person Owen could count on to respect his private life. They had been tramping together for fifteen years, bailed each other out of tight spots, attended baptisms and confirmations, graduations, and weddings. It was Manny who had stood by him after Calen died and Monica walked out. The man had never asked questions or told him how to feel or what to do. Why now?

Finally, Manny nodded. "Ok, I am finished." He nodded toward the galley door as if nothing had happened and smiled. "I saw a bottle of rum under the sink. You interested?"

Owen blinked. Manny had always been a man who could let go of things at the drop of a hat and move on. But this was no simple matter, and he didn't know whether to be angry or amused. He put his hat on as Manny finished the rest of his beer, and said, "I might be."

"Good, I hate drinking alone," Manny said. He slapped Owen on the shoulder. "Let us go inside before we become drowned rats."

Ten

Iquitos, Peru

CLAIRE LOOKED out of her cabin window as another cramp ripped through her. She had been awake since dawn trying to come to grips with what lay in front of her on the bed. She stared out into the ever-brightening sky as the musical voices of dockworkers filtered into her room from her open window. Pregnant. Against all odds, she had been pregnant after all. She put her hand out and drew the bloody towel toward her. What would this child have meant? What choices would she have had to make?

Her mind careened back and forth between her career at Berkley and the vision of what it would have been like to see her child grow up. She was certain it would've been a boy, probably called Alex, because it was the name she had loved years ago when dreaming of having a family. Yet, her career at Berkley was all she had known since the doctors told her she would never get pregnant. What would she have done if she lost her teaching position? She'd seen it happen before. Women in the department took maternity leave and never came back. Sometimes it was their choice and sometimes it was the University's because, yes, there were ways to get around the Family Leave Act.

And there would also be the looks she'd get from faculty, and the gossip. Although she never said anything, it was no secret Jason and she were not getting along near the end. Noah's name would certainly be batted around at the water-cooler, and even though she had issues with him, he had been her husband once and she had loved him; snob and sexist though he was and continued to be.

Tears ran down her face. She leaned forward and gathered the bloody towel into her hands. Holding it, she imagined what he might have become. Would he have had his father's square face and deep blue eyes or would he have had her high cheekbones and dimples? Would he have been tall like her father? Would he have followed in Jason's footsteps or hers? So much she could never know.

Suddenly, a knock came to her door. It was Thad on the other side. "Claire, you awake?"

She carefully set the towel down and cleared her throat. "Yes, but I'm not dressed. What's up?"

"Need to talk."

"Can it wait?"

"Yeah, sure. You all right?"

"Ummm … yes. Just busy."

"Okay, see you on deck?"

"Sure," Claire muttered. She frowned, wanting to cocoon herself in her room, but it wasn't possible, so she got up and threw her robe on. The storage room was ahead of Molly's cabin down the passageway. Tiptoeing out of her room, she headed down to it. When she tried the door, it was locked. *Damn it!*

Suddenly, she heard the sound of footsteps clicking down the passageway. She froze, turned toward the sound to see a tall man casting shadows and heading her way. *Please, not him, not now.*

"Can help you?"

Claire blinked. Thank God, he wasn't Owen. She composed herself as the crewman approached. "Yes, I need a towel."

The man considered her a moment, then pulled a ring of keys from his pocket. "Did your room not have towel?" He said in a deep baritone voice.

Claire snugged her robe around her tight as she stood before the man. "Yes, but I also need one for my hair."

His burnished, ebony face broke into a broad smile. "Of course. Long time since we have senhoritas on board." His dark eyes glanced down her robe. "Did you hurt yourself? There is blood on your robe."

Claire's heart thumped. "No. I just nicked my leg shaving this morning."

The man glanced at the pear-sized stain on her robe. Finally, he said, "Okay. Help self. I leave unlocked for other senhorita. When you done, shut door."

"Obrigado." Claire said, as he pulled the door open. She watched him turn and continue on down the passageway, then entered the small, cluttered room. The shelves were heaped with piles of sheets and large towels. She pulled a set of bedding down along with a bath sheet. As she did so, something deep inside her whispered, bury the child. The next thing she knew, she was searching for something suitable to put her unborn Alex in.

She pawed around the shelves. There were cleaning supplies, dirty rags, boxes of toilet paper, napkins, and paper towels. The only thing that came near to what she wanted was an old wooden cigar box on the top shelf. But it was too small and even if she could fit the towel in, she would not put Alex in a cigar box. There had to be something else. Ten minutes later, the contents of the shelves sat on the floor at her feet.

She sighed, and against her will, forced herself to pull the cigar box down off the shelf. Lifting the lid, she brought it up to her nose expecting the telltale scent of tobacco. Instead, she was surprised to find the fragrant scent of cedar.

She shut the lid, considering. She could make it work if she wanted to. If only 'SAN MARTIN CIGARS' hadn't been written over the front of it. But nothing else was available, so she picked up after herself, tucked the box under her arm, and went back to her room.

Thirty minutes later, Claire pushed through the Galley door into the noisy mess hall. Her team sat across the room apart from the ship's crew. Owen's men were sprinkled amongst the river-boaters, listening to the latest news traveling up and down the river while forking marinated fish, scrambled eggs and bun bread into their mouths. The aroma of brewed coffee permeated the room.

Claire wound her way through the scattered tables toward Thad, Jorge, and Molly. Thad looked up as she approached. "It's about time; you almost missed chow."

Claire sat gingerly, hoping her body wouldn't betray her. "It's okay, I'm not all that hungry."

Knowing looks passed around the table between her team. "Where's our fearless leader?"

"Haven't seen him," Molly said. She slugged down the rest of her coffee and stood. "I'm going for another refill. You want a cup?"

"I'd prefer tea," Claire said, scanning the room. After Molly left, Thad leaned in toward her and whispered, "You feeling okay? You're white as a sheet."

"I'm fine," Claire said.

Thad looked at her. "None of my business, but what went on last night? He was plenty pissed."

"Was he?" Claire said quietly. She eyed Jorge typing on his laptop. "You online?"

"Yes."

"How? We're in the middle of no-where."

"The boat has a transponder. I linked up with it," Jorge said.

"Really?" Claire said, then glancing back at Thad, said, "Don't worry. He's just like Noah. All bark, no bite."

Thad stared back. He didn't look convinced.

Jorge shut his laptop and stood. "It rained hard last night. Going to be hot and sticky today. I think I'll go into town. Get away from the bugs."

"Mind if I borrow that?" Claire said, pointing to the laptop.

He shrugged. "Sure. The wireless is a little shaky, though."

"That's alright, just need to check something out." To Thad she said, "Could you get me a couple eggs? Easy over with a little papa rellena on the side?"

Thad got up and stretched. "You want salsa?"

Claire shook her head. When Jorge handed her his laptop, she turned to him. "I'll drop it off to your cabin when I'm done."

When she was finally alone, Claire dragged the cursor over the search engine's empty field and typed: 'Iquitos cemeteries'. As she sat waiting for the page to load, she darted her eyes back and forth between the screen, Thad, and Molly. *Come on, hurry up!* The screen flickered then loaded the page. More choices. She scrolled down the list, double clicked, and waited again. The page listing the AnaStahl Adventist cemetery came up just as Molly started back toward her. Memorizing the address, she closed the window.

"Find what ya were looking for?" Owen said, sitting beside her with a mug of steaming tea.

Startled, Claire jerked back. "You mind not sneaking up on people?"

He pulled a candy bar from his shirt pocket and tore the wrapper off with his teeth. "Sorry 'bout that." "What happened to you, you look like hell," Claire said.

"Long night. Ya don't look so good yaself."

She caught a whiff of his breath and wrinkled her nose. "Retreat into a bottle last night, did we?"

Owen's eyes turned needle sharp. "Ya like a ill-humored snake, ya know that? I come down here ta make nice with ya, an' all ya can do is hiss at me!" He paused. "Well, let me ask ya something. What bug crawled up ya arse, eh?"

"Hey, Owen," Molly said, returning. She set Claire's tea in front of her.

Owen pushed his chair back and stood.

"It's all right, I can sit over there," Molly said.

Owen bit a large piece of his candy bar off. "Nah, that's all right. I was just leaving."

By the time Claire was finally able to sneak away into town, it was mid-afternoon. As she walked through the narrow streets, heading toward the hills, she thought about Owen's biting remark. She probably deserved it, but then, she really didn't care. He was nothing but a self-serving asshole whose whole world revolved around him. Well, her world was shitting on her pretty good too, and she was in no mood for the delicate ego of a man.

At length, she turned up the main avenue and headed north under the heat of the afternoon sun. Twenty minutes later, she came to a dirt lane that led to the gate of a small cemetery edging up to the forest. She trudged along it, and slipped silently inside the hallowed grounds, veering toward the trees. Here she found a secluded patch of grass. Pulling a small trowel from her backpack, she began digging. When she finished, she sat back on her heels and stared down at the little wooden box, thinking about Jason and all that had happened between them. She knew it was pointless, but she couldn't help wondering how he would have reacted if he had known she was pregnant.

She knew the answer and it unsettled her to have thought about it. She put her fingers to her lips, kissed them and touched the box. At least, here in the cemetery, Alex wouldn't be alone. Her throat tightened as she pushed the pile of dirt in over the box. Then closing her eyes, she recited the rosary. Though she hadn't said it since she was fifteen, the words came easily. "Be at peace, little one," she whispered placing a smooth stone over the plot. "And may the saints protect you."

Eleven

Rio Amazonas – 370 kilometers west of Santo Antonio do Içá.

CLAIRE STOOD on the foredeck looking out over the passing shoreline as the Lírio do Rio slid through the morning mist rising over the river. She hadn't been sleeping the last few nights because her mind was preoccupied with the miscarriage and the tenuous state of the expedition. She looked up at the ever-brightening pre-dawn sky that was threatening rain and eyed the mist-laden riverbank. In the gloom, tall reeds and water grasses waved in a subtle wind. Above them, drooped broad, pumpkin-shaped leaves flopping back and forth on pod-heavy limbs. Down river, flitting shadows skimmed the watery surface.

Against the serene indifference of the river, the Lírio do Rio's diesel engine thrummed . It was not an alien sound to her. She had grown up around diesels as a kid, spending a lot of time in her father's shadow while at the shipyards of Annapolis. This one was a Fairbanks-Morse that should have been retired years ago. She listened to the compressors huffing and puffing below deck, driving the opposing-piston leviathan with heaving strokes. Hopefully the beast would deliver them to Santo Antonio do Içá before hurling its last breath into the air.

The wind picked up, strafing the surface of the water. In the distance, thunder rumbled. Claire liked the sound of thunder along with a soaking rain. It settled her when she felt troubled and uncertain about life. Gathering her hair into a knot, she shoved it under her Giant's baseball cap and pulled the collar of her blouse snug around her neck. *Why all this, and why now?*

She couldn't get the image of her miscarried child out of her mind. She sighed and stood quietly by the rail for some time, trying to figure things out. But no matter how hard she tried to put reasons to actions, she couldn't find an answer. Then her mother's soft, clear voice came to her from out of the past. *God is tapping you on the shoulder, Claire. Listen to him!*

She shook her head. It had been too long since she'd prayed, and she wasn't sure how to begin or even if she wanted to. She wasn't sure she wanted to hear what He had to tell her, especially if it had anything to do with the email she received last night from Noah.

She could still see the imbedded note in it from a friend of Noah's in her mind's eye. It reported that Owen had grown up in the Amazon amongst the tribes, joining them and aiding their resistance against the government-run copper mining industry. But it was the final paragraph in the email that jolted her. Owen had lost a ten-year-old son.

It certainly explained a lot about the enigmatic Kiwi. She looked down into the eddying water rushing past the hull of the boat, reconsidering her recurring thought; was he using her expedition for his own purposes? Maybe he really wasn't that devious. The revelation about his son left her conflicted.

Did she owe him an apology for not putting up with his cave-man attitudes; for calling the shots as she saw them at the breakfast table the other morning? A slight twinge coursed through her abdomen. She took a breath and waited for it to pass. The boat groaned, bobbed, and shifted its direction slightly to port. She glanced up to the bridge and saw Owen out on the afterdeck standing with the quartermaster. Whether he knew she was below him, she couldn't guess, but she had a good idea he did. Not too many things slipped past the Kiwi's keen observations. She saw him lift his field glass to his eyes, look up river, and point to something. A moment later he was gone, and shortly after that, the boat veered hard to port, heading for a small sheltered cove.

Behind her, came the running of feet and orders being barked out. One of the crewmen ran up to her. "Best to go inside."

"Why? What's going on?" Claire said alarmed.

The man pointed to a dark speck moving toward them from way up river. "Jet boat. FARC coming."

Suddenly, Owen pushed through the boat's main deck outer doors. He waved his arms at her, urging her to move it. Claire felt the crewman's hand on her back pushing her toward Owen and the open door.

"Hurry it up," Owen shouted.

When Claire came under the canopy of the upper deck and saw Owen's tense expression, she put aside her need-to-know-right-then and went inside. The crewman led her to the lower deck and showed her to a small, tight compartment forward of the main engine room. Holding the door open to it, was Manny. She looked at him hard.

"Jet boats are coming down the river bearing armed men from the cartels," he said. "Sometimes they board cargo boats looking for supplies. If they find pretty senhoritas, there is no telling what they will do."

Claire felt her body stiffen.

Manny looked away.

Suddenly, Owen's warning three nights ago came roaring back. *So, Owen wasn't kidding when he told me about the skin traders?* Just then, Molly, Thad, and Jorge showed up, bleary eyed and annoyed, along with a member of the ship's crew.

Claire stepped into the small compartment and waved them in. Manny hardened his face and eyed Claire. "You must be quiet until I come get you. Very important, okay?" He pointed toward a large wooden crate. "When I shut the door, push that in front of it, and do not remove it until you hear me come back. I will knock three times, wait, then knock twice more."

Claire nodded, her gaze never leaving the venerable director until he pulled the door shut behind him. When she heard the click of the lock, her heart skipped. Turning toward Thad and Jorge, she said, "Okay, let's get that in front of it, like he said."

Fifteen minutes later, they heard the lock click. Every muscle in Claire's body tensed. For an interminable few moments it felt like all the air had left the room until suddenly they heard three knocks. Thad moved toward the crate, but Claire reached out and stopped him. Putting her finger to her lips, she mouthed the words, "not yet", and waited fitfully for the follow-up knocks. When it came, she let out the breath. Finally she nodded to Thad and Jorge, and a minute later the crate was pushed aside and the door opened with Manny and Owen standing outside.

"That was quick," Thad said to Manny as he stepped out.

"Si. We were lucky. They passed by us very fast."

Owen shot Claire what she believed was a genuine look of apology, but it was more than apologetic. There was something else there. Fearfulness maybe? She couldn't tell. He stepped back as she came out. "We all need ta talk, but let's get our legs under us first, eh?"

The team gathered in Lírio do Rio's mess hall a half hour later around four tables that were pushed together. Owen sat hunched over his cup of coffee and looked at each member of the team in turn. His gaze lingered longest on Claire.

"Folks, we have a game changer here," Owen said. "If the FARC is riding da river this far downstream, there's something going on, an' t'ain't good."

"What's this FARC?" Molly said.

"They're a para-military organization out of Columbia with ties ta drug cartels. Most of their business is up north so we weren't worried about 'em too much," Owen said.

"But now they are moving south," Manny put in.

"Moving south?" Claire said. "You sound as if you knew this already."

"We had our suspicions, but no one knows what really goes on down river," Manny said.

"So, how come we're just hearing about this now?" Thad said, annoyance in his voice.

"Like Manny said, it was just a suspicion, an' we didn't want ta frighten ya for no reason," Owen said.

Thad shook his head and kicked back in his chair. "Un-fucking believable. Jesus, you didn't think we might just be a little bit interested in knowing about this before we got on the goddamned boat!"

"Thad," Claire said. "Enough." She looked at Owen and said, "What now?"

Owen sat back in his chair. "My job is ta guide ya ta this bushman, but bringing ya back safe an' sound trumps it."

"Meaning?" Claire said, pretty sure she knew where this was heading.

Owen stared back at her as if gauging what she might say to his decided response. At last, he said, "Meaning, once we get ta Santo Antonio, I'm thinking on turning this gig around."

Thad opened his mouth then shut it. Molly gritted her teeth and looked down. Jorge stared off into the empty space behind them. Claire took a deep breath. This trip was turning into a colossal mess. She looked upward. Why? Everything she had done for the last five years, the reams of grant applications she had written, the arm twisting, cajoling and yes, even begging for this expedition was evaporating right in front of her.

She closed her eyes. *If this ends here, it's over. I'll never get back. Everything I've worked for will be lost.* She debated what to do. Too much had already been taken away from her. Hardening her resolve, she looked at Owen and cleared her throat. "I appreciate your concern, and I agree, the safety of our team is paramount. But do we know for sure they'll be anywhere near where we're going?"

Manny raised a brow.

"Wait, hear me out," Claire said as Owen opened his mouth. "They're past us, right?"

He nodded. "Yeah, but we don't know where they're heading. Could be five or thirty 'K' down river."

"Or it could be a hundred," Claire said. "Look, why don't we play it by ear? If we see them again, we turn around and go back. But if we don't, I don't see how it endangers us going into the forest."

Everyone looked at Owen.

"It's not about pinching or flogging boats, Claire," Owen replied. "They have interests inland. Da stuff they take usually supplies their bases."

"But how far inland are they? Deep?"

Manny said, "Probably not. They need the river."

"That's exactly my point," Claire said. "We're going deep into the forest. What are the chances of running into them? You said you know the way, Owen. If nothing else, why couldn't we go round about and avoid them?"

Owen was quiet a moment. Finally, he said, "Who knows. Ya may be right, but it's still risky." He waved his hand out over the table toward the team. "Ya all willing ta chance it?"

Thad spoke up. "I wanna go on. At least as far as Claire suggests."

Jorge's gaze came back to the table. "Me, too. I did not come all this way to turn around."

Claire looked at Molly. "What about you?"

Molly looked up, determination in her eyes. "Yeah, at least give it a shot."

Owen ran his hand over his face. "All right, we'll give it a go. But if I see another boat, we're turning back, no if, ands, or buts."

Claire nodded. "Agreed."

They all sat with their decision a minute, then got up one by one and left the table until it was just Owen and Claire left. She stood and came beside him. "I'm sorry for what I said to you the other morning. It wasn't very nice."

"Yeah, me too."

Twelve

Rio Amazonas – Two days later; 120 kilometers west of Santo Antonio do Içá

A LOUD POP woke Owen from a sound sleep. He shot out of bed and bolted into the passageway barefoot wearing only a pair of jeans. Heart pumping, he looked both ways trying to figure out where the noise had come from. It was too loud to have come from a gun.

Several doors down, Claire poked her head out. "What was that?"

"Don't know," he said, starting toward her. "Make sure everyone stays put 'til I find out."

He trotted down the passageway and went out into the thick, laden mist blanketing the boat. Crewmen ran back and forth, radios in hand and looking down at the water over the port bulwark rails.

Owen nabbed one of them as they passed by. "What's going on?"

The man pulled the radio away from his mouth and said, "Big problem. Main compressor line ruptured."

Owen looked out into the silvered gloom. The river was always changing; sediment moving downstream creating shoals where none had been before. Visions of the steel hull peeling off the boat flashed before him. He turned and headed up to the bridge, taking the companionway ladder two steps at a time. He found the quartermaster and officer on duty standing on the afterdeck outside the bridge. They looked up as he came near. "Where's Lino."

"Busy," said the Quartermaster. He leaned out over the rail, directing one of the crew to the bow and circled his finger in the air above his head. The man below powered up the windlass and slowly let out the thick steel chain with the anchor.

The Officer on Duty said in Portuguese, "You need to go back down and while you are at it, kindly remove your lady scientist from the engine room."

Owen sighed. *Just great.* He scuttled down the companionway ladder and made for below decks. On the way, he ran into Manny, Hector, and Rameriz.

"I heard about the compressor," Manny said, joining him as he walked. Rameriz and Hector stayed behind, noting that they preferred the open-air spaces to the tight confines of below decks.

Owen opened the hatch door. "Yeah, we're not going anywhere for a while."

"Somebody is not going to like that," Manny said, following him down the narrow companionway.

"Right," Owen said over his shoulder. He hopped off the last rung and stalked down the dark corridor. As he pulled the engine room door open, he added, "An', I have ta remove that certain somebody from here 'fore she gets us all thrown off da boat. Care ta join me? She seems ta like you best."

Stepping inside the hot, suffocating room, Owen followed a steel-grated walkway lined with pipes, gauges and conduit to the large diesel engine. Standing beside it in a oil stained T- shirts and overalls were two men consulting a clipboard. They looked up when he cleared his throat.

"I was told ya have company down here needs escorting upstairs," Owen said.

"Oh, hi, Owen," Claire said coming around the corner. She set a hefty socket wrench on the motor mount and whisked a gob of soot off her cheek with the side of her hand. Giving him a passing glance, she went and huddled with the crewman and engineer. "The piped connection is toast," she said, pointing at a large iron casting coming out of the block behind her, "but I think we can jerry rig something out of the boiler's hot water line."

The engineer frowned.

Claire rolled her eyes. "Come on–like we've had any hot water?"

Manny grinned as the engineer pursed his lips. "Okay, but we will need a gasket. The pipe is too small."

Claire swept her hand over her hair, pulling it out of her face. "We use the pipe insulation. I need a hack saw."

Owen felt a poke in his side. Leaning toward him, Manny whispered, "Looks like you better leave her right where she is."

Claire snatched the socket wrench up and shoved it toward Owen. "Mind rolling up your sleeves up and pitching in?"

Owen scratched his head. "Sure, what needs doing?"

"I started backing the manifold bolts out. You could pick up where I left off." She cocked her brow as she eyed his bare waist. "Might wanna get a shirt on. That block is plenty hot."

Seven hours later, Owen sat in the mess hall staring at the webpage on his laptop. He had been viewing sites concerning the FARC's movements on the river since Claire ran out of things for him to do a couple hours ago. Sipping his herbal tea, he found himself preoccupied with her. She had left him dumbfounded. Never in his wildest imagination would he have seen her crawling around an engine. He shook his head, then suddenly sensed someone standing behind him. He looked up into Molly's snooty expression. "Can I help ya?"

"More like, can I help you?" she said.

"Wasn't aware I needed any."

"Trust me, you do." She threw her bag on the table, sat beside him and gestured toward the laptop. "Give."

Owen bit his tongue and pushed it in front of her.

"What exactly are you searching for?"

"News of our friends up north."

Molly's fingers danced across the keyboard. "You mean the drug runners?"

"Yeah, 'em," he said.

"You have a name for them?"

Owen drew breath and forced a smile. "Sure, we're on a first name basis."

Molly glared back at him. "You wanna find them or not?"

Keeping his good humor was getting harder by the minute. "Yeah, sure."

"Then I need a name for one of these feckers," Molly said. "Certainly their reputation precedes them?" She reached into her bag and dug her flash drive out. Pulling the cap off, she inserted it, and double clicked. "Name please?"

Owen leaned over her shoulder as she opened one window after another on the laptop. "What's that you're installing?"

"A little helper." She sighed. "Name!"

Owen looked up at the ceiling. "Try, Valderón."

"Thank you," she said. "This might take a while. Why don't you go find something to do … like take a shower?"

Just as he was about to give her a lesson in manners, the Lírio do Rio rumbled, and with it, the engine roared back to life. Suddenly an image of Claire pasted with grease and soot flashed before him. He chuckled. She'd done it, gotten the old beast running again. He smiled despite his irritation with Molly and leaned over her shoulder. "Wait till ya out in da forest a spell. Ya learn da meaning of ripe, yeah."

An hour later, Owen stepped out of the shower, toweled off, and placed the leather thong necklace with his son's greenstone around his neck. After shaving, he sauntered back up to the mess hall and found Molly still at his table working. He grabbed a cup of tea and headed for her.

"How goes da battle?"

Her eyes remained fixed on the screen. "It goes."

"Any luck?" he said sitting down next to her.

She turned the screen in his direction as he sipped herbal tea. When he saw the Brazilian Interior Agency Seal, and the picture of Valderón below it with a full dossier on the drug lord, complete with satellite photography of all his compounds, he almost spit his tea out. "Jesus, ya hacked into da Feds site. And on my laptop."

"Relax. They don't even know we're here," Molly said.

"Right, that's what da mouse says just before da cat pounces on 'im," Owen said, running his fingers through his hair. This was dangerous. Too many people in the Agency would love to find him! Yet ... it didn't hurt that he could find out what certain people were up to. More than that, he was curious how Molly had gotten access into a site his techie back in Christchurch had failed to breach for the last five years. He pursed his lips. "How'd ya slip in?"

"That's a secret," Molly said. "What'd'ya wanna know?"

He put his index finger to her chin and turned her face toward him. "How'd ya get in?"

Molly aimed a defiant glare at him. "I ran a program I wrote."

"What kind'a program?" Owen said, withdrawing his finger.

"A worm. Works like a mirror – reflects the firewalls security measures and encryption protocols back on the host and gains access."

"A worm – wonderful!"

"I'm not a fecking geek," she growled. "I'm a programmer, as if you have any idea what that is."

"I guess that's supposed ta make me feel comfy?" Owen said. He pointed to the screen. "All right, give me da poop an' I'll try ta keep up."

Molly rolled her eyes. "Fine. I'll water it down so I don't confuse ya."

"Ya do that," Owen said, cradling his chin in his hand.

"My worm, unlike other lesser versions, creates an alias on their website. Sort of like how a document aliases itself on your desktop while you're working on it. You know what an alias is, right?"

Owen nodded.

"Good. The beauty of mine is, unless I save the protocols when I close out, it's like I was never there."

Owen had to admit he was impressed. "That is, of course, until someone logs in an' sees there's more than one copy of da system running."

"Not necessarily," Molly said. "My program is read-only so they can log in and do whatever they want and never know I'm there."

"Hey, what's up," Claire said approaching from behind.

Owen turned around to find she had changed into a breezy, white cotton blouse and jeans. "Hey, there ya self," said Owen. He stood and offered her a seat. "Hardly recognize ya without that black slick running down your face."

"I clean up pretty good," Claire said, taking a seat on the other side of Molly. "What're you looking at?"

Owen eyed her niece. "Oh, just a classified website ya shrewd RA managed ta hack inta."

Claire turned the laptop toward her. When she saw a government seal on top of the screen, she grabbed Molly's arm. "What're you doing?"

"Checking out our river rats," Owen intervened.

"This is a classified site," Claire said.

Molly pulled her arm away. "Easy Claire."

"Easy, nothing!" Claire scolded. "People in the States end up in prison for this stuff. God knows what they'd do to you down here."

"It's okay," Molly said. "They have no idea we're in."

"And you know this how?"

Molly pulled the laptop back to her and explained again how she had gained access and anonymity. Claire gave at her a sidelong glance.

Owen got up and stood behind Claire. Putting his hand on her shoulder, he said, "Had my doubts, too, but far as I can tell, it's okay. Thank ya for thinking of me, though. Ya look a little thirsty. Can I get ya a drink?"

Claire looked up at him, and for a minute, he worried he had overstepped his bounds. But her startled expression melted into a smile. "Thanks, I'd like that, and a plate of whatever they're serving."

Claire sat and listened as Owen filled her in on all he knew about Valderón. "The bugger's feared by all da village peoples in Peru an' Brazil, say nothing of local law enforcement," Owen said. "Cross him an' ya end up missing or dead. This here's one of his compounds."

Claire swallowed hard when she saw where it was on the screen. "He lives in Iquitos!"

"Among other places," Owen said. He sipped his tea and pointed to places in Columbia.

The memory of stalking back to the boat after Owen had ticked her off rushed back. "So, where do you think he is now?" she said, studying the map showing the known territories of Valderón's cartel.

Owen shrugged. "His interest lie east near Jutai, but it could be farther off … say around Fonte Boa over here," he said pointing to the map."

"Doesn't look like he's concerned with where we're going," she said. She caught her breath as a cramp slowly drilled through her. *I definitely overdid it today. Not a good idea lifting so soon.*

"What're you looking at?" Thad said suddenly behind her.

"Oh, hi, Poppy," Claire said while tracing the perimeter of the shaded area depicting the cartel's known region. To Owen, she continued, "It's all up north."

Thad tapped her on the shoulder. "What's up north?"

"Valderón," Molly said.

Thad frowned. "Who's Valderón?"

Molly leaned back. "The fecker responsible for chasing our arses into the storage room below decks yesterday."

Suddenly, the screen flickered. Molly said, "Uh-oh, time to check out folks." She reached over and closed out of the window, leaving a deep blue fjord cutting through snow covered mountains on the screen.

"What happened?" Claire said.

"Detection software caught a whiff of us," Molly said. She clicked on the inserted disc icon and opened another window.

"They see us?" Owen said, leaning in and looking over Molly's shoulder.

Molly navigated through several windows ending with one displaying a large black spider. A 'RUN' button was located next to the arachnid. She clicked it and said, "Don't think so, but even if they did, it wasn't enough to track back. This'll make sure they can't."

Let's hope so there, Luv. Don't need da lads in San Paulo digging around my business. But there was nothing he could do about it, and worrying wouldn't solve a thing, so he eyed Molly's choice of spiders while the progress bar filled across the bottom of the screen. At last, he said, "Interesting choice of critters."

Molly grinned. "You like?"

"Very much," Owen said. "Loxosceles reclusa."

When Molly frowned, Claire said, "Brown recluse. Fiddleback."

Owen winked at Molly, "Guess I should've watered it down a bit for ya, eh?"

Molly stuck her tongue out at him.

Claire said, "So, what do you think, Owen? Still good to go." She watched him study the screen, wondering what he was thinking.

At last, he nodded. "All right, but any sign—"

"—Of trouble, yes I know, you're calling things off," Claire said."

Thirteen

Amazon River— 200 kilometers west of Santo Antonio do Içá –

J UAN STOOD in the forward compartment of Valerón's jet boat with his face into the driving rain. Steering the boat was a towering bearded man. Juan ran his hand over his face, mopping the rain away, and eyed Filipe, whom he had grown up with in Lima. Like Juan, the battle-hardened giant had witnessed the decimation of his family from tuberculosis. And like Juan, the man had felt the touch of hunger from months of living on the narrow, dirt streets above Villa El Salvador. The man knew where Juan had come from, and had spent years with him on the river and in the forests of Peru. He was the one man Juan could count on in a tight spot.

He turned and passed a measured gaze over the wet, sullen faces staring back from under their rain ponchos. Recruited by Valderón, these eight privileged sons of the Columbian cartels, along with another eight in the boat beside them, could never begin to comprehend not knowing where they were going to lay their heads at night. They only knew the luxury of their father's mansions. And though they had been trained with the best rifles, none of the armory could match the power of one Anopheles mosquito.

Well, they would find out soon enough what life was like in the forest, and they would learn about rain that came down in torrents.

And when it wasn't raining, they might also learn about the sting of the Assassin nymph or the deadly strike of the eight-legged Brazilian Wanderer.

Tapping Filipe on the arm, Juan pointed to a sheltered inlet ahead then hand-signaled the accompanying boat on their flank. "I need to piss. We'll take twenty over there. How we doing on petro?"

Filipe looked down at the gauges with his sharp, coal-black eyes. "Half tank. We'll need to fill up when we get to Santo Antonio."

Juan nodded, turned around to face the men. "Listen up. We're heading in for a breather. Ya got business to do, do it, cause we're not stopping again 'til we get to Santo Antonio."

"How long will that be?" someone asked from the back of the boat.

Juan looked at Filipe, and the man consulted the GPS on the front console. He held up three fingers then eased the throttle back, dropping the front of the broad thick-hulled aluminum boat into a slush of swirling water. Juan peeled his life vest off as Filipe steered the boat around a cluster of spindly branches pushing up through the gray, dappled surface of the river. Tossing the vest into the hold in front of him, Juan said, "Three hours."

There were moans and someone muttered something about, 'not signing up for this shit'.

Juan let the remark go, but he knew who had said it, and it would not be forgotten when the time came to report back to Valderón.

Filipe brought the boat into shallow water, and when they got close to the shoreline, pushed forward on the throttle, launching the boat halfway up onto the gravel beach. As the other boat came along side, Filipe reached over, unlatched the hatch door leading to the forward compartment and flipped a toggle switch. A small engine whined under the console, and slowly, a long, thin gangway unfolded like a long spider leg over the bow and onto the shore.

Juan hopped up onto the gangway, looked up and down the shrouded river and marched over to shore. Jumping down, he planted his boots on the stony riverbank and went under the forest canopy to empty his insistent bladder. As he stood before a towering beech, listening to the rain pelt the leaves above, Filipe came tramping up.

"What?" Juan said.

Filipe found a tree beside him. "Benito is a big pain in the ass. I say we do him here."

"Patience," Juan said, zipping up.

"Patience?" Filipe said, raising his brow.

"Si, and keep your voice down, will you?" Juan said, "Unless you want all of Brazil to know our business."

Filipe drew breath. "Right, sorry."

Juan nodded toward a large stump thirty meters away. "It's okay. Now, when you're done watering that poor tree, join me over there." He trudged through the soft feathery carpet of fern and moss and waited for Filipe to finish.

A minute later Filipe was beside him.

"What is wrong with doing him now?"

Juan cracked his knuckles and stretched his neck from side to side. "Two things: Miguel and Sosa."

Filipe frowned. "We could do them, too."

"You're really itching to use that new Beretta, aren't you?" Juan said, nodding toward the 9mm pistol tucked under Filipe's leather vest.

"Si," Filipe said and grinned.

"Not now, after we leave Fonte Boa we'll do 'em as planned. We have to be careful, Filipe. Valderón will not like hearing that his precious idiot of a nephew is dead. Until then, Benny-boy stays alive. Comprende?"

"Si. And Miguel and Sosa? What about them?"

"If necessary, we do 'em later, too. But only if we have to! I want to keep this to a minimum. If Valderón smells a rat, we're fucked, okay? Look, I know you don't like the son-of-a-bitch, but we've planned this for too long to take chances here, no?"

Filipe nodded and rubbed his beard. "I still get first shot, right?"

"Yes, you're first in line," Juan said.

"I wish this rain would end."

"Me, too," Juan said, slapping a bug on his neck. "Let's get back at it. I want to make do Içá before six."

A snarl of thick gray clouds greeted Juan as the jet boat headed for the wooden docks of Santo Antonio do Içá. The hard, cold rain that lashed them three hours ago had long since lifted, and in its wake, left a world of muted greens. Juan chewed on his cigar, and pointed to an empty berth at the end of a long pier. Filipe steered the boat toward it.

"We'll fill our tanks in the morning," Juan said after tossing a bumper over the edge. Turning around, he addressed the men. "I don't care what you do here, but keep your noses clean. I don't want to have to come dig you out of a cell. If I do, you'll wish you'd stayed there."

Filipe killed the engine, letting the boat float up to the pier as Juan tied a mooring line around a dock cleat. Twenty minutes later, both boats were tied off and secured for the night. Filipe shut the hatch door to the jets and watched the men heading off down the dock. "Where you want to eat?"

"Not hungry." Juan said as he stowed his gear. He wanted to think about the next few days.

Filipe shot him a quizzical look.

Juan tossed his spent cigar into the water. As he took inventory of the rifles, he waved his friend off. Ten minutes later he had his Glock semi in his lap, and was gazing out over the river under the fading sunlight. The pistol felt warm and comforting in his hands as he played with his silencer. How he loved the flicking sound of a bullet flying out of it.

His first thought regarding Benito before he left Iquitos was to have a boating mishap; send the beady-eyed son-of-a bitch into the water. The river was wide at Fonte Boa, and a well-aimed bullet from his silenced Glock when the man went into the water would insure he never made it back to shore. And wouldn't it be tragic if Miguel and Sosa went into the water, too; and if, in Filipe's distress, he turned the boat around and ran Benito's two friends over?

"Nice boat," said a soft, lilting voice on the pier above.

Juan looked up into long-lashed, chocolate-brown eyes and stuffed his pistol behind his back under his belt. She was tall, and the smile on her lips was full. A small beauty mark dotted her cheek.

"Is this yours?"

"Si," he said, gauging her to be no more than twenty.

She swished her bright yellow dress around her long legs. "I bet it goes real fast."

Juan nodded. "Fast enough." He watched her gaze sweep over the hull and back to him. As they chatted about where she was from and what she did, he felt his body stir. "So, you're a waitress."

"Si."

"I bet you get nice tips," he said.

"I do alright."

His gaze drifted down over her pert breasts. "It's Friday. Business must be brisk. Why are you here and not raking it in?"

She gazed out over the river. "I like watching the boats." She flashed him a smile. "Can I come aboard?"

Juan eyed the slender beauty. She seemed nervous and fidgety as she pulled her long, black hair around her neck. But the docks were empty as far as he could see so he got up and positioned himself under where she stood above him on the pier. He looked up as she swung onto the ladder and traced the curve of her calf to the soft sweetness of her thighs. Raising his hands, he clutched her waist as she stepped down into the boat.

"So, what do you do that you need such a fast boat?" she said, turning and patting his shoulders with her hands.

"Deliveries," Juan said enjoying a quick feel of her ass.

She giggled and broke free of him. "I like your vest," she said, finding a seat beside the gunnel. She crossed her legs and made herself at ease.

"Do you?" Juan said. "You want a drink?"

"Yes … what do you got?"

Juan went over and dug a bottle of pisco out of his gear bag. He held it up and shrugged. Perhaps five or six shots remained in it. He unscrewed the top and took a seat across from her. "Here."

"Looks like you're running low," she said taking it from him.

"I have more coming," he said. As she tipped it back and took a swallow, he mused delightfully on the screwing he was going to give her.

"So," she said, pulling the bottle from her lips and handling it back to him. "Are you alone or do you have friends around?"

"They're in town. Maybe eating at your cafe right now. You're probably missing a very nice tip."

"I'm sure I am." She paused, darted a furtive glance around the boat and pointed to a large, metal chest behind the driver's seat. "What's in there?"

Juan took a turn on the bottle, turned around, and smiled. "Just guns."

For a minute she stared at him, and he could see her trying to discern whether he was serious or not. Finally, she rolled her eyes. "Very funny! But seriously, what's in there?"

Juan shook his finger. "I wish I could tell you, but if do, I will have to kill you."

More nervous laughter parted from her soft petal-like lips. "Okay, keep your secret." She was quiet for a few more minutes. Again, her gaze flitted around the boat, and up over the pier. At last, she said, "How 'bout we take a walk? I know a nice private spot nearby where we can get to know each other better."

Juan cracked his knuckles, knowing exactly what was going on. "I don't think so. I have a better idea, though."

"And what's that?"

"How 'bout you stop bull-shitting me?"

"What do you mean?" she said, getting up and gliding toward him.

He set the bottle down, stood, and grabbed her. Holding her firmly, he looked into her eyes. "I think you have friends hiding somewhere, no?"

"I don't know what you are talking about. Stop! You're hurting me."

"Oh, you know what I'm talking about. We're going to stand right here and you're gonna play your little part." He gripped her face fiercely with his hand and kissed her hard and long. If she had friends out there, they'd be coming for her soon. He pricked his ears as she tried to push him away. A moment later, a soft baritone voice came calling down to him from the pier above.

"What are you doing amigo?"

"Saying good-bye to my wife," he said, turning around. He eyed the hatchet-faced, black man scowling back at him. The gun in the man's hand was a .38 special, and an older model, too.

"Get away from her," the man said as two other men came beside him.

"I don't think so," Juan said, sizing the other men up. Though it was now dusk, he could still see they weren't armed, and if they were, they couldn't get to their pistols very easily. "I think you boys need to mind your own business before you get hurt."

The gunman laughed. "I don't think you understand who has the gun here, amigo," he said, eyeing the girl with a knowing glance. "Let her go."

"Come get her," Juan said as his hand inched back behind him. When he felt the grip of his Glock, he pushed the girl forward in front of him and fired three shots as the .38 went off. The girl screamed as the men fell. Juan turned the pistol at her head. "You know these men?"

Shuddering, the girl shook her head. "No, I never saw them before." She put her hands to her face.

Juan smiled. "Really?" He stepped toward her. "Let's find out, shall we? Up you go." He pushed her toward the ladder. When they were on the pier, he shoved her forward to where the men lay. The gunman had a bullet through his head; the man beside him, a chest wound. The third man, the short one, was gushing blood as he struggled to breath. Juan bent over him while keeping his gun pointed on the girl. The man had been struck in the abdomen. He probably wouldn't live. Juan stood and went over to where the .38 lay clutched in the gunman's hand.

"Come here," he said to the girl.

She shook her head, tears flowing down her face and staining her cheeks with mascara.

"I said, come here!" he growled, aiming the gun at her. "And shut your mouth, or I'll do you, too!"

Her eyes widened and her body stiffened. Swallowing hard, she came forward on wobbly legs.

"Get his gun. Now!"

She squatted and reached for it as if afraid to touch it.

"Don't get any ideas," he hissed, as she pried it out of the gunman's hand. "Get up!"

She stood with the .38 dangling in her hand. Juan grabbed her arm. "Come over here. We're going to find out if you're telling the truth or not." He forced her down to her knees beside the man. "Put the gun to his head … Do it!"

The wounded man's eyes fluttered open and he looked up at her fearfully.

"I don't know him," she cried. "Por favor."

"So, you do know him, eh?" Juan said, pressing the muzzle of his Glock against her ear.

"No, no, I don't know him!" Her face became a wretched grimace. "Por favor!"

Juan reached over and wrapped his fingers around the gun in her hand. "Here, let me help you," he said, forcing her finger over the trigger. As he made her press down on it, she screamed and recoiled into his chest.

"Such a pretty young thing," he whispered into her ear while removing the .38 from her hand. "You know, you shouldn't hang with men like that. They are very bad for you." He deftly moved his finger from the trigger guard onto the Glock's trigger. "I'm sorry. This will only hurt a second," he said, and then he shot her.

Twenty minutes later, Filipe strode down the pier with a large plastic bag of groceries in his arms. When he came along side the boat he looked down at the bodies. "What happened here?"

Juan pulled a corner of the canvas over the girl's head and lit a cigar. "Local welcoming committee."

Filipe dropped the bag down to him and mounted the pier ladder. "Thought you said to keep things low key."

Juan put the bag by his gear. "I did, but you know how uninvited guests piss me off." He grabbed a pail and set it in front of Filipe. "Fill this and find a brush to take care of that mess up there, would you? I don't want people asking questions in the morning."

Filipe took the pail and nudged the corner of the canvas back with his foot. Gazing down at the girl, he said, "Hermosa."

"Si, very nice to look at," Juan said, peering down at her. "Too bad. She would've been a nice diversion for us tonight."

Filipe pulled his foot away and the canvas slipped back. "But you are getting married. What would Reyna think?" Filipe jested.

Juan smiled and tagged his friend with a friendly jab. "Nothing, unless you were to tell her. When you're finished; find something to sink these cock roaches to the bottom of the river."

Juan tied the final knot around the canvas-wrapped bodies when Filipe came back. He watched the big man swing onto the ladder with a thick section of concrete on his shoulder. "That's not very big."

"Is that so?" Filipe said, touching his foot down into the boat. "Here, you take it then."

When Juan grabbed the chunk of concrete, his muscles screamed. With a thud, he dropped it onto the bodies.

Filipe grinned and went up to the bow to untie the mooring line. "Where you want to sink these peons?"

"Anywhere away from the main channel," Juan said. He unleashed the rear mooring line and sat back on his heels as Filipe climbed into the driver's seat and started the boat. Under the thrumming whine of the jet engines, the boat slowly pulled away from the pier. "I need to use the running lights. Is okay?" Filipe said.

"Si. Dig the flashlight out of the storage compartment next to you and toss it back. I can hardly see anything back here," Juan said as the boat pirouetted in the dark water. He bent forward and wound the rope around the concrete sinker as Filipe popped the compartment open.

Ten minutes later, they were skimming over the river's glassy surface. "What a pain in the ass," Juan muttered, looking up at the first stars of night.

Fourteen

Amazon River - 130 kilometers east of Iquitos –

OWEN PULLED a candy bar from his shirt pocket and tore the wrapper open. Looking out from the window of the Lírio do Rio's bridge, he surveyed the rain-swept river, wondering if continuing the expedition was the wisest thing.

The ship's captain, Lino, stepped away from the helm and came beside him. "I'm told your anthropologist is quite the mechanic."

Owen glanced at the man and nodded.

"Tell her, I said thank-you," he said, then added, "Last night a friend of mine heard the FARC passed through do Içá. He believes they're expanding their territory southward. Are you sure you want to take your friends into the forest?"

Owen eyed Lino's thin, bronzed face looking for ... what? He didn't know ... a reason to turn around maybe? But the classified data they'd hacked into said otherwise. "Down south? How far?"

Lino shrugged. "Hard to say. There is a report that a village along the Rio Juruá was hit a little while ago."

"What do ya mean, 'hit'?" Owen said, straightening. When Lino looked away, Owen said, "How many?"

"Fifteen or twenty dead, mostly old men and women and a few who tried to resist. Spears and arrows are no match for guns."

Owen's hand clenched and his jaw tightened. He wanted to strike something, hurt someone; kill the bloody bastards. He looked up at the ceiling, fighting the rage welling inside him.

"The news from Fonte Boa is that they are conscripting men and women. And there are also large cargo boats with armed men going down the river, too. Some are saying an operation in the basin is underway."

Owen's heart sank. If this was true, it was definitely a game changer. "Deep in da Basin? Where?"

Lino shook his head. "I do not know."

"And nobody's saying," Owen said, slapping the wall. He didn't know what pissed him off more, that no one was willing to do a thing to help the forest people or that he was suddenly leading an expedition into harm's way.

"The FARC is very powerful," Lino said grimly. "People are afraid."

"Yeah, what they don't know, mate, is that their silence ain't gonna save 'em in da long run. You know it an' I know it." Owen glared out the window. "And here I am going inta who-knows-what-kinda shite." He drew breath and shook his head.

"What are you going to do?"

"Don't know." He paused. "Ya heading back ta Iquitos after we dock in do Içá?"

"No, we are going to Fonte Boa, then we will turn around. You can stay on board if you want. No charge."

"Thanks. But I think I'll be getting off here. What I need is a crate a rifles instead of them bows below deck."

"Maybe, but even if they could use them, what good would it do? You cannot save all the men and women of the forest."

"I expect ya're right about that," Owen said, pressing his lips together. He narrowed his gaze on the captain. "But if it could save one village, it'd be worth it, in my mind."

They fell silent as the rain slashed against the window. Finally, Lino stirred. "Here," he said, nudging Owen in the side with his elbow.

Owen looked down at a thick roll of Brazilian reals in the man's extended hand. "What's this?"

Lino leaned in close so no one could hear. "There is a man in do Içá who might have something you might be interested in," he said, then pulled away and eyed him knowingly.

Owen stared back. He had known Lino a long time, and if there was one thing he knew about the shrewd captain, it was his love of the river folk. "Thanks. I don't know what ta say."

"Nothing to say. You fixed my boat," Lino said, then turned and walked back to the helm.

Owen sat up in bed the following morning after a night of fitful sleep. Beside him on the nightstand, sat thirty-five hundred reals: $1,600 American. He gazed at it, thinking about what Lino had whispered to him yesterday. He'd said he wanted rifles; well, now he could have them. Except the money wasn't his, not technically, anyway. Claire was the one who repaired the engine. If he told her what he was going of do, she'd go ballistic. There were no right answers, because the lines were blurred when it came to doing the right thing.

He ran his hand through his hair as a knock came to his door. "Yeah?"

"It is me, boss," said Manny. "You awake?"

Owen reached over and dragged a pair of pants on. "Yeah. Come in."

The door opened, and when Manny saw the money on the nightstand, his brow rose. "You been rolling bones?"

Owen felt a smile on his face but it didn't last long. "I wish." He paused. "We got a problem, mate."

"I does not look like a problem to me," Manny said.

"Trust me, it is," Owen said. He told him what he had heard from Lino. "I'm turning this gig around."

Manny nodded. "She is not going to like hearing that."

"Probably not, but she doesn't have a choice. It's too risky not knowing where those sons-of-bitches are. When we get ta do Içá, I'm getting off with my bows an' they're staying put: comprende? Don't look at me like that," Owen said. "Ya're staying here. I need you ta make sure she remains on board."

Manny frowned.

"I'm sorry, but it's the way it has ta be," Owen said. "I know what I'm doing. An' I need ya ta make sure they get back ta Lima safe an' sound. Can ya do that for me?"

"Si. What should I tell the Jackass back in Lima?"

"You tell 'im I had business needed tending to," Owen said. "'Sides, I may make it back 'fore ya." When Manny cocked his brow, Owen told him the Lírio do Rio was heading to Fonte Boa before heading back. "You'll be river-bound for two week's till ya're off it an' on da road."

Manny nodded toward the money. "So, what's this? Their refund?"

"Something like that. Lino gave it ta me for getting da boat back up and running."

"Si, you are such a grande mechanic," Manny said waving his hand.

Owen scowled. "Don't get all noble an' shite on me. I'm gonna give it ta her … least most of it."

"Of course you are," Manny said. "So, when are you going to tell her you are not coming along?"

"Don't know, why?"

"So I can make sure I am as far away as I can be when she finds out."

"Very funny," Owen said. He paused then continued, "I'll need a couple of lads ta porter for me."

Manny sighed. "You're sure about this?"

"As sure as I can be. Look, we've tramped a long time together, right? Ya know how I feel about this. The Manaqüi mean a lot ta me. They're in danger and they need those bows more than ever. Fact is, they need more than bows."

Manny's eyes widened. "Surely, you are not thinking what I think you are," he said.

"Don't worry," Owen said, "I haven't gone around da bend just yet. But there may come a time when there's a need, yeah."

A long silence followed. Finally, Manny said, "We will meet again, right?"

Owen met the penetrating gaze from his venerable old friend. "Of course we will!" But in his gut, something told him this might be a one-way trip.

Later that night, Owen pushed through the double doors and stepped into the crowded mess hall. His mind was made, but it didn't make what he had to say to Claire any easier. He wondered if he should address the whole group or pull her aside. It would be easier telling everyone at one time with Manny there, but a part of him wanted to let Claire know his decision in private. He owed it to her.

He watched her chatting with Manny at the table. Her long, dark hair was pulled back over the tip of her ears. Manny leaned toward her and said something that made her laugh. God, she was beautiful. But it was more than beauty; it was her deep passion for what she believed in that possessed him, even if it was grossly misdirected. He studied her fine-featured face from across the room, admiring the beaming smile she was giving Manny.

Their differences concerning the peoples of the forest weren't so far apart; they just looked at them differently. She wanted to keep the tribes pristine; untouched, allowed to exist as they had been since time out of mind. He wanted to save them, but to do it, he would have to violate all she believed in.

He took a breath, grabbed a cup of tea, and pasted a smile on. Walking up to their table, he said, "So, how'd like da rain?"

Molly looked up at him as she corralled a fork-full of papa rellena on her plate and growled. "It was lovely."

"Good, cause ya're gonna see a lot more of it," Owen said, pulling out a chair and sitting. He nodded toward her half eaten dinner. "That looks pretty good."

"It passes," Molly said.

Claire said, "I'll be glad to get off this boat and into the forest."

Manny eyed Owen furtively.

Owen said, "Yeah, me too." He took a sip of tea. Even though he had convinced himself he was doing the right thing, he felt like a cad. He opened his mouth then shut it when he saw her smile at him. Suddenly, he wanted to kiss her.

"So, how much longer to Santo Antonio?" said Thad, kicking back in his chair.

"We'll be there tomorrow - late morning," Owen said, roused out of his musings. Then someone behind him started strumming a guitar.

They all turned to see Paulo warming up an old twelve-string Martin. A few minutes later, he was plucking notes that drifted out over the room. It was a song Owen knew well, and it brought back memories of childhood on the tributaries that flowed into the great Amazonas.

As another man joined in with a soft lyrical voice, singing words of love and loss on the river, Claire stirred and eyed Manny. "What a beautiful ballad. What's it called?" she said when the song ended.

Manny broke out a cigar, nipped the end off, and said, "Sonhos de Rio. It is a very old song. My mother used to sing it to me when I was little."

Paulo started another ballad, and an hour later, the rum was flowing and voices were raised in song. A lively number got Claire's foot tapping. She stood and pulled Manny to his feet. "Dance with me?"

Manny smiled and they went to an open spot between the tables. Five minutes later, Owen, Thad, Jorge, and Molly stood in a ring of clapping crewmen and porter's around the dancing couple.

Out of the corner of his eye, Owen could see Thad tipping his beer back as he watched Manny and Claire nimbly twirl around the floor.

Molly said. "God, look at them. They're so good out there."

"Sorta hoaky if you ask me," Thad said.

The comment drew a curious gaze from Owen.

"That's cause you can't do it, Poppy," Molly said. Her eyes sparkled as she watched Manny spin Claire around.

"Right, and I wouldn't want to," Thad said. He grinned and elbowed Jorge, but Jorge kept his eyes on the dancers.

Molly shot Thad a frown.

"What?" Thad said.

"Nothing. You're hopeless," she said.

Owen felt a smile crease his face. He could sense Molly wanting to get out on the floor. He bent back toward Thad. "Ya're missing a chance, mate."

Thad looked at him quizzically.

"Molly," Owen whispered, "she wants ta dance. Ask her out."

Thad snorted. "I don't see you out there."

"That's cause I got two left feet, an' Molly here ... well, she wouldn't wanna dance with an old bloke like me anyway."

"I'll pass," Thad said. He lifted his beer to his lips and drained the last of it. When he turned to Jorge and found him chatting with Molly, he pursed his lips.

"I'd love to dance," Molly said, taking Jorge's hand. She looked back over her shoulder at Thad as Jorge led her out onto the makeshift dance floor.

Owen crossed his arms and watched the young Brazilian exchange student spin and twirl Molly around to the lively guitar and vocal melodies. The kid was quite good, and as they danced, bright smiles creased their faces. Owen glanced back at Thad, who stood looking on with a pained expression, and dropped back a step.

"Eh ... everything all right?"

Thad hardened his expression. "Yeah, I'm fine."

"Right," Owen said. "None of my business, but I've seen how she looks at ya sometimes. I think she likes ya. If ya stop busting on her, ya might have a shot."

Thad bent toward Owen. "Her uncle's the chair of the department I'm trying to get my thesis through. Any more suggestions?"

"Ahhh, forbidden fruit," Owen said.

"Something like that."

"Ya like her, though?" Owen said.

"She's all right," Thad said with a crooked smile.

"More than all right, I think," Owen said. "She's a looker. Ya better watch out, Jorge'll steal her away."

Thad laughed. "That's rich!"

"Come again," Owen said.

"Well, look at her! She's a hundred miles an hour, flat-out, all the time. Jorge's too laid back. He held up his empty bottle. "I'm going for another. You want one?"

"Sure, why not?" As Thad slipped away from the circle, Owen turned his attention to Manny and Claire. He wanted to be Manny, holding Claire in his arms, swinging her lithe, graceful body around. But he wasn't sure he could even manage a slow two-step.

The song came to an end, and both Jorge and Manny bowed to the ladies. As they walked toward him, Owen saw Paulo gear up for another song. He cleared his throat as Claire came near. "You guys look pretty good out there."

Claire pulled a lock of hair away from her eye as Paulo started slowly strumming. "Manny did all the work. I just followed."

"That is a lie," Manny protested, grinning. He drew a handkerchief out of his pocket and wiped the glistening dampness from his face. "Boss, she is all yours. I need a beer."

Claire gave Manny a casual glance as he headed for the galley door. To Owen, she said, "It seems as though I've been passed off."

"Yeah, he has a way of delegating duties," Owen said companionably. "But in this case, I don't mind filling in. I'm not as good a dancer as Manny, mind ya, but I'll give it my best go if you're up for it."

"I might be," Claire said, eyeing Jorge and Molly, who had returned to the floor and were spinning slowly to the dreamy rhythm of the guitar.

Owen took Claire's hand and led her out next to them. As they came together, the warmth of Claire's body seeped into him like butter into a warm biscuit. She felt even better than he imagined she would, and the smile she shot him stole his breath. He closed his eyes, soaking in the barrage of delicious sensations running through him. Here was a woman he could spend time with. "I want ya ta know ya're aces in my book, yeah," he said, pulling back.

"Thanks. You're not so bad yourself."

"Way I see it, we're a lot alike, us two. We care about things that matter, yeah."

"Really? Such as?"

"Well, da forest for one."

Claire tilted her head slightly, and her gaze narrowed. "Go on."

Owen took a deep breath. Suddenly, it was more than just enjoying the feel of her slender, warm body, more than listening to her sweet voice when she hummed along to the music, more than inhaling her intoxicating scent. He gauged her curious expression and decided she wasn't baiting him.

"I was eight when my pop brought me down here, yeah. As an ichthyologist, he was interested in da links between native diets and da role of fish in da resistance ta pathogens. Anyway, I grew up playing with da local lads of da Manaqüi, an' so you could say, I have a strong affection for 'em."

"I can see that, and that's what puzzles me," Claire said. "Why the bows?"

"Yeah, I figured ya'd bring that up," Owen said. "I have my reasons."

"I can't think of one that makes sense to me. You have any idea the damage you're doing to these people you love?"

"All too well, but what ya're not understanding, is that these people are being pushed ta da brink. Their land is being raped by copper mining an' pharmaceuticals. This bushman we're looking for, he's a prime example. We're past da balance of power between da tribes here. These people are fighting for their lives."

Claire was quiet a moment. Finally, she said, "Certainly, there're other ways? The government–"

"–is these people's worst enemy!" Owen said as his foot nipped her toe.

"Ouch!"

"Sorry, bout that. I'm not very good at this."

"It's okay," Claire said, patting his shoulder. "So, you were about to say."

"Yeah, right. Anyway, it's all spin an' propaganda with 'em."

Claire wrinkled her brow. "How can you think that? There are reams of restrictions against interfering with these tribes."

Owen laughed grimly. "Not when it comes ta business. Believe me, what ya read in ya papers up north is what they want ya ta believe. It's all shite, all of it. An' when ya add da cartels coming down an' conscripting da poor bastards ta run their coca operations, they don't stand a chance."

The song ended, and she looked at him a long time. Whether she bought what he'd told her, he didn't know, but she certainly was thinking about it. As they started off the floor, she said, "So, how old were you when you left?"

"Da forest?"

"Yes."

"Sixteen, just after my pop had his run in with a nasty little river critter."

"Oh? What was it?"

"A Payara; candiru."

"Is it poisonous?"

Owen shook his head. "If it were only that easy! No, this little guy has its own bit of hell in store for ya ... I need some air," he said. He pointed in the direction of the rear doors leading outside. "Wanna join me?"

Claire nodded, and as they stepped out onto the stern deck, he saw her tighten her brow as if she had been stuck with a pin. "Ya all right?"

"Yeah, just a twinge. Comes and goes. So, you were saying?"

"Right. It's a thin little bugger that's almost transparent in the water," Owen said stepping up to the bulwark rail. "If ya're a man, it scares the hell outta ya."

"Why?"

"Cause of what it does if it finds ya. See, it's like this; ya're out spear fishing an' while ya're diving ya need ta take a leak. Big river, ya're out in da middle of it, fifteen, twenty minutes back ta shore. Ya think nothing of it. But this here critter, he senses ya gift in the water an' makes a bee line straight for ya. Then da fun begins."

"Fun?"

"Yeah. It thinks ya're female, so it slips inta ya plumbing where it climbs up inside ta get acquainted."

Claire blinked. "That's wicked scary!"

"Ya don't know da half of it. Imagine a nasty set of spines digging inta ya innards. How ya feeling now?"

Claire shivered. "What did your father do?"

"Nothing he could do. They had ta surgically remove it. Unfortunately, by da time they got da critter out, it paralyzed him from da waist down. Five years later, he died of complications. That's why ya rarely catch me in da water, especially where da little ankle biters are playing, if ya understand me."

They fell silent as the river slipped under the boat. Finally, Claire stirred. "I'm sorry. It must have been horrible to watch him go through that."

"Yeah, it wasn't easy." He looked at her hard. "One thing I understood quickly after that, was that this river doesn't take hostages. But enough of that shite," he said. He took a deep breath and looked up. "Look at that awesome sky."

Claire was quiet a moment, then said, "Yes, it's beautiful."

Owen glanced at her furtively. "Reminds me of you; inspiring."

She swatted his arm. "Stop!"

"Just calling 'em as I see 'em," he said, turning toward her. He felt his breath catch as he stared down at the playful smile tugging at her lips. "Ya're quite stunning, ya know?"

She stared at him discerningly and said, "Are you making a pass at me?"

"I might be. That a problem?"

She opened her mouth then shut it and looked out over the water. For a moment, she stood there in thought under the waxing moon. Finally she turned back, looked up at him with a searching gaze. He sensed her fighting some unknown battle, and wondered how it was going to turn out. At last, she said, "Owen, despite how you aggravate me, I like you. But I can't complicate my life right now. There's too much -"

"Yeah, yeah, I know. We'd just end up killing each other in da end," he said.

She smiled diffidently.

He looked out into the night as their bodies brushed against each other and felt the underlying current of tension coursing through her. God, how he wanted her. "Well, it's getting on, an' we got a big day ahead of us tomorrow," he said, dreading the thought of what he had to tell her.

She pulled away and they stared at each other without saying a word as the dark water slushed against the boat.

Finally, she pressed her lips together, turned and walked away.

Fifteen

Amazon River – Santo Antonio do Içá

THE FOLLOWING morning was bright and humid with just a whiff of a breeze coming over the river. Claire climbed the companionway ladder and drifted halfway down the upper deck. Her thoughts were a turbid maze of confusion. Standing there, she eyed the tiny port of call that was rapidly approaching. It was teeming with boats motoring in and out over the dark waters. Men were loading and unloading cargo from the holds of vessels that had seen too many years in service. The high-pitched trebling of crakes flocking around the docks for the remains of fish filled the morning air.

This was Santo Antonio do Içá; their last stop before entering the forest. But for all that she had longed for this moment over the last three years, it fell short of her expectations. She thought about last night; about what she had almost allowed to happen between Owen and her. Falling into his arms would have been a disaster, but God, it would have felt nice. The memory of their bodies touching under the starred sky, of looking up into his longing gaze wouldn't let go. Like it or not, she had wanted to kiss him, to feel his arms around her and she didn't know what to do about it.

The sound of someone coming up the companionway ladder roused her from her musing. She turned and saw Owen heading toward her, his hat in hand. She tensed.

"Morning," he said. "Figured I'd find ya up here."

She smiled, determined to keep her focus on the expedition. "Did you?"

"Yep. Said ta myself, if I was her, I'd be wanting some time alone ta think about things."

Oh, great, he wants to talk about last night. "Owen, let's not go there, okay?"

"What? Ahhh, that! Forget it," he said, waving his hand dismissively.

In the awkward silence that followed, she realized he was talking about the expedition. She relaxed as dread melted away. Finally, she said, "Nice day out there for it."

"It is," he said, turning a friendly eye at her. "How'd ya sleep?"

"Good." She paused, thinking of what more to say. "So, this is Santo Antonio do Içá? It's smaller than I thought it'd be."

He cocked his brow. "We are in the middle of da Amazon."

"Right," She said, feeling like a tourist. What the hell was wrong with her? Why was she suddenly tongue-tied? She gathered her wits and said, "So, I assume we catch a ferry across the river?"

Owen's face darkened. "Yeah ... ummm ... that's something we need ta talk about."

Oh, Jesus, what now? She studied him, trying to determine what that meant. "Is there a problem?"

"Kinda ... Actually, yeah, there is." He paused and looked toward the approaching piers. "Captain pulled me aside yesterday. Told me a village down south was attacked by one of the cartel's death squads."

Claire felt her eyes widen. "Oh, my God! When?"

"He thinks Tuesday. Anyway, it didn't turn out too good for 'em." Struggling for words, he took her hand in his and squeezed gently. "Claire ... I'm sorry, but I can't let ya go down there. It's just too dangerous."

Claire felt the air run out of her. She had known the status of the expedition was touch and go, but she thought the odds were in their favor after seeing the classified government documents on Valderón.

Downcast, Owen dug into his pocket and pulled a roll of money out. "Here, it's not much, but it's da best I can do right now."

"What's this for?" Claire said as he put it in her hand.

"Ya hired me ta take ya into da forest. An' I can't, so this is–"

"A refund?"

He shrugged. "Guess ya could call it that. There'll be more when ya get back."

Claire wasn't sure how much money was in her hand and she didn't really care. Suddenly, she felt the toll of the last three weeks crashing down on her. She folded her fingers around the wad of money and stuck it in her pocket. She thought about the lost opportunity and what it meant to her career, say nothing of facing Noah, she sighed. "You're absolutely sure about this?"

Owen nodded solemnly. "I am."

She felt her throat tighten as she struggled to contain the host of swirling emotions. "Right. So we turn around and go back?"

"Not exactly. The Lírio do Rio has cargo ta deliver in Fonte Boa, so ya an' ya team'll be heading there 'fore doubling back."

Claire narrowed her eyes. "You're not coming?"

He looked away. "I have business across da river. I'll join back up with ya later on."

"Delivering your bows?"

He didn't say anything; he didn't need to. He could see she knew exactly what was going on. "I see," she said. She pressed her lips together and glared at him. "Tell me, did you ever intend on taking us into the forest?"

"What ya talking about? 'Course I did. Why would ya ask?"

She felt her body stiffen. "'Cause from where I stand right now, it feels like I'm being used. This is just a delivery operation, isn't it? Paid for by my grant."

"Not at all," he retorted.

Claire shook her head. "You'll pardon me if I find it just a little curious that at the last minute you come up with a village being attacked;

and conveniently, you just happen to have two crates of bows on board that you just have to deliver."

"What is it with ya? Ya just can't let go of things, can ya? Well, ya wanna go tramping in da forest, be my guest, but 'fore ya head out, ya might wanna consider ya team." Putting his hat on, he turned, took two steps, then wheeled around. "I'm not a cheat, never was, an' never will be. Gidday!"

As he stomped off, Claire clenched her fists. "And good riddance."

"That wicked woman," Owen muttered as he climbed down the companionway ladder. Well if she wanted to be an idiot and head into the forest, so be it. He'd wash his hands of her. But in his gut, he knew he'd never let it happen. Like it or not, she had wormed her way into his heart. He marched down to below decks, passing busy crewmen as he went. He needed to calm down. Logically, he knew it was all saber rattling. That's what Monica had always done when she wanted him to give in. Usually it worked, and the one time it hadn't, he wished it had. Calen would still be alive.

He shook his head and forced the unwanted memory away. Claire was a lot of things, but stupid wasn't one of them. She wouldn't endanger the lives of her team. Besides, Manny would be there. He'd make sure people kept their heads on straight while he was gone.

He pushed through the heavy metal door into the crowded hold. At the far end under a swinging light bulb, Manny and Inacio were busy uncrating the bows and stuffing them in large canvas bags. The men looked up as Owen shut the door.

"Make sure ya wrap them arrows up nice and tight," Owen said to the young porter as the boat swayed and creaked.

"You are back, and still in one piece," Manny said.

"Yeah … she's not happy, but she understands," Owen said, walking ahead down the center aisle. He ignored the odors of rotting fruit and bananas stacked on pallets as he searched for his pack and rifle. "Keep an eye on her just da same."

Manny cocked a brow. "What are you not telling me?"

"Nothing. Just do as I ask, okay, mate? I can't afford ta be worrying about 'em."

"Okay, I will keep my eye on them."

Owen sighed as he dug his pack out of a pile of gear. He never planned it to be this way. It was supposed to be an easy drop off to his forest friends while Claire's expedition was busy checking things out down south: sweet and simple. No one would know, no harm – no foul. But somewhere along the way sweet-as turned into bad-as.

He thought about the man Lino had spoken of as he pulled his rifle out. In his heart, he knew introducing rifles to the Manaqüi was out of the question. They were just too damned complicated, and they'd ultimately either end up rusting away in some forgotten hole or killing some poor innocent blokes. Besides, the Manaqüi couldn't just run down to their local sporting goods shop for another box of ammo when they ran out.

Even his redesigned re-curved compound bow had its issues. Although it was easily repaired with hand-made parts and provided a level of accuracy well beyond the long bow, not all tribes liked it. Still, those who were willing soon became excellent marksmen, eventually converting most of the naysayers. The problem now was that there wasn't a lot of time for convincing people.

Manny reached down beside him, lifted a bag out of a box, and handed it to him.

"What's this?" Owen said, opening it and pulling out a handful of chocolate bars.

Manny shrugged. "Something for the trail."

"Yeah. And da box there by ya feet; what's in there?" Owen said.

"That you will have to wait to find out about when you get back," Manny replied, waving a finger.

Despite his sullen mood, Owen slapped Manny on the shoulder. "Okay, ya keep ya little secret. I'm off."

An hour later, Owen was on his knees outside on the pier making a final check of his gear. Beside him lay two long canvas bags cinched at the top. Above, on the main deck of the Lírio do Rio stood Claire, Molly, Thad, and Jorge looking down with unhappy faces. He drew breath and averted his gaze to Hector and Ramirez, who stood beside him with full packs. The broad-shouldered men with burnished bronze skin were no strangers to the rainforest, and for where he was going he needed the best of the best.

Satisfied that everything was in order, he drew the strap tight over the pack, secured it in place and sat back on his heels. Looking out over the broad river, he studied the distant shoreline bordered with trees that appeared no more than mere bushes. Soon he'd be under them, looking up sixty feet or more into a tangled network of woody vines and moss-ridden branches. He skinned his teeth, then grabbed his machete and rifle. "You ready?" he said to his two porters.

"Si, Boss," Hector said, lifting one of the canvas bags.

"What about you, Rammy, you set?" Owen said, getting to his feet and tucking his sheathed blade under his belt.

"All set, Boss," said the other porter.

Owen strapped his pack on. "Hey, mates. Drop da 'Boss' stuff, eh? We're not guiding anymore."

The men smiled. Hector said, "We are being watched."

"Yeah, I know," Owen said, wanting to look back. He tilted his head toward the assumed audience looking down from above and behind. "Let's get off this stage 'fore we get our heads handed ta us."

They marched down the pier with Owen leading the way to a haphazard grid of off-loaded cargo. The ferry, which would transport them across the river, was a short, squat vessel a hundred yards away. Owen couldn't wait to be aboard it. Even after he was well away from the Lírio do Rio, he could still feel Claire's gaze burrowing into his back.

Claire watched Owen melt into the sea of crates and humanity from the deck of the ship, and turned to Molly. "Crank up your lap-top. I want to find out what the real truth is. I'm so pissed. I should've done this a week ago. Damn it!"

As Molly skated below deck to her cabin, Thad said, "But even if he's lying, we're still stuck here on this boat."

Claire gripped the bulwark rail, squeezing it hard. "Not necessarily, Poppy." She pulled out the wad of money Owen had given her and showed it to him. "If the Jungle Boy is lying, we'll hire our own guide." To Jorge, she said, "Find Manny. I want to talk with him."

Jorge nodded and struck off, leaving just Claire and Thad looking out over the port. Thad said, "You think there's enough there?"

"We'll find out. I have a better idea though."

Thad tilted his head. "And that would be?"

"You'll see. Let's go inside."

Under the shadow of the rear upper deck, Claire and Thad gathered around Molly and her laptop at a large, long table outside the mess hall. As the computer booted up, Molly said, "Where should I start looking?"

Claire thought for a minute. If she were trying to find out what was going on locally, she'd tap into one of the social networks. "Google … Santo Antonio do Içá … tourist info and see if they have a Facebook page."

Just then, Jorge returned with Manny in tow. With him was Inacio's brother, Paulo. They came beside Claire and looked down at the page loading on Molly's laptop. Manny said, "What do you need senhora?"

Claire turned. Even though she liked Manny, she was trusting no one at this point except her own team and her own eyes. She let a moment of silence hang between them, then said, "We're checking your boss's story, and if he's lying you have some explaining to do."

Paulo frowned. "Owen does not lie!"

"We'll see," Claire said, defiantly. A page came up on the screen. Molly scrolled down it and clicked on a link named, 'Traveler's Warning'. The following page showed nothing, except a small article about some tribal squabbles 230 kilometers away. Claire glanced at Manny knowingly. "Try … Recent Armed Attacks on Villages in the Amazon Basin."

When that came up empty, she threw out several more suggestions to Molly. But they all turned out to be nothing as well. Finally, she narrowed a pointed gaze on Manny and crossed her arms. "Well?"

"Means nothing," Paulo said.

"I don't believe I was talking to you," Claire said to Paulo.

"It is all right, Paulo" Manny said. "What are you saying, senhora?"

"Come on. Don't play games with me."

Manny scowled. "Why are you doing this? What do you hope to accomplish?"

"I want the truth," Claire said, looking at the laptop screen from the corner of her eye. "I want proof your boss isn't swindling the university. More than that, I have a chunk of my life tied up in this expedition. I'm just not going to stand by and watch it go floating down the river with him."

"I know what you are thinking. Forget it."

"I have no intention on forgetting anything. I have in my pocket a fair amount of money I'm sure someone down here wouldn't mind taking for guiding us."

Manny furrowed his brow, and his face hardened. "That would be a very big mistake, senhora – a very big one! You have no idea who knows what down here. There are many who would take your money and leave you to die in the forest. You will stay on the Lírio do Rio."

Claire bristled and motioned him away from Paulo. Lowering her voice, she said, "Or what? You going to kidnap us? I don't think so. I think you're going to take us into the forest, that's what I think. Because if you don't, I'll find someone who will. So what's it gonna be?"

Manny glared at her, but she didn't care. She was done playing nice. "I do not think so. You are not listening to me." He glanced at her team. "Follow me, I want to talk with you alone." They walked out of the mess hall and strolled along the back of the boat. When they were out of earshot of the porters and the boat's crew, Manny looked at her hard.

"Owen does not lie. If he says the FARC is down there, I believe him." When Claire opened her mouth, Manny put his hand up. "Wait,

I am not done talking yet. I wanted to go with him, too! But it is more important that I stay here."

"To keep us in line," Claire scoffed.

Manny shook his head. "You are so wrong about him. You have no idea what kind of man he is. He would take a bullet for you and any of your team," Manny said, softening his voice. "Yes, he brought down some arcos. Nothing he hasn't done before, but it has never prevented him from honoring a contract. If you go forward with this, you are risking the lives of your team and me. Is that what you want?"

Claire drew breath. If it wasn't for her admiration of him, she would've have dismissed his warning altogether. But he had a point. Regardless, she needed irrefutable evidence there was a threat, and as far as she could see, there wasn't any. At last, she said, "Of course that's not what I want, Manny," she said quietly. "But we're going."

Manny sighed. "I hope you will not regret it."

Claire eyed him, waiting for him to say more. When he didn't, she said, "Please make the arrangements."

"Very well, I will need to pick up two porters before we strike out. If I can find them by the end of the day, we will leave tomorrow, otherwise the next day at the latest. I assume that is agreeable to you?"

"Yes, that'll do. And Manny –"

"What?"

"Thank you."

"Do not thank me! You might have just sentenced us all to die," he said, and walked away with hunched shoulders.

Into the Forest

Sixteen

Santo Antonio do Içá

CLAIRE LOOKED out over the water toward the distant shores of Santo Antonio do Içá from the back of the ferry. It was 7:00 AM, and already the heat was building into another beastly humid day. She tied her hair up in a knot and thought of Owen. It had been two days since he'd abandoned her and headed into the forest on a mission of his own. Their bitter parting still gnawed at her as well as what Manny had said afterward. Was she really risking her life along with her team's by going on with this expedition? Was her quest to find the 'Lone Bushman' interfering with her judgment? The questions chipped away at her resolve as the ferry headed to a small village with no name on the other side of the river.

A sharp twinge caught her breath. As her stomach roiled, she wrinkled her nose at the earthy breeze laced with diesel rushing over the ferry. She closed her eyes. I'm all right. It's just my body getting back to normal. She turned, pushing away the memory of the miscarriage and stepped to the large pile of supplies and equipment that would accompany them into the forest. She needed something to do, something to silence the ominous voice that was whispering inside her, telling her that all was not well with her body.

Kneeling on the other side of the pile was Manny, who had his arms elbow deep in his backpack. Lingering in the background was Paulo and the rest of their porters. Manny looked up as Claire pulled an aluminum shipping case off the top of the pile. Even though he wore a smile, she knew he wasn't happy, and therein was the problem. She respected him too much.

She opened the shipping case containing the Sat-Lynk transponder, and took inventory: eight spare lithium ion batteries, four coax fire-wire cables, a retractable high gain antenna neatly packed away in bubble wrap and strapped down.

Suddenly, a small commotion caught her attention on the port side. She looked up to find Inacio and Paulo pointing to something out in the water. Another porter was yelling to a man on the upper deck of the ferry. The boat slowed and a moment later, was idling in the water.

"What is it?" Claire said to Manny.

The director got up and went to the rail. A minute later, he returned shaking his head. "The river has claimed another poor soul."

Claire sighed. *Christ! What next? But this is the Amazon, and it's not like I haven't seen it before. Except lately every time I turn around something bad seems to pop up.* She got to her feet and went over next to Paulo. The porter shot her a withering look and stared out over the choppy waters. About ten yards away, the remains of a dark brown pant leg with a boot bobbed in the water.

"Excuse," said one of the ship's crewmen coming up behind her. He pushed past her with a long gaff and ordered the onlookers away from the rail.

As the boat maneuvered toward the floating leg, Manny came beside her. He opened his mouth to say something, then stopped and took her by the hand. "Are you all right?" he said.

"I'm okay," Claire said, taking a deep breath. She managed a weak smile.

Manny cocked his brow. "Why don't you go inside, lay down?"

The door to the enclosed portion of the boat suddenly swung open. Claire froze. The last thing she needed was for Molly to see this. She patted Manny's arm as Thad poked his head up behind Molly's shoulder.

"What's going on?" Thad said, furrowing his brow and looking at the commotion at the side of the rail.

Claire pulled away from Manny and marched over to her lanky RA. Pushing Molly and him back inside, she pulled Thad aside and lowered her voice. "They found a body in the water."

Thad's face darkened and he looked at her quizzically. "Hey, you all right?"

"Yeah, I'm fine. Just the heat is all. Can't sleep."

"I hear ya there." He fell silent and looked out the door's portal window at the action on the deck.

Claire cleared her throat and nudged the daypack on the floor with her foot. "What's in there?"

"A few souvenirs," he said tearing his eyes away from the door. "So, what do you think happened?"

"I don't know … Souvenirs? What kind of souvenirs?"

He grinned. "A little rum, some tequila, and some pisco."

"Snitched them off Owen, did we?" Claire said, shaking her head.

"The way I look at it, he owes us," Thad said.

"Well, just remember this isn't a party we're going to here," Claire replied. She felt another cramp building. "I need to use the bathroom. And keep Molly away from the door, would you?"

Thad frowned. "Yeah, right."

An hour later, they were docked on the other side of the river and off-loading gear and supplies. Claire stood on an old wooden dock, looking at a half dozen tar-papered houses with corrugated metal roofs and wooden doors. Sitting atop thick log pilings burrowing into the dark sandy soil, they were not so different than what she'd seen in parts of Africa. People built their houses with what was available.

Leaning against two broad-leafed capirona trees was a simple but serviceable rack fashioned from thin branches and tied together with vines. On it, were fish hanging out to dry in the warm humid sunlight. A cluster of colorful woven baskets and carved wooden bowls sat on the ground below.

Claire eyed a group of old, dark-skinned men, bare to their waists sitting around a large wooden table mending nets. While none of them looked up, she was quite sure they knew she was there. Two women were digging roots in a small garden not far away from the men. One of them was keeping an eye on the barefoot group of children who were gathered near the water's edge. Their beaming coffee-colored faces were smiling as they pointed to Claire and her crew.

At length, she swung her daypack over her shoulder and started down the dock. As she stepped onto dry ground, she said in Portuguese, "Holla, are you the welcoming party?"

One of the older boys came forward with a toothy smile. He ogled Claire with large, brown eyes and in Portuguese said, "What's all that stuff up there?"

Claire knelt so that she was at eye level with him. "What's your name?" she replied in stilted Portuguese, while admiring the thick matt of burnished, black hair sweeping over his shoulders.

The boy continued to look past her. "Abilio."

"That's a nice name," Claire said. "Are you their leader?"

Abilio shifted his curious gaze back onto her and puffed his chest. "Si."

"I thought so," Claire said. She turned around and pointed to the expedition's cargo. "That's our gear. We're going into the forest."

Just then, Claire saw the woman who had been watching the children start toward her. As the short, round woman came close, Claire stood and offered a greeting.

The woman ordered Abilio behind her and eyed Claire suspiciously. "What do you want?"

"Nothing, I was talking with this bright young man," Claire said, carefully. "Is he your son?"

Suddenly, Manny came beside Claire. "Graca, is that you?"

The woman looked up, and a smile came to her round face. "Manuel! What is all this here?"

"I am guiding this woman and her people into the forest," he said. "This is Claire."

The woman shot Claire a fleeting glance. To Manny she said, "Cloud-Walker came through here three days ago. How come you not together? You always together. Something wrong?"

"No, not at all," Manny said.

Graca cocked her brow. "Hmmm ... I think you are not telling me everything. Jose is out fishing with the others. You will stay for café da manhã, no? He would like to see you."

"I am sure he would, but we have a long way to go today. But perhaps some of your famous papa rellena to go?" Manny said.

The woman frowned. "You can stay at least to sit and eat! There is cuy, also? I made just this morning. It is my very best."

"Of course," Manny conceded, eyeing Claire sidelong.

Graca nodded then turned and marched up the riverbank with the children swarming after her.

Manny waved his hand toward the woman's retreating back, and said to Claire, "After you, senhora."

As they followed the woman, Claire leaned toward Manny and said, "Cuy, that's the dish Owen mentioned when we arrived in Lima, right?"

"Si, roasted guinea pig. It is a delicacy, and it would be impolite to refuse. It is not bad. You will like it, I think."

"I'm sure, I will," Claire said. *But Molly won't. She'll have to get used to it though, or starve. Hmmm ... Cloud Walker, where'd I hear that name before? Ah! Noah's email. Something about Owen being some kind of mystic with the tribes.*

"Manny?"

"Si."

"Cloud-Walker, what's up with that name?"

"I do not understand. What do you mean?"

Claire sighed. *Stop using slang Claire and start thinking like these people.* "I'm sorry. I meant, why do they call him Cloud-Walker?"

Manny eyed her discerningly, and Claire could see he was debating whether he would answer. Finally, he said, "I do not know the whole story, but I will tell you what I can. When Owen was a child, he spent a lot of time playing in the Manaqüi village near his parent's research station. In the village, lived a powerful old medicine man. One day, Owen came across the old man on his way home through the forest. Owen told me the man had collapsed while gathering herbs and roots. Anyway, he helped the man to his feet and back to his hut. In the act, he earned the man's respect. Soon after, Owen became a regular visitor to the man's hut, and there the man taught him the secrets of the forest."

"Manny, I find it hard to believe any elder tribesman would take a child of a white man into his world."

"Si, it is hard to believe, but it happened. Remember, Owen grew up among them."

"But he didn't live with them," Claire said. "He lived with his parents."

"True, but he was with them more than he was with his parents. And his parents were well respected and liked among the Manaqüi."

"Still—"

"I understand your skepticism," Manny interjected, "but sometimes there are exceptions, and Owen was that exception. They looked at him as one of their own, and so his adaptation of their world came early, and by the time he stumbled on the man out in the forest, he was well known to him."

"All right. For the sake of argument, I'll accept that for now. So tell me, what are these secrets he learned?"

"He does not tell that to anyone. You see, when a tribal elder gives you secrets, they are to be kept just to you. That is the way it is. Anyway, in the eyes of the tribe, Owen gained great stature," Manny said. "And it is also said, the man taught Owen the espírito walk."

Claire raised her brow. This was ridiculous, but Manny was so sincere, she didn't have the heart to call him on it. "So, they think he's a ghost?"

"Si, some do!" Manny said. "And when the old man passed away, some said, he had given Owen the power of the Cloud-Walker. Rumor spread of course, and soon after, Owen became known to all as, 'the white man who walks like a shaman'."

An hour later, Claire backed away from Graca's table. The roasted cuy wasn't bad at all. It had a smooth texture similar to beef tongue and a slightly gamey flavor akin to roast duck. The rest of her team, except Molly, finished their plates. The redhead flat-out refused to eat anything. Jorge made a hasty excuse that she wasn't feeling well, which wasn't so far from the truth. But sooner or later, Molly would have to give up her eschewing of native foods.

More importantly though, was what Graca and the old men weren't saying when they talked about the goings on in the forest. Most of it revolved around fishing and hunting; how it was a good year so far. The remainder centered on a festival they were looking forward to. Nothing was said of the FARC or of any other civil unrest, which left Claire feeling more confident in her decision to continue the expedition.

As the old men went back to their nets, Manny headed over to the porters who were taking their rations by the dock. Claire bent down and retied the laces on her boots. A little way off, Molly and Jorge were going through their packs. She saw Jorge sneak Molly a sandwich he had filched from the ferryboat galley. Molly smiled, and her hand lingered over Jorge's as she took it. Beyond, Thad furtively looked on, glum-faced as he slung his backpack over his shoulder.

Claire shook her head. "Hey Poppy, do me a favor?"

He started. "Yeah, what?"

"Grab me another bottle of bug juice. They're in the first-aid bag on the dock, over by the Sat-Lynk case." As he went for it, she decided he was going to walk with her the first day to remind him why he was there.

Claire waved Molly and Jorge to their feet when Thad returned. As Thad handed her the bottle of repellant, Manny came up behind him and said, "You ready?"

Claire nodded.

"Okay," Manny said, rubbing his hands together. "Here are the rules. You all stay behind me, and in line. Do not stray off the trail. Trust me when I tell you there are many things ahead that can hurt you very bad, even kill you."

He looked at each of them in turn, holding Molly in his gaze longest. "Now, if nature calls, yell out and either I or one of the porters will stake a path for you. Do not, I repeat, do not pick flowers or plants. There are many stinging insects that like them, not to mention that some of these plants, which I will show to you along the way, are poisonous.

"Last of all, we have a long tramp ahead of us and it is essential we get to where we are going before sunset. And most important, be vigilant of where you put your feet. Use your tramping poles at all times. Remember where you are. This is not a walk in the park. This is the Amazon. Many things live here that do not play by your rules. Okay?" When no one raised an objection, Manny took a deep breath and said, "Let us go."

Seventeen

C LAIRE STABBED her hiking pole into the black soil and stepped over the giant buttressed root. Her team, along with the porters, had been following Manny for over three hours on a thin path cutting through a never-ending blanket of undulating trillium. The resinous perfume of the forest lay all about them. Above waved a dense, tangled network of spidery branches and vines. Thick clusters of tree fern and piassava palms dotted the understory, their giant fronds reaching up to catch the spray of precious sunlight raining down.

Claire reached over her shoulder for her water bottle as she walked. The path ahead crisscrossed roots that dove into patches of false daisy and guajava. She squirted a quick drink, wiped her brow with the back of her hand, and pushed on in silence. No one had said a thing in the last hour. Show and tell had been replaced by the incessant background whine of insects. She ducked under a low hanging frond and stepped down into a narrow, earthen channel, sloping into a guess.

A few yards ahead, Manny strode effortlessly over the jumbled landscape, arms tight to his sides, elbows bent and hands raised in front of him gripping the shoulder straps of his daypack. As he picked his path, the long machete sheathed under his belt swung back and forth in lockstep with his legs. Claire marveled at his endurance. For someone in his fifties, he had the speed and agility of a man half his age, and there was no sign he was tiring any time soon. He hopped out of the channel, turned around. Satisfied the troop was keeping up, he moved on into the gloom.

Claire drew breath and picked up her pace to keep in stride with him. Behind her, the snapping of twigs under booted feet announced the passage of the tiny caravan through the pristine and primordial forest. Coming down the river on the boat, she had tried to imagine what the Amazon would be like once they entered it, but her imagination had fallen far short of the mark. Although they were only three or four miles into the dense jungle, she felt as if she were in another world, where dinosaurs once stretched long necks high into the trees.

She stabbed her pole in the soft earth, stepped up out of the channel and saw a majestic tree fern ahead whose tall, feathered crown was lit by a golden sunbeam. When Thad stepped up beside her, she said, "Look at that beautiful thing! Here, hold these. I wanna a picture of it."

"It's nice." Thad said, taking her hiking poles. "Hey, I finished the preliminary outline draft of my thesis. Mind looking it over?"

Yeah, sure," Claire said, snapping a shot. She tucked her little digital camera back into her pocket and took her poles back from him. Looking down the channel, she saw Molly and Jorge twenty yards back, walking close together with Molly leading.

"I thought about what you said on the plane," Thad said.

"And?"

"And, I'm going to stick with my theory."

"I see. Okay, give me an argument then."

Thad was thoughtful then said, "Okay … let's take the Maori, for example. They came to New Zealand around 1300 CE. The land they set sail from was rich and fertile, so lack of food wasn't an issue, and so far as I can see, there was no pandemic or natural disaster that would have created severe hardship, yet they paddled for a thousand goddamn miles? Why? It's not population pressure. Hell, they had eight square miles per person before they left."

"I dug into that a little bit after our conversation on the plane," Claire said. "Did you know there's a paper out that theorizes a red tide of biblical proportions decimated their fishing grounds? That might be the cause for leaving."

"For a whole year or more?" Thad said. "Cause that's what it would take to force such an exodus."

"Really? And you know this, how?" Claire said. She pointed ahead and started off after Manny, who had turned around and was waiting for them.

Thad followed close behind. "They had other sources of food. They'd look to that first before venturing out into the unknown I think."

"Ahhh, you're guessing then."

"You have to make a few assumptions," Thad argued. "From all I've read, the Maori people were practical people. To up and leave over one bad fishing season just doesn't make sense. And a red tide that displaces the entire south pacific people who were thriving? All at one time? I don't buy it."

"Okay, so what's your theory?"

Thad was quiet a moment, then said, "I think they were pushed out, and I think it was a cultural cleansing."

"By whom?"

"The Mongols."

"The Mongols? Really?"

Thad pressed on though. "They were in the midst of empire building during that time. Everyone knows that."

Claire ducked under a low hanging branch. "All the way down the peninsula?"

"Why not?" Thad said.

"Okay, let me get this straight," Claire ventured, switching poles and slapping a mosquito. "You're saying every south pacific culture that ventured out over the ocean 7,000 years ago was on the brink of annihilation by the Mongols? Yet at the same time you reject the red-tide theory because they were all leaving at the same time? Sounds like a contradiction to me," Claire said, and waited for his response.

"Not really. History is ripe with these kinds of invasions. Alexander the Great, the Roman Empire, Genghis Khan, for example."

"You're right, but they came much later," Claire argued. "Besides, why would some cultures be allowed to thrive and others destroyed?"

"Acquiescence. Those who subjugated themselves to the Mongolian pantheon of beliefs would become an asset to the empire."

"Maybe, but it's a thin point." Claire answered. She pushed a low hanging branch out of her way and held it for Thad to pass by. "Look, you might be right, who knows, but there's no way of proving it. Again, I urge you; settle on one culture, examine it, make good assumptions based on evidence we already have and form your thesis around that."

"But I –"

"I know. Look, I'm not saying to abandon the idea, just don't use it as a thesis. Noah will eat you for breakfast, if you do."

Thad was quiet a long time. Finally he turned around and looked at her. "Is that what you did?"

"Did?" Claire said, planting her pole in the soft ground and hopping over a muddy soft spot on the trail.

"Held off writing about the African-South American trade connection until now?"

"Yeah, something like that," Claire replied, gritting her teeth. She paused, fighting the impulse to snap back, and added, "Look, sometimes, you have to wait for it. Don't let your impatience get the better of you."

Thad laughed. "Impatience?"

"Yeah," Claire said. "Talk to me about Molly."

"What about her?" Thad said, lifting a palm frond blocking his path. He held it up for her as she passed underneath.

Claire shot him a sidelong glance. "You've been moping around like a whipped puppy ever since Jorge got her out on the dance floors the last night on the boat."

Thad snorted. "You think I'm jealous?"

"The thought occurred."

"Well, I can assure you, I'm not."

"Good, cause I need your head in the game down here," she answered, patting his shoulder. "Come, we better get a leg on it or Manny'll get upset.

Juruá River – Yagüani village – seventy kilometers south of Fonte Boa

The first light of dawn frosted the distant treetops as Juan lifted his infrared binoculars and focused on the murky riverbank. Filipe stood next to him, guiding the slow-moving jet boat on the black waters of the Juruá. Even with the best high-tech navigation equipment on board, traveling on the treacherous, serpentine river under cover of night was dicey. Beside him, an LCD display glowed. They were nearing the first of three villages that were part of the initial phase of Valderón's operation. He lowered his binoculars and tapped Filipe on the arm. A second later, the whine of the jets died along with those in the companion boat behind them. In the silence that ensued, the distant echoes of macaws filled the void.

As the boats floated under the first light of dawn, Juan and Filipe searched the tall, wading grasses and bushy camu-camu trees for an opening to run the boats ashore. A half-kilometer upriver, Filipe pointed to a spot amid the low-hanging branches of capirona and piassava palms. Pointing the boat toward it, he brought the jets back to life for a final burst. The bow leapt, and the boat slashed through the grasses onto the thick quagmire of mud and decaying vegetation. The big man flashed a smile at Juan as the other boat came alongside and cut its engines.

Juan frowned. "It is a good thing I was holding on or that shitty smile of yours would be missing a few front teeth." He turned around and eyed the stern-faced men who were gathering their gear and weapons. *They are tired and in a nasty mood. Good! It will make what we have to do that much easier.* He collected his rifle, jumped overboard into the ankle-deep mud and rapped on the side of the boat. When he had their attention, he said, "All right, get set up. I want to be ready to move in a half hour."

As Juan waited under a giant jabillo tree for his men to gather round, he tightened the straps of his flak vest over his Gore-Tex top. Filipe knelt beside him under the pale light of an LED lantern, pulling clips of ammunition out of an open canvas bag. He piled them on the ground next to a bundle of plastic zip-ties and a large manila envelope secured to a clipboard with a rubber band. He sheathed his knife, took up the clipboard, and powered up his digital short-range text communicator. The screen of the SCRIBBLER flickered and came to life, it's cursor blinking and waiting for input. Checking the range indicator, he saw they were a hundred meters upriver of the village. That was good. He flipped the lid on the data device, slipped it back in his pocket and tugged the rubber band off the envelope.

If I work this right, Benito, you will be out of my life before the day is done - hopefully, by one of the roaches. Hmmm ... Let's see, where is it best to send you? He thought as he pulled the plastic aerial photo out and studied it. He looked at the dozen thatched roofs circling the long house on the photo. To the north and west sides of the village was dense forest. To the south, brush and scrub followed an undulating riverbank.

As the men filled in around him and Filipe, he passed the photo around. "Listen up. We will divide into three teams; one coming in from the north; one from the west, and the other fanning to the south."

As Filipe passed the clips out, Juan eyed Benito. "You come in from the west with Sosa, Miguel. Pedro and Emilio, you back them up. Next he turned to Filipe. You take Jose, Adao, and Nuno. Herberto and Marco you back them up. The rest of you are with me to the north. "We will take up positions here, here, and here," he said pointing to specific places on the photo. "I will text you on your SCRIBBLER when to move in."

"What about cross fire," one of the men said.

"Have you forgotten already? The clips Filipe is handing you are armed with rubber bullets."

"Rubber bullets?" another man said, with a smirk.

"Si, rubber bullets, asshole. We are here for able men, women, and children to work the operation, unless you want to do all the work."

There was general laughter all around. Someone said, "And the others? What of them?

"I will deal with them afterward," Juan said, staring at their large bearded faces.

Filipe shot them a lop-sided smile and ran a finger across his throat.

One of them named Luiz frowned.

"What? Is there a problem?" Juan said, zeroing in on the man's indignant expression.

Luiz shook his head. "No problem."

"Good. Make sure it stays that way." He looked around, gauging each man, then slapped a clip in his Glock. "Let's go." As the men dispersed, Juan pulled Filipe aside. "Keep an eye on that son-of-a-bitch. I do not trust him. And one more thing."

"What's that," Filipe said.

"I have been thinking, if one of the roaches fails to take Benny down, how are you with a bow?"

"I do all right," Filipe said.

"Good, just make sure to keep out of sight and aim high. Extra points for through the eyes."

Filipe smiled.

Fifteen minutes later, the teams came out from under the forest and fanned out. Juan positioned his men just outside the perimeter of the trees and eyed the village from behind a large kapok. Twenty meters away, in front of the long house, wisps of thin smoke rose into an ever-brightening dawn sky . All was quiet as mist gathered off the shushing river beyond. Juan mashed a mosquito on his arm and panned the grounds, listening for awakening children. He needed a battle to deal with Bennie, otherwise this would have been a done deal already.

Slipping his SCRIBBLER out of his pocket, he punched in a message to Filipe and Benny, asking whether they were set and ready to go, and hit the send key. A minute later, the device hummed in his hand. "All set." Juan pocketed the device and raised his hand, motioning his team to fan out left and right.

Now, came the tricky part. He kept his head low and slipped into the small clearing north of the village, taking a position behind one of the huts. From inside, he heard the murmuring of voices through the bamboo-clad walls. *They're waking up. Time to flush the toilet.* He reached into his vest pocket and pulled out a small canister of gel accelerant and sprayed a thin coating on the wall, then dug a lighter out of his pocket. As he lifted the tiny flame to the wall, a twig snapped behind him. He wheeled around and found himself on the business end of a spear, inches from his face.

The large, hulking man jabbed the tip of it at him, motioning him to move aside. Juan collected himself, and glanced furtively around. The deadly weapon moved closer as the native's unforgiving gaze assessed him. Suddenly, over the man's shoulder, Juan saw Benito running up. As his lieutenant's shot rang out, the native man spun around. Juan dropped to his knees, rolled on the ground and fired three rubber bullets at the man's back. A loud grunt followed as the man arched backward before falling to the ground. Juan got up and made sure he stayed down with a quick jab to the head with the butt of his rifle.

As Benito ran up, men with spears and bows poured out of huts, shouting to each other. Suddenly, the forest erupted with gunfire and the air was full of arrows. Juan panned the grounds, calculating his next move as Benito joined him.

"You all right?" Benito said.

"I'm fine," Juan snapped, angry at himself, then out of the corner of his eye, he saw a man on their right flank sighting them with an arrow. Instinctively, he brought his rifle up, pushed Benito aside and fired.

Benito nodded. "Thanks."

"Don't mention it," Juan said. He slapped Benito's shoulder. "Go!"

Juan struck off between the huts, his finger on the trigger of his rifle. He let go a flurry of shots, taking down a pair of natives who were circling around behind one of his team members. As he dispatched the empty clip, an arrow bounced off his flak jacket. He looked up, spotting the native who shot it and slapped another clip in. But before he could fire, the man twisted and spun to the ground. Filipe came around the corner of the hut with his thumb up.

Fifteen minutes later, thirty-six men and women were zip-tied and lying in the long house. The bad news was that Benito was still alive. Juan gave Filipe a sidelong glance and got a shrug back in response. But how could he blame him? He himself had let a golden opportunity slip through his fingers. He let his disappointment go. There would be other chances.

He called Filipe and Benito over to where he sat under the outstretched roof of the long house. When they walked up, he had them sit, and said, "We will make this our base camp, use the long house to hold the roaches. Take their weapons and stack them in one of the other huts.

"We spend the night here then?" Filipe said.

"A few of us, si. The rest of us will strike out for the next village later this afternoon, make camp, and then hit it at the same time we hit this one." He reached into his pocket and pulled out a map. Unfolding it and laying it flat beside him, he said, "It is about a four-hour march from here through the forest."

"What, no photo?" Benito said.

"No, no photo. When we get close, we will scout it out. We need to be careful about this one. They have the advantage there, cause they know the forest around them better than we do."

Benito put a cigarette to his lips and flicked his lighter. "You mean careful like we were just now?"

Juan frowned. "Very funny."

"So, who stays back?" Filipe said.

"I think Carlos and Marco. And now, I must take care of business. Filipe, get a fire going and get the men out fishing. We need to keep our prisoners fed, not to mention ourselves."

He rose with mixed emotions. Killing unarmed roaches was necessary, but he didn't much care for it. But as the main man, it was imperative he led by example. Never let anyone do your dirty work for you, lest they get a big head. That was Valderón's problem. He had forgotten how to get his hands dirty. Juan would not let that happen to him.

He walked over and circled the sorted group of old natives and little children who were sitting on the ground looking up with confused and frightened faces.

"Miguel, Sosa, get them up. It is time," he said, exchanging the clips in his rifle with live ammo. With a sigh, he set off along the river's edge through the thick brush with a small contingent of lieutenants. After a five-minute hike, he came to a field of tall grasses. It was as good as any place, he supposed. Standing to the side, he watched Miguel and Sosa push the old men, women, and children in a semi-circle, facing away from their executioner.

When his lieutenants were out of harm's way, he gritted his teeth and lifted his rifle. As the natives fell before him, an old man with a painted face and pierced lips turned around. A haunting, penetrating gaze shot out from the man's deep-set eyes and drilled into Juan like an arrow.

Juan let go of the trigger and stared back, determined not to let the defiant challenge go un-met. But the face staring back at him didn't flinch. Anger coursed though Juan then as he realized the old man had won the silent battle of wills. He gripped the rifle in his hand savagely, aimed high and obliterated the man's face into a mass of bone and blood.

Eighteen

Twenty-five kilometers northwest of the Marauá village

A SKITTERING RUCKUS in the canopy brought Owen out of an uneasy sleep. He looked up through the mosquito netting of his hammock as a dark dream melted away and saw a troop of spider monkeys bouncing around in the leafy labyrinth of sunlit branches. A tiny bead of morning dew touched the corners of his lips as he watched them. At length, he pushed the netting away, sat up, and stretched. On the other side of his tiny camp, Ramirez kneeled on the ground going through his gear. A meter away from Ramirez was Hector. He'd had the last watch of the night and was squatting beside the tiny propane stove, heating water for morning tea. The men looked up as he rolled out of his hammock, then went back to their business. Appreciating their silence, Owen slapped his hat on and went out among the variegated ferns to relieve his bladder.

As he took care of business, he bent his mind on the day ahead. They'd been tramping though the stifling heat of the forest on a straight course for the Manaqüi village for five days now. He chose this route through the forest instead of the much-used hunting paths for two tactical reasons: first, to avoid a chance encounter with the FARC, who would definitely outnumber them, and second, to get to the village as fast as possible. If Lino's sources proved correct, the Manaqüi village they were headed for would need everything he could give them and more.

Zipping up, he looked into the muted green perfusion. If his bearings were right, they were twenty-five kilometers from the village, and with two decent slogs, would be there by late tomorrow afternoon. But they were cutting across the forest, and there was no telling what obstacles might get in their way. Maps of the basin were vastly incomplete, and even satellite imagery failed to locate tributaries running under the dense green canopies. As treacherous as the thin, winding waterways could be, it was what they often swelled into that concerned him most. The dreaded Igapós was to be avoided if at all possible.

He slapped a mosquito on his neck, turned to join the men back in camp, and ran into Hector, who was already waiting for him with a cup of tea. "That mine?" Owen said, mashing another bug on his arm.

Hector handed him the cup. "Si. They are voracious this morning, no?"

"Yeah, yeah. One wonders what they eat when we're not around ta feed 'em. How was watch?"

Hector waved a hovering mosquito away from his face. "Quiet for the most part. I heard a big cat just before dawn, though."

"Yeah, it's a panther. We've been trespassing through his territory since yesterday afternoon. He knows we're here an' he's not happy about it," Owen said, rubbing a bug bite.

Hector yawned. "How far is the village, do you think?"

"A day, day-an'a-half, depending," Owen said. He sipped his tea and nodded toward Hector's lower leg. "How's da spidey bite?"

Hector shrugged. "I have had worse."

Owen eyed him sidelong. Having been bitten by a wolf spider once or twice, he knew Hector was lying. "I'll throw another dressing on it 'fore we strike off. You an' Rammy ate yet?"

"Si."

"Good. Well, I best get my gear together. Got another long day ahead of us. Let's hope our luck holds out an' we don't run across trouble out there, eh?"

By mid-afternoon, the heat was stifling. Owen took his hat off and wiped the sweat from his brow with his arm. The machete in his gloved hand felt like it weighed ten pounds and a blister was growing on his palm. He took a breath and looked at the barricade of broad-leafed trompa, jarra, and heliconia barring their way. He'd been hacking through it for the last two hours, along with fighting the network of woody vines and roots underfoot. Sheathing his machete, he slipped his water bottle out and squirted a drink into his parched mouth.

"You okay?" Ramirez said, stepping beside him.

Owen nodded. "Yeah, yeah. Just needed a breather," he said, taking his glove off to inspect a large transparent bubble on the palm of his hand. "Reach in my pack an' grab my med kit, would ya?"

As Ramirez pulled it out, Hector stepped beside them and scattered the swarm of tiny gnats flitting about their faces. Looking up, he squinted at the blazing sun pouring down. "I will be glad to get through this crap."

Owen squeezed a drop of salve onto his hand and stretched a Band-Aid over it. "Me too."

"You want me take the lead?" Ramirez said.

Owen shook his head. "Nah, I'll be fine." He glanced at Hector as he handed the med-kit back to Rameriz. "How's da leg?"

"It is good."

Owen pulled his glove back on. "Well, back at it. Sooner we're outta this shite, da better."

"Not to mention, away from these gnats. They are worse than mosquitoes," Hector said.

"Yeah, they do seem ta like ya," Owen said. "Must be that cheap aftershave ya're wearing."

"You mean that stuff I borrowed from you?" Hector said, shifting his pack on his shoulders.

Owen grinned and, unsheathing his machete, struck back out into the dense understory.

An hour and a half later, they were sitting on a moss-and-lichen-covered log eating their noon meal. Owen was glad to be out of the suffocating tangle of trompa and ivenkiki, but now a new threat was looming. He nibbled his lunch, thinking about the soft, punky soil underfoot and the scent of rotting flora. Pitcher plants had begun to appear in increasing numbers in small stagnant pools of brackish water.

He finished his lunch and looked down upon a mass of ants crawling over a piece of papa rellena that had escaped his plate and fallen to the ground. As he watched the bugs navigate around a puddle with their burdens, he considered his options if he came across an Igapó.

One thing he would not do is pass through its murky waters unless there was no other way. But that also might mean them going kilometers out of their way, and there was no guarantee they'd fare any better up or downstream. Who knew what other barriers might await them there? He brought his knee under his chin and retied his bootlaces.

Looking out over the dark, tangled forest, he pulled his pack onto his lap, and said, "Hey, mates. I think things are gonna get soggy in a hurry. Might wanna break your gaiters out, yeah."

"Might need more than gaiters," Hector said.

"Let's hope not." Owen packed up his gear. Once everyone was set, they started off into the gloom of the primeval forest, following a game trail that zigzagged past rotted stumps and fallen trees. From time to time, Owen jabbed his tramping pole into the soft sandy soil, testing for ankle-breaking holes.

As they went, the sullen forest looked down upon the wayward travelers with indifference as it grudgingly gave passage through its undulating landscape. Owen looked up often into the gray moss-ridden network of twisted landi. Mangrove trees draped with thick blankets of gray-bearded moss and lichen were appearing in greater numbers. The resinous odor of decay grew stronger, until there it was: the dreaded Igapó. Owen sighed as he stepped to the foot of it and panned the haunting, still waters that stretched as far as he could see in either direction.

Ramirez and Hector came beside him. Hector said, "O meu dues."

"Yeah," answered Owen. "My God, indeed." He sat on a fallen kapok and considered which way to chart a course. To his left, the understory was pocked with ragged stumps. The ground to his right was flat and level around the jagged shoreline. But the further one tramped, it narrowed to a thin ledge hemmed by a steep slope. The difference between the two was that the one to his right was in the general direction he was striking for.

He studied it, taking in the occasional cluster of mangroves hugging the shore. They didn't bother him so much as the thought of coming to a dead end with only two choices. He didn't want to double back and start over, but taking his chances and wading out into the unknown depths of the murky waters wasn't a pleasant thought either.

He called Hector and Ramirez over. Both men agreed the route to their right was better. With that settled, they unpacked their waders and poled around the shoreline under scurrying capuchin monkeys high above in the branches. Despite the innocuous goings on above them, Owen knew there were deadly ambushes waiting below the surface of the water for the unsuspecting.

As they scrambled over mangrove roots and limbs, the path veered steadily away from where he wished to go. At last, he stopped, and looking over the water, pulled his GPS palm pilot out. "We're three k out of our way. Ya know I don't wanna go wading out into this here hellhole, but I don't see a way around it. And I sure as hell don't wanna be spending da night here."

The men nodded.

"All right then," Owen said stepping into the water. "Button your knickers an' say ya Hail Mary's. Here we go."

They gingerly felt their way out into the swamp, poling the soft muddy bottom. Each step was grudgingly given up to them as they sloshed through knee-deep water. A hundred meters out, the bottom started to fall away. Fifty meters later they were chest-deep in it. They waded through the next ten meters, with their arms up, choosing every step along the rising and falling bottom until slowly, the water dropped back to their knees.

"So far, sweet as," Owen muttered. He reached out, pushed aside a veil of thick draping moss and jabbed his pole into the black water, feeling more and more confident. Raising his pole, he pointed toward a grove of mangrove and landi. "I think I see solid land beyond those trees. Let's make for it."

Ten minutes later, he stepped on shore only to see another wide expanse of black water before them. He groaned as Hector and Ramirez came beside him. "Looks like it's back into da soup for us," he said, and struck back out into the murky waters, charting a zigzagging course eastward from tree to tree until they came upon a wide-open channel. He took his hat off and looked each way.

"Damn. I don't like this a bit."

Ramirez pushed a spidery branch to the side and stuck his pole into the soft, mucky soil. Stepping forward, he said, "I will try."

Owen watched as the man waded into the channel up to his chest. At length, Ramirez turned around. "The bottom is flat and level here. I think this is the river section."

Owen nodded and followed him out into the water, with Hector following. "I think you're right, Rammy. There's a current here," he said. "Be careful an' take ya time."

Suddenly, Hector tapped Owen's shoulder and pointed at a long, s-shaped ripple slicing through the water. "Look! Over there."

Owen panned the channel and saw the disturbance downstream. It was near an island of thick, floating water grasses perhaps thirty meters away, and it was coming straight at them. Whatever it was, it was big. Owen felt his body tighten.

"Rammy, stop where ya're at!" Owen warned as his gaze locked onto the wide, arching swells moving across the surface. He felt his mouth go dry. Licked his lips as he slid his machete out of its sheath.

"What is it?" Ramirez said.

"I don't know. Could be a 'conda," Owen said watching the rippling water. The surface went still then. "Shite. Where da hell is it?"

Nineteen

THEY STOOD frozen for the next five minutes, searching the channel. Suddenly, Hector nudged Owen. "There, by that fallen mangrove tree. See, it has caught something."

Owen let go his breath and slid his machete back into its sheath. "Let's get this tiki-tour over with. I've about had it for one day."

They made their way out of the swamp and spent the next three hours tramping through a tangled confusion of woody vines, snarling brambles, and undergrowth until at last they walked out under a gray sky into high, waving pampas grasses hugging the winding Juruá River. He pulled his GPS palm pilot out and scanned the ragged shoreline as Hector came up behind him. In the muted daylight, swarms of tiny midges jittered frantically over the rippled surface of the water. Hector set the large bundled canvas of bows down and wriggled out of his pack.

"As soon as Rammy's done back there watering da lilies, we'll make for that point over there," Owen said. "If my little compass here isn't lying ta me, da village should be just beyond it."

"I'll be glad to lay my head down tonight," Hector said, looking down river. As he cranked his neck back and forth, stretching thick-knotted muscles, he frowned. "Uh, oh."

Owen stopped fiddling with his palm pilot and looked up. "What?"

Hector put his finger to his lips and crept ahead into the dense scrub under the low hanging tree branches with his shoulders lowered.

When he came to a thick patch of ivenkiki, he stopped and looked downriver over it. Owen frowned. He didn't like being on the other end of a need-to-know situation. He crept through forest understory and slipped next to his porter in the tangled vegetation to see two large jet boats amid the tall waving reeds.

Hector turned an uneasy gaze toward him. "Where do you think they are?"

Owen lifted his binoculars and searched the nearby trees and thickets. When he didn't see anything, he shook his head. "No idea, but we'd better find out, an' soon." He tucked his field glasses away, and unsheathed his rifle. Tapping Hector on the arm, he added, "Best pull a bow out of ya gear an' ready an arrow." He glanced back toward the forest, thinking about his next move when Ramirez walked out from under the trees with something in his hand.

The man looked upriver, then turned toward them when he heard Hector whistle. Approaching them, he said, "Look what I found?" He extended his hand and showed Owen the butt end of a spent cigar. "The ashes are fresh. I think we have company, unless the Yagüani have learned how to grow and roll cohibas."

Owen pointed toward the jet boats sticking out past the grasses into the river. "Arm yourself an' stash da bows someplace safe in da bush while I figure out what ta do."

After surveying the immediate area, Owen came back and drew a rough diagram on the ground showing the basic layout of the Yagüani village as he remembered it. He had no idea if it had moved in the last three years or not. Yagüani were prone to move their communities up and down the river during the rainy seasons. Yet the fact that the cartel's jet boats were here led him to believe otherwise.

He wondered how many cartel men had been on the boats. By appearances, at least twenty, and armed with automatics, more than enough to subdue fifty or sixty men, women, and children. He shuddered. He'd seen too many pictures of the FARC's butchery.

"There's only three of us," Ramirez said, rousing Owen out of his grim thoughts."

Owen nodded. "Yeah, I know, but for all we know, we're pinned in here like a bug on a board right along with 'em. I don't know 'bout ya, but I don't care for tucking my tail 'tween my legs an' running."

"Si, I do not like it either," Ramirez said. "So, how do we attack?"

"Didn't say anything 'bout attacking. Just looking things over. Seeing what they're up ta so we're not taken by surprise if we decide to do something later on. That's where mistakes are made an' ya end up dead."

"Can end up dead just by looking too," Hector put in, pursing his lips.

"Yeah, yeah. Ya're right. But at least it's on our terms," Owen said. He looked at them, holding each in his gaze. "Look, ya know me. We've tramped together a long time. If ya want ta take a pass on this one, I won't hold it against ya, but I'm going in."

The two porters frowned and were thoughtful for a minute. Owen knew they had family back in Lima, and he had a mind to order them to go back. But just as he was about to open his mouth, Hector said, "I will come"

"Me, too," Ramirez said. "So what now?"

Owen bit his lip. These men didn't sign on for a life-and-death battle. But it was too late now. They had made their decision. He said, "We plot a course ta da village. I think our best approach is from da north," he said. "Da forest is pretty dense along da edge over there: lot's of ways ta blend in. From there, we can see most of da village."

"If it is still there," Hector said, rubbing his chin.

"Yeah, yeah," Owen said. "But I have a strong feeling it is. These swamp rats are looking for slaves ta run some kind of operation, least that's what Lino said." He poked his stick at the diagram representing the long house etched on the ground. "Anyway, if da bloody bastards took prisoners, this is where they're holding 'em, I guarantee it."

"Then what?" Hector put in.

"If they're in there, then we decide our next move, like I just said."

"Which would be?" Ramirez said.

"Don't know, Rammy. 'Fraid we're gonna have ta play that one by ear," Owen said.

"In the mean time, why don't I set up a surprise for 'em when they come back to their boat?" Hector said.

"Good idea, mate," Owen said. "An' I'm thinking ya got just da present for 'em, eh?"

Hector smiled grimly.

Fifty kilometers south of Santo Antonio do Içá

Claire stuck her tramping pole in the soft, light brown earth and came to a halt on the thin game trail winding back and forth through the forest. Taking a deep breath, she wiped the river of sweat running down her face with the back of her hand. Beside her was a deep ravine populated with giant tree ferns. She looked over their feathered crowns as tamarins and marmosets bounced from limb to limb in the leafy canopy above. Suddenly, a yellow-breasted aracari swooped down from a lofty branch and landed nearby. The long-billed bird of paradise plucked a berry from the ground and flew off into the steamy forest.

Several meters ahead, Manny turned and looked back. "You need a break?"

Claire slipped her water bottle out of her pack and drained the last few drops. "How much farther before things level off?"

Manny marched toward her as Thad, Molly, and Jorge came up from behind with the rest of the porters. Manny looked into the gloom and said, "Another half hour maybe. How is the tummy?"

"It's okay. Must be this change of diet. It doesn't like what I'm feeding it," she said, although she didn't believe it for a minute.

Molly said, "So, this village we're headed for, how much longer to that?"

"Actually, we are in their territory now," Manny said, "which is probably a good time to have another little talk."

"More rules?" Molly said.

"Si, more rules," Manny said. "Okay, the Jadatani are a hunter-gatherer people who are friendly enough, but they very fussy about certain things. So, names for example. Do not ask them their names. It is considered very rude. Second, and very important, do not stare at them very long under any circumstance, and whatever you do, do not attempt to take their picture. In fact, just leave your cameras in your packs. If they offer you food, take it. It is considered rude if you refuse. One bite and a little smile is all you need to do."

"And what exactly might I be expected to eat?" Molly said with a wary tone.

"Probably an anteater McMuffin or a McMoth with cheese and ant sauce," Thad said, grinning.

"Very funny!" Molly said, and swatted Thad's shoulder with a hefty backhand. She turned a grave expression onto Manny again, who was fighting a smile himself.

He looked off, then turned back to her. "It is probably better I do not tell you."

"I don't eat bugs!" Molly said, indignantly.

Manny shook his head. "Not to worry, they will not serve you any. Insects are reserved for initiation rites." He turned his attention back to the group. "A couple more things. We will make our camp outside of their village. Do not go out of it without me with you. Same rules as on the trail, and you also do not want to find yourself somewhere you do not belong. Another thing. If you have personal items you do not want to let go of, leave them at our base camp in your packs. The Jadatani like jewelry and interesting clothing, and will want to trade with you. Refusing a trade is considered rude."

He eyed Thad, then. "Also, do not ask to hold or touch their bows, spears, or knives. They consider these things like part of their bodies." He paused, and here, turned toward Claire and continued, "Nor are their children to be sought after. Let them come to you, and whatever you do, do not pick them up.

"Last, but not least, look to me often. These people, while outwardly friendly, can be unpredictable. I do not want anyone hurt, so if you see me get up and put my hat on, that means, time to go back to base camp. No arguments. Okay?"

When everyone nodded, Manny said, "Good. Let us get back at it. We still have a good slog ahead of us before making camp, and I can assure you somewhere along the way, we will be met by a scouting party. When that happens, remember what I said about looking at them and keep your mouths shut. I will do all the talking."

True to Manny's word, they were soon met by a band of Jadatani hunters who stepped out of the forest undergrowth. In the men's large bony hands, were longbows and spears. One of the men had a bow exactly like the one Owen had brought aboard the boat. The hunters moved forward like stalking panthers, their dark eyes darting back and forth between the aged Peruvian guide and the expedition team.

They were not tall men, perhaps a little over Claire's five-foot-four, but with their weapons in hand, their height increased dramatically. She subtly took in their bronze complexioned skin and long faces framed with jet-black hair, chopped at the ears. Broad shouldered and stoutly built, the men wore nothing but streaks of dark brown and white paint except for a simple thong. To Claire, they were utterly marvelous to look at.

The man with the bow spoke, and Manny answered. A short conversation ensued among the forest hunters. The lead man relaxed his grip on his bow and came forward. As he assessed Manny, Claire could feel the rest of the hunters' gaze upon her team.

This is what she lived for, meeting new peoples and cultures, learning their ways and languages, what they believed in, their myths and legends. She spied the paint they wore, studying it a little closer. Body markings held many meanings from tribe to tribe. She assumed these were hunting symbols, giving power over their quarry, but who knew. Yet it was the fractured language they spoke that fascinated her the most. It was unlike anything she had ever heard, and what was more, Manny knew it! She would have a long talk with him after they were settled in at base camp for the night.

One of them approached and looked her team over, eyeing Molly's shock of red hair. He was the youngest of them, or so Claire guessed, and had a long bamboo splint piercing his broad nose. A strong, musky odor wafted about him. After he gave their team a close inspection, he went back to the lead man standing beside Manny and uttered several choppy, fragmented words. The leader bobbed his head then uttered something to Manny.

"We are to follow this man beside me," Manny said, turning around. The Jadatani leader made a side-to-side motion with his hand and jabbed his bow out towards his party. One by one, the hunters melted back into the forest as if they'd never been there.

Twenty

Jadatani village

THE EXPEDITION team followed the Jadatani hunter through the forest along a meandering stream until they came to a broad clearing. Across a small grassy field, Claire saw a large oval compound crafted from bamboo and thin, upright logs. The leader led them forward to a small opening past a plot of tilled earth, lush with fluttering heart shaped leaves. Among the sprouting plants knelt a group of bare-breasted women who looked up from their work as the team approached.

In the field beyond, Claire saw children and toddlers gathering grass into bundles. Startled, she remembered her miscarriage. She closed her eyes and steeled herself; trying to force the memory away, reminding herself that it was best it had happened. But try as she might, she couldn't make herself forget.

The lead hunter said something to Manny then ducked through the low opening into the compound. "You are to follow him inside," Manny said. "I will come right after I get our porters started on setting up camp." He stood aside as Claire bent her head and entered after the Jadatani hunter. Inside she saw a thriving community: men stripping bark from long, slender branches and braiding rope, others butchering and dividing a tapir fresh from a hunt, women weaving baskets and sorting berries and roots on heliconia leaves. Everywhere she looked, something of interest was going on.

Before long, men, women, and children looked up from their tasks. Ten minutes later they were jostling one another to get better views. As they gathered around her team, Manny came beside her. Leaning in close, he directed her gaze to a wiry man at the far end of the compound. "See him? That is the medicine man." To Molly, he said, "Your red hair will be of great interest to him. He will want to touch it. It would be most generous if you allowed him to." When Molly shrugged, Manny smiled and said, "All you need to do when he looks at it is to hold a lock of hair out toward him. Do it purposely. That is how he will know he is invited to touch it." He glanced at Claire, Thad, and Jorge. "This is how they make physical contact. They look intently and wait for you to offer. Remember, the key is to be purposeful. If you have any question in your mind whether you have been invited to touch them, do nothing."

"What about the other way around?" Thad said. "Is it rude to refrain from accepting an offer?"

Manny looked at the tall RA discerningly. "Si! Good question." He glanced around at the team. "It is extremely rude to deny any offering, so be very careful of, how you say, 'body language'?" When they all nodded, he went on. "This applies to women," and here Manny's gaze strayed to Claire and Molly, "as well as men. Do not look at them with anything more than a passing glance."

Molly's eyes grew wide. "You mean they might think–"

"Si," Manny said, answering her unsaid question, "they will feel obligated to lie with you if they think you are offering yourself to them as a gift. The women will not like it, so be on your guard!" He looked back toward the far end of the compound, where the wiry, old man and three very round women were speaking with the hunter. Although they were a fair distance away, Claire could feel their pointed glances coming across the open grounds.

Claire dipped her head but kept a furtive eye on their conversation. How much power do women wield in the tribe, she wondered? But it was the old man that held her attention. He was wearing a pair of faded Levi's. She glanced at Manny. "I assume a gift from Owen."

Manny shrugged. "Si. If you are wearing anything you want to keep, best to stuff it in your pocket, because here they come."

"I'm good," Claire said, pocketing her wolf charm bracelet. She watched the old man leading the three women toward them with the hunter who had met them on the trail. "Molly, Thad, Jorge, anything you don't want to let go of, better get rid of it now, and quick."

Jorge reached behind his neck and unclasped a silver necklace holding a figure of Saint George. As he slipped it into his pocket, Manny greeted the old medicine man whose toothless face displayed four deep-brown helical lines that ran from ear to ear. The women who came with him had piercings through their faces and ears, and a plethora of dark, brown dots covering their bodies. They stood off to one side and looked on impassively with the rest of the tribe.

Claire furtively assessed the newcomer's markings and those of the tribe behind them. Several of them she had seen before in text books: black and brown +'s and o's arranged horizontally across their faces, squiggled lines running down their bodies.

The medicine man stepped toward Claire and considered her with an enigmatic expression. Claire met his gaze briefly and smiled as he looked her over. Manny pointed to her and said, "ū qüi ãhé."

The man said nothing and moved to Molly who stood rigid. Manny said, "It is okay, Molly, relax. He is curious."

"When do I show him it's okay to touch my hair?" Molly said.

"Same way you know when I want to touch you," Jorge said softly beside her, and grinned.

Molly blushed, and whispered, "Jorge! Stop."

Claire cocked her brow. *So you've made it past running your tongues down each other's throats. Better keep it in your pants, young man. I'm not bringing Molly home pregnant.*

The old medicine man noted Molly's blush, made a toothless smile and thumped the heels of his bony hands together suggestively. Molly looked to Manny, and said, "What did that mean."

Manny cleared his throat. "He believes you are spending time together in the hammock at night making bebês."

When Molly dropped her jaw, Thad frowned. Claire looked upward. *Jesus, they're at it already!* The old man eyed Molly queerly though, obviously baffled by her sudden discomfort.

Manny quickly said something to him, bringing back his smile. Winking, he said to Molly, "I told him you were trying to keep it a secret from your mother."

"And who might that be?" Claire said in a neutral tone.

"Why, you of course, senhora," Manny replied. He turned back to Molly. "I think now would be a good time to offer him a lock of your hair."

Molly glanced at the medicine man anxiously and reached up to loosen the elastic thong holding her ponytail. When she shook her long, wavy red hair, ohh's and ahh's traveled through the tribe. Molly blushed again and looked down as the medicine man stepped closer. Claire sensed Molly's unease and said, "Think of this as research for that paper you're going to write when we get home."

Molly gave a crooked smile and tentatively extended a thick length of hair to the old man. He reached out and dragged his gnarled fingers slowly through it, then closed his eyes and jiggled his head up and down, saying, "Mâ-taüi-oo-ma-tupu da la püoh-tãça," which brought murmuring from the tribe.

Manny said, "He says, 'life-force of firebird is strong in her,' which is very good. Macaws are sacred to the Jadatani; scarlet-feathered ones especially."

The medicine man pulled his hand away, and opening his eyes, stared deeply into Molly's for a long time as if he were conversing with her soul. Claire watched the silent exchange between them. Part of her was jealous of what was taking place, and another part worried for Molly. She had witnessed such encounters before - in Africa - and the troubled dreams they could bring.

Finally, the medicine man released Molly from his gaze and moved on to Thad and Jorge.

An hour later, Claire was sitting on a split log under a broad thatched canopy with Manny beside her. Across from her sat three Jadatani men picking purple berries off a heliconia leaf and popping them into their mouths. They had been casually conversing with Manny for the last twenty minutes. Claire lifted the drinking gourd from her lap and sipped a swallow of rainwater. *He certainly knows them well enough. He's been here a lot!*

She eyed Molly who was several yards away, and at the moment, the center of attention with the Jadatani women and children. Manny tapped her on her shoulder, rousing her from her musing. "Yes?"

"They want to know what is in the equipment packs we have brought with us. I have told them it is special gear for the expedition, but they are curious. They would like to see it," Manny said. He eyed her knowingly. "What should I tell them?"

Claire paused, scrambling to think of a way out of appearing rude. The last thing she wanted was to have to explain why she wouldn't trade her high-tech equipment for a handcrafted basket. "Tell them they are welcome to look, but these items are to us like the spear and knife are to them, and so are not for trade."

Manny gave her a subtle nod of approval and translated it back. The men seemed to accept Manny's explanation and fell into whispered conversation between themselves. She wondered what they were thinking. Although she trusted Manny - perhaps more than she should - she was at the mercy of his translations.

Her attention went to the powerful, long-limbed man sitting next to Manny. The man wore a wide armband of white feathers with three long red ones pointing upward. A long thin bamboo shaft pierced his nose and thick black paint covered his gaunt cheeks, giving him a fierce look. She thought of him as Longface. At the moment, there was a definite feeling of wariness coming back at her from his dark penetrating gaze. She tried to ignore it as she waited for the men to speak again. Suddenly, Longface said something and motioned Manny to translate for him.

"He wants to know where we are going," Manny said.

Another pointed question. Claire looked up to get her bearings. The sun was on her right, which meant south was dead ahead – sort of. She pointed a little to her left, which brought raised brows from the Jadatani men. Longface shook his head emphatically and uttered a string of words. Manny translated, "He says, that way is no good. Bad spirit lives there."

"Bad spirit?" Claire said, carefully.

"Si. They avoid that part of the forest."

Claire was intrigued and mystified. "You know about this?"

Manny nodded. "I am sorry. I forgot about it. It has been a while since I have been among them."

Claire paused, pondering her next question.

Manny slapped a mosquito on his arm and looked at her hard. "You think this bad spirit is our man?"

"I do," Claire said.

Manny said, "The Jadatani rarely speak of such things. Let me see what I can find out." He turned to Longface and spoke. Longface paused, and answered back. Manny turned to Claire and said, "We are in luck. He is going to get someone who saw it."

Claire watched Longface stride across the compound toward an old man in a hammock. A mangy dog lying under the old man's feet looked up as Longface neared, then lowered his head again. The men spoke for several minutes, until the old man pulled himself to his feet and limped behind Longface. Claire's gaze went to old man's misshapen leg, bent at an odd angle below the knee. Claire guessed it was from a fracture a long time ago. As Longface helped him sit, the old man turned to Manny and smiled companionably. The two men seemed to know each other. Finally, the old man began to speak in a slow-metered, reedy voice.

When he finished, Manny said, "He and I go back a long way, but I have never heard this tale. Anyway, here it is. He rambles on quite a bit. I will try to get to the point, though. Before his injury, he was a hunter. One day, he saw a man with a head of a fîjâr walking in Tu-ahn-anch-uha: the 'Dreaming Land.'" Manny paused, and must have seen her confusion, because he added, "A fíjâr is a jaguar. Jadatani believe in shape shifters. They are bad spirits to them and to be avoided at all costs."

"What is this 'Dreaming Land?" Claire said.

"I do not know. I have never heard of it until now."

The old man eyed Manny and said something.

Manny nodded and turned to Claire. "He wants to know why you want to go there?"

"Tell him," she said, sipping another drink of water.

Manny turned to the old man and spoke at length, gesturing as he did so. After he finished, the old man shook his head and reeled off another reply. Manny said, "I told him we are looking for a man who lives alone. He says: no one lives alone there. Only bad spirit."

Longface spoke, then tapped Manny and gestured toward Claire. "He wants to know why you want to find this man who lives alone," Manny said.

Claire waved a bee away from her face. *One thing's for sure, they are direct! The problem is; how do I answer their questions without appearing evasive.* At last, she said, "Tell him we're trying to help him."

Manny shook his head. "They will not understand that. All the people of the forest know how to take care of themselves. Tell you what, I will handle it." He turned back to Longface and spoke for some time. As he did, the man's gaze shifted to Claire. Slowly his stoic expression melted into understanding. He made a few pointed comments that were answered by Manny and nodded acceptance at whatever was being said.

As silence settled in between them, Claire leaned toward Manny and whispered, "What did you tell him?"

"I told him you are searching the forest for a man who has great visions of the Before Time."

"The Before Time," Claire said.

"Si, it is the time before."

"Before what?"

"Ah, now you see," Manny said.

"See what?" Claire said, confused.

Manny shrugged. "The problem. They do not know what is before anything, only that something must have been."

"Interesting! I also find it interesting Owen never mentioned these people."

Manny shrugged. We will talk about that later, okay? When we are alone?"

"Yes, by all means. Anything else I should know?"

"I do not think so," Manny said.

"Well, one thing's good, our man is most likely in the direction we're heading."

"Except we will not be able to strike out that way when we leave," Manny said.

"Yeah, I know," Claire said rubbing a mosquito bite. "They definitely won't like us disturbing their bad spirit."

Longface and the rest of the men rose and walked away without another word, leaving Claire and Manny looking on after them. It was now mid-afternoon, and the oppressive sun in the cloudless sky was baking the compound. Claire waved a host of flies away from her face and looked around. The men, women, and children had since retreated to their hammocks. Thad came and took a seat across from her and was observing a man trim a fletching on an arrow several feet away. Jorge remained next to Molly and was watching some girls draw 'S's' on their faces.

Manny tapped her arm and waved his hand. "So, what do you think?"

"They're beautiful," Claire said.

"I have never thought of them as beautiful before, but si, I guess you could say that. You know, these are the people Owen grew up with as a child."

"These people?" Claire said surprised, although she didn't know why she should be. Every time she turned around, something new popped up about the Kiwi.

"Si."

"But Owen said his parent's research station was on a river," Claire said. "There's just a stream here."

Manny sipped a drink of water and pointed southwest. "Over there down a slope is a large tributary feeding into the Rio Javary to the north. Later on, I can take you to it and you will be able to see where Owen grew up. The station is abandoned now. Most of it scavenged and reused by the Jadatani. Some of it is right behind us," he said nodding toward a wall of flat weathered boards. "Anyway, these people are very precious to him. The man you met with the bad leg; he is called Tupu or 'Feather'. I have known him for ten years, but Owen, he used to play with him when they were boys."

Claire was taken aback. The man appeared to be in his late sixties. "So, Tupu's in his mid-forties then?"

"Si. They are a most hardy people, but the forest, it wears them down. If it is not a fall from a tree or a poor diet, it is illness. Chagas and malaria are everywhere and they do not discriminate against who they attack," Manny said. "Few ever make it to my ripe old age."

Across the compound, Claire saw a man with a long bamboo pipe placed to his mouth. On the other end of it was a man who had positioned it over his nose. When a man blew into it, the other man pulled back quickly and looked away, as if he was in great pain. Two other men beside them were gyrating in slow, undulating motions. One of them was turning slowly with his arms up, the other walking back and forth like a chicken. Both were singing lyrics that repeated over and over in flat monotones. Manny narrowed his eyes on the men and frowned.

Claire said, "Is that Yopo they're blowing through the pipes?"

"Si," Manny said. He snatched a berry from the basket beside them. "I had better call your team over here in case things become uncomfortable."

Claire and her team retreated to base camp outside the Jadatani compound just before sunset. They were tired and hungry, but very excited. They dished up rations of rice and beans with marinated hard-boiled eggs from the mess tent and found chairs outside under the fading sky. Manny pushed aside several small beetles that had landed on his plate. "It has been a long day and these old bones are tired," he said. "Tomorrow, we will head for the river and follow it south for a couple hundred meters before turning back and heading northeast."

Thad said, "Why? Last I looked, our coordinates are back that way."

"It's in deference to the tribe," Claire said. "They believe a bad spirit walks where we're going. We don't want to distress them."

"Oh," Thad said. He was quiet a minute. Suddenly, he spoke up. "They certainly liked you, Molly. Look at all that artwork on your face."

Molly stopped picking at her meal, turned to Jorge and smiled demurely, stretching the concentric brown circles and squiggly lines drawn over her jaw down to her neck. "I kind of like 'em. What do you think?" she said tilting her head for him to get a better look.

"They are nice," Jorge said, peeling a jagua. He broke apart the orange-sized fruit and offered Molly a wedge.

Thad shoveled the last forkful of beans into his mouth, sat back, and said, "Yeah, not bad, Mol. Anyway, today was off the charts, wasn't it? I mean, there's a whole library right here just waiting to be written."

"By you, of course, I'm sure," Molly added in a sarcastic tone. She popped the wedge of jagua into her mouth and looked off, eliciting a frown from Thad.

Claire took a deep breath and waited for a grinding cramp to pass in her abdomen. Her wince caught Manny's attention. He furrowed his brow as she set her fork down and wiped her mouth with a napkin. "I think I'm gonna turn in. Thad, would you mind taking care of my plate?" When he nodded, Claire tapped Molly on the arm. "Walk with me?"

She rose and waited for Molly to join her. As they headed for her tent, Claire said, "Everything alright?"

Molly shrugged. "Sure, why."

"You seem preoccupied. You had quite an experience today."

"Yeah, it was different," Molly said, fidgeting. "It's really weird. I keep seeing his face in my head."

"I remember an experience I had in Togo with a tribal shaman. I dreamt about him for weeks afterward. Don't worry, it'll pass," Claire said. She was quiet a minute, mustering up her nerve to say what had been on her mind since they entered the compound hours ago. Finally, she said, "Can I ask you a question?"

"I guess."

"Are you on the pill?"

Molly started. "What?"

"The pill, are you on it?"

Molly frowned. "What does that have to do with anything?"

Claire drew breath. "I saw how you acted when the medicine man made reference to you and Jorge being intimate. The last thing we need is a pregnancy in the middle of the Amazon."

Molly blinked. "I'm not a child."

"A fact I'm well aware of. Please answer my question."

"Fine! If you must know, yes, I'm on the pill. Anything else?"

"No, that'll do … Molly?"

"Yes," she said, her tone chilled.

"Regardless of what happened between Noah and me, I still consider you family, and families care about each other." Claire smiled diffidently and took Molly's hands in hers. "Jorge is a nice guy. Just take your time, okay?"

"Yeah. Sure, whatever."

Claire sighed and pulled her close. "I promise I won't intrude again," she said. Drawing back, she put her hands to Molly's shoulders and patted them. "Well, I suppose I better let you get back to Jorge before he wonders what happened to you."

Molly shrugged, and as she turned and walked away, Claire felt like she had lost another piece of her diminishing family.

Twenty One

Yagüani village

OWEN TOSSED his hat to Hector, stepped into a dense thicket of heliconia, and snuck up to a curtain of ovate leaves. Through their jagged cracks, he could see the Yagüani longhouse. Over its thatched roof, a thin trail of white smoke rose into a slate sky. He carefully parted the leaves in front of him and lifted his field glasses to his face, hoping against all odds the tribe was okay. But the empty grounds before him were quiet. He sighed. *Not good. Da area should be teeming with men, women an' children.*

He lowered the glasses and backed out slowly to where Hector and Ramirez waited under low overhanging branches. Raising a finger to his lips, he pointed to a mound of tall pampas grass to the north. The men nodded and slipped away with bow's cocked-and-ready in one hand. Owen followed, placing each step carefully so as not to make a sound.

When they neared the riverbank, Hector crouched and wedged his way into the pampas. Owen lifted his head just far enough to see over the waving grasses and spotted two barrel-chested men in dark Gortex shirts. They were sitting on a log in front of a sputtering fire by the longhouse, smoking cigarettes, and bitching about the bugs. Their rifles lay beside them along with their vests and dirty dinner plates. One of them poked at the fire with a stick.

Owen ducked back down, pointed to himself then back to where they had just come from. Mouthing the words, 'I want ta make sure they're it,' he slunk away and circled around to the other side of the village under the cover of the forest. As he came out from under the trees, he saw several birds circling in the sky upriver. A foul odor hung in the air. He dismissed the telltale signs of death on the river and burrowed into the tangled brush.

When he came close to the edge of the clearing, he pricked his ears and listened. One of the men said in Portuguese, "These fucking bugs are driving me crazy. How do those baratas stand living here in this shit-hole?"

The other man spoke up with a deep booming voice. "You better get used to it. We're gonna be here awhile. Give me another butt."

"What are you? A chimney! Take it easy, we're gonna be here all night, and I'm not going back to the boat for another pack with it starting to getting dark ... Bom Dues, what's that smell?"

"I think somebody shit their pants in the shack back there," the deep voice said, laughing. "If it bothers you so much, go change their diapers."

"Fuck you."

"Where you going?"

"To take a piss. You wanna hold it for me?"

"With what, a pair of tweezers?" said the man with the deep voice. He laughed. "You know you've been a miserable prick since we left do Içà. What's crawled up your ass?"

"What do you think? This fucking jungle! I didn't sign on for this shit. Fucking Valderón. And Juan, he's no better. He follows the asshole like a bitch-puppy."

"Si, but that bitch-puppy can kick your ass, amigo. Be careful to keep your opinions to yourself or you might end up with a 9mm enema. Hey, when you're done watering the lilies with your little squirt gun, bring back another piece of jerky."

"Fuck you!"

Owen gritted his teeth. *Those dirty rat bastards!* They've left these blokes behind ta watch their goodies while they're gone looking for more.

More booming laughter followed. Suddenly Owen heard steps coming his way. *Shite!* He unsheathed his knife and wriggled back on his belly as quickly as he could, but not nearly as far as he wanted. The man's shadow darkened the edge of the brush. A minute later, Owen heard a telltale rat-a-tat-tat pinging the leaves a couple feet away. He turned his face as the muscles in his arms and legs coiled.

The sound of a zipper being zipped was followed by a shadow moving over Owen's head. The grass parted and all at once, the man was staring down at him. "What the hell –" Owen scrambled to his feet, knife in hand and lunged at the man. They fell to the ground and rolled over. Suddenly Owen was on his back. His weapon hand pinned to the ground. The man outweighed him considerably and was incredibly strong. He looked down at Owen with grinning eyes as he tore the knife from his hand.

The blade came up and readied itself for the downward stroke. Owen shot a hand up and seized the man's wrist. Slowly the tip of the weapon inched closer to Owen's chest. "Adeus, asshole." The man said.

Something whizzed over Owen's head.

Phh-womp!

The blade dropped, pricking Owen's shirt and slipped off. Owen felt the man list to the side. Saw the man raise his hand to his throat, his dark eyes bulging. Blood oozed from the corner of his mouth. A gurgled gasp followed, and then silence as he fell to the ground on his face.

Hector came running up as Owen got to his knees. "I saw you out here playing and figured you could use a hand"

"Yeah, yeah, nice shot," Owen said. He stood and dusted the dirt off his shirt. "I take it ya took care of da other swamp rat?"

"Si. Rammy dealt with him."

"Good, let's see about our friends," Owen said. "From what I heard, da other rats are off collecting more labor so we have a window here if we wanna do something 'sides hit an' run."

Hector slung the bow over his shoulder. "What do you have in mind?"

"Setting up a little homecoming party."

Hector nodded as Ramirez came running over. Ramirez said, "It looks like there's only the two of them, but we better not hang around here long. Who knows when the rest of them'll be back?"

"No worries, Rammy," Owen said. "They're far afield rounding up more labor. Won't be back till early morning. Let's see about our friends."

They marched to the longhouse and stepped inside. In the dark shadows, murmuring voices ceased as Owen stood adjusting his eyes to the dim light. He wrinkled his nose and panned the far corner.

"There they are. Help me get 'em up an' outta here." He broke into stilted Yagüani, and said, "Everything going ta be all right. Men who did this are gone. Hold still. We cut free."

Fifteen minutes later, thirty-six men and women stood outside talking all at once, asking questions and telling Owen what had happened. The question foremost on their lips was, 'where are the children'?

Owen looked back to where he saw birds circling in the sky and frowned. In Portuguese, he said to Ramirez, "I gotta bad feeling here. Rammy, do me a favor, aye? Tramp up along side da river a couple hundred meters. Let me know what ya find." To Hector he said, "Go fetch da boats. We've got work ta do here, an' not a lotta time ta do it. In da meantime, I gotta get these people settled down an' thinking straight.

He noticed then for the first time, that many of them had dark bruises on their chests and abdomens. He eyed the semi-automatic rifle lying near the fire discerningly.

"They used rubber bullets on 'em," Owen said looking off as he watched Ramirez tromp into the field. He turned back searching the angry and confused faces around him for a rigid and determined expression. He needed someone who could control his anger and channel it in the right direction. He spied such a man near the back of the throng. He was taller than most, broad shouldered with a thick crop of black hair sprinkled with gray. A long, shell necklace hung around a thick, bronzed neck.

The man's gaze was slowly sweeping over the village, taking everything in. Here was a man Owen could talk to. He went through the crowd and pulled him aside.

In Yagüani, he said, "Men who did this are coming back." He put his hand out and waved it across the grounds. If you want ta remain here, ya must fight."

The man pointed toward the rifle lying near the fire ring and said, "What can we do against those?"

Owen went over and picked up the rifle. He turned around and faced the crowd that was gathering behind him. "We use this against them."

"But they have many of those. How can one defeat them all?" another man said, which brought several comments from the crowd.

Just then, Ramirez came stomping back through the brush. When Owen saw his face, he knew what he had feared had happened. He closed his eyes, swallowing the burning rage inside him, and said, "I have something new ta show you." He broke back into English. "Rammy, gimme your bow."

Ramirez came forward with fire in his eyes, and as he handed Owen his weapon, spat on the ground. "The porcos butchered them. I will kill them!"

"Yeah, yeah, but we need ta keep our heads in da game mate," Owen said, taking the bow from him. To the elder Yagüani, he said, "This not da same as yours. It's," he struggled for the word, "stronger, more true. When ya aim, arrow go where ya want. Faster, farther. I have enough for many men, but I need ta show them how ta shoot."

The Yagüani took the bow in his hands and looked at it skeptically. "Where does the arrow go?"

Owen took the bow back and grabbed one of Ramirez's arrows. "Watch." He lifted the bow up and slid the arrow into the modified riser and fitted it to the innermost string. "Look there. See that capybara at edge of da river?" When the man nodded, Owen pulled the string back and let the arrow go. It sprang off the bowstring with a whoosh and raced across the clearing into the animal with a thud. The elder Yagüani's eyes widened along with several other men who had been watching.

"Ya see?"

The man nodded.

"Now ya try."

Owen put the bow in the man's hands and stood behind him positioning his arm this way and that so the backlash of the cable-string wouldn't slice into the man's arm. The man pulled the arrow a third of the way back, stopped and frowned. "It gets easier da farther ya pull back," Owen encouraged. The man tightened his grip on the bow, clenched his jaw and pulled back again. When the arrow was drawn halfway the man smiled and pulled the rest of the way with comparative ease. He sighted the arrow and let it fly. It missed the target, but not by much.

Owen said to him," I have way ta win back ya home. Ya help me?"

The man asked for another arrow. As Owen gave it to him, he said to Ramirez, "Make sure no one sees what ya saw back there in da bush 'til this is all over. I'm working on a plan that depends on people being patient. Last thing I need is someone rushing out at da wrong time."

Four kilometer's southwest of the Yagüani village

Juan stepped over a gnarled root and swatted a leaning trompa stalk out of his way. His raid had gone exactly as planned except that Benito was still alive. The man seemed to have the fortune of a cat. Sosa, however, did not. Juan allowed a rare smile to come to his lips at the memory of Sosa's death. The beauty of it was, it had happened without one bit of forethought. What were the chance of the thrown spear connecting with the back of Sosa's head from thirty feet away? If lightning could strike twice more like that, life would be perfect.

Filipe caught him up. "One down, two to go."

"Si, two to go."

"Don't worry, I will make sure they do not come back from our next raid."

"Just remember to keep your berretta where it belongs, comprende? I want their miserable lives to end from an arrow or a spear," Juan said, stepping down into a muddy swale.

"Too bad Bennie wasn't on the other end of that spear. That was one hell of a shot!" Filipe said.

"It was."

"Maybe we should bring the roach who shot it along on our next raid. See if he can do it again," Filipe said with a hint of sarcasm.

Juan glanced back over his shoulder at his life-long friend as he picked his way along the path. "That is one of the things I like about you, you're always thinking. So, once we get back, I want you to notify the cargo boat in do Içá to come along. We should be all set to start clearing the forest downriver by the time they get here."

"Hey boss," came a shout from behind.

Juan stopped and turned around. From the middle of the long line of prisoners stretched out on the winding trail, he saw Miguel waving. "Si, what is it?" he shouted back.

"We got a problem back here," came a reply. "Emilio twisted an ankle."

Juan frowned. "Okay, we'll take five." He popped a cigar out of his vest pocket and bit the end off. To Filipe, he said, "Go back and see what the hell's wrong with him. We have another hour ahead of us. Tell him to get it fixed. I don't want to be stopping every ten minutes for the son-of-a-bitch."

Filipe nodded and started off.

Once he was alone, Juan lit his cigar and looked out into the tangled profusion of woody vines. To his surprise, he discovered he missed his honey-eyed Reyna. He wondered what she was doing right now. In his mind's eye, he could see her sitting by the pool in a saffron silk robe studying a brochure of a college she would never attend as long as her father had anything to say about it. Valderón kept those who were near to his heart close, and his enemies dead.

For that reason, Reyna had no love for her tyrannical and overbearing father. Perhaps that's why Juan trusted her to a point, and had on occasion opened up to her about his life on the streets of Lima. To be honest, besides Filipe, she was the only one who really understood him. The question was; how would she react after he made his move on her father? Loathing parents was one thing, rejoicing in their death was quite another. But he couldn't worry about it now. He had to stay focused, follow through with his marching orders until he was sure he had the leverage and support he needed from the rank and file lieutenants under Valderón, and most of all, he needed Benito and Miguel dead.

Filipe came tromping back and stood beside him. "Emilio said he'd keep up. If not, just go ahead. He'd catch up later."

"Or he could be target practice for that new berretta you have, hmmm," Juan said, curling his lip. "Okay, let's move on."

The sortie and their line of prisoners treaded the threadbare trail for the next four kilometers in relative silence. Juan walked alone deep in thought with Filipe and the rest following single file. Since they'd struck back on the trail for the Yagüani village, he'd been thinking about Valderón and counting up those he knew he could depend on to back him up when it came time to strike. He had fifteen lieutenants in his pocket so far. Did he need more? How soon should he make his move after he returned to Iquitos? As far as the hit was concerned, that was not an issue: he would do the deed. The question was, how to reorganize the cartel?

He strutted along, pushing fronds and low hanging branches away, when suddenly he realized the forest had gotten quiet. Too quiet! He stopped and panned the outlying trees and ferns.

"What's wrong?" Filipe said from behind.

"I don't know." He went for his rifle, and just as his hand touched the grip, the air hissed with arrows. Suddenly, men were crying out behind him. The sound of gunfire erupted in the forest. An arrow flew into Juan's vest with a thunk and stuck. He looked down. It was a machine-made arrow. What the hell? Another one whipped past his ear. He dove into the tall ferns beside the trail and took cover, watching the unfolding battle.

Pulling his SCRIBBLER out, he texted Filipe.

'WYRRE U?'

A moment later, the response came.

'BEHID - OP TRAOL - TOOK ARIW 2 LEG - BLEDD BAD - WHDRE U?'

Juan gritted his teeth. He needed to know more of what was going on. As his heart thumped, he fought to assess his options. The safest thing was to wait things out, see what he was up against. But his gut told him Filipe needed help. Any other man he'd leave to fend for himself. But not Filipe!

'STA. WIL B THRE SUON'

The gunfire ceased. Juan pocketed the SCRIBBLER and scanned the trail, rifle in hand. Whoever had ambushed them was out there survey-ing the situation. He waited, his finger on the trigger guard. *They're coming soon. Who are they?* An ill feeling came over him as he kneeled in the tall ferns.

Finally, the surrounding bush crowding the trail began to move, and out of it poured painted men with compound bows. Juan snarled. Where the hell did they get those? Then, following from behind came a white man with a rifle. A semi! Son-of-a-bitch!

His grip on the rifle's fore stock tightened as he watched the man step onto the trail and turn a body over with his foot. Bringing his rifle up, Juan aimed. Just as he was about to put his finger on the trigger, something snapped on the ground behind him. He whipped around just as a machete came crashing down, ripping the rifle out of his hand. A mind-numbing pain raced up his right arm.

The blade came at him again. He lunged to the ground and rolled aside. Kicked the legs of the enemy out from under him and fled into the forest. Groping his vest, he searched for his Glock. Saw blood pouring out of a wide gash above his wrist. A root caught his foot and sent him tumbling forward. He lay there gasping until he realized he'd lost his pistol in the leafy ground cover.

As he rolled over to look for it, a dark shadow fell on him. He turned and looked up into cold, black eyes. A painted face pitted with bone piercings scowled back. Juan froze. He had seen the face before. The man was a Yagüani! The machete switched hands. As the man swooped down toward him, Juan kicked up and connected with a knee. The man stumbled to the side as Juan scrambled to his knees.

Seizing the moment, Juan drew the blackjack from the sheath on his belt. He coiled to lunge at the man, but felt something dig into his leg. Glancing down, he saw the grip of his pistol under his shin. The Yagüani sprang to his feet. Drew back his machete. Juan dropped to his knee and slung his Glock up, firing three, quick silent rounds. The startled Yagüani jolted backward, eyes wide and thumped to the ground beside him.

Juan nudged him with his foot making sure he was dead, then sat grimacing as the world swirled before him. First order of business was to stop the bleeding. He ripped the shredded remains of his sleeve away and wrapped it around his gaping wound as tight as he could stand it. That helped, but he knew he needed more. He wondered where Filipe was, but with no way to determine the enemy's position, he couldn't chance moving just yet. Clenching his jaw, he listened to the lyrical voice of the white man trickling through the bush.

"We will meet again someday, amigo, and things will much different, I assure you!" he muttered then withdrew further into the forest.

Twenty Two

Yagüani village

O WEN HANDED Hector his rifle and took a deep breath, trying to calm his thudding heart and regain control of jittery nerves. He'd been in firefights before, and they always left him shuddering. Killing men, even when it was necessary, was bad business and he didn't like it, especially when he was the one dealing out the death. He went over to the side, away from the others to take a minute alone and collect himself. There would be dreams regarding this ambush in the future – there always were - and he wasn't looking forward to them.

Hector called over, "You alright boss?"

"I'm fine, just catching my breath," Owen replied, reaching down under his shirt and pulling the necklace with his greenstone out.

"Okay. You want me to make sure the rats cannot cause any more trouble?"

"Yeah, yeah, do that," Owen said, kissing the stone. He put it away and surveyed the forest. "An' check da surrounding area. I'm pretty sure I saw a couple of 'em slip inta da bush."

"Si. What if we do not find 'em? They could still cause trouble," Hector said.

"They might, but more than likely, they're trying ta find a way back ta their boat."

"'Cept their boats aren't there are they?" Hector said. "I must tell you, it will be nice riding home on the river instead of tramping through the forest."

"Ya, right," Owen said, eyeing the ragged line of startled and wary Pauapo captives on the trail. On the ground scattered before them, lay five of the cartel's men. Three of which were dead with arrows piercing their bearded faces. The other two were breathing hard and moaning. Owen went over and kicked aside their assault rifles and looked down at them.

His first impulse was to leave them there and let the forest finish them off, but thought better of it. It was better to let the tribes decide. He looked up. "Let's bring these bastards back with us. See what da cartel has in mind. He nudged the wounded men with his foot and broke into Portuguese, "You'll wish for death once these lads get after ya, yeah." He motioned to the elder Yagüani who had helped organize the ambush against the cartel raiding party. "We want these two alive."

The man looked down on the wounded cartel soldiers disdainfully. After a long pause, he nodded and called a warrior over.

"Doku," Owen said, appreciatively. "Now, ta get these people un-tied." He walked down the trail with the elder Yagüani at his side, stopping here and there to assess casualties. Many had the deep bruises that the Yagüani had suffered. More than a few had broken noses and swollen cheeks. One by one, he snipped the zip-ties on their wrists and severed the long attached rope connecting them to one-another.

When he neared the end of the line, he found Ramirez trying to calm an angry young Pauapo boy. On the ground behind the boy, lay a woman, who had taken an arrow to the chest. Owen dropped to a knee beside the woman and drew her lids shut. The boy glared at him.

"I think she is his mother," Rameriz said. "And seeing how that is my arrow, I believe he blames me."

"I think he blames all of us, mate," Owen said, eyeing the scowl on the bone-pierced face staring back at him. "I'd give a year's salary right now ta be able ta talk ta him." To a by-standing Yagüani, he said, "Can ya tell him I'm sorry for what happened ta his mother?"

The Yagüani pointed to Owen, put his hand over his heart and spoke. The boy shook his head and spat on the ground near Owen's feet.

The Yagüani man said, "He not believe."

Owen sighed and sat back on his heel. "Tell him we did not come ta hurt his mother. We came–" he searched for the Yagüani word, "-ta protect."

The Yagüani relayed the message, but the boy remained defiant. Suddenly, one of the Pauapo men nearby came over and grabbed the boy by the shoulder. After he uttered a barrage of sharp, biting words to the boy, he turned to the Yagüani and held his hand out for a knife.

The Yagüani nodded and handed his weapon over.

"What's going on?" Owen said, concerned for the boy's life.

The Yagüani man said, "Child will be burden. May need to die." As the Pauapo man cut the zip-tie loose, the man added, "To live, he will need to prove he is a man."

Owen swallowed hard, but knew he couldn't interfere.

Just then, Hector came running up. He pulled Owen aside. "I found a dead Yagüani in the bush along with these," he said, holding a rifle and a pair of field glasses. "They were well off the trial. I also found this." He pulled a hand-held palm device from his pocket. As Owen studied it, Hector added, "The rifle has live ammo. No rubber bullets. There's another rat out there. Shall I form a search party?"

Owen looked off into the curtain of tree ferns, trompa and nettles crowding the sides of the trail. He had a feeling whoever it was out there, was more than the just another soldier. "I'd like ta snatch da bugger, but finding him would probably cost a life. Aint worth it." He eyed a green tree boa slipping over the branches of a strangler fig above him. "Let da forest take care of him."

"That is, if he stays in the forest," Hector said.

Owen considered that for a moment, then said, "He'll stay put for a while, believe me. He knows he's outnumbered an' in a tight spot. Without his rifle an' field glasses, an' whatever da hell that thing is, he's in a hard spot."

"But desperate men do desperate things, no?"

"I suppose ya're right 'bout that. But it usually ends up bad for 'em. And believe me, after da Yagüani see what da dirty rat bastards did ta their children, it will."

It was late afternoon when Owen stepped out of the longhouse where he had been interrogating three of the cartel men. As expected, he didn't learn anything he didn't already know. The Yagüani were to be conscripted workers for the cartel's coca operation. A boat was coming, they said, with more men, but Owen had the feeling they were lying.

He eyed the group of Yagüani who were constructing a large rack out of bamboo by the riverbank. Despite what the bastards in the longhouse had done, he pitied them. From his short time amongst the Yagüani a few years back, he'd seen how they dealt with enemies.

As he stood there thinking, he remembered the device Hector had handed him on the trail. He dug into his pocket and pulled it out. The index-card sized instrument was unlike anything he'd ever seen before. He turned it over several times trying to figure out how the seamless, brushed chrome device opened. But there was no button to push anywhere.

"Where da hell is it?" he muttered, holding it up to the sun so he could see every little scratch. At last, he noticed a small, raised oval bulge on the back. When he pushed down on it, the front of the device lit up with an alphanumeric keyboard on a blue screen. A minute later he was reading several text messages in Portuguese.

'WYRRE U?'
'BEHID - OF TRAOL - TOOK ARIW 2 LEG - BLEDD BAD - WHDRE U?'
'STA. WIL B THRE SUON'

Owen scratched his head. How were they able to text in the middle of the Amazon? And there were two of them, though one of them would be dead by nightfall. Yagüani poison, if not quick to kill, was lethal.

He scrolled down a little further and read their texts from yesterday morning.

'BB IN POSITION - AIM HIGH'
'NO WORRY HE DIE 2DAY'
'GOOD - GO NOW - B READY'

Then he saw two more texts, sent a couple of days ago. But these had an odd symbol beside them. He studied the little green circle with an inverted 'v' on top and realized it was a satellite connection. The boats were equipped with a transponder. Impressive.

'20 K OUT'
'WILL HOLD IN DO ICA TIL EVERYTHING SECURE AND READY'

As the Yagüani elder and the remaining tribe headed toward him, Owen depressed the power button on the back of the device. It was time for the prisoners to be dealt with. The elder stepped before Owen and stabbed a long spear in the ground. Owen met his deadly gaze, nodded, and headed toward Hector and Ramirez, who were on board the jet boats going through the cartel's gear and equipment. They looked up as he approached.

Hector held a canvas bag up and said, "There is at least fifty clips in here and a pair of infrared night goggles."

Ramirez tossed Owen a bottle of tequila. "And eighteen bottles of that, along with several bottles of rum and vodka."

"They were a thirsty crew," Hector said.

"Yeah, yeah," Owen said.

Ramirez plunked a case of cigars and two cartons of cigarettes onto the gunnels and nodded toward the assembled bamboo racks off-shore. "What are those for?"

"Ya don't wanna know," Owen said. "What's da fuel status?"

Hector went and bent down over the helm and said, "About four hundred liters. Enough to get back to Fonte Boa."

Just then, a chorus of angry voices came from the longhouse. Owen spun around to see the wounded prisoners being led toward the racks.

He turned to Hector and Ramirez. "I wanna be out of here as soon as we can be. Hector, ya take this boat. Rammy and I'll take da other."

His porters darted glances, then nodded as the angry throng behind them grew louder.

"Now, Rammy!" Owen said.

He ran over to the other boat and pushed it out into the river as Ramirez hopped down and followed. Hector gunned the jets on his boat and Rameriz did likewise on theirs. As they moved out into the current, Owen saw the cartel men being tied to the racks.

Ramirez said, "It does not look good for the swamp rats."

"No, it doesn't," Owen said.

"Now, what happens?"

"Watch," Owen said, idling the boat.

With morbid fascination, Owen and Ramirez watched the three racks with the men tied onto them being staked in the river. When the Yagüani pulled back, the only thing that could be seen above the surface of the water were the men's heads.

Ramirez said, "Fish food?"

Owen snatched a guava from out of his pack and was quiet a long time. Finally, he said, "Yeah. They ring da dinner bell by sticking 'em in the side with a spear. Get da blood in da water and let nature do da rest. If da buggers are lucky, they'll bleed ta death 'fore nightfall."

"Otherwise"

Owen bit into the fruit and gunned the jets. "They get eaten alive."

Twenty Three

Emergency Base Camp

THE NARROW game trail the team had been on for the last two days seemed to Claire like it would never end. She stuck her pole into the soft green earth between the tangled roots and took a deep breath. Her legs were tired and sore, her arms ached, and her abdomen felt like it was going split apart. She wiped the river of sweat running down her face with a damp rag.

"Something wrong?" Manny said, suddenly standing beside her.

Claire looked at him with bitter irony. Knowing now what was wrong with her, she nodded and said, "You don't happen to have an antibiotic in that little goodie bag of yours, do you?"

Manny frowned. Peering closely at her, he said, "Anti-biotic? Are you hurt? Where?"

"It's internal," Claire said, and winced as a sharp cramp shot through her. She spied a moss-ridden stump and staggered over to it and sat.

Manny came and knelt before her. "Internal? What are you talking about?"

"I had an incident … on the boat. I thought–" But another wave raced through her and took her breath.

Manny put his hand to her head. "You are burning up!"

Claire gritted her teeth. As she sat, the line of porters and her team tramped up behind them.

Molly said, "What's wrong?"

Manny pursed his lips. "She is sick. Go back and tell Inacio I need the med-kit."

Clearing her throat, Claire said, "You're kidding."

Manny shook his head. "Just antiseptics and some anti-venom."

Claire sucked air and rasped, "Ironic, isn't it? In the middle of the ... greatest freaking pharmacy in the world ... and we ... I can't get ... a stinking milligram of what I need."

Manny looked up, then leaning in quietly said, "When we were in the Jadatani village, one of the women there came to me. She said she sensed a angry spirit in you."

"Really?"

"Si. She also gave me something for it."

"What?"

"A tea and something made from the local roots."

Claire looked at the grave expression staring back at her. "And?"

Manny stroked his chin. Looking out into the dense maze of the jungle, he said, "She said your body was fighting an angry spirit child. I did not think much of it, but now ... was she right?"

Claire averted her eyes, unable to answer. Then again, it didn't matter. It was out and her silence condemned her. At last, she told him about what had happened on the boat and also of the improbable odds of her ever getting pregnant."

Manny was quiet while the whine of insects filled the space between them. "Well then, I suspect you will know what to do with what she gave me," he said handing her a neatly wrapped leaf package.

Claire unfolded the leaf and eyed the gray paste inside. Her options were limited. Still, the idea of coating her insides with something that was cooked up in the middle of the Amazon under less than sterile conditions wasn't her first choice. And who would do it if she couldn't? Molly? Oh, Molly would definitely not like that.

At length, Manny shook his head and said, "You are supposed to be the smart one, no? Doctor and all?"

Claire nodded, but the look on Manny's face told her he doubted she was listening. He shook his head. "What were you thinking? Bom Deus! You could die out here, and there is nothing we can do about it." Standing, he called out to the entourage of porters and barked out orders. Afterward, he turned to Claire. "Let us hope it does not come to that, no?"

That evening, Claire lay on a cot outside of her tent. Camp had been made on a wide flat stretch of ground near a rushing stream. Beside her sat Molly. She watched her niece's fingers fly across the keyboard of the Sat-Lynk. The med-kit had produced a bottle of painkillers, which offered some relief. But it wasn't what she needed to halt the infection spreading inside her. She thought of the medicine Manny had told her about earlier, trying to find another way out of this mess she had gotten herself into. But every option led back to the unpleasant idea of acquiescing to the Jadatani remedy. *You did it this time, girlfriend. God, please get me out of this. I didn't come all the way down here to die!*

Molly called Manny over from his supervision of the camp set-up. "I've made contact with a clinic in do Içá, but the soonest they can get anything to us will be next week."

Manny shook his head. "She won't make it that long. Can you contact Lino?"

Molly shrugged and pursed her lips. "I'd need his transponder address for that, which I assume you don't have. Why?"

"I was thinking we could get a message to Owen," Manny said. "He should be back in do Içá or very close to it by now. Wait, I have an idea. Ask if there is anyone at the clinic who knows Lino."

As Molly typed away, Claire could hear Manny's urgent voice conversing with Thad and Jorge some ways away. She assumed it was about her as she watched one of the porters get a fire going. Her eyes grew heavy and shortly afterward she felt a damp cloth put to her head. She looked up to see Manny kneeling beside her.

Suddenly, Molly said, "I got a reply back from the clinic. There's a nurse who works the evening shift that knows Lino. She'll check to see if he's down at the dock. If he is, she'll tell him to get a hold of Owen."

Manny, said, "Good! Let us hope we get a bit of luck. We're going to need it."

Claire drew breath and cried out as the sudden searing pain woke her from a dreamless sleep. Around her, she heard hushed voices. "This doesn't look good. She's burning up."

Molly came and kneeled beside her. As her soft finger swept a lock of hair away from Claire's eye, she leaned close, and said, "Help is on the way, Claire. I got a hold of Lino. He's back in do Içá. As soon as he sees Owen, he'll let him know."

Claire closed her eyes. Just wonderful: Owen freaking Nightingale to the rescue. I'll never hear the end of it if I live through this.

"Are you thirsty?"

Claire shook her head and took another deep breath. Then suddenly, everything went eerily quiet. She opened her eyes to see everyone in stunned silence looking toward the banks of the stream. Finally, she heard Thad say, "Holy shit!"

Manny's voice cut in. "Nobody move."

"Don't worry, I'm not going anywhere," Thad said.

"What is it," Claire said, blinking up at Molly.

Molly looked down at her wide-eyed. "We've got company."

Claire forced herself to sit up, and slowly took in the tall, powerfully built men aiming arrows at them from the edge of the campfire light. The lead man was huge, and a long, ragged scar ran down his chest. He stepped forward and spoke in a language she could hardly believe she was hearing. She repeated the ancient Egyptian words under her breath as the men moved forward, tightening the circle around the camp.

As they did so, the lead man swept his thick black hair over his shoulders and spoke in a demanding tone. Claire widened her eyes as she took in the braided necklace bearing several large stones around his muscular neck. In the center of it was a large, bone tile with what looked like a cartouche. She blinked. *I'm dreaming. I must be. This isn't possible!*

But Thad whispered, "Look at the symbols on his arms. "They're Egyptian."

"In the middle of the Amazon?" Jorge whispered back.

"Quiet," Manny shushed.

The man came to a halt before the team and planted himself defiantly in the leaf litter. Again, he spoke, and this time Thad answered back in an ancient Egyptian dialect. "Welcome, noble one, to our humble fires."

The man's eyes bulged, but he quickly recovered and regained his rigid expression. He said, "You know our words. How is that?"

Claire said, "They are the words of my people long ago."

The man was quiet a long time as he considered her. Finally, he said, "Your people?"

"Yes," Claire said, in the old tongue.

"What's he want?" Molly muttered.

"I said, quiet," Manny said.

The man glanced toward Molly and hardened his face. "Where have they gone?"

Thad said, "To Atum and the afterlife."

An audible gasp shot around the ring of warriors behind their leader. The man raised his hand and silenced them. "You know Atum?"

As Claire felt her strength start to fade, Thad interjected, "Yes, he is the God of all. We revere all the gods of old, Atum most of all."

The man was quiet a long time. Finally, he said, "We are the Haja-mawri, and I am, Mahl-attu-ani."

As Thad introduced Claire, she focused on the ancient symbol engraved on the bone tile around the leader's neck. *Jesus, he's wearing an Ankh.*

The man saw her looking at him, and fixed her with a riveting gaze. Suddenly, he stepped forward with awe plastered on his chiseled face. He raised his arm and motioned his men to lower their weapons, but not all the way. "It has been foretold you would return," he said, yet bearing doubt in his eyes. He looked at Thad then at Manny and the rest of the encampment before returning his attention back onto her. Claire sensed indecision in him, and with it, the balance between life and death. At last, he released her from the iron grip of his steely gaze and slowly removed his necklace. "It is required that you be given a token of welcome. This is all I have."

The meaning of what had just transpired was not lost on Claire, and the last thing she wanted was to pass out in front of this man. She licked her lips. "And I gratefully accept it." She was about to say more when her body gave out.

The next thing she knew, she was in her tent looking up into a dim yellow lantern light. Manny had his back toward her, and with him was the Hajamawri leader along with Thad. She listened to Thad tell the Hajamawri man that she was between the worlds right now, which was no lie, and that it would be a while until she could travel to their village. It appeared to satisfy the man because a moment later, he nodded and left with Thad following close behind.

"She's awake," Molly said.

Claire looked down and saw Molly sitting near the foot of her cot with her long face full of trepidation.

Manny turned and came to her side. Looking down at her, he said, "Claire, there is no more waiting. You must try the Jadatani medicine."

Claire gazed wearily at Manny. Applying the salve up inside her was unpleasant business, but she was in no position to do it. She took a deep breath, and barely above a whisper looked down and said to Molly, "I can't do this myself. I'm going to need you to help me, sweetie."

Molly nodded, but Claire saw her swallow hard.

"Here, drink this," Manny said, "It will ease your pain." He lifted her head and put the bitter tea to her lips.

As Claire drank, Molly said, "Are you sure about this? I mean, what if..."

"It'll be alright." Claire glanced up at Manny, mouthed the words, "Time to go."

Manny squeezed her shoulder then he and left Molly and her alone. A moment later the tea began its work, and the room began to spin into a spiraling miasma of distorted images.

Amazon River – Santo Antonio do Içá

Owen veered toward a sheltered inlet off the main channel three kilometers east of Santo Antonio do Içá. He wasn't sure where the cartel's operation boat was docked in town and he wasn't interested in finding out the hard way. He spotted an opening between the waving river grasses, and gunned the boat up onto shore out of sight within the dense thicket of camu-camu. Shutting the jet engines down, he hit the switch to the boat's pneumatic gangway as Hector pulled in beside him.

After drawing aside the front panel of the segmented windshield, he gathered up a long nylon rope and hopped up on the causeway. Ramirez went to work removing the boat's GPS monitor along with a few other electronic goodies that might be of interest to the local pawnshops back in Lima. The rifles and ammo they had confiscated from the cartel raiding party would be hidden aboard the boats until he could figure out how to dispose of them.

At length, he stepped onto the spongy shoreline and tied the boat up, wondering if he was making a mistake in not destroying the weapons. But Ramirez reminded him he could get a good price for them and perhaps help offset what he owed Claire. He unsheathed his machete and went to work in the dense, spindled brush. Although the area was fairly secluded, he wanted the boats covered. He would leave nothing to chance.

Hector came beside him and wrapped his arms around a growing pile of trompa and camu-camu. "I will be glad to eat some real food."

"Me too. How's da leg?" Owen said, slicing into a tall trompa stalk. The plant fell at his feet and dropped to the side.

"It is much better," Hector said, walking over to the jet boat and throwing the brush over the gunnel. From over his shoulder, he called back, "So, are you ready to deal with the senhora?"

The mention of the feisty anthropologist made Owen look up. As her face flashed before him, he said, "Not really."

Hector came back and grabbed another armful of brush. "She is going to give you an earful. I do not envy you."

"Yeah, I'll get it good, but I did what I had ta, an' a good thing, too," Owen replied. But even though he knew he had done the right thing, he felt unsettled. For the first time, he found he was tired of fighting the good fight.

"Maybe telling her you saved two villages will satisfy her," Hector said.

"I doubt it," Owen muttered, trying to force himself to forget her. He looked up from hacking the camu-camu in front of him and gazed out over the river, battling his conflicting feelings toward Claire. Hector broke into his musing. "You all right, boss?"

Owen started and looked at the man. "Yeah, yeah. Come on. Let's get these boats covered up an' get ta town. First round's on me."

Owen stepped out of the high grasses and gazed down upon the quaint picturesque city of Santo Antonio do Içá. From where he stood, it looked like a blue, red, and cream-colored bead necklace hanging off an elegant bronzed arm. Beyond the city, the afternoon sun was brushing its golden rays on the rising hills.

He took it in and sighed as he thought about the reunion with the testy anthropologist. Whether he'd get an earful or the silent treatment, he didn't know. Monica had been good with giving him a deaf ear, knowing that it pushed his buttons. Fact was, Claire pushed his buttons too, albeit in a different way. He had never met anyone who could get in his face and challenge him the way she did. Nor did he think she was aware of just how keenly it affected him.

The men tramped down the twisting gravel road into the heart of the city. The first order of business was a cold beer and real food.

The return to the Lírio do Rio could wait, though he sorely wished Manny were with them. He could use a little recon regarding Claire's disposition.

He plodded along the busy, cobbled street with Hector and Ramirez following behind. It was near dinnertime, and the aromas of garlic, cilantro, and roasted meat were drawing people out of the stores and shops to the open street cafés. Owen casually surveyed his choices as he walked among the colorful citizens of the city and settled on a little eatery with wrought iron tables and cushion-covered chairs.

"I don't know about ya two, but I'm knackered," Owen said, plopping his pack on the ground beside him and sitting.

Hector dropped his pack as well, stretched, and pulled a chair out. As he sat, he let out a sigh. "Ah, it feels good to relax again. My ass hurts from sitting too long in that boat."

"I have to piss," Ramirez said, slipping his bulging pack off. "I will be right back. When the waitress comes, order me a shot of tequila with a beer."

Owen reached for the menu wedged between a jar of salsa and a napkin holder. As he perused it, a woman in a crisp, white dress with flowery embroidery came to their table. She set a basket of chips before them and flashed a broad smile. "Holla, how are you today?" She said.

"Mighty thirsty," Hector said, giving her deep plunging neckline a casual glance.

"What can I get for you?"

"Three tall jars ... er, glasses of beer, an' a shot-a tequila," Owen said, and watched her walk away. He took a glance at the menu and put it down. "Don't know 'bout ya, Hector, but a nice steak an' taters is gonna hit da spot."

Hector nodded toward the departing waitress. "And I will take her for desert."

"Ah, come off it, mate. She's way too young for da likes of ya."

"Oh, no, she is just right." He paused, looking out over the busy street. "So, have you decided what you are going to say to your feisty anthropologist?"

"Not yet."

"You know, a man could forget about many troubles with a woman like her around," Hector said, thoughtfully.

Owen hid a frown behind a good-natured chuckle and averted his gaze toward a white stucco cathedral with a tile roof down the street. The man didn't know how close he had guessed to the mark.

"Hey, look who I found," Ramirez said.

Owen turned around to find Lino standing sober-faced beside his porter. Owen felt his stomach twitch as he locked eyes with the man. *Uh-oh, I don't like this.* "What's wrong?"

"Manny! Son-of-a bitch," Owen said, slamming his fist on the table, nearly spilling his glass of beer. But inside he was shaking. "Damn her! I'm gonna kill 'em both 'less da forest does it first."

But Lino shook his head. "Manny did his best to keep her onboard, but she was very determined. Said she would hire someone else to take her into the forest. What was he to do? You know how some people are."

"Yeah, yeah, I know," Owen said. He picked his beer up and drained it in one long gulp, then threw a handful of reales on the table and picked up his pack. "So much for relaxing. So, who's this nurse?"

"Her name is Juanita. I will take you to her," Lino said.

As they walked, Owen filled Lino in on what had happened down south, then said, "How deep in da forest are they?"

"Five days east of the Jadatani village," Lino said. "I have their coordinates back on my boat. It is a very desolate spot they are in. I assume that is where you were leading them?"

"Yeah. By da way, I have a bit a merchandise for your mate in town."

"Do you?" Lino said, and cocked his brow. Keeping pace with Owen's long strides, he said, "Sounds like you ran into our river boat friends."

"Ya could say that."

"Well, you don't look the worse for it," Lino said. "What exactly do you have?"

"Depends on how reputable ya contact is. Last thing I need is for da goodies ta fall back inta da hands of those dirty swamp rats. Speaking of which, have ya seen an unusual boat floating 'round down by da docks?"

"To answer your first question, the man is quite friendly towards the forest people, so I do not think you have to worry. This boat - I take it - is associated with your 'dirty swamp rats'?"

Owen rounded the corner and headed toward a mission-style stucco building at the top of a hill. As he passed the church, he said, "That's right. They're waiting on a message that ain't ever gonna come."

They walked a minute in silence, until Hector spoke up from behind. "Hey, Boss, I have been thinking. Maybe we should send a message."

"What're ya talking about, Hector?"

"Think about it. They may decide to go looking for them, and if they do, would they not go to the last coordinates?"

Owen thought about it. Hector had a point. "So, if I'm reading this right, ya're saying: send 'em on a tiki-tour?"

"Exactly."

"Good idea." He pulled the strange data device he had lifted off the raiders out of his pocket. Tossing it back to Hector, he said, "Why don't ya shoot 'em an invite." To Ramirez, he said, "Ya up for another slog?"

"Sure, when do we leave?"

"As soon as I get da meds," Owen said, and thought about the jet boats, but where they were going deep in the forest, they would be of little use. To Lino he said, "I'm sure da ferry's gone. How much for a lift over da river?"

"Put your money away, amigo. This one is on me," Lino said. He dug into his pocket and pulled out his cell phone. Flipping it open, he called the boat and told them to get ready to leave the minute they got there.

Twenty Four

Three kilometers southwest of the Yagüani village

JUAN GRIMACED as he plodded through the dense forest hauling Filipe, whom he'd found left for dead in the tall forest undergrowth. "Come on amigo, we're getting close, I know it. Soon, we'll be at the boats and headed out of this shit hole," he said, trying to ignore the relentless throbbing ache in his arm.

Filipe groaned. He was getting weaker by the hour. "Okay, we stop for just a minute. Need to check that leg of yours anyway." He looked around for a place to sit and saw a fallen tree ahead. Another groan. "Yeah, I know, it hurts like a bitch." He hauled Filipe to the tree. Sitting him down, he peeled back the strip of black Gortex he'd tied around the leg to stem the bleeding. The ugly red-ringed puncture wound was oozing thick gray pus.

Pulling the bandage back over Filipe's wound, he surveyed the surrounding forest. "We have to be close to the river by now. Where the fuck is it?" He reached into his pocket, pulled out a small digital compass and tapped a button. It flashed NNE. He looked back at Filipe. The man was listing awkwardly on the tree and his eyes were shut.

Juan took a deep breath, gritted his teeth, and laid an arm on the big man's shoulder. "Okay amigo, siesta time's over, you lazy ass."

Filipe opened his eyes and a tiny smile crept across his crooked lips. "Who you calling a lazy ass?"

"You!" Juan said. "Here, put your arm around my neck."

Filipe frowned. "I can walk!"

"Como inferno! Do it or I'll kick your ass all the way to Iquitos and back."

"In your dreams," Filipe said, but he put his arm around Juan's neck all the same.

Juan braced his legs against the fallen tree, and with a ferocious effort hauled the man up with a grunt. With sheer determination, he bore Filipe's considerable weight for the next half hour through the tangled understory of thick ferns and ivenkiki until at last he hit the trail they had used to raid the Yagüani village.

Staggering over to a large, moss-covered root, he sat Filipe down on it. As he gathered his breath, he gauged the distance to the boats. It was no more and half a kilometer. "Not far now," he said, standing back up and looking down the trail. As he mopped his forehead with the back of his hand, he heard a thump. Suddenly, his heart sank. He didn't need to turn around to know the man he loved like a brother was dead. He went over to him, looked into lifeless eyes.

For a long time, Juan sat in numb silence reliving their sordid past and plotting revenge on the 'white bastard'. Finally, he put his finger to Filipe's lids and pulled them shut. "Well amigo, it looks like the clouds are getting ready to piss on us, so I better get you to the boat, no?"

He got to his knees and dragged the man over his shoulder. Ten minutes later, he was standing at the water's edge with Filipe's body at his feet, stunned and speechless. The boats were gone … they were gone! He clenched his jaw and kicked at the ground with reckless fury. He couldn't believe it. The white bastard and his roaches had stolen them.

He closed his eyes and tried to think. Every muscle in his body wanted to storm back to the village and tear them apart, but his wits won out over the urge. What he wanted was revenge. He stared out over the waving river grasses, drinking in bitterness like a man quenching a deadly thirst, then turned his gaze onto Filipe's body. "I will find him amigo, this I promise you. And when I do, I will kill him slowly, very slowly."

An hour later, Juan stepped away from the brush covering Filipe's body near the reedy shore. It wasn't much, but it was the best he could do. He hadn't the time, the means, or the energy to bury his friend. He went and sat by the Juruá River, which flowed northward to join the Marañon in Fonte Boa. As he did so, he felt the labors of two days without sleep catching up to him.

There were so many things he wanted to say, but he had no idea where to begin, so he just stared numbly, trying to make sense of everything. Suddenly the memories came flooding back. He laughed grimly and in a low voice, said, "I remember when we first met in the barrio, amigo. We were just crianças. You were the big shot in the vizinhaça, ordering all the little shits around. Do you remember that? You thought I was just another turd until I knocked you on your ass. You gave me the beating of my life for it, but you respected me. After that, we took what we wanted from whomever we wanted.

"And do you remember our first raid? Lago Tauari, I think it was. We were as green as the crianças. But we learned fast, eh? Those were the days, drinking tequila until we puked our guts out and doing the senhoritas. Guess I'll have to pick up your share now. I will miss you, o meu amigo. You deserve better than this, but perhaps you don't care. What is life anyway but people going around pissing on each other?"

A large raindrop splashed on Juan's face and then another. He looked up and laughed grimly. "You asshole. You think you're funny, don't you? I was gonna say a few words to you before I left, but now you can kiss my ass."

He stood, looked down at the makeshift grave for a moment, then struck out northward along the riverbank as the rain intensified.

On the trail, eighty kilometers northwest of the expedition team's emergency camp.

Owen scrambled down a sharp, root-tangled incline and came to a breathless halt. Beyond, through the trees, he saw a wide grassy field rising up to meet pink and red painted clouds. He reached for the water bottle in the side pocket of his pack and drained the last of it. He had been tramping through the forest at a bruising pace non-stop with Ramirez at his side since the first light of dawn. Suddenly, hunger and fatigue slammed him. He could go no further. But he had made the four-day tramp to the village of the Jadatani in three days. As he capped the water bottle, Ramirez came beside him and stood. Hector would have been with him also, had he not insisted the man stay back and have his leg looked at. Besides, it wasn't brawn Owen was looking for on this trip, it was speed.

"Well, this is about all we can do for one day, mate," Owen said.

"You think we'll make it to her in time?" Ramirez said.

Owen knitted his brow. "Of course we will. No worries, right?" But over the last hour, he had had to admit that the possibility of failure had been creeping into his thoughts and gnawing at his resolve. He steeled himself. She had to be all right!

Twenty Five

CLAIRE OPENED her eyes and blinked into the fuzzy haze surrounding her. As the world came into focus, she saw Molly's beatific face lying in a snarl of red hair beside her. It quite surprised her for a second. She looked up at the muted shadows moving back and forth over the top of her sunlit tent as the lingering fragments of strange dreams drifted before her. As they gradually slipped away, memories of a tall powerful Indian replaced them. Was that a dream as well? Everything was a blur.

She heard murmuring voices outside, and a waft of smoke brought the aroma of cooking meat into her tent. Her stomach growled and she discovered she was quite hungry. Breakfast! She licked her lips and stared back down at Molly. As she watched her sleeping, the tent flap was pulled back.

Claire looked up to see Thad coming in. He kneeled beside her and put his hand on her forehead. "Hey, you're awake. How ya feeling?"

"Better," Claire said.

"Her fever has dropped," Manny added.

Claire turned toward the director's voice behind her, wondering how long he'd been there. "Hey!"

He smiled. "It is good to see you back among the living. You gave us quite a scare."

"How long have you been here?" Claire said.

Manny moved around beside her as Molly woke. "A while. Are you thirsty?"

Just then, Molly lifted her head up in surprise. "Claire."

Claire smiled and took Molly's hand in hers. To Manny she said, "I could eat." She leaned forward and the world starting spinning again.

Manny said. "Lay back down. You need your rest. You have had a couple of very long days."

"Days?" Claire said.

"Si. You have been in and out of it for a while," Manny answered. "Thad, why don't you go fix Claire a plate."

Claire grudgingly lay back on the pillow. "I had these weird dreams about a strange tribe."

"Did you?" Manny said.

"Yes, and they spoke an old world language." She noticed a grin come to Manny's face. "What?"

"Did they wear a necklace like this?" he said, pulling a leather thong with a bone-tile ornament on it out of his pocket.

Claire shot up. "It was real!"

"Lie down," Manny said, and after she did so, he told her all that had happened. When he finished, Claire could hardly believe her turn of fortune. This was luck beyond luck, and her curious mind went crazy wanting to discover everything about this undiscovered tribe.

On the trail – east of the Jadatani village

Owen and Ramirez spent the night with the Jadatani getting reacquainted with old friends; taking much needed rest and a meal. But mostly it was to get news of Claire's brief stop there. What he heard from one of the elder women took his breath away. He thought about what she said: that Claire's body had recently removed an unwanted child. How she knew this, Owen couldn't begin to guess, but having grown up amongst the Jadatani, he didn't doubt it for a minute. They had uncanny abilities concerning illness and disease in people, especially the women.

The next morning they woke up to a soaking rain. He and Rameriz gathered their gear and headed out into the forest. By the time they reached the northeast tributary, it was a downpour.

Ramirez said, "The only saving grace about this hosing is it keeps the bugs away."

"But we're losing time," said Owen. He pulled his GPS device from his vest pocket and took a reading: 3° 49' 54" S Lat, 67° 42' 23" W Long. He entered the coordinates of the stranded expedition. Fifty-two k. He bit his lip. At the rate they were traveling they wouldn't make it to Claire until the day after tomorrow. He pocketed the device and pointed down river to a fallen Kapok bridging the muddy, serpentine tributary. "If we cross there, we'll cut a few hours out of da trip, yeah? With any luck, we'll run out of this hosing 'fore long."

They sloshed down the slick, muddy trail toward the giant root-mass, and as they went, Owen's thoughts turned again to Claire. In his mind's eye he could see her lying on her cot, soaked in sweat with her hair matted to her face. On its heels came the memory of Calen in his final hours as Malaria drained the life out of him.

The wind and rain picked up as they came to the foot of the fallen tree. Glancing down at the dark, brown waters below, Owen assessed the danger of falling into a roiling current. Suddenly, a streak of lightning flickered through the leafy shroud above and thunder boomed after it. From far off, came a sharp thwack.

Ramirez slipped out of his boots and rolled his pant legs up. "Here, take Claire's meds just in case," Owen said, reaching into his pack. "I'm not as steady on these slippery buggers as I used ta be." He flipped the small, round bottle to his porter and watched the man climb barefooted up onto the tree. With his boots laced to his pack, Ramirez started across the wet, silvery bark.

Owen waited until the man was on the other side, then shimmied up and started walking along the broad, undulating trunk. Below, the rush of the water splashing against the trunk sent vibrations through the silver behemoth.

"Boss, look out!" yelled Ramirez.

Out of the corner of his eye Owen saw a large, gangly limb careening downriver. Before he could take another step it was there, crashing into the kapok and knocking him off. A mind-numbing thud sent him into darkness. The next thing he knew he was submerged in the dark, murky water. Lunging to the surface, he sucked for air and spat. Floundering, he struggled against the current, but it was too fast so he let it carry him down stream and skillfully managed to move himself toward shore and out of the fast moving water. As he pulled himself up on shore, Rameriz came running up.

"You okay?" Ramirez said helping him up.

Owen bent over catching his breath and glanced at the man. As he did so, a gnawing pain grew in his mouth and with it was the taste of blood. *Shite.*

"You are bleeding," Ramirez said.

"Yeah, well onward. Time's wasting."

Emergency Camp

Claire sat in a canvas-folding chair, sipping herbal tea outside her tent. She was feeling better, although she was quite tired. She finished typing her little white lie to Noah on the Sat-Lynk laptop then read it back to herself, making sure her explanation was airtight regarding the lie over the dying battery. Hopefully it would suffice in answering his twenty-something emails he had sent over the last seventy-two hours demanding status reports. After she shot it back, she shut the lid, set the laptop down, and took out the Hajamawri necklace from her pocket.

She studied the symbol on the bone tile. The ancient marking was daring her to believe the unthinkable. Proving her trans-Atlantic theory was one thing, discovering a tribe that spoke the ancient language and used symbols created three millennia ago half way around the world was quite another.

"Do you ... think they ca—ca—come from across ocean?" said Inacio, suddenly beside her.

Claire looked up as the camp stirred with porters going about their business. "Oh, hi, Inacio. How are you this morning?"

"Very ga–good, thank-you," he said, his curious eyes ogling the necklace.

Claire knitted her brow and broke into Portuguese. "To answer your question, I don't think so. Civilizations evolve and with them, their customs and beliefs. It is amazing though to see this symbol here in the middle of the Amazon."

Inacio nodded. "What does it mean?"

Claire said, "It is called an Ankh, the symbol for eternal life."

"Do you ba—ba–believe in heaven?"

"I believe I want to," Claire replied.

"They say … when you are ve–very sick, sometime you se-see bright lights … and pe–people who have gone be–before you," Inacio said.

"Yes, I have heard that, too," Claire answered. She patted the chair beside her, inviting him to sit, and continued. "The night when the Hajamawri came, I thought they were ghosts and if it wasn't for what everyone said, I would've believed it."

Molly's bubbling laughter came ringing out from inside a tent across from them. *Ah, we're awake!* Claire looked at her watch then frowned as she saw Jorge pulling back the tent flap.

Inacio looked at her sidelong. "I think … the, the … senorita and … and Jorge are in amor."

Claire considered his astute observation. The young porter had a lot more on the ball than anyone knew. "What makes you think that?"

"The … the wa—way they look at each other," Inacio replied.

Claire cocked an eye and smiled. "Yes, I think they are. Do you have a girlfriend back home waiting for you?"

Inacio blushed. "There is someone I…I…like, b—but s—she does not … kn-know."

"Why haven't you told her?" Claire said, though she was pretty sure she knew why.

"I … I not smart like others. S—she would la-laugh at me."

Claire frowned. "You are a bright young man. Never let anyone tell you different. And besides, how do you know she would laugh at you? She may be as nervous as you are."

Inacio beamed. "You think so?"

"Yes, I do," Claire said as Jorge started toward her."

Paulo popped out from behind a tent several yards away. "Inacio! Come here."

The young porter started, then got up. "My hermano ne–needs me. I go now. Gracias."

Claire watched him trot away, then, seeing Jorge heading back from the mess tent, waved him over. "Morning."

Jorge flashed a broad grin. "Good morning. It is going to be a hot one today."

"Yes, it is," Claire said. "Have a seat."

Jorge sat and offered her a part of the mango he was eating.

Claire thanked him and after popping a wedge of it in her mouth, said, "Sleep tight?"

"Si."

"Up a tad late last night, weren't we?" When Jorge didn't answer, Claire pushed on. "Relax Jorge, I'm not going to bite you. Noah however, is a different story, and you don't want to get on the wrong side of him."

"I know," Jorge said.

"Not as much as you think you do," Claire said. "I was married to him once upon a time."

"You were?" Jorge said, astonished.

"That's right. Being the new kid in town, you wouldn't know that. Anyway, it wasn't one of my stellar decisions. I assume you know Molly's his niece?"

Jorge's eyes grew large.

"Calm down, life isn't over." *Yet*, Claire thought. "You just need to be careful with her. Hurt her, and he will nail you to the cross, and when he's done, I'll filet you."

"Oh, I would never do anything to hurt her," Jorge protested.

"I'm sure you mean that, but things happen. Just make sure you don't." And I'll do my best to keep the old hound at bay. Speaking of hounds, I wonder if the Kiwi's gotten back to Santo Antonio do Içá yet. If he has, I bet he's plenty pissed off right now. Not as pissed off as I was though, and still am.

On the trail sixteen kilometers from Emergency Camp

The next day, Owen stood in a waist-deep field of waving grasses, looking up at a fading gray sky. The last twenty-four hours had been bloody hell. The ache in his face was killing him. He took a breath between clenched teeth, steeled himself, and pulled his GPS device out.

They were sixteen kilometers away from where Manny had made Claire's emergency camp. He waved the flitting swarm of gnats away and assessed the small clearing about them. If he weren't in such a damned hurry, it would be an excellent place to lie over for the night.

He shed his pack. "We'll take five here," he muttered, clamping his eyes shut. He raised a hand, gingerly touching the swollen mass on his jaw. He had done more than taken a healthy knock to the chin yesterday.

"I think maybe we should camp here for the night," Ramirez said, coming up from behind.

Blinking, Owen turned and met the man's concerned gaze.

"You look like shit."

"Yeah, I know, an' every word I say leads ta new adventures in pain." He drew a shallow breath. "No worries. I'll be all right. If ya don't mind, I'll be holding off on da chit-chat from now on."

They sat in silence a moment, catching their breath, then struck out again under cover of night with Owen leading the way. Every step had to be chosen with care now, especially through the thick blanket of ferns where fer-de-lances and bushmasters hid. Owen swept the beam of his flashlight side to side, keening his ears for the sounds of a big cats. At last he came to a halt and closed his eyes.

"How much further, you think?" Rameriz said.

Owen drew breath and looked out into the murky forest. Above them, from the faint network of spidery branches, came the sounds of skittering monkeys, and from the distance, the sound of squawking macaws. It would be dawn soon. He looked up and said, "Another five k." He plodded to an overturned tree and sat.

Ramirez tramped after him and took a seat. "How you feeling?"

Owen shrugged "One more slog and we're there. Only problem is, I'm running on empty." He delicately ran a finger over his enflamed mouth and did the math. If they continued at their present rate, they'd arrive in three hours, give or take, providing they didn't run into any unforeseen obstacles.

He leaned forward. Unforeseen obstacles, indeed. This whole adventure down the river had been nothing but a Tiki Tour. But then, the last five years of his life had felt like that, too. Every choice he made seemed to put him in a world of shit. He thought back on the rescue of the Yagüani. Was it all in vain? Eventually, the cartels would get back there. And when they did; who would stop them?

But he did the right thing, damn it! And why did Manny let Claire muscle him into taking her into the forest? Why was she so goddamned headstrong? And why couldn't she listen? A vision of her standing next to him at the bulwark rail in the stern, sipping her beer and looking out over the river came to him. It was right after they boarded the boat in Tarapoto. He could still remember her vanilla perfume and the smile on her face as she pestered him with questions about the river.

He tried to get up, but his body wouldn't go. He'd hit the wall. Ramirez helped him sit back down, and as he did, the world spun. For a moment, he thought he saw a long shadow slipping out of the gloom but then, the world went black.

Emergency Camp

Claire looked down at Owen as he lay sleeping on her cot. For the last thirty-six hours, the Jadatani 'dreaming tea' had delivered him from the agony of his swollen jaw.

Dipping a rag in cool water, she kneeled and ran it over Owen's forehead. The swelling on his face had gone down, but it would be another day before she could determine the extent of the injury to his jaw. Until then, the improvised cloth strapping over the top of his head and around his chin would have to do. If the jaw were broken, it would need to be wired shut. But how, and by whom?

She frowned, trying to think of a way to set the bone if it was broke. If it wasn't done right, it could lead to all sorts of complications. Damn him, anyway. She wanted to be angry with him, but she couldn't help adoring what he'd done for her, even if it was in vain.

But her thoughts were on the story Ramirez had told her about the cartel raiding party. After hearing it, she found herself eating crow for doubting Owen. Still, if she hadn't gone with her gut, she would never have met the elusive tribe.

The unflappable kiwi twitched and creased his brow. Claire watched his eyes flutter under his cracked lids. He was coming out of the drug-induced sleep.

"Don't try to talk," she said quietly as he stirred. "Your jaw may be broken." He winced, blinked, and then looked at her with apparent amazement. "Yes, I'm all right," she said, "but you're not."

He tried to sit up, but she pushed him back. "Whoa, not so fast there, Jungle Boy."

He shook his head and waved her hand away.

"Owen, stop ... stop...! Fine, suit yourself," Claire said as he forced her hand off him and bent forward. She watched him close his eyes and grab for the side of the cot. "Dizzy?"

He nodded.

"It's the dreaming tea we got from the Jadatani. It's fairly potent," Claire said. She reached for her water bottle. "Thirsty?"

He eyed her and nodded again.

"Just a sip. Use the straw and keep your mouth shut - as if you could," she said, giving him a saucy smile.

He shot her a sullen expression and winced.

"Oh, and don't do that either," she said, watching him squeeze his eyes shut. "In fact, keep your expressions to a minimum for a while, unless you enjoy getting your ass kicked."

Handing the water bottle back, he pointed to her and shrugged an unspoken question.

"Long story, Jungle Boy. I'll tell you later. Right now, I need to take a peek under your bonnet."

Owen rolled his eyes.

"You know, I sort a like you being muzzled," Claire said as she peeled the cloth away. "Keeps things civil between us."

Owen frowned as she studied the dark puffy mass around his jaw and drew the cloth strapping back in place. Sitting back on her heels, she said, "Ramirez told me about your little party with the cartel boys. God knows what the long-range effects will be on that village."

She paused and shook her head. She knew she owed Owen an apology, but it wasn't coming easy. At last, she said, "I shouldn't have doubted you, but you should have told me."

He pantomimed writing then pointed to her pack. She went over and dug a notebook and pencil out. When she came back, she said, "I suppose you'll be demanding a bell next?"

He snatched the notebook and pencil from her hand, scribbled a note and showed it to her.

Claire read it. "Yes, I know. I could've asked the captain. But for all I knew, he was right in your back pocket."

Owen nodded and looked off toward the open tent flap a long time then wrote again. After he finished, he handed her the notebook. She looked at the words in silence.

Finally, she said, "Me, too. I know you didn't think of it as leaving me high-and-dry, but that's how it felt. And the others felt the same way. These kids worked hard and gave up a lot to be here. I wasn't gonna fold up and walk away without a solid reason. If you'd been straight with me from the beginning, I would've taken you a lot more seriously."

He took the notebook back.

"Yes, I know what you said in Tarapoto. But seriously, the way you said it? How was I to believe it? Don't look at me like that. I still don't approve of giving those bows to the tribes, but I see your point ... to a degree, that is."

He wrote again.

"No, I don't want to argue either."

Owen turned the page and eyed her a long time. Finally he wrote again and handed her the notebook.

Claire took it, and as she read, felt her resolve melt. "I know you feel responsible for what happens to me," she said, eyeing the man who'd walked a two-and-a-half days non-stop with a possible broken jaw to save her life. That she hadn't needed the anti-biotic after all was beside the point. Did he deserve a second chance, or in his case, a fourth? Her heart said, absolutely. Her pride told her 'no'.

At last, she said, "Why don't you get some rest and we'll talk later? By the way, I have a big surprise for you."

He grabbed the notebook from her and jotted down the word, "what."

"You'll find out. Get some sleep now."

He frowned, but gave her back the notebook and pencil. Closing his eyes, he laid back and nodded off to sleep. Claire shook her head as she slipped out of her tent. *Damn him! Every time I get him out of my system, he turns around and does something nice. Ughhhh!*

Twenty Six

Twenty-four kilometers northwest of the Yagüani village

J UAN FOLLOWED the course of the river for two days before being turned into the forest by a flooded plain. As he tried to navigate around it, the dense jungle pushed him further and further away from the river until he was utterly lost. He scrambled up a slope choked with ferns and looked back down into the deep ravine. His wounded arm throbbed and the blisters on his feet threatened to burst with every step. He could go no further until he had a breather.

Spying a fallen tree a little way down the other side of the ridge, he stumbled to it and sat, basking in relief while squirrel monkeys played in the trees above. What he wanted was to lay his head down and sleep, but he knew it was a bad idea.

He checked his wounds and plotted what to do next. He was fairly sure he was striking north, but without a compass it was impossible to be sure. To continue in the present direction would mean finding a way down into the deep gully and up the other side. His other choice would lead him to who knew where.

He eyed the bloody gortex wrapping around his arm and gingerly pulled the bandage back. The long, deep gash was oozing thick, gray goo, and angry red streaks ran around its jagged edges. He didn't need a doctor to tell him he was in deep shit.

He waved a mosquito away and pulled the bandage back over the gash. The steamy jungle waved in front of his tired eyes as he searched for a path down into the gloom. Then, though the cacophony of skittering monkeys, he heard the sound of trickling water. He sat bolt upright, training his ear toward it. There was a stream somewhere nearby.

Then suddenly, a blinding pain shot up his arm. He gasped, and looking down, saw a large black ant clinging to his hand. Suddenly another bolt of blinding pain ran through him and another. He looked down and saw a horde of them crawling over his legs and lap. Others were pouring out of a hole in the tree. Jumping up, he frantically swatted his shirt and pants, but the stinging insects were everywhere, shooting jolts of electrifying agony up and down his body. Staggering, he raced down the steep slope. As the fire raged in his brain, his legs went out from underneath him. The last thing he heard was a loud crack, before everything went black.

Emergency Camp

Owen woke up to find Manny sitting beside him. He looked up at his old friend, who was puffing on a cigar and reading a cheap paperback novel. Golden rays poured in from outside along with the pleasant aroma of Papa Rellena. His stomach growled. There was a million questions he needed answered, mainly: how had Claire gotten better? She had told him nothing when he questioned her earlier. He reached over and tapped Manny's leg.

"Hey, Owen. How you feeling?"

Owen's jaw quickly reminded him that he'd been better, much better. He shook his head, sat up, and pointed to the pad and pencil Claire had left beside her pack. When Manny handed it to him, he wrote, "What time?"

"Around four. You have been sleeping most of the day. You hungry?"

Owen wrote. "Starved."

Manny got up and went out. When he came back, Claire was with him. She had a bowl and a bamboo straw in her hand. "You're going to have to suck your dinner through a straw," she said. "I've mashed it up as good as I could."

Ankle biter food. Just great! He took the bowl from her and frowned at the slurry of potatoes and herbs. After a couple of sucks on the straw, he put the bowl down and wrote, "How long am I gonna be muzzled?"

"Until the jaw heals," Claire said. She shrugged "Probably around a month or more. Hard to tell."

A month? Holy shite! He wrote again, handed it to her and managed a meager smile. "Guess ya'll be enjoying that, eh?"

Claire crossed her arms and smiled back. "Despite what you think, I don't enjoy watching someone suffer, even if they annoy the hell out of me. And by the way, that's a nasty scar on your hip. What caused that, or shouldn't I ask?"

Oh, just great! She had my pants off.

"It's not like I haven't seen it before," Claire said to him, half rolling her eyes.

Manny chuckled, and said, "He had a little argument with big cat."

"Of course he did," Claire replied, shaking her head. She nodded toward Owen and his bowl of half-eaten pureed potatoes. "Eat your dinner before it gets cold."

Owen grabbed the notebook and wrote: "So what's the big surprise?"

"Oh, that," Claire said. "We've made contact with a tribe no one has ever seen before. And guess what?" She waited for him to egg her on. "They speak an ancient form of Egyptian. My theory is validated!"

Owen looked over at Manny, who was nodding reluctantly back at him. *That's nuts? They're jacking me up? That's all right though. Suppose I deserve a little bit of my own medicine.* He set the straw down and handed her back the bowl. Picking up the pad, he winked at Manny and wrote, "I guess that calls for a drink."

Manny snubbed his cigar and said, "I have a bottle of rum in my pack."

Claire pursed her lips. "Well, I'll take that as a cue you two want to be alone." To Owen, she said, "Remember, keep that jaw shut!"

Owen nodded, picked up the notepad and wrote. "Will do my best." But he knew there was no way he could keep his mouth idle for a month. People talked through their teeth all the time. Women especially. He watched her leave, and as he did so, ogled her tight little behind.

When she was gone, Manny pulled out paper cups and poured them each a shot. "So, you had a run in with a tree?"

Owen groaned. *Rammy!* He motioned for the paper cup. Taking it, he drained it and went for the notebook. But just as he was about to write, he set it down. *Fuck it.* He pulled the bandage off and tossed it to the side. Through his teeth, he said, "Someone has a big mouth?"

Manny laughed. "Ah, a voice rings out in the dark. But you better be careful. If she hears you, she will give you hell."

"Yeah, yeah. Tell me something I don't know."

"You think it is wise taking that off?" Manny said, nodding to the discarded bandage.

"Probably not," Owen said. "But I'm not going through da next few weeks with this contraption on. So tell me, what's with her sudden turn-around? Last I knew; she was on death's door."

Manny poured another shot, drank it down, and told him everything that had happened since they parted in Santo Antonio do Içá. When he finished, he leaned close, and said, "She did not leave your side from the minute you were brought in until you woke up this morning."

Owen was dumbfounded. "Really?"

"Si. You know, you two need to stop pissing each other off."

"Yeah, well, I'm working on that. By da way, mind filling in a blank for me?" Owen said.

"If I can."

"Just before I took a nap out in da bush, I thought I saw three of her new forest friends. Was I imagining it?"

"No," Manny said, and sat back in his chair. "They and Ramirez brought you in. It is lucky for you they met us first, or you would not be lying here right now."

"Right. Speaking of which, when do I get ta meet 'em?"

"Don't know. They come and go."

Suddenly, a loud argument erupted outside. Manny sprang from his chair. Owen got to his feet and lumbered out after him. Standing in the middle of three very agitated porters, was Claire. Manny put his fingers to his mouth and whistled. When he got their attention, he said, "What is the matter here?"

Claire said, "Inacio fell into a pit out in the forest."

Paulo said, "My brother is hurt bad." He shot Claire a blistering scowl. "It is all your fault! We should not even be here. If we had stayed on the boat like the boss ordered, none of this would have happened."

"We can debate that later," Owen said, earning a frown from Claire. "Where is he?"

As Ramirez, Thad, and Jorge stepped out of the command tent, Paulo said, "Follow me. I will show you."

"Rammy, get a rope," Owen said. "Thad, grab a couple flashlights. Jorge, da med kit."

Manny tapped, Jorge, on the shoulder. "I will get the kit, you go help Thad."

Molly came running up from the river, towel in hand. "What's going on?"

As Thad ran past her, he said, "One of the porters fell into a pit."

"When? Where?" Molly said, alarmed and bewildered.

Owen marched over to her and pointed toward his retreating director. "Molly, grab everyone's tramping poles, an' bring 'em back here, okay?"

Molly nodded, and after she hurried off, Claire marched up to Owen and eyed him fiercely. "Where's the sling I made for you?"

"It wasn't comfy, so I took it off. Now don't look at me like that. I'm fine! See?" He put his hand on her shoulder, parted his lips and showed her clenched teeth as he spoke. "No worries. Come on, time's wasting."

Claire followed Owen to her tent, thinking about what Paulo had said. He hadn't liked her since he set eyes on her, and now he had her by the short hairs. Suddenly, she felt unsure of herself. Was Inacio's accident really her fault? It wasn't like she had ordered him out into the forest. Yet she had to admit that forcing Manny to go against Owen's orders was having dire consequences, and if Inacio was dead; what then? She shuddered at the thought, but. she would not be intimidated, not now when her leadership was needed.

And she was damned if she was going to listen to Owen moan and complain because his jaw ached, when he could very well prevent it. *Men! They're just overgrown boys, preening and bragging about their toughness. But when they come home all banged up and bloodied, it's us women they cry to.* She picked up the sling Owen had discarded on the cot and shook her head. "At least wear it to bed."

He dug his machete out of his pack and nodded. "Fair enough."

Claire blinked. She had been prepared for an argument. "Good. You'll thank me later, believe me."

"I'm sure I will," he said. "Let's go, they're waiting on us."

They all met back up at the edge of camp and followed Paulo through the forest until they came to a grove of bananas. Paulo pointed toward a small, dark depression in the leafy ground cover. "There, by that rock."

Owen frowned.

"What's wrong?" Claire said.

"That, and those over there," Owen said, nodding to the rock Paulo was pointing at and the banana grove, "are not supposed ta be here." His gaze drifted outward over the rocky terrain as he walked. "They're all over da place," he muttered.

"I don't understand," said Claire.

Owen turned. "The geology; it's all wrong here. An' those banana trees over there are cultivated."

He strode ahead, and as they followed him, Manny spoke up, "Stones are rare in the basin."

"What about my brother?" Paulo barked.

"We're working on it mate," Owen said. "Got to be careful. There just might be another hole around here. Don't want to compound da problem."

"Ummm ... guys, take a look over there," Thad said.

"What?" Owen answered looking up.

"Over there, through the trees.

Owen squinted and saw a steepled shape covered in thick vegetation. Claire came up beside him. "It's a stepped pyramid."

Owen couldn't believe it. The Mayan people had never come this far south, yet here it was. But at the moment there were other things more pressing. "It'll have ta wait," he said, and stepping toward a dark hole, put his hand out to keep everyone back. He bent down on hands and knees as Manny joined him.

"Thad, hand me your flashlight," Owen said. Flicking it on, he aimed a narrow beam down and saw Inacio lying on a rocky ledge with his leg bent the wrong way. Owen looked at Thad. "Give a yell down would ya?"

Thad leaned over the hole and called down. "Hey, Nace, you all right?"

There was no reply.

"Damn," Owen muttered.

Manny whispered. "You think he's—"

"Let's hope not," Owen answered back. "Question is: how are we going ta get him out?"

"Looks like he's got a broken leg," Thad said. "Whatever we do, someone's gonna have ta go down there."

"I will go," Paulo said coming up from behind.

Owen shook his head. "Hang on, mate. No one's going anywhere 'til I check da situation out. One injured lad's enough for one day."

Thad said, "Judging by the air wafting out this hole, I'd say there's a system of caves below. And it could go down a long ways. If he comes to down there and rolls the wrong way—"

"Right," Owen said as he circled the perimeter of the hole. He shook his head, assessing his options.

"Look, I've done a bit a climbing, and I know a thing or two about getting out of tight spots," Thad said. "We need to get down there, and quick."

Owen looked up. The kid was right, and being the only one there with any experience scaling walls, he was the logical choice. "All right then, I guess ya're our man." To Rammy, he said, "Take da rope we brought with us an' find something ta tie off ta."

Five minutes later, Thad was descending into the hole. As the darkness swallowed him, Claire lay at the earthen rim and watched the beam of his flash-light pan the chasm walls. Finally, Thad called up. "Okay, just a couple more feet and I'm down." The rope went slack. A long silence followed. Finally, Thad said, "I'm gonna need the med-kit and that other length of rope."

"Is he alive?" Claire said and held her breath waiting for the answer.

There was no word from Thad for a moment then finally, he called back up. "He's knocked up pretty good, but yes, he's alive. Got a nasty fracture though. Not going to be easy getting him out of here."

"We'll figure something out," Owen said. He turned toward Manny. "We're gonna need a few more lines."

"This is all we have," Manny said, handing Owen the rope. "We were not planning on exploring caves or climbing mountains."

"What are we gonna do?" Claire said anxiously.

Owen got up and surveyed the network of woody vines around them. "We make our own. Tell Thad we're gonna put something together up here an' get it ta him." He handed Claire the med-kit, then put his hand to his jaw and winced. "Think I'm gonna stop talking for a while."

"Good idea," Claire said. Bending over the edge of the hole, she called down, "Med kit's on the way. Owen's working on the rope. You need help down there?"

Thad's small, muffled voice came back. "Negative. Pretty tight on this ledge. Inacio's lucky he landed where he did. There's a drop off of another fifty feet at least to the bottom, and ... good God, Mary and Jesus!"

"What, Poppy?" Claire said.

"Claire, the lower walls ... there's markings on them, hundreds of 'em." He paused, and she could see the beam of his flashlight bouncing back and forth in the impenetrable darkness. Suddenly, he yelled back up. "Claire, they're cartouches and ... and pottery. Loads of it ... all over the place! Wait, there's more. Oh, my God."

"What?"

"I think this is some kind of burial chamber."

Claire glanced back at the ziggurat and closed her eyes. This was not the way she wanted to be vindicated. "We'll deal with it later. Take care of business, first."

"Right! On it," Thad said.

Twenty Seven

Twenty-four kilometers southeast of the Hajamawri Valley

A THROBBING ACHE jolted Juan's eyes open. He looked up into the variegated gloom of the forest canopy and grimaced. *Where am I? Oh, my fucking head!* He closed his eyes, rolled over, and put his hand to his temple as a blinding wave of pain shot into his brain. When it eased, he got to his knees and dragged himself to a log and sat. Looking down, he saw the tip of the long gash on his wrist peeking out from under the field dressing. A dark, red ring was now all around it. On his pant leg below the knee, a dark bloody stain leered back. Bright red blotches dotted his hands. Suddenly, the memory of the stinging ants running over his lap came rushing back and he jumped to his feet.

Rage consumed him. He hated this goddamned forest and everything in it. After he took care of Valderón and the white man, he'd burn it all down. But for now, he was stuck in it with no idea of which way to go. The only thing he knew was that he was at the bottom of a deep ravine with no flashlight and a long daunting hike ahead.

He reached inside his vest for his Glock. *Where is it?* He looked up the steep vegetated slope and checked his holster again. *Where is my fucking gun?* He ignored the aches in his battered body. Without the pistol, he was screwed. He scrambled to where he had landed from his tumble and raked his fingers through the leaf litter. Nothing! *Where is it?* Again he checked his holster and patted himself down. *This is the last thing I need right now.* He got to his feet and traced a path through the dense vegetation, sweeping his feet from side to side as he went. Around him, the forest thrummed with the shrill of crickets and frogs. The whine of mosquitoes was everywhere and a ravaging hunger gnawed at him. A tiny pinprick stabbed his arm, then another on his neck, and another and another. He gritted his teeth. The only thing that mattered right now was the pistol. He tacked back and forth up the ragged slope, groping every tendril, vine, and woody root that sprang out of the damp, dark soil. Night was creeping into the impassive forest. If he didn't find it soon, he would be pinned down until morning with only his scout knife to defend himself.

Twenty minutes later, he found the weapon lying in the fern halfway up the slope. He held the pistol flat and tight to his chest and gripped the handle fiercely. The forest was now in deep shadow. Only a hint of the massive trees could be seen through the gloom. A little ways up-slope, he saw a kapok. He scrambled to it and hunkered down between two of its finned, buttressed roots to wait out the long, miserable night.

As he sat with his back against the tree with pistol pointed outward at the malevolent darkness, he bitterly mulled over his broken plans. Five long wasted years of climbing the ranks and positioning himself to achieve his ultimate goal had vanished in a heartbeat. The narrow-minded Valderón would live on. It was all wrong! What really cut into him though was the death of Filipe. The man was gone, and along with him, the only friendship that had ever mattered.

As the sobering thought sank in, he assessed the stark reality of his situation. He ejected the clip from his Glock and counted the rounds left in it. Four precious bullets and he was no game hunter by any means. His lighter was getting low of fluid and would perhaps provide enough flame to start two or three campfires. His arm? Screaming at him! No water, and he hadn't eaten in three days. The odds of making it out of the forest alive were not in his favor.

The following morning, he dragged his exhausted body up from the kapok and stood. He felt like he had gone fifteen rounds with Filipe, and what was worse were the damned blood-sucking mosquitoes that had feasted upon him during the long fitful night. He resisted the urge to dig at the red splotches on his arms and plotted a course down the treacherous slope to level ground. Ten minutes later, he struck a small gurgling stream running along the bottom of the ravine. He dropped to his knees and took a long drink, then cupped a handful of water and splashed it over his face.

Feeling somewhat refreshed, he washed out his blood soaked bandage before starting westward along the banks of the waterway, confident that it would join with another. And where there was a confluence, there was often a village nearby. He kept that thought forefront in his mind as he struck out under the dense canopy.

But the going was slow and difficult. Every step was met with resistance by the thick, broad-leafed kamarampi and yellow flowered cat's claw that crowded the edges of the zigzagging channel.

By late afternoon, the heat and humidity had skyrocketed. Soaked in sweat, he stopped for another drink and wrung out his shirt. How many kilometers he had put behind him, he didn't know, but it felt like a hundred and still there was no sign of coming out of it, nor any hint of humanity. He gingerly pulled the bandage off and trimmed away a dead flap of skin with his scout knife.

As he tended the wound, a rustling in the leaves up-slope made him freeze. Looking up, he searched the undulating landscape. Thirty meters away, he saw a small peccary with its nose in the scrub. He slipped his Glock out and crept toward it, picking his steps with care until he had it firmly in his sights. As he took aim, the animal jerked its head up, and for an instant, it stared straight at him. Juan hesitated. Just as he was about to pull the trigger a flash of black zipped past him toward the animal.

All at once, the forest erupted with loud huffs and barks, and the leafy understory exploded with stampeding peccaries. Behind them came a streaking jaguar. In stunned silence he watched the cat chase its target down. Seconds later the king of the forest had the animal by its throat.

Juan backed slowly away, keeping his gun aimed with his finger on the trigger. How long the cat had been hiding in the brush was anyone's guess. He drew breath and melted back into the trees as the bitter defeat of losing a meal hit home. Whether he'd come upon the forest pigs again didn't matter. He was savagely hungry and all he could think about was the taste of roasted meat. He sneered at the berries on the bush beside him. He'd had his fill of them.

For the next three days, Juan drove his exhausted and famished body along the banks of the widening stream. On the evening of the third day, delirium swept down on him. But the fast-rushing stream whispered the promise of humanity right around the next bend, so he pushed on into the darkening shadows until they gathered into a black shroud. Finally, he could go no further, so he sat and surrendered. With fumbling fingers he built a meager fire by the stream to chase away the relentless assault of bugs, then fell into a dreamless sleep.

The following morning the clatter of branches and the chattering of spider monkeys awakened him. He opened his eyes. The tiny fire he'd built on the bare earth before him had died hours earlier. He sat up and licked his parched lips as the acrid odor of smoke mingling with the tang of soil wafted about him. If he was going to make it out of here alive, he was going to have to get mad-dog mean. Otherwise …
No, there was no otherwise about it!

As he pulled himself up onto his knees, he discovered he couldn't feel the fingers on his wounded hand anymore, Nor did he have any strength in it. He eyed the dark purple and sallow hues that had spread over his fingers and up his arm and sat back on his heels.

Looking out into the gloom, he knew he was running out of time. He gripped one end of the gortex swatch with his left hand and the other with his teeth. As he pulled the knot tight, a jolt of nausea rushed through him. Fighting it back, he got to his feet and stalked off along the banks of the stream. As he followed its jagged course along the pitted landscape of vines and upstart saplings, he saw the sloping walls of the ravine melt away until they were all together gone. In their wake, they left a broad expanse of gray bearded trees and rotted stumps draped with lianas and mosses.

Sweeping his tired gaze over the muted forest floor, he traced the stream's course as far as he could see. His stomach growled as he popped a handful of berries in his mouth. "Fucking 'A'. How much more of this shit is there?" he muttered. He huffed and continued on. But with every kilometer he put behind him, there seemed to be ten more ahead. After a while, he wondered if he was going to die like a bug under someone's boot. Up until Filipe fell, he had never given death more than a passing thought. It was merely a fact of life, and it happened to other people. But now, alone and lost in the unforgiving arms of the forest, it took on a new meaning. No one would come looking for him, and no one would care. Well, maybe Reyna would, but then it was only because he was her ticket out from under the foot of her tyrannical father.

He frowned. As much as he wanted revenge on the white man, it was Valderón he really hated. The man sent him into this shit hole for what - to expand the cartel's territory? Anyone with half a brain knew starting a coca plantation in the middle of the forest was idiocy! The man needed to die, and he was going to enjoy plugging him. He held onto that thought as he plodded along, but the notion of never getting out of the forest gnawed at him until vengeance was no more than a shadow in his mind.

Stumbling up a small incline, he leaned against a moss-ridden cinchona. For the past two days he had trudged blindly through the forest following the fast-running stream, but now he had nothing left. He bent his head back and looked up at the threatening arms of the dark canopy. Unseen, within its thick shroud, he felt watchful eyes stabbing down.

Death was methodically closing in: tightening its grip. Even the friendly stream that flowed beside him was mocking him. He ran a hand across his face, mopping a thin sheen of sweat away as biting flies buzzed around his head in broad, looping figure eights.

Ahead stood a battalion of gray-buttressed giants and beyond them, dark murky shadows. He drew breath, and through his fading sight, took in the daunting landscape. The forest was pronouncing judgment and rendering its sentence. His back slid down the tree, and as his body melted into the tangy green mat of ivenkiki, a soft murmuring of far away guitars came whispering in his ears.

Emergency Camp

Owen pulled the tent flap back and stood aside as Paulo and Thad passed him with Inacio strapped to the cot. Manny and Claire followed. As Claire ducked under his outstretched arm, he noticed her focused expression. He'd seen that look before: back on the boat when she was working below deck on the engine. She was all business, seeing what needed to be done, then doing it. He went in after her and watched while she and Thad rechecked the splint and the field dressing on Inacio's broken leg. As he stood there, he found himself conflicted, and he didn't know what to do about it. Paulo's right: if she hadn't pressed Manny to bring her into the forest, none of this would've happened.

Manny stepped up beside him and looked on as Claire and Thad went about cleaning the scrape over the young porter's eye. At length, Manny cleared his throat. "This is my fault."

"Don't beat yourself up, mate," Owen whispered. He looked down at Claire and added, "'Sides, he's in good hands." From the corner of his eye, he saw Paulo frown and give Claire a sullen look.

Claire shot Owen a guarded glance then turned back to Inacio lying on the cot. Running her fingers over the large bump above Inacio's eye, she probed the soft, fleshy mass. "The leg'll mend," she said, "but who knows what going on up here?" she added, tapping her temple. Turning to Thad, she said, "Hand me your flashlight."

Thad dug it out of his back pocket and gave it to her. Flicking it on, she checked Inacio's eyes then sat back on her heels.

"Well?" Manny said.

Claire's face darkened. "His left pupil's dilated, and his reflexes are sluggish. Add being unconscious for over an hour along with the bruising around the eye, and it's safe to say he has a concussion."

"It's a grade three," Thad added, checking Inacio's pupils as well.

"So, what now?" Paulo said.

Claire sighed. "We wait and see."

"What do you mean, we wait and see?" Paulo hissed. "This is your fault. If he dies –"

"Shut up, Paulo," Owen barked. "Ya got a problem; from now on ya take it up with me!"

"Stop it!" Claire shouted. She wheeled around and pinned an icy glare on Paulo. "I don't recall asking either of you to go traipsing around the goddamned forest looking for bananas. And if I'm not mistaken, aren't you supposed to check with Manny or Owen before you go out on your own? Or am I missing something?"

"Ya're damned right he's supposed ta," Owen growled.

"Coming from a man with a injured jaw who refuses to keep his mouth shut." She shook her head. "Guess you don't care if you end up deaf and losing your teeth. But what the hell do I know. I'm just a woman, right?"

Owen blinked. "Hey, I'm not da enemy here!" He said trying to figure out how he'd gotten backhanded.

"And neither am I," Claire snapped. To Paulo, she said, "Thad and I are doing all we can. If you think you can do better, be my guest. I'm tired of being blamed, and I'm tired of being lied to," she said, flashing a withering stare at Owen. "If you think I don't care, you're wrong. I care about every member of this crew."

Paulo's furrowed brow melted, but his fiery gaze remained. Manny spoke up. "We know you do, senhora." He looked at each of them then went on, "All this arguing is doing no good. We have more important things to do then stand around lobbing threats and accusations. Claire, Thad, is there anything further that can be done?"

Owen watched Claire collect her thoughts. As she settled down, Thad said, "Well, he shouldn't be left alone for any amount of time for one thing. Watch for slurring of speech, complaints of bad headaches and nausea."

"Very good, I'll take the first watch," Manny piped up.

"And I'll take the next," Paulo echoed.

Claire stood, and as she pulled the tent flap back to leave, Owen noticed the sag in her shoulders. *Yeah, it's been a long slog for all of us, and it isn't getting any easier.*

The following morning, Owen saw Claire sitting on a log down by the fast-running tributary. How long she had been there, he didn't know, but he knew why she was alone. He stood beside a large flowering heliconia several yards back from shore and quietly observed her gazing out over the broad channel. On her lap was an open notebook and a pencil twitched in her hand.

"Well, you gonna stand there watching me all day, or are you coming down?" she said over her shoulder.

Owen smiled and trod down the steep slope. When he came beside her, he said, "How ya doing?"

"I've been better."

"Yeah, I hear ya. Don't worry none about Paulo. His bark's worse than his bite."

"Thanks, but it's not Paulo I'm worrying about." She nibbled a fingernail and sighed.

"I know."

"You know what sucks?"

"What's that?"

"I'm this far," she said, raising her hand and putting her finger a hair away from her thumb, "from the greatest anthropological discovery of the century, and I feel like crap."

"Nace'll be fine," Owen said, ignoring the twinge in his jaw. He pulled a candy bar out of his shirt pocket and tapped her shoulder. "Here."

"What's this?" she said, looking up.

"A woman's best friend. Seeing how I can't eat it, I might as well give it ta someone who can."

She gave him a dim smile and set her notebook down. When she peeled the wrapper back, the inside drizzled onto her hand. "It's a mess."

"Yeah, there is that. Heat an' humidity have a way with chocolate," he said, chuckling. "Considering where he was, Thad did a hell of job setting that bone."

"Yeah, he did." She was quiet a moment, then said, "I'm scared, Owen. Inacio could die. And the truth is, it would be my fault. I was the one who forced Manny to bring us down. If I hadn't pushed him, none of this would've happened. Ultimately, it's all on me."

"You know what I think?"

"What?"

"I think shite happens," Owen said. "Ya can go crazy wondering about da what-if's."

"Maybe. But it's not that easy letting go of them." She took a deep breath and let it out. "This was supposed to be my vindication. I spent ten years writing grants trying to convince people to let me test my theory, and then finally, I get it, and everything goes to hell."

"Right."

"Right? If you only knew."

"Try me," Owen said.

Claire looked off over the water and was quiet again. Finally, she said, "Three weeks before I left for this excursion, my fiancé, Jason, says he needs to branch out, explore life a little. 'Oh, and by the way, I've taken a job in New York'. Then a week before I leave, my ex, Noah, who's department chair, decides to torpedo the expedition by changing out my RA. I get that all straightened out, and I get a letter from dear old Jason with my townhouse key. No note, nothing. And it goes on and on."

"Sorry 'bout that. I know it sucks. By da way, how's da tummy?"

Claire turned and looked at him, and as she did so, her face wrinkled and her eyes glassed over. She turned away and brought a finger up to her cheek. "It's good."

"Manny said ya went through a hell of a time."

"Did he?" she muttered.

"You all right?"

He saw her swallow. "I'm fine." After a couple of deep breaths, she said, "Did you ever lose something you didn't know you wanted until it was gone?"

Owen nodded and thought about what to say next. She had voiced a thought he'd been trying to avoid much of his life. He took a deep breath, removed his hat, and sat beside her on the ground. Only two people in the world knew the haunting secret that had dogged him for the last six years. One had left him over it; the other person had carried him through the dark days. He closed his eyes for a moment, sighed, and studied a low-hanging vine skidding over the surface of the fast running current. Finally, he said, "Yeah, I do. A long time ago, someone I cared about died down here.

"He was a kid, an' you know how they are. Living in da moment, forgetting things, taking chances. Anyway, it was supposed ta be an education an' all: teaching him ta see da world differently instead of learning 'bout it from da ass end of a tellie."

His throat tightened and he paused to collect himself. This was about easing her pain, so why was he about to spill his guts? She didn't need to know this, and he certainly didn't want her pity. The thwapping of water against the grassy shoreline drummed in his ears as he watched a brilliant-blue dragonfly dart back and forth over a flowering lily. But it was too late to stop talking now, not the way she was looking at him. At last he cleared his throat. "Yeah, malaria's an evil thing. Boils ya in ya own blood. An' being where we were so deep in da forest, an' without meds an' all, there wasn't anything I could do."

"What about quinine?" Claire said softly.

"Yeah, there is that, but keeping it down an eight year old long enough for it ta work is quite another thing. Anyway, by da time help arrived, it was too late, yeah. He'd be fifteen next month." He pressed his lips together and picked up a pebble. After he threw it out into the water, he looked up to see her standing in front of him. He averted his gaze.

"Owen?"

"Yeah?"

"Look at me?"

All at once, he wanted to run away. He felt her hand on his shoulder and shuddered.

"Don't condemn yourself."

"Why shouldn't I? He died on my watch. He had his whole life ahead of him, an' I –"

"Loved him?" Claire said.

Owen closed his eyes and clutched the green stone necklace under his shirt. Swallowing the knot in his throat, he steeled himself. "Yeah, I did. Look, I'm sorry."

She bent down in front of him. "For what?"

"Putting that on ya."

She looked into his eyes. "It's nice to know there's a heart under that Neanderthal exterior of yours." She gave him a crooked smile and reached out to take his hand. "Can I see it?"

"What?"

"The necklace."

He pulled it out and set the stone in the palm of her hand. "It's beautiful. The design: it's Maori, I assume."

Owen nodded. No one had touched his son's pendant since the day he had laid the boy to rest, and it brought a myriad of feelings he wasn't prepared for: comforting and yet invasive, as if she had barged into the sacred space that only he and his son shared. He gently took it back and slipped it under his shirt. Quietly, he said, "It's called a triple twist. Two vines growing together."

"Like father and son?" Claire said, though it was more a statement than a question.

"Yeah."

She moved back to her seat on the log and though his gaze was pointed out over the water he could feel her soft brown eyes caressing him. Finally, she said, "How's the jaw?"

He let out a deep breath; glad she'd changed the subject. "It aches, but I'll pull through. So ... what's next?"

"What's next, what? Oh, you mean the tribe," Claire said quietly. "Well, in a perfect world, we'd observe and wait. But with all that's happened, it's out of the question unless you'd consider leaving me here and coming back in say ... six months..."

He glanced at her sidelong and raised a brow.

"Yeah, right, didn't think so."

"Sorry, Luv. I always leave da dance with da lady I came with."

"It's, 'I always leave with the one that brought me...' Never mind, it's just me being me."

Suddenly, they heard feet tramping down the slope behind them. Owen turned to see Thad standing a few yards away. Claire frowned, then jumped up. "What's wrong, Poppy?" she said, heading for him.

Thad shook his head. "Nothing. They're back."

"Who?" Owen said, putting his hat back on.

"The Hajamawri."

Owen followed Claire and Thad back up the trail. When he came to the clearing, he saw a dozen tall, robust Hajamawri tribesmen waiting for them at the far end of their encampment. Claire marched over to them with Thad, and after an animated conversation, turned around and shot Owen a smile.

"A ceremony is being prepared in my honor," she said.

Owen drew a pensive breath and glanced at the men standing beside Claire. Their long chiseled faces looked on with stoic expressions. All of them had bows strapped to their backs with thin cords. A few had finely tooled flint blades tucked under a leather band around their waists. He wondered where in the world they'd found flint.

"When?" Owen said, but he knew that it was right now. His gut tightened as he made eye contact with the lead tribesman. They may have called them honored guests, but the gaze looking back at him made him nervous.

Claire said, "Tonight. Their tribal elders are anxious to meet me."

"Yeah, yeah, of course. Let's hope that's all it is."

"What do you mean?" Thad said, wrinkling his brow. "They're not gonna eat us."

Owen shot him a furtive look of caution. "So far, yeah. But cross some hidden taboo, an' we're likely ta end up on da business end of one of them there spears," Owen said, darting a quick look at the rigid-faced tribesmen. "Not that we have a choice."

"Owen, we'll be okay," Claire said.

The leader said something to Thad then, and when he was finished, Claire said, "He's says, we need to leave. It's a long walk to their village."

"Yeah, yeah, I'm sure it is," Owen replied. As he strode ahead toward Manny to chat about what would happen should things go south, the leader pointed to Jorge, Molly, and Thad. Owen looked upward. It appeared they were all to be guests. This wasn't good, not good at all.

Beyond the Veil

Twenty Eight

"**I** DO NOT like this," Manny said, as Owen took him aside. "We do not know their customs. You could end up dead and not even know why."

Owen looked over his shoulder at the tall Hajamawri leader. The man was getting impatient. "So, what do ya suggest? Tell 'em thanks, but no thanks. I don't think so, mate. We'll just have ta be careful is all."

"It is not you so much I worry about," Manny said. He nodded toward Molly who stood fidgeting under the watchful eyes of one of the Hajamawri. "She is not so perceptive and does not know the ways of any of the forest people, nor do Thad and Jorge, for that matter. They could get you–"

"Yeah, yeah. But it seems a waste of time, don't it? They coulda put an arrow in ya da night they came on ya."

"And they would have, except for Claire and Thad."

"Yeah, hearing someone speak their language certainly must'a been an eye-opener for 'em," Owen said. He paused, then went on, "Look, I don't like it any more than ya do, but I don't see a way around it, an' I sure as hell don't wanna offend them, or we could all end up dead."

"Owen," Claire called over. "They want to go — now!"

"Right, coming." To Manny he said, "Keep ya eyes peeled an' ya ears up, ya hear?"

Manny nodded. Owen took off and joined Claire, who was waiting with the Hajamawri at the edge of camp. The leader eyed him shrewdly, then turned about face and marched into the dense, humid forest.

As Owen followed Claire and her team, he furtively eyed the men walking beside them. Although they were large-boned, thick-bodied men, he had no doubt they were hunter's, skilled with bow and blow dart, knife and spear, and capable of running long distances.

A couple kilometers down the trail, the ground began to rise steadily among the towering trees. The team trudged along, stepping over gnarled roots and woody vines. The flora took on an otherworldly appearance, and there were many plants Owen had no name for. His gaze went to a flock of toucans in the branches above, then settled down onto a massive rhododendron pushing up through a grove of tree ferns. He shook his head in wonder as he took in the unknown species. There was cataloguing work here enough to keep botanists busy for a lifetime.

But it was the large outcroppings of gray rock popping through the thick green blanket of ground cover that confused him. In all his long years of tramping the Amazon, he had never seen a landscape like this.

"I can't believe the size of the orchids, and did you see that vine back there?" Claire said. "It must have been a foot in diameter,"

"Yeah, I did," Owen muttered, pushing away a hanging liana blocking the path. "This forest feels all wrong ta me."

"How do you mean?"

"Well, take a look around. It's like God scooped up a mix of seeds an' dumped 'em," Owen said. He shook his head and went silent, not wanting to alarm her about the deep, troubling thoughts growing in his mind.

After a few minutes, Claire said, "You okay?"

"Yeah, yeah. Just thinking's all."

"About what?"

"Ah, nothing really. Just da good ole days with my mates here in da forest," Owen lied.

Claire sidestepped a waist-high fern. "You mean the Jadatani?"

"Yeah, yeah," he replied, glad to have been given an out.

"Tell me more about them."

Owen shrugged. "Not much ta tell. I was a tyke at da time. We fished, explored. All that nonsense."

"Hmmm … I seem to remember hearing a different story not all that long ago."

Owen shot her a sidelong glance and thought back to the night before he ducked out on her. How he'd wanted to kiss her that night. He blinked, and when he glanced at her, saw a smile on her face. "Something I should know?"

She looked at him. "Don't think so."

The leader ducked under a low, hanging branch dripping with lichen and came to a halt. As the team followed the man under it, Owen wondered what was going on with Claire. She had been quiet for the last half hour, as if debating inwardly. Perhaps pondering what new discovery she was going to make. He smiled, liking the way her expression turned inward when something was on her mind.

Suddenly her eyes grew large, and when he turned to see what had caught her attention, his breath ran away from him. Thirty meters ahead was a broad dark opening in the side of a sweeping, steep hill. He blinked. *What da devil? Another cave.* He eyed it in disbelief as the Hajamawri piled in around them.

The leader pointed ahead and said something to Claire. She nodded then turned to Owen. "Their village is through there."

"What'd'ya mean, through there?" Thad said, wiping the sweat off his brow.

"He didn't elaborate," said Claire.

Molly piped up suddenly and pointed to their left. "Look!"

Claire and Owen shifted their gaze. "Jesus, it's a obelisk," Claire said, and went to it.

The Hajamawri watched her while murmuring quietly to each other. Claire put her hand on the smooth, dark stone and traced the engraved cartouche with her fingertips. "It says: 'Only those of pure heart may enter the Valley of Ra.'"

The team looked back and forth at each other, but no one said anything. Ten minutes later they were in the dark passage, picking their way around strewn boulders and rocks. Behind them, the pale sunlight cast their long shadows on the fractured stones. Then, up ahead, a firelight bloomed in the darkness, revealing a gallery of intricately carved reliefs depicting daily life of a long forgotten people.

As the statues of nobility and commoners paraded ahead of them, Claire said, "I can almost hear their voices reaching through the millennia."

Thad tapped his shoulder. "This is gonna blow their minds back at Berkley. We're gonna re-write history!"

"And destroy a people in da process," Owen said under his breath.

Claire turned back to Owen, and said, "Any research by my department will be designed to preserve the tribe's way of life."

"Yeah, yeah," Owen said. "But it'll still change 'em. Can't be helped. Hell, we're changing 'em right now."

The cave bent to the right and around the corner was a stairway cut into the rock. The leader bounded up it, and as they followed, the passage lightened. Owen felt a fresh, cool breeze brush his face and a mist dampen his skin. Something big was waiting for them ahead.

"Mother, Mary and Joseph," Jorge said. "Where are we?"

Owen said, "Not a clue."

Claire exchanged glances with Owen as they stood on a narrow promontory just inside the rocky passage. Above them, light rained down and within, the air sparkled. To their left, was a thin waterfall gushing over a broad gray shelf of rock that went down to a guess. Claire eyed a broad archway of chiseled stone over them as the Hajamawri leader pointed to a low wall of fitted stone with a harrowing switchback stair hugging the cliff walls to their right. Owen eyed it dubiously.

Drawing an audible sigh, he started down behind the leader. Claire and her team followed. When they came to the first step, she caught her breath.

Molly shrieked. "Fecking Christ, you gotta be kidding me!"

"We take it one step at a time," Owen said.

"Careful, Owen. That's a long way down," Claire warned as Owen peered over the edge of the wall.

"Yep, an' da less we look, da better." He turned and eyed the following Hajamawri. To Claire, he said, "Tell 'em not ta push too hard, would ya?"

Claire passed the message back in the ancient language as Owen called Molly to him. But Molly shook her head. "No way! I'm not doing this."

"We don't have a choice, kid. Ya be in between us an' I'll have a hold of ya. Nothing's going ta happen."

"Molly, come on," Claire said, quietly. "I'm scared too, but we can't turn back. Take my hand."

Molly tentatively reached out and when their fingers locked, Claire could feel the harrowing fear in her R.A. At last Molly moved, and as the treads passed under their feet, Claire heard tiny stones peel away and ping down the eroded stairway. As they went, Molly's fingers dug into Claire's hand, and more than once brought them both to a halt until she could find her nerve to go on. But when they came to the first switchback, there was no moving Molly any further. Claire eyed the dozen terrifying steps ahead with nothing to grab onto except each other.

"Don't look down," Claire said, steeling herself as Molly's iron grip threatened to send them both tumbling forward. Claire sucked a deep breath, and said to Owen. "She's petrified. We're going to need help."

Owen turned around and said, "Hey kid, look at me. I want ya ta take a deep breath an' let it out. Relax. We got all da time in da world here. We'll go one step atta time."

But Molly shook her head and squeezed her eyes shut. "I can't!"

"Yes, ya can," Owen said calmly. "What I want ya ta do is sit an' scoot down on ya butt, like ya used ta do when ya was a tyke. 'member that?"

Molly continued to shake her head, but allowed him to help her sit.

"All right, now," Owen said, "Claire ya sit in back of her an' I'll be in front. Here we go."

Slowly, they made their way around the hairpin turn until at last the narrow treads widened and a friendly wall came beside them.

"Okay, there, ya did it," Owen said. "Tell 'em back there we need a moment here before moving on."

After Molly got her nerve back, Owen got them moving again. Claire took her time, concentrating on each step as they descended along the cliff wall until at last they came to the tips of the outstretched tree canopy. As they were about to duck under it, a flock of scarlet macaws screeched overhead. Claire stopped, and looking up, saw the faint outline of a colossal ruin across the valley.

The sun was high overhead when the team saw the first hint of the Hajamawri village through the dense grove of towering tree ferns and banana. Claire tapped Owen on the arm and tilted her head toward the thatched roofs peeking through the waving broad-leafed thicket. "Looks like we're here."

"Yeah, yeah," Owen said.

Claire saw his eyes darting around. "What?"

"In da trees beside us. We're being watched," he said.

Molly started to turn her head to look, but Claire reached over and grabbed her hand. "Keep your eyes forward, Mol. You'll see plenty soon enough."

"I know how to handle myself," the girl whispered under her breath.

"Then please start acting like it," Claire said quietly.

Owen added, "This aint no meet an' greet, Mol. These blokes here been living by 'emselves a long time, an' there's a reason for it. They don't like company. We give 'em cause ta not like us an' we'll end up as bug breakfast on a pole somewhere … Thad, Jorge; ya hear me back there?"

"Don't worry, this isn't our first rodeo," Thad said.

Owen frowned.

Claire said, "Poppy, can it. Owen's right. All of us, watch their leads, and be mindful of your expressions, especially smiling."

Emergency Camp

Juan stumbled out of the forest undergrowth into a sunlit glade and stared at the bivouac of canvas tents, wondering if he were in a dream. As he panned the small encampment though weary eyes, several people turned their heads. Somewhere, someone was cooking. Juan inhaled the aroma of sizzling meat and herbs. His ravenous hunger roared as his gaze, settled on a pump-action rifle lying across a chair with an oil-rag over its barrel. A meter or two from it stood a tripod with a high-gain antenna. A middle-aged man in tan khaki's emerged out of the far tent twenty meters away and started toward him.

Juan slipped his hand inside his vest and wrapped his fingers around the grip of his pistol. Walking beside the old guy was a tall, bronzed man, Peruvian maybe. Behind the Peruvian stood a small folding table. On it, was a bulky, silver laptop with an open notebook.

"You are a long way from home, amigo," the middle-aged man said in Portuguese, then leaned toward the Peruvian and whispered something into the man's ear.

Juan considered the long bush blade sheathed under the men's belts. "Si."

The middle-aged man wrinkled his leathered face as he stepped up to him. As his discerning gaze drifted down Juan's injured arm, he said, "What happened?"

Juan licked his lips. "Nicked myself with my scout knife."

The man wedged a cigar between his teeth. "That looks like more than a nick," he said, lighting the cheroot. He snapped his lighter shut. As a cloud of smoke veiled his face, he said, "You have a name?"

Juan gauged the penetrating stare appraising him. He had looked into eyes like these before, a long time ago: eyes that saw right into his thoughts. They'd belonged to the only man he'd ever feared, a man who ran the powerful Brotherhood gang in Lima. But this was not Leandro Alzira, nor was he afraid. Finally, he said, "Juan, and you are?"

"I am the director here," the man said, and called back to a watching camp member to get the med-kit.

"So, you're the boss man, then?" Juan said pulling his hand away from the Glock.

"No, the boss is out right now."

Juan glanced at the rifle again, mulling over what he would say to the man in charge when he arrived. He wasn't quite sure what he'd stumbled upon, and wondered when the question of how he'd gotten to the middle of nowhere alone would be brought up. Nodding toward the tents, he said, "What is all this?"

"It is a research camp," the director said.

"What are you researching?" Juan said.

"That is not for me to answer. Right now, I suggest we get that arm looked at," the director said. "Come." He led Juan over to a table and had him sit.

Juan settled into a canvas folding chair and lifted his arm for the man to look at while fighting to keep a steady eye on the large Peruvian.

"I need you to take your vest and shirt off," the director said.

Juan shook his head. "Vest and shirt stay on. Rip the sleeve."

The man shrugged. "Okay, but it would be much easier with the shirt and vest off."

"Don't worry about it. So, am I to call you Director forever?" Juan said, watching him grab the end of the ragged garment and rip it past his elbow.

The man pulled the cigar from his lips and flicked the ashes to the ground. "Name is Manny," he said, removing the makeshift bandage around the wound. Frowning, he shook his head. "Your wound is gangrenous."

Juan stared back at him expectantly. "And?"

"I am not a medical doctor, but looking at it, I think you are going to lose the hand, but we will see. Now, I need to pare back the dead skin and check how bad it is. You will be wanting to take a pass on this, I think." He called over to one of the other men. "Bring me my pack. It is in my tent." He turned back to Juan. "I have something that will ease your pain."

"And that would be?" Juan said.

Manny unsheathed his blade and handed it to the Peruvian to run it over the fire.

"It is an anesthetic. You will be out for just a little while, not-"

"I'll be fine," Juan interjected. "Do what you gotta do."

"Tough man, eh? Okay, have it your way. Might I at least suggest a drink to take the edge off?" Manny said. "I have a bottle of rum in my tent."

"Si, a drink would be good," Juan said, preparing himself as the director rummaged through the med-kit.

"So, how is it you are out here all alone amigo?"

Juan paused. Although he'd been expecting the question, it came sooner than he thought. He scrambled for a moment, then said, "Plane crash."

"Really? You are lucky then. People usually do not walk away from those."

Juan frowned. *Lucky, my ass.* "Si."

"Were there others?" Manny said, shooting him a glance while laying out fresh dressings and tape.

"One other. He died in the crash," Juan said as Filipe's face flashed before him.

"You the pilot?" the Peruvian said.

"Si." Juan stretched his neck. "So when is this boss man due back?"

"Hard to say. He was invited to a nearby village." Manny said then paused. "So, you are flying a little far south. What are you looking for?"

"Surveying. I work for the Ministry of Defense," Juan said, delighting in the reply that had come off the top of his head. Sometimes, he surprised even himself with what came out of his mouth.

Manny nodded as the man returned with the bottle of rum and a couple of mason jars. Unscrewing the top, Manny poured out drinks for the both of them, and said, "Kind of figured you were military, seeing most men do not go around wearing Kevlar." He handed Juan a jar and raised his upward. "Well, here is to your recovery."

"Si, my recovery," Juan said, and downed the drink in one long gulp.

Twenty Nine

C LAIRE FOLLOWED Owen through the narrow gap in the trees, which were wading in manioc and cassava to a small open field of fescue grasses. Fifty yards in front of her was a ring of thatched shelters. Gathered in front of them and looking her way was a scattering of curious men, women, and children. Some were dressed in muted loin clothes, others, not at all. But what caught her eye was what was behind the village. She ogled the eroded stone ruin built into the side of the steep valley wall.

A tap on the arm startled her. She glanced at Owen who was nodding toward a withered dark figure heading their way. She studied the man. He wore a tan sheath over his thin boney shoulders. Around his neck was a strand of bone tiles. A bright red streak of paint ran from the tip of his nose to a crinkled forehead. When he was close, he leveled a primordial gaze that held her frozen until at last he dipped his head.

"I am Iotep," he said in the language of the old kingdom, "keeper of the word which has passed down to me by those who have gone to A-o-bis. Long it has been told you would return. Welcome High One."

Claire nodded approval, and saw Owen draw breath beside her. Although he had no idea what the old man had said, she knew he knew the danger they were in if she didn't walk the fine line between telling the truth and keeping up appearances. But what was the High One to these people? She allowed a thin smile to come to her lips, and said,

"It is good to be here. My feet are tired from the long walk, and it is hot out. Is there a place we may go out of Ra's shining face?"

"Yes, come and rest," the man said, and flashed her a toothless smile. He turned, motioned to the waiting crowd at the edge of the village, and all at once they scattered like mice.

When the old man was far enough ahead of them, Owen said, "Care ta share what just went down?"

"His name is Iotep," Claire whispered, "and he said he is the 'keeper of the word'. I'm guessing he's a tribal historian. It seems I'm thought of as the High One, which I'm thinking is an ancient queen. The old kingdom held such views in their 'Book of the Dead'. Anyway, I told him it was good to be here and that I was tired from the long walk."

"Thank God he doesn't think you're a goddess," Owen said.

"Yes, or we'd be screwed," Claire replied.

Owen was led to the shade of a massive, thatched pavilion. He, along with Thad, Jorge, and Molly, sat within a ring of a hundred curious Hajamawri men, women, and children. Claire was taken to a round bamboo hut by Iotep and a large, ruddy man who wore a red, beaded sheath. Owen assumed the stern-faced giant was the village leader. Somewhere inside the hut, a discussion was being held that would determine their immediate future.

As he looked about him, gauging the mood of the surrounding throng, he thought back to his time amongst the Jadatani. The murmuring people ogling him were not so different from the indigenous tribe that lived a hundred kilometers to the west, except for one thing: they didn't paint their bodies, although a few marked their faces. Most of them wore bone-tile necklaces. Thad, who sat to his left, whispered that the markings were of Egyptian origin: spiritual identifiers. Owen didn't know about that, but he knew whatever they were, it was best not to stare at them.

A banana leaf of grubs and bush meat was being passed around. *Lunch. Yummy.* He eyed Molly as it came to him. Since chewing was out of the question, he passed on the meat and picked a couple of grubs off. Handing it off to Thad, he tucked the delicacy between his lips, rolled it around his teeth to the back of his throat and swallowed. The Hajamawri man to his right nudged him with an elbow and smiled. Owen nodded. *Yes, very tasty.*

When the leaf came to Molly, she looked up, and as she did, Owen could read her mind. The expression of, 'Oh-no, I'm not eating this fecking thing,' was pretty clear on her face. He stared her defiant expression down. *Eat Molly. We don't wanna piss 'em off.* But his silent warning went unheeded. She started to pass the leaf off to a hefty middle-aged woman beside her until she found herself on the other end of many pointed stares. Again, she looked at Owen, but this time there was terror in her eyes. Reluctantly, he saw her pick a chunk of bush meat off and stare at it while those around her watched expectantly. Finally, closing her eyes, she popped it in her mouth and courageously smiled at the woman beside her. Unfortunately, the woman insisted she take a few more.

Molly was saved when Claire emerged from the hut. As the anthropologist strode toward the pavilion with Iotep and the Hajamawri chieftain, Molly flashed Owen a smile. The crowd parted, creating a path to the center. Iotep and the tribal leader followed and took up seats across from Owen, sweeping their piercing gazes around the circle.

At last, Claire spoke. As she did, Thad translated. "She says, she's come to them with a message from Ra."

"Jesus," Owen muttered. "I hope she knows what she's doing."

Thad went on. "She's telling them Ra is pleased with them because they've protected His land."

Claire looked over to Iotep who was the 'keeper of the word'. When the man smiled, Owen wondered what was going on behind his all-seeing eyes.

Claire went on, fixing her attention on the curious, awe-struck expressions of the tribe. As she did so, Thad continued translating. But Owen wasn't paying as close attention to Thad's words as he was to the body language of those around him. Not that he could do anything about it if things went south.

Finally, Claire stopped talking and turned toward Iotep and the chieftain, holding them in a queenly gaze until at last, she released them and strode toward Owen. The Hajamawri men who sat beside him got up and cleared a wide berth for her to sit.

As she sat cross-legged, Owen leaned in her direction. "So, should I be getting my affairs in order?"

Claire cleared her throat, and keeping her eyes straight forward, broke into a thin smile. "Not unless you decide to do something to screw things up."

"So, how'd ya figure out what ta say?"

"I listened and let the old man talk."

"Smart girl!"

"I keep telling you that," Claire whispered, slapping a mosquito on her leg.

"So what's da big guy's role over there? Been trying ta figure him out," Owen said, putting another grub to his lips.

"What is that you're eating?" Claire said.

Owen swallowed an' rolled an eye her direction. "Lunch." He opened his hand to show her his twisting and curling meal. "Want one?"

Claire shook her head. "I'll pass."

"Figured ya would. They ain't half bad though."

"Right." Claire said, keeping her voice low. "Now hush and I'll tell you what I know, which isn't much. The big guy across from us is Donata. He's the equivalent of what would be called a vizier in the old kingdom. An overseer and keeper of the peace. At least that's the way I read it."

Owen nodded. "Well, he won't get any arguments from me, that's for sure."

"Or me either," Claire said, "Now, for the interesting stuff. It appears they thought I was an incarnation of this High One, a powerful woman who commanded the building of Haja-al-amawri temple behind us. Apparently, she entrusted it's keeping to the seffi, a word I've not heard of before – but I assume was a selected group of men within her inner circle. My guess is that these seffi either slowly died off or took mates within the tribe. Either way, the duties of looking after the temple shifted from the Egyptian elite inner circle to this indigenous tribe at some point."

"Now, what's going on?" Owen said, interrupting. He nodded to the animated conversation between Iotep and Donata across from them.

"They're discussing how they should celebrate our arrival. It appears we're invited to dinner."

"As long as we're not da main course, I'm in," Owen said.

As the tribe went about its business regarding the evening celebration, Claire slipped away to look at the temple ruins. As she walked along the narrow meandering path leading into the forest behind the village, she discovered she was not alone. Behind her, three young village girls - maybe ten or twelve years old - followed from a distance. She smiled, waved them toward her, and a moment later was looking down at three very round curious faces.

After answering several questions about where she was going, and how come her skin was so light, she led them toward the massive temple, whose crumbling walls could now be glimpsed through the cracks of the green menagerie. Pointing to the ruin as they walked, she asked what they called it. The oldest girl with shoulder length black hair spoke up, telling her it was the home of A-o-bis where the ancestors lived. *In other words, where they buried their dead,* Claire mused.

Finally, the forest gave way, and suddenly before her stood a broad open court of stone clothed in thick ivenkiki, manioc, and fern. Upon it stood a towering statuette of a striking woman in a long sheath gathered at her waist by a thin belt. Claire's gaze drifted over the statue's upward looking almond-shaped eyes and shivered. It was a face she knew well. She'd been looking at it in the mirror all her life. *No wonder these people think I'm the High One.*

A familiar voice called out behind her. "Well, looks like ya hit pay-dirt."

Claire glanced back to see Owen standing at the edge of the forest looking on. He was right. Her career was about to rocket into the stratosphere. A vision of her standing in front of a packed auditorium applauding her discovery flashed before her. Yes, life was going to be very good when she got back. No more laughing stock. She'd be the center of attention, the one everyone wanted to talk to. Except there was one problem: Owen. He would not stand by and idly watch as she paraded her findings in front of the academic world.

In truth, she knew he was right. Sooner or later, news of the tribe would leak out from the halls of academia and when that happened the tribe and it's culture would be destroyed forever. And then there was the growing feelings for him she was trying to deny. He was a good man, misdirected maybe, but sincere in his love for the people of the forest. More than that, he had put his life on the line for them, and also for her, now that she thought about it. She mused on what had happened with him on the riverbank earlier that morning as she stood in front of statue. He had opened up to her, trusted her, and now she would throw that all back in his face? *Damn him.*

He cleared his throat. "Ya know, once ya let da polecat outta da bag, there's no getting him back in." He paused letting the words drill into Claire; then added, "But I guess it doesn't really matter now does it?"

Claire looked off, unwilling to meet his condemning expression. *Am I really playing God? Yet isn't it for the greater good. Mysteries will be unraveled and a better understanding of the migration of the ancient peoples will be learned.* Her heart whispered in her ears and she knew the answer. Yet, she had to prove herself. Then it hit her. The cave! It had all the evidence she needed to convince Noah and her outside interests. At last she cleared her throat. "Yes, it does, Owen."

Owen eyed her cock-eyed. "Really? You'd abandon everything an' go back empty handed. Somehow I have a hard time swallowing that one."

Claire frowned and looked off toward the three Hajamawri girls who were picking berries at the foot of the temple. "You think I'd really expose them?"

"On no, Luv, not at all. It's da blokes riding ya coattails I don't trust. People have a way of forgetting what's right an' wrong when it comes ta fame an' fortune."

"Who says I'm going to have people riding my coat-tails?"

Owen drew back and looked at her hard. "Come again."

"You heard me," Claire said. "I plan on coming back alone–well, there'll be a few trusted friends along. Interested?"

Owen grinned. "That's a tall order there, yeah. Usually folks coming back with nothing ta show for it are shown da door in my world."

"Who says I'm going back empty handed?"

"Go on," Owen said, placing his hands on hips.

Claire looked up at the statue. "One can only wonder what's in that cave Inacio fell into."

"Right. An' da answer's, no. We ain't going down there," Owen said.

"We don't have to explore the whole damned cave," Claire said. "Just a quick look around."

"A quick look-around, my arse," Owen said.

Claire smiled. She knew by his expression she had him.

The feasting and dancing went deep into the night until at last the clouds opened and sent a soaking rain to drown the fires. Owen stared up into the inky black night that had crept inside their hut and listened to the distant rumble of thunder. The steady drip, drip of water running off the roof and splashing into puddles outside their door joined in with the quiet snores of Thad and Jorge. In the woven hammock beside him, was Claire. Feeling her eyes upon him, he rolled onto his side and said, "You awake?"

"Yeah."

Her flat reply made him pause. "Ya all right?"

"Yeah, just thinking."

"'Bout what?"

She was quiet a moment then said, "You. We're a lot alike: all wrapped up in our missions, determined to do the right thing."

Owen thought about what she'd said. She was right, but there were some things no amount of doing right could ever correct. He pursed his lips, and said, "I tell myself da same thing."

"Why do people like us need to control everything?"

The question caught him off guard, and he took a minute before answering. "'Cause we're not good at trusting, I reckon."

"Or paying attention to people who care about us," she whispered.

Owen thought about that and as he was about to answer back, heard her stir in her hammock. A few minutes later, rhythmic breathing ensued. He sighed, then rolled over and went to sleep.

Thirty

CLAIRE WOKE from a dreamless sleep. It was just past dawn, the sallow sky above creeping in through the cracks of the thatched roof. Outside the hut, a thin blanket of mist was draping itself over the village. A ribbon of smoke streamed up over the smoldering embers of last night's bonfire.

Lying in his hammock beside her was Owen. He slept on his back, and his long, lean body was stretched out over the woven swing. She sat up and studied the crow's feet spreading out from his eyes. A faint crescent scar hid just within the hairline above his right brow. Why hadn't she ever noticed that before? He also needed a shave, but she kind of liked the stubbly look on him; gave him character.

His nose twitched, and she saw his eyes move behind closed lids. She wondered what he dreamed about. Did his son fill the lonely nights left unguarded by duty? Could she live with the ghosts of his past? She didn't know what to think. She more than liked him, but there were so many impossible obstacles between them: hardheaded opinions not the least of them. And then there was the matter of distance. She wouldn't follow Jason, so what was any different about Owen? The answer to that, she already knew. She just hadn't admitted it to herself. No, it could never work. Let it go. But the memory of him bearing his soul by the river wouldn't go away.

She looked off through the opening of the hut and out to the rising mist, contemplating her future. The expedition was a bittersweet success. A nice young man had almost been killed. She had lost a child she didn't know she was carrying and had almost died herself. That she had discovered something beyond her wildest imagination did not lessen the guilt she carried. And in her heart she knew Owen was right. People would pile on her coattails once they heard of her find, and sooner or later a grab for grant money would ensue, say nothing of the cultural destruction to the Hajamawri. A long time ago she heard someone say that discovery was a violent act, and as she sat in the dark contemplating it, she knew it was true.

By mid-morning the team was following Mahl-attu-ani and two Haja-mawri hunters back to their Emergency Base Camp. As Owen brought up the rear, Thad dropped back beside him and said, "You know, the more I look at this valley, the more I'm thinking it's an extinct caldera."

Owen pressed his lips together, then said, "Ain't no volcanoes in da Amazon, mate."

"Well, according to you there ain't supposed to be any rock formations, stepped pyramids, or caves either."

Owen sighed. The kid had a point: but a volcano? He just wouldn't believe it. At last he said, "Ya could be right, but looking around an' all, I'd put my money on an impact crater, though that's as likely as a month a sunshine in Milford."

"Milford?"

"It's in da fjord-land's, down-under on da southern tip of New Zealand," Owen said. "Lotta rain down there."

"You miss home?"

"Sometimes. Ya get used ta it." They walked another hundred meters without a word until Owen said, "So, tell me, how long ya known Claire?"

"'Bout seven years," Thad said. "Why?"

Owen ducked under a vine and veered around a fallen tree. "Just wondering. Ya think highly of her, don't ya?"

"Yep," Thad said. "She cares about us students unlike most of the tenured profs."

"Meaning?"

"Meaning; they only care about furthering their careers on our backs," Thad said.

"I see. Ya know, I read up on her a bit 'fore I took this gig. This trans-Atlantic connection isn't exactly main-stream thinking, is it?"

"Nope," Thad replied. "Most of the faculty thinks she's whacked." Thad stopped and stared at Owen curiously. "You trying to hook up with her?"

Owen blinked. *Where did that come from?* He eyed the young man shrewdly and shrugged. "I like her. Why?"

"Well, don't. She's been through a lot."

"Haven't we all," Owen muttered and sidestepped a deep rut. "Careful, there's an ankle breaker there." He pushed ahead, sweeping away a tall, broad-leafed stem. "Anyway, I bet da folks back in Berkley aren't pleased: her getting this grant an' all."

"No, they're not," Thad replied. "They're jealous as hell. And it pisses 'em off she got it over their petty little mundane projects."

"I bet," Owen answered. "So what's this Noah like?"

"The department chair? He's a pompous ass. No one fucks with him, though, unless you wanna see your project deep sixed."

"He can do that?"

"Technically, no," Thad said as a branch snapped underfoot. "But he has a lot of influential friends, if you know what I mean."

"Yeah, yeah. Why'd Claire marry him?"

"One could only guess. She's never said and I don't ask."

"Right." Owen was quiet a moment, piecing more things together about Claire's past. Finally, he said, "So, her having been hitched ta Noah an' getting this grant must have folks in a lather."

"Yep. And I know what you're thinking: conflict of interest."

Owen heard the whine of a mosquito and a moment later felt a prick on his neck. Mashing the bug, he said, "It did cross my mind."

"Yeah, and you're not the first to think it. But what you don't know is he's her worst critic. Had his fingers into everything and damn near sandbagged me from coming."

"Really?"

"Yeah. Not sure how she pulled me coming off, but she did."

Owen nodded. "So, I'm thinking this bloke must have a couple redeeming qualities, eh? She married him after all."

Thad groaned. "Redeeming? No. What he is, is smooth. A real player, and the girls on campus eat his Scottish shit for breakfast."

Owen was perplexed. "Claire doesn't strike me as someone who eats shite."

"Oh, don't get me wrong, she doesn't. But the man's smart, too. He knows his biz. And unlike a lot of the meatheads on campus, he's fairly open to new ideas. That's probably what attracted her to him in the beginning. But sooner or later the asshole in him finally came out."

"Must have been interesting: both of them in da same shack," Owen said.

"Shack?"

Owen paused. Americans were so literal. "House."

"Oh. Yeah. You don't know the half of it," Thad said, as the trees parted in front of them revealing the long, giddying climb back up the narrow switchback stairs.

Two hours later, the team ran into Manny on the trail just outside camp. After a warm welcome back, the director came to Owen and pulled him aside. "We have a house guest."

Owen cocked a brow. "What'd'ya mean?"

"Some guy from the interior department. His plane crashed in the forest down south."

Great. The last thing I need is a soldier in my midst, 'specially one from da Department of da Interior. "He injured?"

"His hand is severely injured. I think he will lose it."

"What about da others in his crew?"

"Dead."

"What's going on," Claire said drifting over.

Owen ran his arm over his forehead. "Manny says we got an injured soldier at camp."

"Injured? How bad?" Claire said.

Manny repeated his story. "I think he has gangrene. I cleaned out the wound as best as I could. It is pretty deep."

Claire looked up at the waving branches and let out a sigh. "What next? Okay, let's get back."

Owen and Manny nodded, and as they followed Claire, Manny whispered, "His name is Juan. And I do not think I trust him. He is, how-you-say, just a little tight-lipped. And–" Manny waited until Claire was a little further ahead–"There is a bulge beneath the man's vest."

Owen glanced at Manny. "Wonderful. Who's looking after him?"

"Rameriz."

"Good. Well, let's get a move on 'fore these damned skeeters make a meal outta me."

Juan sat up on his cot when he heard a female voice come into the camp. A woman. And an American by the sound of it. He eyed Inacio sleeping across from him and slid his Glock inside his vest just as the tent flap was pulled back.

"Hi, I'm Claire, the expedition leader," the woman said in decent Portuguese, and this is Thad, my assistant. "I'm told you're injured. Mind if I take a look?"

"No, go right ahead."

Claire watched as he pulled his sleeve back. After a cursory glance, she said, "How'd you get it?"

"I nicked myself with my scout knife," Juan said.

"Your director, Manny, thinks I'm going to lose the hand."

"He may be right," Thad replied.

Just then a shadow darkened the opening into the tent, and as it did, Juan's eyes grew large. White bastard! Manna from heaven – revenge is mine.

"Hey, mate. Heard ya had a spat in da forest," the man said.

You have no idea, senor. "Yes, my plane went down. Engine trouble. And you are?"

"Owen, Owen Macleod at yer service." He turned to Claire and Thad. "How bad's it?"

"It's infected. I don't know," Claire said. She turned back to Juan. Owen said, "So, ya're bunking with Nace here. How ya doing?"

"We are doing all right," Juan said, resisting the urge to pull his Glock out and finish things right there. He winced as Thad probed the wound. "So, you two are casados?"

Claire and Owen glanced at each other hesitantly then said, 'no', in unison. Juan kept his smile to himself. *But you like each other, don't you? And I bet you've been in each other's pants. Maybe I'll let you into mine, eh, senora. See what it's like to have a real senor, no? Bet you would like that. Maybe do you right in front of your white bastard lover before I kill him. Oh, I am going to think hard about how this, very hard.*

Owen stepped out of Juan and Inacio's tent and bee-lined toward Manny and Rameriz, who were sucking up coffee. "Ya're right, Manny, he's packing."

"I told you. What, you do not believe me?"

"Yeah, yeah, course I do."

"So, how do we go about prying it away from him?" Rameriz said.

Owen was quiet a moment. There was no simple way about it. Juan would never let go of his gun. For good or bad, he knew he'd have to force the matter. One gun in camp was enough, and besides, a pistol was of little use in the forest other than for killing men. At last, he said, "We've two choices. Try an' persuade 'im ta let go of it, or make 'im give it ta us."

"And who do you suggest will try and persuade him?"

Owen pursed his lips and gave them knowing glances.

Manny snickered. "Right. You have such a magical way with words."

"I do just fine," Owen replied.

"Right. Your mastery of the senhora is beyond belief," he said, and then shooting Rameriz a grin, added, "Has her eating right out of his hands."

"Very funny," Owen said.

Manny laughed, but soon lost his smile. Narrowing his gaze on Owen, he said, "But seriously, I have a bad feeling about this feder-allie. He is very secretive and when he thinks no one is looking, I see him assessing things. He is making plans."

"I agree," Rameriz said.

Claire wrapped a fresh wide, cloth bandage over the gash on Juan's arm and sat back. Thad had done the best he could but he was no surgeon, nor was she, and she had no intention of becoming one.

One thing was for sure, though: Juan had a high threshold of pain. Either that, or he was a master of concealing it. Only once did he flinch as Thad probed the underlying dermis. The rest of the time, he stared at her with cold, calculating eyes.

"What's wrong?" Juan said, as Thad got up and left.

"Nothing, just thinking." She followed Thad to the doorway and called for someone to bring Juan a plate of food. After she came back, she said, "I assume Manny showed you where the river is."

"Meaning?"

Claire smiled. "You could use some soap and water."

Juan leered back at her with devilish eyes. "So sorry I offend you, senhora. One forgets how one stinks until a pretty senhora such as yourself reminds them. I will make sure I am more presentable for you in the future."

"I'll get you a towel," Claire said, not caring for Juan's indulging tone. "Oh, by the way, I'd appreciate it if you parked that gun you have under your vest away until we're back in do Içá." She nodded toward the table outside the tent. "One of those things out there is more than enough around here."

Juan raised a brow. "You're very observant."

"My father was a military man," Claire said, unzipping the bag and setting a bottle of pills in front of him. "He was never without one when he went out in the field." She pointed to the bottle. "Take one of those every four hours. They're an anti-biotic. I don't know how much good they'll do considering the state of your wound, but it's the only other thing I can offer you. If you'll excuse me, I'll go get you that towel."

As she turned to leave, Juan said, "Senhora?"

"Si?"

He looked up from studying the bandage around his arm. "Agradecimentos."

"Don't thank me just yet. Like I said, we don't have a lot of hope for saving your hand."

Later that evening, Claire settled down to answer several emails from Noah. She sat back after typing a short response on the Sat-Lynk to one of his needling questions regarding their progress. As she sipped chamomile tea from a tin cup, she thought about the stepped pyramid, the cave, and all that had happened to herself and the people she cared about. She had done the best she could, and seeing how things had settled down some, the only thing left was to move on.

Claire set her tin cup down and typed another paragraph, tip-toeing around specifics regarding the Hajamawri, and the discovery of the ziggurat and the cave. The less Noah knew, the better. She needed time she didn't have to learn about these new people before she could even attempt to draw up a preliminary hypothesis. And despite everything that had happened, like it or not, she needed to get into that cave.

"Hey there, Luv. Busy writing da boss up north?"

"Something like that," Claire said, looking up. She was getting used to being called Luv by him, and she kind of actually liked it now. She finished typing up the last part of the email, and sent it off. With a nod toward Juan, who was sitting at the far end of the camp with Paulo and the porters, she added, "He seems to be making friends quickly."

"Yeah, he is," Owen said, taking a seat beside her.

She shut the lid of the Sat-Lynk and set it aside. Taking up her cup, she said, "You go along with his story?"

"Don't know 'nuff right now ta say one way or da other."

Claire sipped her luke warm tea. "I don't think he's telling us everything."

"Yeah, what makes ya think that?"

"The gun under his vest."

Owen blinked.

"Oh, come on, give me some credit. I'm not blind," she said, rolling her eyes. "But I guess you can't help it. Men are conditioned at an early age to believe the only things we see are clothes, flowers, beach houses, and candy."

"That right?" Owen said, cracking his knuckles.

"Yeah. Don't take it personally. Anyway, back to my point. My father was a career Navy man. Always carried his piece in plain sight, even in the field. I don't know about your country, but shoulder harnesses aren't standard issue in our armed forces."

"Mine either."

"Maybe it's a preference of his to wear one: people have their reasons when it comes to arming themselves. Anyway, I told him to pack it away until we get back to do Içá."

Owen coughed and shot her a wide-eyed expression. "Really? An' how did that go?"

Claire shrugged. "Don't know, don't care. I don't like guns. They're a menace." When Owen's glance strayed to the rifle sheath leaning against the tree beside his tent, she added, "That includes rifles, too."

"For our protection, Luv. Speaking of which, I think I'm gonna see if our guest is telling the truth 'bout himself."

"Oh, and how are you gonna do that?"

"I was chatting with Molly an' it seems we can delay an email being sent out, so I'm gonna let the bloke use the da computer and see what he does."

"Good idea," Claire said, She took a deep breath and tilted her head back, stretching tired muscles. At length, she turned and looked at him searchingly, accessing approachability. He had changed since the he left her at the boat. He was accommodating, willing to listen, and softer around the edges, and after this morning, vulnerable. At last, she said, "I have something to say, but I don't think you're going to like it."

"Put that way, I'm sure I won't, but go ahead, shoot."

"About the ziggurat and the cave. I need pictures, and I need to get down there and look around. I don't want to come all this way and leave empty handed."

He let out a long, shallow breath. "Ya're not giving up?"

"No."

"When?"

"Day after tomorrow, maybe."

"Ya'll go one way or da other, I suppose," Owen said, glancing over his shoulder at Juan.

"I'd like it better if you supported it, but yes, I'll be going either way," Claire said, softly. "Look at me. I'm not going to do anything crazy. I just want to see what's down there. It could go a long way towards my getting another grant to come back."

Owen blinked and turned a guarded glance toward her. "Caves are dangerous."

"We'll be careful."

"We'll? Who's we?" Owen said, alarmed.

"My team, silly. You don't think I'm going down there alone, do you?"

Owen shook his head and ran his fingers through his hair. "Owen, this is my life's work," said Claire. "Everything I've done over the last fifteen years has been geared for a moment like this. I can't do it alone. I need people who know what they're doing, and what to look at. I need Thad and Jorge."

A long silence followed. Finally, his wrinkled brow relaxed, and eyeing her gravely, he said, "Guess I'll be coming along with ya then."

Claire felt a smile come to her lips, and without thinking, stretched her hand out and laid it over his. It was only supposed to be a pat, but she couldn't tear her hand away and ten minutes later they were still sitting with fingers entwined.

Thirty One

J UAN SAT by his tent, gobbling a second helping of breakfast. He hadn't slept well because there were too many things running through his mind. That, and his hand was killing him. He glanced out over the camp as he popped a piece of sausage into his mouth. The area was subdued and quiet. A group of porters murmured among themselves around the small open-air kitchen downwind. The Americans were hovering under a screened tent around a long table piled with papers and equipment. A thick mat of morning mist was rising off the forest floor.

He wiped the sweat from his brow with the back of his hand. It was going to be another oppressive hot and humid day. As he chased the last forkful of sausage, beans, and powdered eggs around the plate, he thought about the conversation he'd had with Inacio an hour ago. He had learned about a deep pit in the forest. He reached down for his mug of tea and sipped it as he contemplated a plan he'd been working on over the last half hour. It would take more than a little finesse to kill the blonde bastard and get away with it.

What he preferred was to get Owen away from everyone for a private conversation with a bullet. But with the sly director following Owen around like a puppy, it was nearly impossible. And if it wasn't Manny, then it was the shapely anthropologist Claire or one of her minions. A very astute and attractive woman, this Claire was. He'd have to be careful around her. He glanced in her direction and watched the conversation she was having with the young redhead in the screen tent and felt his body stir.

But there would be time enough for that later. He had to stay focused. If only his English were better. Only a third of what he heard made any sense. But he had one thing in his favor. The man named Paulo. Paulo was upset with the anthropologist about what had happened to his brother Inacio.

He sucked his lip as another wave of pain rode up his arm. As it passed, he took a deep breath, and skinned his teeth.

"Little twinge there, eh mate?" Owen said.

Juan started and looked up. How the hell had he snuck up on him? "It's nothing."

Owen reached over and pinched Juan's shirtsleeve. "I see Claire snatched one of my crabhoppers for ya."

Juan nodded. "Si, it's a little tight around the chest. What happened to your face?"

"Had me a little tumble back in da woods. Hurts like da dickens, but not near as bad as that, I reckon," Owen said, nodding at Juan's arm. He waved a fly away. "Say, I was thinking ya'd probably be wanting ta get a hold of someone up north. They must be wondering about ya." He pointed toward the antennae across camp from them. "We've got a satellite dish. I'm sure Molly could getcha patched right in ta 'em."

Juan's heart lurched. Sneaky bastard. He's trying to trick me. He feigned a cough and looked away.

"Ya all right?" Owen said.

"Si. Something went down the wrong way," Juan said. When Owen didn't reply, Juan cleared his throat. "There, it is gone. And agradecimentos, I was just about to ask you about that."

"Of course ya were," Owen said, eyeing him pointedly.

Fuck you, asshole. "Of course you don't mind if I log in by myself. It's a secure site."

"I'm sure it is, seeing it's da gov an all."

"Si." Juan replied. He sat back and watched Owen's eyes dart back and forth. *Got you asshole. You think I'm an idiota? So now, what to do, eh, amigo? Let me contact my lieutenants or weasel your little pansy-ass out of your own trap?*

Owen scratched his head. "Well, don't see any reason why not. Lemme check and see 'bout it. Sit tight, be right back."

As Owen marched over to Molly and Claire, Juan smiled and watched the ensuing conversation. Occasionally, Claire and Molly would glance his way. He had Owen right where he wanted him. At length, he pulled the bottle of pills from his pant's pocket and popping the top, brought it to his lips. Tapping the bottom, he sent a caplet tumbling into his mouth. As he washed it down with a gulp of tea, Owen came striding back.

"Well, looks like ya're good ta go."

Juan cocked a brow. "Really?"

"Yep. Whenever ya're ready, just go over an' let her know," Owen said. "Anyway, Like I said, we'll be heading north soon enough."

Juan smiled. *You have no idea what you just did to yourself asshole!* "Really? How is that? You have a man with a broken leg in there," Juan said tilting his head toward the tent behind him."

Owen sat. "True 'nuff. But it's nothing more than strapping him ta a litter an' hauling him out."

"Then why wait?"

"Believe me, wouldn't be waiting 'cept he has a nasty bump on da noggin. Don't want him seizing up on us out on da trail." Owen mashed a mosquito on his arm. "By da way, been meaning ta ask. How's da hooves?"

"What?"

"Feet? Ya been tramping a fair bit, an' we've a slog ahead of us back ta do Içá."

"My feet are good," Juan said, waving a fly away from his face.

Owen nodded. "Damn biters. They get hungry first thing in da morning." He pointed at Juan's shoulder. "I saw a nasty welt on ya arm when Claire was working on ya. Had a run in with a bullet ant, eh?"

"Ah, it is nothing."

Owen curled his lip. "Right. Piece a cake." He went quiet and Juan wondered what was going on in his sly little brain. Suddenly, Owen stretched, and leaning forward cast an unwavering gaze at him. "Look, I'm not opposed ta firearms 'round camp, but they make da lady nervous, if ya understand me."

"Not to worry, I put it away in a safe place," Juan said, concealing a delightful thought. "But now, if you excuse me, I would like to go ask your director if he wouldn't mind parting with a cigar. It is has been a long time since I have had the pleasure of a smoke."

"Yeah, sure 'nuff, mate," Owen said getting up. "I got chores ta do anyway. The lady runs a tight ship." He turned and took a step, then spun back around. Pulling a shiny object out of his pants pocket, he said, "Oh, by da way, ever see one of these gadgets? I found it out in da forest a while back."

When Juan saw the SCRIBBLER in the man's hand, he had all he could do to keep a straight face. "Let me see it."

Owen stepped over and handed it to him. "Interesting little thing. Looks like one of them smart phones or whatever they call them these days. I gave it a go trying to figure it out, but I'll be whacked if I have any idea how ta open it."

Juan held the silver plated communicator up to the sun and eyed the smooth contoured bump that opened the lid. Shrugging, he handed it back. "Never seen anything like it. Where did you say you found it?"

"Back in da woods. Anyway, we'll jabber more later on."

That night, Claire gathered her team along with Owen and Manny under the screened tent. As predicted, Juan had used the computer and of course erased the sent message. What the man didn't know, was that the message had never been sent.

Claire pulled Molly aside. "Any luck retrieving the sent email?"

"Not yet. He did a pretty good job covering his tracks."

"Meaning what? It's lost?" Owen said.

Molly pursed her lips. "No, but I need an ap so I can to get to it."

Owen pressed his lips together. "Shite. It didn't send though, right?"

"No, it didn't go. That I'm sure of."

"Well that's good," Owen muttered.

"The fact he was so careful, raises suspicion to me," Manny said.

"Me, too, mate. Anyway, lets tend ta matters at hand."

"You mean the cave?" Manny said, and frowned as he watched Thad, put the final touches on the loose sketch of the underground chamber.

"Yeah." Owen said, and turned to Thad. A moment later they were listening to how the foray into the underground chamber would be done. When Thad finished going over the last detail, Manny shook his head.

"I do not like it," Manny said. He turned and eyed Claire paternally. "I know this is important to you, but we are not equipped to be going into caves. What if someone gets hurt? You saw how hard it was to get Inacio out."

Claire stepped beside him. "Manny, I know you're only looking out for our best interests, and I adore you for it, but I need to get down there if I want a chance at coming back. It's just a quick trip down to look things over, collect a couple samples, and then back up. We'll be careful, believe me."

"It is not about you being careless I worry about," Manny said. "Caves have their own ideas. My brother's nephew died in one."

"Sima Pumacocha," Owen said.

Thad looked up. "He was in that expedition? Oh, man!"

"What?" Claire said.

"It happened in 06," Thad said. "A team of cavers went down to do routine mapping of a cavern in Peru. It was supposed to be an in-and-out deal in one day. They were on their way back out when a cave wall collapsed and trapped them. The crew up top sent for help, and the next day, potholers were coming from all–"

"Potholers?" Molly said, piping up.

"Tunnel rats, spelunkers," Owen said.

"Anyway, by the time help arrived it was too late," Thad added, and sighed.

"Did they ever get them out?" Claire said, eyeing Manny's haunted gaze from the corner of her eye.

Thad shook his head and they all were quiet for a moment. As Claire stood, thinking about how Manny was feeling and what to say to him, she noticed Paulo standing outside the tent looking in. Suddenly, an odd feeling came over her, though she had no reason to think he was doing anything wrong. It wasn't like anyone had anything to hide. Yet something in the way he looked at them gave her pause. She took a deep breath, and said to Manny, "I'm sorry."

Manny stirred. "It is all right. You did not know. Again, I say, forget the cave. Surely there is enough stuff already to take back to write your next grant?"

Claire sighed, not wanting to argue the point with a man she held in high regard, but she had to see it. "No, there isn't. I need hard, tangible evidence if I'm to come back."

Owen said, "It'll be okay, mate. Claire says it's a burial chamber, so people been in an' out of it. It's not like SP-1."

"Not sure that was the best choice of words," Thad said, shooting Owen a sideways glance. "But he has a point. The hole Inacio found is not an entry point that would be used for the purposes of burials. This cave will have an exit point somewhere, maybe multiple exits. And the fact that its contents are still relatively intact tells me its architecture is stable."

Manny shrugged and looked at Owen warily. "It seems I am being overruled. Okay, I will not argue it any further." He turned his gaze toward Claire. It was the look she'd seen back on the boat when she muscled him to bringing her down into the forest. He held her in his sights a moment, then said, "I hope he is right for all your sakes," then pulled out a cigar and put it to his mouth.

Juan rinsed the disposable razor in the tin water basin in front of him and looked into the small, square mirror on the table. He felt like shit, but he didn't mind. Soon, he would have reinforcements coming his way. The idiots had even given him the geographic coordinates of where they were. He tilted his head and dragged the razor over his chin. As he shook the thick soapy lather from the blade into the water, he saw Paulo ranting about something to one of the porters across camp from him. Juan watched the man's hands wave back and forth as he spoke to the men around him. Whatever it was about, it had Paulo in a snit; therefore it was something he needed to know about.

Tossing the razor in the basin, he toweled his face off and lazily shuffled across the camp toward them. As he neared the men, he could hear Paulo spitting out a biased opinion about some field trip the American scientists were planning later on in the week.

"Is stupid," Paulo grumbled. "Going down into that hole. What happens if something goes wrong? Huh? It will be our ass's going down to pull them out. I do not know about you guys, but I did not sign up for this crap."

"But the Boss–"

"Has gone soft over that American bitch," Paulo said, shaking his head. "We need to get Inacio back to do Içá. That is the only thing that matters, not some fucking artifact."

"So what are you suggesting? Leave? This is not the back woods around Lima, Paulo. None of us know the way back," said a short, stout porter that reminded Juan of Sosa. "And besides, I trust the Boss."

Paulo grunted. "I used to. But he's on a leash. She tugs, and he goes. We don't have time for this. We need to get Inacio out of here."

"May I say something?" Juan said, stepping forward.

Paulo eyed him speculatively and shrugged. "Sure."

Juan swept his gaze around the small circle of men. Most of them were no more than twenty, if that, with the exception of Paulo and the Sosa look-a-like. Maybe he could create some dissention and peel away a few of the men from the camp in the process. At length, he said, "Who has the power here? Hmmm? You are the ones who carry all the shit, no?" Heads nodded. "You put up the tents, no? Cook the food? Do all the crap they don't want to do?" Again, heads nodded. "That's what I thought–so use it! Demand that Manny return with those who want to go home now, and let your boss take the Americans back after they're done playing in their little shit-hole. But, I don't want to tell you what to do. This isn't my party, hmmm?"

Not yet, anyway! Juan thought.

"See, he agrees!" Paulo said, boldly, panning the nodding faces around the circle.

"It makes sense," one of the men said.

Paulo shifted and was about to say something, but Juan tapped his arm and subtly shook his head. When their eyes met, he mouthed the words, 'Wait on it.'

Another man spoke up, "I am all for going home, but what about our pay? I have family, and I need the money."

"The Boss is a good man. He will pay."

"I say let them go down. What is a couple more days?"

"It could end up being a couple of weeks," said another.

Finally, Paulo could wait no longer, and said, "So, who is with me?"

The men all looked at each other and shrugged. The Sosa look-a-like said, "I am."

Another man said, "I will stay, but I think other's should not have to if they do not want to."

"Me, too," said another, and one by one each of the men made their choice.

When all of them had spoken, seven had elected to leave. Seven less men he had to worry about. He stepped away, and as he walked back to finish shaving, he grinned.

Thirty Two

OWEN HAULED a large, thick pack out of the supply tent and plopped it on the ground beside Claire's chair. She looked up from checking her list and watched him kneel beside it to undo the straps. As he rummaged around, pulling out hand-held lanterns and zip-lock bags of extra batteries, she felt a tiny smile come to her face. In many ways he reminded her of the Noah she had known and loved ten years ago: a man who had stolen her heart with a smooth Scottish brogue and gleaming, blue eyes. And that was precisely why she'd felt antagonistic toward Owen in the beginning. After all, he had that melodic voice and eyes a woman could drown in. Already, she was up to her neck and treading water with him.

Yet, she couldn't help feeling tugged toward him and the indelible scars he hid behind a no-worry mask. She knew he was searching for meaning, for a reason his son had died. But there were no answers that would ease his guilt and pain, and there never would be.

He looked up and shot her a boyish grin, winked, and went back to hunting for batteries and gloves. "Well, at least we got things rigged up out there today," he said over his shoulder. "That Thad of yours is quite handy around ropes an' such."

"He's has a lot of experience," Claire said. "I want an early start tomorrow, say, around six."

"Molly aint gonna like that," Owen said, keeping his nose buried in the pack. "Manny tells me she's been keeping company with Jorge, yeah? Which makes sense, seeing how she's been turning out well after nine in da morning."

"Don't remind me," Claire said as Owen lifted a pile of work gloves over his head and dumped them at her feet. She checked them off the list. "So, how much you think we can fit in our packs?"

"How much what?" Owen said, backing his nose out of the pack and looking at her quizzically. "Oh, ya mean artifacts an' stuff. We could get a fair amount in, I suppose. I assume ya cleared it with da gov 'bout such things?"

"Of course. We're not tomb-raiders, Owen," Claire said, a little stronger than she intended. "I'm sorry, that was a bit harsh."

Owen shrugged. "It's okay, I know ya didn't mean anything by it."

Claire felt like a jerk. "No, it wasn't. You're just looking out for us. In my line of work, that doesn't happen a lot." She smiled. "I'll try to remember you're on our side from now on ... So, what else? Oh, something to wrap specimens in. I think I saw some–"

Owen shot her a glance.

"What?"

He was quiet a minute and looked off into the woods. Finally, he said, "Leave 'em there."

Claire set her pen down. "Why?"

He sat back on his heels, "The dead belong ta da Lady."

"The Lady?"

Owen nodded toward the forest beyond their tents. "Once she claims 'em, she likes 'em staying put. An' when they don't, she gets a might surly."

Claire was amused and delighted all at once. "Oh, really?"

But Owen was quite serious. He leaned forward and held her with a deep, penetrating gaze. "Look, I know what ya're thinking, but it ain't that at all. I've seen things I can't explain, an' I'm telling ya, no good'll come of it. 'Sides, aint there other things down there?"

Claire drew breath. Just as she was about to answer, she saw Paulo leading a group of porters their way. Suddenly, she had a bad feeling. Getting up, she said to Paulo, "Something wrong?"

"We want to talk to the Boss," Paulo said. "Alone, if you don't mind."

Owen stood, and from the corner of her eye, Claire saw his muscles tense. "You can say whatever ya need ta, ta da both of us. What's da problem?"

"We've been talking. We're leaving first thing in the morning. Inacio needs a real doctor," Paulo said, defiantly. He looked at Claire with dagger-eyes. "No offense, Senhora."

Claire stiffened. "None taken," she said in Portuguese, then noticed Juan sitting outside his tent smoking one of Manny's cigars. The man blew a stream of smoke into the warm, humid air, tapped the ashes off the cheroot onto the ground and glanced her way.

Owen said, "That what ya think? See here, mate, 'Nace ain't going anywhere 'til he's fit ta travel."

"We are not waiting for another accident to happen. This place is cursed," Paulo said, and got nods of approval from the men around him.

"Cursed?" Owen said. "What'da'ya talking about?" When Paulo looked toward the path leading to the cave, Owen shook his head. "Oh, I see. Ya're worried about our little excursion. Well, ya're not going down, so don't worry 'bout it."

"We're not, cause we're not going to be here," Paulo stated emphatically.

"Paulo, it's just down and up to collect a few things," Claire said. "There's no reason to –"

"What? Worry? Who do you think will be ordered to come after you if you get hurt? It will be one of us. I do not go into caves!" Paulo cried. "People die in them!"

When murmurs of agreement rippled amongst the men, Owen put his hand up. "Look here. No one's ordering anyone ta do anything they don't wanna."

"Is that so?" one man said from in back.

"Yeah, like any of us could refuse," Paulo ranted. He puffed his chest, and added, "You are not the boss of us in this matter."

Owen shot Paulo a searing gaze. Claire nibbled her lip as she watched his face tighten. Finally, he said, "That so? Well, guess ya're on ya own then. Good luck getting back."

"Is not a problem. Manny will take us?"

"That what ya think; well think again." Owen said in an icy tone.

"Look, I know things have been difficult," Claire interjected. We've all had a hard time, but were any of you forced to come?"

"Yeah, you all signed up, remember?" Owen said. He eyed the men, one by one to drive home the point.

At length, the porters nodded. Paulo looked off toward the looming forest and grunted when one of his followers changed his mind and stepped beside Owen.

"Well, what about it then?" Owen prompted.

Silence followed as everyone looked at each other. A tall, broad-shouldered man Claire knew as Alonzo spoke up. "Why do you have to explore this cave?"

As Claire opened her mouth to answer, Owen put his hand on her arm. "Cause, I promised her, that's why. She paid us ta bring her down here –"

"And that is what we did," Paulo burst out. "We did everything we were supposed to."

"I know that," Owen said.

"Look," Claire said. "I'm not asking anyone to put their lives in danger."

"Senhora, we know what you believe, but you cannot predict the future," said a gaunt, dark-skinned man named Hernandez. "You have found your lost man, no?"

Before Claire could answer, Paulo blurted, "Hell, we found a whole fucking tribe of them!" He shot Claire a withering scowl. "What more do you want?"

"She needs tangible evidence," Owen said, raising his voice. "This is an expedition, an' our job's ta give her what she paid for. Way I look at it, she's gotten da short end of it."

Claire widened her eyes.

One of the men spoke up. "Not by us."

"No one's saying that," Claire interjected. She glanced sidelong at Owen, wondering if she had heard him right, then turned and eyed Paulo. "Believe me, I came here to work, not to play doctor."

"Well, if you'd kept your little ass on the boat, you wouldn't have needed to," Paulo snapped back.

Owen spoke up. "Watch ya mouth, mate."

"Or what?"

"Ya'll deal with me, is what!" Owen shouted. He put his hand to his face and winced.

"You all right?" Claire said.

"Yeah, I'm fine." He drew a long breath through clenched teeth, and leveled a threatening gaze at Paulo. The two men stood locked in a test of wills until Paulo finally looked away. Owen put his hands on his hips, and to the men standing around him, said, "The reason she went against my orders is 'cause I screwed up an' wasn't straight with her. Any questions?"

Claire blinked.

"But you had your reasons," a man in back said.

"Yeah, I did. But I had no right ta put my agenda ahead of hers. She paid me ta guide her, not leave her stranded on da boat." He paused, and after a moment to let things sink in, went on, "For my part, I'm gonna make it right. But if you're still hell-bent on leaving, go ahead."

Claire felt her jaw slacken as she looked at Owen in wonder. Noah had never admitted to a mistake, nor had Jason or any other man she had known.

"Very well, we will wait two days then," said Alonzo. When the other's agreed, Paulo's frown deepened, and with a disgruntled look, he spat and stalked away.

Later that night, Juan plopped onto his cot and pulled his boots off. He had sown the seed to divide the camp. He thought about his next move as he chatted with the stuttering young porter for a time, hearing about his inconsequential life back in Peru. That the Americans had chosen to put him together with Inacio was almost too good to be true. The information he'd gathered from the injured man had gone a long way in deciding his plan to get even with Owen. But Inacio's uses were quickly coming to an end.

As Inacio rambled on about his brother and the future business they were planning, Juan plotted his end game, After he worked out all the details, he waited for Inacio to nod off. *Should I kill you now, or later?* He thought, glancing over at the man. *Later would be better. And how to get a hold of the rifle? Again, the swarthy director was the issue. The man guarded it like one of Valderón's pit bulls.*

He scratched his head, bringing a sharp rampaging pain up his arm. "What I wouldn't give for a quiet moment with you, amigo," he muttered as he sucked a breath and peered down at his arm. There was no denying it anymore. He was going to lose his hand. Well, someone was going to pay for it. He dug his pistol out from underneath his cot and tucked it under his pillow. Very soon, he'd have his revenge. Yes, very soon.

Thirty Three

O WEN STEPPED out into the warm morning mist. It was just dawn and the camp was silent among the towering kapok and capirona giants. In the distance he heard the sound of water splashing along the banks of the tributary that flowed south of their camp. Stretching, he inhaled the perfumed scents of orchids and flowering Brazil nuts then headed toward the mess tent to start a pot of morning tea.

Pulling the mess-tent flap aside, he went in to find Manny already up. They talked a moment about the day ahead, and about Juan and how it was curious he had befriended Paulo so quickly. But Owen would concern himself about that later. He wanted time alone to think. Fifteen minutes later he was standing at the edge of camp, overlooking the fog-veiled banks of the channel. As he sipped his tea, he watched the muddy water flow into the gloom and closed his eyes, falling into sync with the ancient rhythms of the great Earth Mother, Papatūănuku. With her, he knew where he stood. It was living in the manufactured world of men that was hard.

He shook his head. Why was life so damned complicated? He'd finally come to terms with Monica's leaving, and had gotten back to enjoying his own company. And then she came along and turned it all upside down. Which meant what? He didn't really want to be alone after all? Sometimes he didn't understand himself.

He thought of his admission to her two days ago on the banks below, and saw her beautiful brown eyes gazing back. The memory brought a smile and he looked upward into the ever-brightening sky streaked with soft pinks and golds.

As he lifted his mug to his lips, Claire stepped beside him. "Penny for your thoughts?"

Owen startled, almost spilling his tea. "Give a man a warning next time, Luv." He wiped his hand on his shirt. "So, ya ready for ya big day?"

"Ready as I'll ever be," Claire said, stretching her arms over her head. "How's your jaw? You wearing that sling I made you?"

Owen nodded. "Every night, like clockwork. Kids up?"

"Barely, but yes." She was quiet a moment then said, "Can I tell you something?"

"Sure," Owen replied, acutely aware of her being inches away from him.

She tugged his sleeve, and when he looked down, he saw her gazing back anxiously. After a deep breath, she said, "I'm sorry. And thanks for sticking up for me yesterday with Paulo."

Owen drained his tea, hooked his pinky finger around the handle of his mug, and said, "Ya know, when ya been doing things a long time by ya'self, ya think ya got it all figured out. That ya know better than those around ya. My father, bright man he was, told me once, 'That's when ya start making mistakes'. So it's me that owes ya an apology, not da other way 'round."

"Sounds like we both need forgiving, then," Claire said. She grasped his arm and gave it a squeeze, then turned and walked away.

"Careful," Owen said as Claire stepped to the edge of the dark hole. Although she was wearing an improvised harness Thad had rigged up, he wasn't taking chances. He turned her around and rechecked the belaying line attached to her harness, and gave it a tug.

"You're making me nervous, Jungle Boy," she said, smiling as she wrapped her hands around the abseil line coming down from overhead.

"Just making sure my future gets down in one piece," Owen said.

"Future?" Claire said, cocking a brow.

"Ya know," Owen said, scrambling not to look like an idiot. "Getting cited in one of ya papers so I can get outta this tourist-trampin' racket."

"Right." She waved her hand, shooing him away. "And do what, move to San Francisco?"

They traded knowing glances with each other. Finally, Owen said, "Yeah, yeah, something like that," He took a deep breath and joined Rameriz and Hernandez on the line.

As he dug his heels into the soft earth, Thad went forward and stood beside her. "Here's your camera. Now, just lean back and let them do the work," he said, as Molly and Jorge looked on.

Owen watched her clip the camera lanyard to her belt and check her flashlight. Finally, she looked down, raised her hand and gave the thumbs-up.

Twenty minutes later, Claire, Thad, and Jorge were down. Owen tucked his light in his back pocket and grabbed the abseil line. As he wound the rope around his leg like Thad had shown him, he saw Molly look up from organizing the layout space for items to be catalogued and bagged.

"When you get down, tell Jorge to be careful for me," she said.

Owen tipped his hat and just as he was about to drop into the hole, stopped and whistled to Rameriz. "Aye, throw me a box of matches, would ya? There in that pack over there beside Molly's tarp."

"Planning a camp fire?" Rameriz said, smirking.

"Not really, why? Ya wanna invite?"

"Only if there's rum involved," the man said over his shoulder. He dug the matches out and tossed them to Owen.

"Soon enough on that one, mate," Owen said, stashing the little box in his shirt pocket. "All right, here goes."

"Be careful," Hernandez said.

"Believe me, I plan on it. An' thanks for coming along this morning. Means a lot, mate ... Oh, crap."

"What?" said Ramirez.

"My hat. Here take it, would ya?" Owen replied, handing it to him. The porter put it on and smiled. Owen frowned. "Don't get too comfy with it, an' don't stretch it out. I finally got da damn thing ta fit right."

Owen gave the thumbs up, and as the two porters grabbed the line, pushed off solid ground and hovered over the hole. It had been a long time since he'd rappelled down anything, let alone into a cool, damp, suffocating darkness.

He relaxed his grip on the line, and a minute later saw Claire's flashlight spraying the tall, cavernous gray walls below. To his right, in the dim sunlight filtering down from above, he saw Thad and Jorge mounting lanterns on tripods. The LED bulbs flickered then shot out a burst of white light.

Claire's 'wow' echoed in the expansive cavern. "Look at the pottery. And the jars - there's hundred's of them. Oh my God, what's that?"

"It's a boat," Thad said. "A fucking boat just like the one in Giza! Are you thinking what I'm–"

"Way ahead of you," Claire said as Owen touched down. He watched Claire sweep her gaze over the sprawling chamber. On the walls around him were thousands of cartouches. Towering stone columns reached up into the dark recesses of the vaulted ceiling. Suddenly, he felt very small in this alien world.

Claire pointed to a dark triangular opening fifty meters across from them. "There! See it?"

Owen dropped down to solid earth and untied himself, then saw the longboat sitting on a massive slab of schist.

"Pretty cool, huh?" Thad said, joining him.

"Yeah, yeah, right."

"And it's intact, too!"

Owen cocked an eye. *'Intact'. I don't think so, mate,* he thought, eyeing the vessel from where he stood.

"What's the matter?" Claire said, stepping beside him.

Owen shrugged. "Just wondering what they made it out of."

"Probably, cedar," Thad said.

"Aint no cedar in the Amazon," Owen said, guessing the boat's length at around twenty meters.

Claire flashed a wry grin and winked. "Who said they built it here? I'm going for a look. You coming?"

"Yeah, yeah, be right along."

She took a deep breath and broadened her grin. Owen had never seen anyone so captivated. Her eyes sparkled as she raised her arm in the air and bounded off like a kid let loose in a toyshop.

Juan slipped into a dense tangled network of leafy vines and ferns and surveyed the extent of the shadowed clearing before him. In the middle of it stood a three-legged log scaffold with a rope dropping down into a small, dark hole. Beside it sat the Portuguese man named Rameriz and beside him, another he recognized as Hernandez. Back a ways from them, the redhead was busy playing with her science toys. Juan checked his clip. Four bullets. He gave the silencer on the end of his pistol a good twist and readied himself.

His only regret was not being able to put a bullet in the bastard's head, but being marooned in the cave with no way out would have to suffice. At least the man's death would be slow and agonizing. At length, he slid back out of the thicket and stood, tucking the Glock behind his back and under his belt. After a final check of the readiness of the scout blade under his vest and a quick dusting off of leaf litter on his pants, he was off and walking into the clearing. The porters, who were talking to each other, looked up startled when they saw him approaching. The redhead, who was kneeling on a tarp, sat back on her heels.

Juan said, "Manhã."

"Manhã," Hernandez said getting up. "What brings you out here?"

"I was bored and thought I'd take a walk," Juan said. "So, this is the cave I've been hearing so much about." He peered down into the hole and saw lights shining back up. "Quite a drop," he added, and looked back at the porters.

"Si," Rameriz said, eyeing him shrewdly. "I would be careful if I were you, walking around out here. There could be others like this. Last thing we need is someone else falling in."

"Right," Juan said, as he strategically placed himself on the other side of the gaping hole. He gauged the distance between them and him to be around five meters. Close enough for a sure hit, but far enough away in case one of them charged him after the first shot. Slowly, he slipped his arm behind his back and gripped his pistol. "Well, I will leave you to your duties, but before I go, one last thing."

"What is that?" Hernandez said.

Juan smiled. Whipped the pistol out and put a bullet in the man's head. As he swung the pistol around to take care of Rameriz, the man leapt to the right. But the bullet found the man's side nonetheless. The redhead screamed. Rameriz cried out as he rolled on the ground.

Juan gritted his teeth and ran forward, shoving his gun under his belt as he went. The last thing he had wanted was to get into hand-to-hand combat. He ripped it out of its sheath. Dropped to his knees beside the porter and raised the blade over the man's chest.

But before he could drive it down into the man's chest, he was jolted forward. Suddenly, sharp teeth bit into his arm. He yelled out. The knife dropped. Reaching up, he grabbed red hair and yanked. A sharp cry pierced his ear as nails dug into his face. Rearing back, he threw a vicious elbow. Connected with ribs. He heard a grunt and the redhead was gone. Juan scowled. Rameriz had rolled away from him and the knife lay between them.

As Juan lunged for it, Ramirez's foot kicked it away. A second later, something hard slammed into his jaw. He winced, tasted blood. The ground spun. Blinking, he shook his head as another blow drove him to the ground. Again, the redhead was on him, clenching his wounded arm. All at once, a wicked jolt ran through him sucking his breath away. Gritting his teeth, he rolled his body and threw her off. Heard her yelp as he got up.

By the time he got his wits back, Rameriz was on his feet. A dark, red stain covered the porter's shirt and trailed down onto his pants. The man eyed him grimly then averted his gaze to the knife lying a meter away from them. Juan ran his sleeve over his mouth, gauging his opponent while surveying the clearing. The redheaded bitch was gone. Where the hell was she? He glanced back and forth, then behind him. He wouldn't underestimate her again. But she wasn't there.

Fuck! She's running back to camp. I gotta finish this quick, he thought.

Rameriz wavered, turned his head and spat.

Any other time, Juan could wait and watch him bleed out. But he had to get to the girl. Still, he had to be careful. The tall muscular porter was mortally wounded, but he was a still force to reckon with. And what was more, the redhead had opened the wound on his wrist. He looked down and grimaced at the open cut sending wave after wave of burning agony up through his shoulder. The thought of pulling his gun out and ending it consumed him, but he needed the remaining two bullets.

Rameriz eyed him like a wounded animal, and in that moment, Juan knew it was now or never. He dove for the knife and grabbed it. The porter fell on top of him. Pinned him face down onto the ground. Ramirez's iron fingers groped for Juan's grip on the blade.

Suddenly, Juan's eyes widened, and he saw his death before him. Clenching his jaw, he summoned all his strength and arched his back. With a quick thrust, he kicked and rolled over, throwing the porter off him. The man landed on his back with a thud. Juan whirled around, raised the knife, and brought it down. But Rameriz twisted and the blade missed, slicing the man's shirt. Juan pulled the knife back for another stab, but Ramirez's hand shot up and locked his fingers around Juan's arm. For a moment, the blade hung in the balance between them. Then slowly, Juan pressed his advantage, saw the fear in the man's eyes as the tip of the blade touched his chest. A moment later, resistance vanished, and the blade plunged in. A rushing breath escaped the man's lips. For good measure, Juan twisted the blade and sat back, huffing.

Fighting to keep from passing out, he gritted his teeth and re-applied the bandage to the gaping wound on his arm. *Now to find the little red-headed bitch.* He wiped his blade off on Ramirez's shirt, and saw a bloodied stone on the ground. He picked it up, and was about to sheath his knife when he saw the abseil line waving back and forth. Puzzled, he crawled over to the scaffold and looked down. To his surprise, the redhead was hanging on the rope and looking up. *The little spitfire must have fallen in and grabbed the line on the way down.* Smiling, he put his blade to the nylon cord and called down to her. "Better hurry senhorita. I don't know how long I can keep my knife from cutting through this rope."

Thirty Four

CLAIRE RAISED her camera, shot several photos of the statue of Horus then ran to it and put her hands on the cool damp stone carving. She could spend the rest of her life here and not come close to deciphering the mysteries about this hidden world. But her time was limited, and the dark, antechamber waited in front of her. She flicked her flashlight on and felt her heart race as she entered the tomb. Inside the musty chamber, was a sprawling collection of gold statues, plates and regalia beyond the wildest imaginations of any thief. She took several more photos, and then shined her light over them, following the spreading beam to a stone dais. On it, was a stone sarcophagus and eight canopic jars. She resisted the urge to run to it, and went instead to the decorated wall before her. As she ran her finger along its hairline joint, she studied the lines of pictorial text, many of which were barely readable. But those that were, spoke of a favored one who called himself, Haja-al-amawri or 'Follower of the Stars'. Claire read on, and saw that the man had been sent with an armada of over a great sea, in search of a mystical herb rumored to grow in a land of tress. A little further on, she read of a sacred valley, called, The Dreaming Land. Her eyes widened. *I've heard this name before. The Jadatani talked about it!* She studied the faded red and yellow ochre's and lapis lazuli further, until suddenly she saw the symbol of Hatshepsut!

It was placed prominently among the iconography of Osiris, Ma'at, Horus and Atum. But there was also another symbol she did not recognize of a woman who was referred to as the *High One*. Things were beginning to take a new twist and so she looked back at the sarcophagus. Could the *High One* be in it? She started to read the text again and found there was a great deal written about the woman, but before she could get too far into it, Owen was at the chamber entrance. Behind him, she heard Thad's voice echoing off the walls in the outer hall.

Owen said, "We got a problem."

"What?"

"Molly's on her way down."

Claire frowned. "What the hell? I need her up top. Why is she coming down?" She tore herself away from the wall and stalked out of the room. When she came out into the vast kidney shaped hall, she looked up and saw Molly sliding down the abseil line a hundred feet away. Thad and Jorge were directly below her, looking up and yelling for her to stop.

Owen rushed up behind Claire. "She's coming down too fast. I can't yell account of my jaw. Tell her ta slow down."

Claire shook her head in exasperation and shouted out Owen's order, but Molly wasn't listening.

"Damn it! She's gonna hurt herself," Owen growled, and he took off running toward Thad and Jorge. As Claire came after him, the rope snapped and Molly came tumbling down, landing on Jorge and Thad; sending them into a scattered heap.

Claire put her hand to her mouth in stunned silence and came to a halt on the undulating cavern floor. For a moment, she struggled to believe what she'd just seen then came to herself and rushed to them.

Owen was untangling the three of them as she rushed up behind him. Jorge, who had taken the brunt of Molly's fall was lying on his side, moaning. Thad was on his hands and knees, coughing. Molly was sprawled between them, rope strewn over her body, legs draped on Jorge's back and her head on the ground.

"Is she all right?" Claire said.

"Yeah, she got da wind knocked outta her is all. Damn lucky Jorge an' Thad was here, else she'd gotten hurt a lot worse."

Claire breathed a sigh of relief and dropped to her knees beside Molly. "What were you thinking of?"

But before Molly could say anything, a voice came rumbling down from above. Claire looked up. Within the bright sunlight blotting the hole fifty feet above, was a muted face looking down. "*Hola, senhor.* I see the *senhorita* made it down in one piece."

"Juan, is that you?" Claire called up.

"*Si.* It looks cozy down there. I wish I could come down and join you, but things being what they are, this will have to do."

"An' why's that?" Owen called up.

A derisive laugh trickled down. "Surely you can figure that out, no?"

"Oh, I have a good idea. So who exactly are ya?" Owen said.

"Oh, really? I'm disappointed in you, *amigo.* I cannot believe you have forgotten me so soon after our little party down by the river. But, perhaps so. You were very busy butchering my men as I recall."

Claire leaned toward Owen. "What's he talking about?"

Owen's face darkened. "He's a FARQ. A soldier of one of da cartels."

Juan's voice rained down again. "So, has your memory come back?"

Claire gritted her teeth, and shouted, "Butcher? You're the one who slaughtered those women and children!"

"Is that so, *Senhora*? Perhaps you would have had me leave them to starve to death? No, I did them a favor; believe me. But, no matter." He paused and went on, "So *amigo,* how does it feel to be on the other end of an ambush? I trust you are enjoying it? I know I am, and it should comfort you to know your companion, Rameriz, died quickly at the end of my knife. I wish it could have been you, but he will have to do. And now, I have some parting gifts, so if I were you, I would have the *senhora* move away from where she is sitting, unless she wants a front row seat."

The hole brightened a moment, and they heard something being dragged to the rim above. As the hole darkened, Owen picked Molly up and said, "Don't know what's coming down the chute, but we best get back."

Juan called down, "Look out!"

A dark mass came hurtling down, hit the ledge above and bounced off, landing a ten feet away. Claire felt something spray her face and arms. She wiped her cheek and looked at the red splatter. *What the – oh, my God! It's blood ... Hernandez! Oh, no!* Tears flooded her eyes as she looked at his bloody and twisted body splayed out on the cavern floor.

Molly shrieked.

"Fucking animal!" Thad cried out, leaping back.

"Got another one for you," Juan called back down.

A couple minutes later, Ramirez's body came hurtling down and landed a foot away from Hernandez. Juan's cruel voice returned, echoing through the cavern. "Well, I am off, *amigo,* as I have business with your director. Cannot have him snooping around here looking for you, no?

"Before I leave though: I would like to tell that bratty redhead of yours something. Is she there?" When Owen refused to answer, Juan laughed. "I see my gifts left you speechless. I'm very glad you liked them. Fortunately, the little redhead bitch did not ruin my surprise. I worked very hard on them. But you know *crianças*; they get so excited over gifts.

"*Hola*, Molly is it? You forgot your toy. I assume you want it, so here it is." A click-clack noise trickled down through the cavern as a rock tumbled to the ground several feet away. "Next time, be more careful with it," Juan said with a threatening tone and then his shadow slipped away from the opening above. After several minutes of silence, they realized he was finally gone.

Juan looked through the screened opening in the tent he shared with Inacio and saw the young porter sleeping on his cot. Though his arm was killing him and his body ached, he smiled and slid into the tent. Oddly enough, the one part of his plan he had the least control of, had turned out exactly as he'd hoped. He sat on his cot, and keeping a keen eye on Inacio, played with the bandage, fixing it back to his arm the best he could. Later, he would steal into the supply tent and snatch another gauze pad and some tape. In the meantime, he had his antibiotic. He opened the bottle and popped one into his mouth.

Having done all he could for himself, he lay back and closed his eyes, replaying his triumphant revenge. The only thing he hadn't planned on was the little redhead putting up such a nasty fight. He put his fingers to his head, feeling the swollen bump over his ear then ran them down over the dagger-like slash she'd left across his cheek. He had to admire the way she came after him. There were men in Valerón's compound that didn't have half her courage.

As for Owen, he wished he could've seen the expression on his face after his two porters came crashing down around the man. It would have gone a long way in offsetting his loss of putting a bullet in his head. But it was, what it was, and very soon he would execute the end game.

Owen sat catching his breath with his back against the wall looking numbly across the tumbled slabs of stone. For the last hour and a half he had put his anger and rage into building a cairn for his friends.

He closed his eyes, fighting the gnawing headache in his temples, and as he did, felt a cold sweat coming on. Taking a deep breath, he tipped his head back onto the damp wall. *Sorry mates. Know it aint much, but it's da best I can do. Should'a listened ta my gut. Everything 'bout him was wrong. It's all on me.*

Claire coughed beside him and roused him from his musing. He turned toward her, and in the dimmed lantern light, saw her sitting with her hands wrapped around her knees. She hadn't said a word in twenty minutes and the heartbreaking expression on her face mirrored the emptiness inside him.

Finally, Molly's monotone voice broke the silence. "So what now?"

"What'd'ya mean?" Thad muttered.

"Well, help isn't exactly on the way," Molly replied.

"You don't know that," Thad answered.

"No, I don't, but from where it sit, I'm not seeing a happy ending here."

Thad grunted. "You never see a happy ending in anything, so what's new?"

"How would you know?" Molly hissed.

Thad snickered and shot her a scowl. "That's easy, ever take a look at what you read sometime: Fallen Honor, Death Becomes Them—gimme a break! You never see anything except doom and gloom. Get your eyes out of a damn book for once and pay attention to those around you."

"Pay attention to those around me?" Molly said, raising her voice. She bent forward, and fixed him with a savage glare. "Is that what you think?"

"Yes!"

"Well think about this Poppy: while you were down here playing preppy dog, I was up there trying to save Ramirez's life, so you can kiss off."

Thad opened his mouth to reply, but nothing came out. He stared at her a minute, then looked away licking his wounds.

Suddenly, Claire said, "We need to stop bickering and start thinking or we're all going to end up dead." She glanced at Owen then straightened her shoulders and stood."

"Agreed," Owen replied getting to his feet. No one was going to come looking for them. Juan had the element of surprise on his side, and he'd already managed to drive a small wedge between him and his porters. He thought of Manny, and an ugly vision flashed before him. But he couldn't dwell on things he couldn't control. People were depending on him here, so he drove it out of his mind. It was time to move on, but he would not forget. "Okay, ya're da experts here, but

I'm thinking 'less there was a collapse in here back when, there's a way out?"

"That's what I'm thinking," Claire echoed. "And we need to start searching for it." She turned to Thad, blinked and rubbed her temple. After another deep breath, she said, "There should be a seal-stone in here some where. Thad, you're with Owen; Jorge, Molly, you're with me."

"I think we should stay together," Owen said.

"But splitting up, we could cover more territory," Claire argued.

"I know, but right now, I'm real uncomfortable with that."

Claire pursed her lips. "Okay. In the meantime, let's turn the lanterns off. I have a feeling we might need them at some point."

"Right," Owen answered. "We'll use our flashlights."

As Jorge shut the lanterns down, Thad said, "I'm not a cave rat, but I think this is no different than climbing. Let's daisy-chain ourselves together just in case there's a shaft or something we might fall into."

Claire tilted her head in agreement. "Well, rope we have."

Owen eyed Claire, Jorge and Molly as they walked ahead with their flashlights bouncing over the rock walls. They had been skirting the edge of the mammoth tomb for the last fifteen minutes, with no sign of any way out. But that wasn't the only thing Owen was concerned about. In situations like this, it was important everyone play well together. He eyed Thad sidelong having a good idea the argument between the young RA and the girl had more to do with hurt feelings than the situation they were in. At last, he said, "Let it go, mate. I know what it's like when ya have feelings for people an' can't let 'em out. But right now, I need your head in da game. You're da best we got down here."

Thad frowned. "Lately, everyone seems to know how I feel better than me. How is that, huh?"

"Maybe we see things ya don't. Sort'a like da proverbial, seeing-da-forest-through-da-trees."

"I see just fine," Thad muttered.

"Yeah, I know," Owen said as a sharp pain rifled through his brain. He blinked and put his hand to his head.

"You all right?" Thad said.

"Yeah, yeah, I'm okay." Owen said rubbing his temples. He swept his beam over the arching wall ahead and pointed to the seemingly endless stream of cartouches on them. "They were busy little blokes, weren't they? What's all this say?"

"I'm no expert, but from what I can tell, the writings tell the story of an Egyptian armada coming to the Amazon," Thad said. He pointed to a symbol of a man with three stars over his head standing on what looked like a large boat. There was also a woman standing next to him with long dark hair, and around her waist, was a belt of gold.

Owen went forward and looked at it. Although the figures were small, much attention had been paid to a curious ring on one of the man's fingers. He pointed to the serpentine shaped stem, projecting off the top of the band. "Looks like a snake."

"It is," Thad said. "Egyptians were quite fond of them."

Owen nodded and went on, "What's that in his other hand?"

"A leaf. Coca, I guessing," Thad answered. "The writing below it calls it, *The Herb of Ra*, which he was probably sent to bring back to Pharaoh along with a new kingdom to rule."

"An' so, da first drug wars began," Owen muttered. He leaned closer to the cartouche.

Thad nodded. "Maybe so. Anyway, the man's name was Haja-al-amawri. Sound familiar?"

"Christ, ya!"

Thad smiled. "Now, this pic here indicates Haja-al-amawri was near a large city when he learned of a spirit land deep in the forest." Thad aimed his flashlight at a series of cartouches showing a deep valley with the sun hanging above it. Suddenly, he came to a halt. "That's wild."

"What?"

Thad put his hand to the cartouche and traced two white spiral lines rising from the valley floor to the sun. "These lines."

"What're ya talking about?" Owen said.

Thad traced the marks with his fingertips. "These, if I'm reading the text below them right, say, 'Haja-al-amawri dwells in the Dreaming Land awaiting his wife whom he left behind in search of Ra's blessing.'"

Owen grunted. "Whatever that means."

Thad shrugged. "Yeah, right." He shook his head.

Owen started back off to catch up to Claire, Molly and Jorge. When Thad caught back up to him, Owen listened to the RA theorize what the story meant. After listening to the his assumptions, Owen said, "So, ya're thinking what? That this Haja-al-amawri bloke here believes da forest is da throne of da Sun god."

"Something like that," Thad said steering his light to a series of faded cartouches. When a colossal, colonnaded structure appeared on the wall, he stopped and said, "Jesus, that's what we saw in the forest above."

Owen raised his brow.

Thad's eyes widened like a kid in a candy store then ran to fresco and read, "Sacred is the narrow way to Ra within. Blessed are the high one's who know way." He glanced back at Owen. "There's a chamber inside the ziggurat, just like the pyramids."

"Then what's all this?" Owen said.

But before Thad could answer, Claire called back from ahead. "I think we found it!"

Owen averted his flashlight toward her and saw a large wheel-shaped boulder ahead. A minute later, he was standing next to her looking at the hulking stone. "How'd they get this monster in place from da outside?"

"They didn't," she said, as Thad came up behind them.

Owen was dumbfounded. "So they –"

"That's right. They weren't planning on leaving," Claire replied.

"Yikes," Owen muttered. He studied the cartouches that were painted across the face of the stone. Pictures of snakes, birds, animals, people and boats. One showed several men in profile waiting on what appeared to be a queen or a woman of high stature. At last, he said, "I guess being in high places had its draw-backs."

Thad pointed his light over the ground to the other side of the boulder. "You could say that ... Oh-oh."

"What?" Claire said.

"They chocked it!"

"Uh-huh," Claire answered. "It's what they did in the pyramids, why would it be any different here?"

Owen saw the rocks wedged in underneath the stone. "So we just slide 'em out?"

"If it were only that easy," Claire said, panning her light left to right. "See those notches in the floor on either side? Those are there to hold the fulcrum while they worked the *seal* in place. Those chocks are dug right into those notches."

Owen accessed the two and a half meter high stone that weighed at least a thousand kilograms, and said, "So, unless I'm missing something, ya're saying we have ta lift it over 'em."

"Exactly!

Thirty Five

OWEN'S HEADACHE intensified as he tried to figure out a way to move the stone. He blinked, trying to focus, but everything was blurred and shifting, and breathing was getting difficult. No matter how deeply he inhaled, he found it harder and harder to get enough air.

Claire eyed him, concern on her brow. "You're feeling it too, aren't you?"

He nodded and ran his tongue around the inside of his mouth, trying to get rid of the dry, acidic tang. He eyed Thad, the glancing at Claire knowingly, said, "I think there's something down here gasin' us. I can't see straight."

"Could be CO2, although we're not very deep," Thad said.

"Whatever it is, we better figure out how ta move that rock, an' get out of here quick," Owen said, trying to still the panic in his heart. Things were ganging up on them and siphoning away their dwindling chances by the minute. "I'm open ta suggestions ... anyone?"

They were all quiet for a moment, and then it hit Owen. "What about da boat?"

"What about it?" Claire said.

Owen eyed her warily. What he was about to suggest would be blasphemy to a scientist, but their choices were slim and none. "There might be something we could scavenge off it ta make a lever."

"Are you kidding?" Thad gasped. "It's irreplaceable."

"Yeah right," Owen said, "And so are we."

Thad shook his head. "There has to be another way."

"Well, I'm listening," Owen said.

When Thad didn't have an answer, Owen nodded. "What I thought. Look, we gotta make a decision here while there's still time."

When Claire nodded, Thad rolled his eyes. "You can't seriously be thinking about letting him rape that boat, Claire? It's–"

"Our only hope outta here," Claire said, cutting him off. "Unless you wanna hang out with the king and queen."

"And if that's da case," Owen added, "be my guest. Me, I'm all for getting out an' livin' ta tell about it."

Claire said, "What do you have in mind?"

"Well, there's some long planks on da boat," Owen answered. "I'm thinking we can band a few of 'em together an' make us a lever."

"All right then, do it."

"I can't believe this," Thad cried.

"Put a cork in it," Molly said, glaring at Thad.

Claire spun and leveled a withering gaze at Molly, backing her down. She turned to Thad. "We need to all start working together here. Understand?"

Thad stiffened his jaw. "Understood, but I'm going with him when he does the deed."

Owen fought back a wave of dizziness and started off. As they walked, Thad said, "You really think 3,000 year old cedar can stand the stresses of lifting that rock? It'll snap like matchsticks."

"Let's hope ya're wrong, mate" Owen said. "Our biggest problem is at da fulcrum. That's were da stresses are da greatest."

"I suppose you could use a few of those flat rocks Jorge found and make a flitch plate out of it," Thad said.

Owen looked at Thad and patted him on the back. "That's using da old noggin. Excellent idea!"

Ten minutes later, Thad and Owen were at the boat hacking away the knots holding it together. As Thad worked alongside him, he said, "Take it easy! We're here to scavenge, not demolish."

"Right," Owen said, trying to see Thad's point of view. But the grating headache made it a challenge.

As Thad gently freed the board and slid it back, he said, "I feel like a criminal."

"I'm sorry, I know this is hard for ya," Owen said. He crawled ahead toward the prow, scrutinizing every board as he went. *Cedar! Here in the Amazon. Now I've seen everything.* He tapped one of the bottom boards, assessing its condition and pointed to it. "Here's another good one."

"Right," Thad said, looking on with a scowl. "I know you blame her for the death of your friends."

Owen sat back on his heels. "No, I don't, an' we don't need that kind'a talk. Come on now, we need ta pull together."

"Sorry, I'm just really pissed."

"So am I, mate," Owen said, "So am I."

A half hour later, Thad and Owen returned with seven planks, each around four meters long. Claire watched the two of them set the boards down near the seal-stone, and a minute later, they got to work assembling the lever under the lantern light. As Owen lined them up, Thad wrapped the nylon rope around them, drawing them together tight with figure eight knots. Once the planks were bound, Owen selected a couple of choice flat stones Molly had found to place on top and bottom at the lower end of the lever. These were tied on with crisscrossing, overhand knots. At the same time, Jorge busied himself wedging a large rectangular stone into one of the grooves under the large wheel-like stone.

At last, Owen took a deep breath and looked at Claire. "Well, it's da best I can do."

Thad stepped beside him, bent over, and gave it a tug. "It's certainly heavy enough."

"The question is: is it strong enough," Jorge said, coming over.

"Ya, good question. But it's all we got," Owen said. "Take five, while I look things over." He drew away from the team and went over to a nearby pool of dark water to splash his face. As he passed her, Claire saw the anguish on his face. Despite his attempts to keep things light and positive, he was wearing down. They all were. She sucked a deep breath, waited for the world to stop spinning, and walked over to him.

"You Okay?"

"Yeah, yeah," he said, wiping his face with his shirtsleeve.

"You, mister, are a lousy liar," she said. She tried to smile, but failed miserably.

Owen winked. "Ya've noticed that, eh?"

Claire looked back at the stone. "You really think we can move it?"

Owen shrugged. "Don't know, but it's all we got."

Claire coughed and cleared her throat. When she saw him looking back at her with knitted brows, she said, "Just a little dizzy. Comes and goes." She rubbed her temples. But the fact was, she felt like crap.

"Now who's lying?" Owen said.

"Guilty as charged," she replied. She looked into his eyes, and saw the weight of losing his friends bearing down on him. All her feelings of hopelessness, guilt, fear, anger, and remorse over lost opportunities felt trivial and petty. Here was a man fighting for their lives in the face of great sorrow. She tried to think of words to convey her feelings for his loss, but they were all inadequate. Most of all, she wanted to wrap her arms around him, tell him how she felt about him, but not here in this place. Not where death and tragedy lurked in the air. "Hey."

"Yeah?"

"Whatever happens, I want you to know … you've changed me."

His gaze held her tenderly for a moment, and she didn't need to ask what he was thinking. She already knew.

They positioned the lever over the large, rectangular stone. Once they were set, Owen gave the thumbs up and with all their might, they jerked downward, thrusting their weight upon it. The stone groaned, lifted slightly then popped back down. They tried again, but the results were the same.

"It's no use," Thad said after a third try. He let go. "It's too big for us."

Owen took a deep breath. "Let's give it a minute ta catch our breaths. Thad, if we give up we all die. We need everyone pulling here."

"He's right Poppy," Claire said. "I've never known you to be a quitter. Don't start now."

"All right, but I'm running outta gas," Thad said.

The team put their hands on their knees. Claire knew this was it. If they failed, they were all dead. She eyed Owen, and they exchanged knowing glances. With a nod, he winked and roused the team. "Okay, one last time. Everyone, on three!"

He counted down, and with a loud grunt, the group gripped the lever and yanked down for all they were worth. The stone grumbled, and slowly Claire felt it rise until all at once it rolled away and flopped on its side with a jarring thud. But, on the other side stood another stone defying them. Claire bowed her head in exhaustion.

Thad said, "What do we do now?"

Juan pulled the pillow away from Inacio's face and straightened out his shirt. The young porter had put up an admirable fight considering his injuries. Surveying the death scene, he then went about putting the details into making it look like a natural outcome of the concussion. Most important was checking for any evidence that could implicate him. Once he was certain all was well, he positioned the young man in a relaxed position with hands lain over his chest and pillow fluffed under his head. When he was satisfied, he casually strolled out of his tent and surveyed the camp. It was quiet and subdued. Men were busy cleaning tools, stacking wood, and going over their gear. A few were sitting at one of the fold-up tables playing cards. Manny was rummaging around in a pack under the screen tent the Americans were using as a command center. Juan eyed him, and when he was sure no one was looking, darted into Owen's tent. He was certain his communication device was in it somewhere, and maybe he'd get lucky and find a handgun, as the rifle never left Manny's sight.

He dug around the bastard's gear, pulling out clothes, disposable razor blades, toothpaste, and toiletries. A small bag holding a comb dotted with green stones was tossed aside as he dug further down. When he came across a billfold, he opened it, whistled under his breath and pocketed the wad of reals folded inside it.

A minute later, he was unzipping the side pouch, and here, he found a small leather book. He pulled it out and leafed through the pages, skimmed journal entries and set it down, dumbfounded. The man was running weapons to the natives. He didn't know whether to laugh or be pissed. But where was his SCRIBBLER? He stuffed the contents back inside the canvas duffle and sat back on his heels, rubbing his chin.

Was it possible the bastard had it with him? He pulled another pack toward him, but just as he was about to open it, heard voices nearby. He got up slowly. He'd have to wait and come back later. After making sure the area was clear, he snuck out, and headed for the supply tent. On the way, he was intercepted by Manny.

"What happened to your face?" the director said.

Juan stopped. "Nicked myself shaving."

Manny chewed on his cigar, considering him with a long look. "You seem to have a problem nicking yourself. What were you using this time; a hatchet?"

Juan smiled. "You are a very funny man, senhor. No, it is hard to shave with only one hand. You have another one of those I can bum?"

Manny eyed him dubiously as he struck a match, lit up, and drew a long toak. "I am starting to run low. You can have this one," he said, offering it to him.

"Obrigado," Juan said taking it. He puffed on it and exhaled. "Not bad for a turd."

But Manny didn't smile. "So, where were you this morning? When I brought Inacio his breakfast, you weren't there."

"I went for a walk to take my mind off my hand. It was killing me."

"Hmmm … Well, there are butifarras in the mess tent when you are ready for them," Manny said.

"So, how long do you think the Americans will be gone?" Juan said, then leaned to the side and spat.

Manny frowned. "Probably late afternoon. Why?"

"Just curious. Paulo is very anxious about his irmão."

"I know," Manny replied. "Now, if you will excuse me, I am going to go see about him." He took a few steps then turned around. "Oh, and by the way, take care when you are out alone in the early morning. I killed a fer de lance last night behind our tents. I would not want to see you get bit."

"I'll keep that in mind," Juan said, feigning appreciation, but underneath, his muscles tensed as Manny strode away. He patted the weapon under his thick canvas shirt and sneered. He had hoped Inacio's body wouldn't be discovered for a while, but it wasn't critical to what he had in mind for the shrewd director. His stomach rumbled. Part two of his plan was about to begin. In the meantime, he might as well grab a bite.

Thirty Six

J
UAN SLOPPED down the last of his butifarras in the mess tent
while watching the comings and goings of the camp around
him. It was only a matter of minutes until Manny would emerge
from Inacio's tent and come looking for him. But he was prepared. They had no way to prove he'd killed Inacio. He had simply
died from injuries sustained from the fall.

Then he would remind Manny that he had a choice in coming down
into the forest and that he had taken the anthropologist interests over
the man's. That would go a long way in keeping Manny in line. The
rest would be easy. He sipped his black coffee and sat back eyeing
Inacio's tent. Manny had been in there longer than he expected. What
was he doing? Then, finally, the man stepped out, and Juan saw him
call Paulo over. The two had a brief animated exchange, after which
Manny handed him something before starting toward the mess tent at
a leisurely pace. Not quite the reaction Juan was expecting.

He sat up and sucked another gulp of coffee as Manny pulled back
the screen flap. Stepping over to the tea-pot on the propane stove, the
director poured himself a cup of hot water and popped a tea bag into
it. At last he said over his shoulder, "How is your breakfast?"

"It's good," Juan said, suddenly uncomfortable. He resisted the urge
to ask about Inacio and watched Manny grab a plate and load it with
the last of the butifarras. "Still hungry, huh?"

"Oh, no. I have had quite enough. This is for Inacio," Manny answered.

What fucking game are you playing with me, old man? Juan thought. "He's awake then?"

"Si, and hungry again," Manny said matter-of-factly. "It is good to see him getting his appetite back, no? He said he was worried about you, that you were in a lot of pain this morning."

How was Manny able to act as if nothing was wrong? He shrugged. "How thoughtful," he said, and keeping a watchful eye on the director, he peered down at the ragged bandage around his hand. When he saw a strip of gauze hanging loosely from it, he froze. He had repaired the dressing right after he got back from taking care of Owen. When had that happened? At once, he retraced his killing of Inacio, saw in his mind's eye the man's fingers grasping and tearing at his arms. He drained the rest of his coffee and got up, "Why don't I take that plate you fixed to him?"

"No, that is all right; I got it," Manny said as his gaze drifted to Juan's arm. He looked up, reached into his pocket, and pulled out a toothpick. As he put it to his mouth, he said, "I would take care of that bandage before you re-infect your arm. Oh, I did some checking on the Sat-Lynk. It appears the government is not doing any survey work this far south. Must be a secret mission you were on, eh?"

The jig was up and Juan knew it. He looked around, and seeing no one was paying attention, stood up and pulled his pistol out. Jabbing it into the Manny's ribs, he said, "You, amigo, are a little too smart for your own good. We're going to take a walk, and you're going to keep your mouth shut, unless you want more of your men to die."

Manny calmly set Inacio's lunch on the table. "So, it is just as I thought. You killed Inacio."

"Shut up, and move!" Juan hissed.

They walked casually across camp, with Manny leading the way. Juan stayed close, his concealed pistol aimed at the director's back. Once they entered the thicket of heliconia, he said, "You think you are smart, senhor, eh? You think I don't see through you? You are wrong. I see everything."

"Is that so?" Manny said, ducking under an overhanging branch. "Well, then, tell me, how do you expect to get back to do Içá?" Manny continued. "It is a long way, and no one knows it except the boss and myself."

"Do not worry. I have friends coming," Juan said.

"Except the message you sent never made it," Manny said. "It was delayed and erased."

Juan waved a cloud of swarming gnats away from his face. *He's lying, he has to be. Another one of his tactics.* "Shut up!"

"Okay, if you're not worried then neither am I."

"I'm not, old man," Juan said. "Keep moving."

"I see you are not wearing your flack vest. Not worried anymore, eh?"

Juan ignored the comment, but secretly admonished himself for being careless as he pushed aside a palm frond. When something rustled in the brush behind him, he jerked around, ready to fire, only to see a bird flitting in the low branches. He closed his eyes and frowned. Why was this old man getting under his skin, making him nervous? No one had seen them enter the path leading to the hole where he had left Owen and Claire to die, so why was he on edge? He collected himself; determined not to be baited again. He put his mind to taking care of business.

After they had walked some way down the winding, narrow path, Manny spoke over his shoulder. "So, explain to me what this is all about. You owe me that at least, no?"

Juan snorted. Manny was playing every card in the deck to divert his attention, but it wouldn't work, not with him. At last, he said, "I own you nothing except a bullet. Keep moving."

But Manny was persistent. "So, you kill for the fun of it then. I think they have a name for people like you. What is it again?"

"Shut up! You know nothing."

"Then what are you afraid of?" Manny said.

Juan jabbed the barrel of his pistol into Manny's back, itching to pull the trigger. But killing the director so close to camp would complicate things. If Manny were found, then his carefully crafted story of how the local cockroaches had kidnapped him would fall apart.

Manny cleared his throat. "Cat snatched your tongue, eh?"

Juan took a deep breath. "I will say one thing for you, amigo, you face death a lot better than most men I have killed. Fuck it, why not - anything to shut you up." He told Manny then all that had happened down south, and how Owen had ambushed him and his sortie. But the death of Filipe, he kept to himself. "Justice must be made, senhor," Juan said, ending his story.

Manny slowed and glanced over his shoulder, eyeing Juan shrewdly. "And you will exact your revenge, how?"

"It has already been done. They are dead," Juan said, pushing Manny ahead. They walked a moment without either of them saying a word. As they strode along the root-tangled path, Juan wished he could see Manny's face. The death of the white bastard would certainly be hitting him pretty hard. He wiped the sweat off his face with the back of his hand, and as he did so, remembered Manny and Paulo talking outside his tent. "By the way, what was it you were saying to Paulo earlier?"

"You mean just before we started off on our little tramp?"

"Si."

Manny was quiet a moment then said, "I told him his irmão was murdered, probably by you. I showed him a piece of gauze I found in Inacio's blanket, very similar to what is around your wrist," Manny said over his shoulder. "He was not happy and he wanted to kill you right then."

"Which he would have instantly regretted," Juan said, not believing him.

"Anyway, I told him to wait with his irmão until I was sure. I do not like accusing innocent men," Manny said, putting emphasis on the word, 'innocent'. "To comfort him, I gave him a radio so he could listen to all you had to say."

Juan grabbed Manny's shoulder and whirled him around. "You lie! Show me this radio!"

"It is in my pocket. Get it yourself," Manny said, staring back coldly. Juan narrowed his eyes and glared at the iron face looking back. "I do not think you understand. I am the one holding the gun, amigo. Empty your pocket, now!"

Manny's gaze drifted over Juan's shoulder, focusing on something behind them. "Or what? You will shoot me?"

Juan knew what he was up to, and scoffed. "You think you can get me to turn around so you can pounce? Think again! It's a bird. I saw it already. You must think I am an idota."

"Not at all," Manny said, calmly. "You are too smart for such a ruse."

As Juan gauged Manny's curious expression, a feeling of unease came over him. Something was up, and when he heard a branch snap behind him, he knew the man wasn't bluffing. Spinning around, he found Paulo standing a meter away with a machete in his hand. But before he could raise his pistol and fire, his arm was jerked back from behind. The gun went off, and the next thing he knew a searing pain was sucking his breath away. He looked down uncomprehendingly and saw the machete buried in his stomach. Coughed. Tasted blood. The blade pulled back, and was jabbed in again and twisted.

"Die, you piece of shit," Paulo hissed, as he pulled the weapon out.

Juan's vision blurred. The trees spun. Voices echoed in his brain as his legs wobbled and collapsed beneath him. Looking up into the fading sky, he saw Manny's grizzled face slide into view. "I do not know who you are, but you will not do any more harm. May Deus have mercy on your miserable soul." The man's face pulled away, and as Juan's sight dimmed, he heard him say to Paulo, "We will bury him later. Right now, I need to find Owen. I cannot believe he killed all of them.

Thirty Seven

"**N**OW WHAT?" Thad said.

Everyone looked at each other. Claire had no idea what to do. If this was anything like the pyramids in Egypt, there was only one door. Why this one exit had been sealed on both sides was beyond her. She took a deep breath trying to get her wind but couldn't. They were running out of time and everyone knew it.

Finally, Owen said, "I remember reading something somewhere, that there was a shaft inta one of da burial chambers in da Giza pyramid."

"Yeah, but it's too small to crawl through, and nobody knows where it ends up," Thad said.

"Just a thought," Owen said.

Claire bent over. Her head buzzed and it was getting harder to concentrate. Then she looked up. "When I was in the burial vault, there was a lot of text on the wall. I wonder. Thad, let's go back and see what it says. There may be something in it that might be useful."

"Like what? A no exit sign?"

"I don't know, but it's worth a shot," Claire said, ignoring his comment. "Come on, let's go."

They fell in behind her as she traipsed back up the long, dark chamber. She didn't know what to expect, but it was better than waiting around to die. And she was damned if she was going to let Juan get away with what he'd done if she could help it. As she walked, Owen joined her, and though they didn't speak, she knew her sentiments were his as well.

At length, they came to the main chamber. Claire took a moment to collect her strength and struck off up the stairs past the statue of Horus. "It was over here, Thad," she said over her shoulder as she entered into the dark burial vault. Her light played over the wall, revealing the scrolling text and cartouches. They all crowded around Thad as he went about the deciphering the ancient language.

For several minutes Thad went back and forth over the ancient symbols and writing until at last he pointed to a cartouche. "Ok, that's the High One, but here's what I don't understand: she's walking over Anubis? It doesn't make sense. The ancients believed they had to go through Anubis to reach Ra?"

"Yeah. I read the same thing. Can we be reading this wrong?" Claire said, trying to think. But her head was killing her. She gritted her teeth and tried to concentrate. "But what else could it be?"

"Hey, Luv," Owen said, bending over beside her. "I don't think we have time ta debate things here. Just go with your gut."

Claire looked at him. He was fighting for every breath just like she was. She turned back, wondering why this High One would be passing over Anubis?"

She pointed to the cartouche. "Why is she doing that?" Claire muttered.

"I don't know," That said. "Weird."

Then Claire had an idea. She focused on the text, reading it three times to make sure she understood it. The symbols multiplied before her and things began to spin. Closing her eyes, she waited a moment for the world to come to a stop, then refocused, and went on, "Listen! 'And the High One ... will rise, and the way ... will be made clear ... clear for her over the bridge ... of Duat to the Land of ... the land of Dreams.' "

She looked back toward the sarcophagus, and all eyes followed her. "And she shall rise," Claire muttered. "Rise, rise, what does that mean?"

She staggered over to the stone tomb, and shining her light down on it, saw the painted face of a woman she'd seen standing in the temple in the Hajamawri valley.

Thad came beside her. "Look familiar?" He said.

"Yeah," Claire replied. But there was no time to marvel at it. She shook her head, fighting overwhelming fatigue and dizziness. "When someone rises," she said, "it's usually from sleep, right?"

"Okay."

"Which might mean, you get up." She paused, as a notion hit her. It can't be that simple. Or can it? She looked up at the questioning looks around her. "It's not a metaphor–it's literal! She gets up!"

"From da dead? What's that have ta do with anything?" Owen said.

Claire closed her eyes as the pounding between her temples boomed and put her knuckle to her mouth. "There's a shaft in here somewhere. Start shining your lights up onto the ceiling."

"Won't it be like Thad said, too small?" Owen said.

"Maybe, but our choices are limited. If you have a better idea, I'm all ears."

After a short debate, Owen and Thad started off to the far end of the expansive vault, playing their lights upward. But all he saw was rock and drawings. Then suddenly from behind he heard Molly call out. "Over here!"

He turned the beam of his flashlight in her direction to see her and Jorge standing by a dark passage leading out of the room. "Hang on, Molly," Claire said from the other end of the room.

Owen traded hopeful glances with Thad then headed toward them, coming up just in time to meet Claire. They ducked through the passage, and a moment later they were standing beside Molly. What he saw when he shined his light ahead, stole his breath.

Thad whistled as he shined his light into a broad round chamber. "That goes down a ways," he said, stepping out onto a rocky ledge.

"Careful, Poppy," Claire said, coming beside him and clutching his sleeve.

"I think we found Duat," Thad said.

Claire ran her light over the jagged walls and narrow ledge that ran around the perimeter of the room. On the other side was a narrow pinnacle of rock that rose up and leapt out over the abyss. A couple meters above it, was a dark opening. "And she rises, just like the text says," Claire muttered. "I bet that leads up to the ziggurat above."

"Maybe," Owen said, "'cept none of us know how ta fly."

Thad joined his light with Claire's. "There's a lip near the bottom of it, see? If there's a handhold above—"

"What're ya suggesting, mate?" Owen said, cutting him off.

Thad shot him a knowing glance. When Owen frowned, Thad said, "You have a better suggestion?"

Owen couldn't think of one. He gauged his remaining strength, wondering if he could pull himself up into the opening, and then what? One wrong move and it was curtains. He sucked a deep breath. "Nope. All right, best get at it."

"Where're you going?" Thad said.

"Where's it look like?"

"No disrespect, but you have zero chance of making it," Thad snapped.

Owen bristled. *You have no idea what I'm capable of.* But he held his retort back. Arguing would only exhaust him. "Thanks for ya concern; but I got it."

As he started for the narrow path beside them, Claire reached out and snagged his arm. "Owen, Thad's right. Look at that hole. It's barely large enough for Thad to fit up. I'm sorry, but he's our best chance. Remember, he's a climber, and we need all the skill we can get right now."

Owen frowned. He had the strength, but she had a good point. The shaft was a tight fit and he was no climber. He eyed Thad, considering the kid's strength. The last thing he wanted was to see him plunge to a certain death. Then again, they were heading for certain death if something didn't happen, and soon. "All right, go for it."

Thad smiled grimly and took a deep breath. He looked at Molly as if making his peace with her, then started toward the harrowing path lying behind Owen and Claire. As he passed her, Claire reached out and pulled him to her. "God speed, okay?"

Thad smiled. "I'll be okay."

"You had better be," Claire replied.

Giving Thad a wink, he said, "See ya up top mate."

Thad nodded, and started off around the perilous ledge that was no more than half a meter in places until at last he made it to the narrow outcrop springing up and over the chasm. Standing before it, he shined his light up into the dark shaft above and called over. "Okay, here goes."

Claire eyed Owen warily, bit her lip. "Great, take your time."

Owen heard Molly gasp behind him as Thad took his first step onto the arching stone. Jorge murmured the rosary under his breath. One thing was for sure: the kid had guts going out on that pinnacle of rock. The question was, could it get him close enough to make a jump and grab the lip of the shaft? From where Owen and Claire stood it appeared so, but who knew until Thad was actually there. Owen assessed Thad's odds of making the leap safely with every meter he climbed, until at last he knew it was insane to try it. He nudged Claire and shook his head.

She bowed her head then called out. "Poppy, Poppy, come back! It's too far."

But Thad replied, "I can make it."

"No, Poppy. Please come back!"

"For what? To die of asphyxiation? No, I'd rather go this way."

Powerless to stop him, they watched aghast as Thad stepped to the very edge of the precipice. Back up a step. *That's right. Gauge it. Take a breath,* Owen thought. *Yeah, yeah, that's it. All right ... and ... now!*

As if Thad had heard him, he vaulted ahead and upward over the abyss. Molly shrieked. In the eternity of seconds that followed, Owen watched Thad's hands shoot up and catch the lip of the shaft. "Hang on, goddamn it," Owen whispered as Thad swung violently forward. As Thad's grunt echoed through the chamber, Owen clutched his fists and willed him not to let go. There was a scuff and then silence as Thad swung back. Owen knew if he were going to lose it, it would be on the backward swing. But Thad held on and a moment later was pulling himself up into the shaft.

"He made it!" Claire cried, putting her hand to her mouth. "He made it!"

"Yeah, yeah, he did." Owen said raising his arms and pumping the air with his fists. Claire returned a hopeful expression, and tilted her head toward the opening of the burial vault behind them.

"We better conserve our energy," she said.

"Yeah, right," Owen replied. "Come on, Molly, Jorge let's get back in.

"You think he'll make it?" Molly whispered as she shuffled along ahead of him.

"Yeah, I do," Owen answered, hoping he was right.

They found places to sit on the floor with their backs against the wall. Over the next hour they talked about family and friends, things they were going to do, anything to avoid their dark thoughts. But eventually they ran out of things to say.

In the shadows though, Owen could hear Molly and Jorge whispering their love for one another. He reached beside him and feeling Claire's hand, took it into his own and squeezed it.

She stirred. "Well, we've done all we can."

"Yeah, yeah." He paused re-thinking the choices he had made on this expedition, and shook his head. "I'm sorry."

"For what?"

"Ya know, all this. If I—"

"Shhh," Claire said, putting her finger to his lips. "Look, I know what you're thinking and you have nothing to feel bad about. You can't always be the hero." She paused. "All my life people have tried to tell me what I can and can't do. I said, 'No! I can do it myself. I don't need your help or anyone else's.' But you know what? Being the hero sometimes means making the hard decisions and stepping back and letting others do the things you can't."

"Really?" Owen said.

"Yeah. Now be quiet," she said.

He put his arms around her shoulder and stroked her hair, thinking about what she said as she nestled her head against his chest. Since Calen had died, he had driven himself to be the perfect leader, but in the end he had failed miserably. Except Claire believed in him. At least, that's how he read it. He felt her head droop forward and slide down onto his lap; listened to her shallow breathing. She was a good woman, better than he deserved. He cleared his throat and muttered, "I love ya, Claire. Maybe next time around, eh?"

Then he closed his eyes to the sullen darkness, ignoring the far away voices.

Thirty Eight

OWEN FELT the sensation of being tugged in the inky darkness surrounding him. Suddenly, he was cold and a far-off voice echoed in his ears. "Set him on the ground over there, next to the senora." A moment later he felt a weight pressing down on him and the voice became clearer. "He's coming around." As warmth seeped through him, a dull ache grew in his head. He shuddered, then all at once, the darkness peeled away and he was looking up at a shadowy face within a waving sea of green.

He coughed, and after several deep, heaving breathes of warm, tangy forest air, he heard the familiar voice of his old friend, Manny. "Ah, you are back with the living. Lucky for you amigo, because I draw the line on where I put my lips."

Owen blinked, coughed again, and brought his hands to his head, pressing them against his temples.

"Don't try to get up yet," Thad said, suddenly beside him. "Your system is still adjusting to the fresh air up here."

Owen nodded; glad to see Thad was alive. As Thad checked him over, Owen looked around. Not seeing Claire, he reached up and grasped Manny's arm. "Claire–"

"Is all right, see for yourself," Manny said, patting his shoulder and pointing to his left.

Owen propped himself up on his elbow and saw her on the ground several feet from him staring back. "I thought we were done for."

"Me too," Thad said, pushing him back down gently.

"What 'bout Molly an' Jorge?" Owen said, wincing.

"Si, they made it as well," Manny replied.

But the look on Manny's face troubled Owen. "Something I should know, mate?"

Manny dipped his head. "Inacio. He–"

"He what?" Owen demanded, trying to sit up.

"He's dead," Paulo growled, suddenly beside him. "The piece of shit, Juan, killed him in his own bed."

Manny waved Paulo away, then looked at Claire. At length, he stared off into the distance then finally turned back to Owen. "You and I, we have gone through much over the years, and you have been an irmão to me, but now I think this shall be my last tramp into the woods. Too much has happened to those I care about. Good men have died, men I have known since they were crianças. Sooner or later, Owen, you will meet the same fate. Is that what you want?" Manny turned his gaze on Claire. "I do not blame you, senora for what has happened, for I have as much to do with it as anyone, but now it is time to decide what is the right thing to do."

Claire bit her lip, tears running down her face.

Manny leaned over Owen and whispered, "Stop trying to fix the world, my friend, before it is too late." He stood, and putting a cigar to his lips, walked over to where Paulo was coiling rope. Owen thought about what Manny had said. He was right. It was time to face down the past that had chased him incessantly.

The entire encampment met in a small clearing some distance away from the tall reeds that guarded the banks of the winding stream. Claire stood silently beside Owen within the whine and oppressive heat of the forest as Manny eulogized their fallen friends that were buried in the sandy soil of the Amazon forest. Over the graves were piles of stones Paulo had carefully stacked, and planted within the stones were three wooden crosses draped with yellow-flowered vines found by Molly and Jorge.

As for Juan, they buried him as fittingly as they could find within themselves to do, well away to the south. There was no cross or marker standing above the devil that had caused so much pain and grief. When Manny finished, he crossed himself, kissed his crucifix, and strode away, his shoulders sagging with the weight of the dead. One by one, the men drifted back to camp, which had been broken down and packed up, ready for their long walk back to Santo Antonio do Içá.

Finally, it was just Owen, Claire, and Paulo left standing around the three mounds. Owen stirred beside her, and she felt his hand start to tug her away. She looked up and shook her head. She needed to make peace with Paulo. Owen nodded at her unspoken words and moved off quietly.

After some time, Claire cleared her throat and, finding the words in Portuguese, softly said, "Paulo? I never intended for any of this to happen."

"I am sure you did not, senora," Paulo retorted. "But this did not have to happen. I do not know what I will tell our mãe. She will be curação quebrado. Leaving him here like this burns my heart, but there is nothing I can do."

"I would carry him back for you if I could," Claire said, her throat tightening.

"But you can't. You can do me a favor though," Paulo said.

"Yes, anything."

Paulo came over beside her and looked at her intently. "The next time you think you have to force people to do your bidding, think about my irmão. Then perhaps you will change your mind, hmmm?"

Claire nodded. "I won't be asking anyone to do anything again, I assure you."

"Good, see that you do not." Paulo said. "For my part, I will try to remember your care for him. He liked you. Said you were kind and that you did not talk down to him like other Americans who come down here. Now, I would like to be alone here if you do not mind."

Claire pursed her lips. It was the closest thing to forgiveness she could hope for from Paulo.

As she shuffled back to camp, she considered what he said. The man was right. She had badgered people when there was something she had wanted. Was that why Jason left her? Maybe. She didn't know anything anymore, except for one thing: her feelings for Owen. She had grown to love him, plain and simple, but admitting it to him would be another matter.

She turned back toward camp, debating her future. As she walked under the draping lianas and tree ferns, she bowed her head, wondering what it would be like living with him. Would they end up in the same tugs of war she and Noah had their entire marriage? Could she endure living in his laid-back world?

She considered what was left of her career. People who handed out lots of money liked results. Obviously, there would be no more grants and no more sabbaticals. That meant her career was pretty much dead on arrival when she got back. But she would not fall into the easy solution with Owen. Too many times in the past she had run from one fire right into another.

Just then, she heard a snap of a tree branch to her right. She looked up and saw a young Hajamawri hunter watching her. For a minute she stared across the distance between them, taking in his cocoa complexion and almond shaped face until he slid back into the thicket and was gone. As she stood there amid the whine of insects with the image of the boy's face in her head, Owen's words echoed back. "We've changed them by just being here." She sighed, and seeing Owen in her mind's eye, smiled. *What I didn't expect was you changing me.*

As Claire stashed her limited notes on the Hajamawri people into her knap sack, she sighed. She knew she was doing the right thing, but it was hard. She wanted more than anything to vindicate herself to her colleagues, show them they were wrong. So, what was she going to do when she got back home? She tried to think of something meaningful going forward, but she just couldn't see that far ahead. The future felt so uncertain. Again, she mused what life might be like if she decided to take up with Owen. But she had never been a good judge of what love was or what it meant when it came to men.

Suddenly she sensed someone coming up behind her. She turned around to find Poppy looking back at her with a guarded expression. He set his backpack down beside him and said, "I know this is gonna sound crazy, but hear me out. I'm in no hurry to get back, and my family, what there is of it, are all back in Greece."

He paused and Claire knew where he was going. It wasn't going to happen, but she decided to let him say his piece. "Anyway, the Hajamawri have a language they can't even read. I could teach it to them, Claire. And in the process, study them. Sooner or later, someone is going to find out about them. It's bound to happen, and then what? Isn't it better to learn as much as we can about them before it happens?"

"I can't disagree with you Poppy," Claire said, "but it's not that easy. I'm responsible for you, and people will ask questions about your where-a-bouts. I'm afraid the answer is, no. You need to come back with us."

"I disagree. It's no one's business what I decide to do or not, and if anyone asks, you can tell them so. If you really need to give them an answer, tell them I decided to leave school and do a little living. It's my decision, Claire. No one else's. I'm not coming, and you can't make me."

"Is this about Molly?"

Thad looked off. "No, not all of it anyway." He paused. "Claire, I need this. I need to have something in my life that's meaningful."

"What about your thesis? Are you just walking away from it?"

Thad shook his head. "Just putting it on hold? Haven't you ever put anything on hold?"

Claire opened her mouth to disagree, but knew her denial would be a lie. She had been putting relationships on hold for most of her life. But Thad wasn't talking about relationships and she knew there was nothing she could do to prevent him from staying. Finally, she said, "How do you know they want you here? You're playing a dangerous game."

"Life *is* a dangerous game, Claire. I want to play. I don't want to be sitting on the sidelines and wake up one day to realize what I've missed."

Claire drew breath. "Well then, I guess you're on your own. One thing I insist on though, is your staying in contact with someone. Take the Sat-Lynk. There's four more lithium batteries left. If you use them judiciously, they should hold out for quite a while, enough so that if you change your mind, you can call for help."

"Noah will have a fit. And how are you gonna pay for it?"

"Don't worry. God knows I'm screwed anyway. How much more can they do to me? Now, you'll need a contact person. I could–"

Thad shot her a lopsided grin. "Thanks, but I already have one."

"Who ?," Claire said.

"Molly."

Claire felt her jaw drop. "Molly?"

"Yeah. Another news flash for you. Seems when they get back to the States she's applying for a visa to come back with Jorge in the fall. They'll be living in Manaus."

"Oh, really?" Claire said. Noah is gonna have a cow over that.

"I can imagine, but that's the plan. I'd love to be a fly on the wall when Noah hears about that," Thad said, his grin growing wider.

"I bet you would. Unfortunately, I think I'm going to have a front row seat." She laughed and pulled him into a hug. "You take care of yourself, you hear?"

"I plan on it."

Three days later, they had put fifty kilometers behind them. In another three days or so, they would near the shores of the Amazon. Owen took up the rear of the slogging column as it trod through the thick understory. Beside him walked Claire, tramping pole in hand. She had been quiet since they struck out and, though he pinned it chiefly on the deaths of their friends, he felt there was something more, as if there was some looming dread upon her.

If it was dread, then it was mutual. Every step he took, brought him one step closer to saying good-bye to a woman he had come to love. He stepped over a fallen log. "So, what are ya gonna do after ya get back ta da states?"

"A mountain of reports," Claire replied. "One thing's for sure, I won't be getting any more grants. You think Thad will be okay down here? I mean, it's not like I had a choice. He was going to do what he wanted anyways."

"Yeah, he'll be fine," Owen said, though he had strong reservations against it. But then, hadn't he once made the same decision Thad was making right now? He survived, so why couldn't Thad? Then again, he'd had previous exposure to how hard life could be in the forest.

"I hope you're right," Claire said. She was quiet a moment, then said, "So, what about you? What's next in your future?"

He shrugged, not really sure what he was going to do, nor did he want to think about it. He pushed aside a branch and thought about what Manny had said. He didn't know how to begin what he wanted to say, or even if he had the right to say it. She had her life and he had his, and they were as far apart as the moon and the stars. But the thought of never seeing her again was crushing him. He had hardly slept the last few nights thinking about it. He drew breath and came to a halt. "Probably'll head back home after I clean things up in Lima."

"Oh?"

"Yeah. Have a couple of visits ta make ta da families of da lads we left behind." He looked away, unable to face her, then came to a halt. It was now or never if he was ever going to tell her how he felt. Clearing his throat, he said, "Hey, Luv, got a minute?"

Claire turned around and looked back at him curiously. "Sure, what's up?"

He waited for the troop to get far enough ahead and then said, "You know me, man of few words an' all. Anyway, I need ta say something 'fore I lose my nerve."

Claire cocked a brow. "Okay."

Owen felt his gut twist. "Ummm ... ya think we could ... could ever, ya know ... stand each other long enough ta make a go of it, hypothetically speaking, of course?"

Claire eyed him wryly. "What's on your mind, Jungle Boy?"

"Well, I have a spread on da North Island. T'ain't much, but it's quiet an' it's not far from da Uni. I was thinking maybe ya might fit in there."

"Owen."

"Yeah, right. Crazy idea. Forget I mentioned it."

But Claire reached out and took his hand. "You know, in the beginning I wondered if the two of us could survive a whole day without killing each other."

"Me too," he chuckled, finding it hard to breath. The words were right on the cusp, but they wouldn't come.

Claire eyed him for a moment and he wondered what she was thinking. At last she said, "And I thought the same thing. But now, I wonder if I could spend a day without you."

Owen took in her beatific face, felt his heart race. Gathering courage, he looked at her and said, "Yeah?"

"Yeah."

Owen licked his lips. "What would you say if I said ... ummm ... I ... I love ya?"

Claire's eyes widened. "That depends. Do you?"

Owen swallowed. "Yeah, I think I do. Ya're da first thing that's making my heart beat in a long time."

The words hung suspended between them like the sparkling morning mist until Claire put her hands to his cheek and broke the silence. "I guess it's mutual then."

"Yeah?"

"Yeah, yeah," Claire said as a tiny grin spread across her face.

He pulled her into him, planting a long tender kiss on her lips. When they parted, a twinge raced through his jaw making him wince.

Claire tapped him on the cheek. "You screw that kisser of yours up and I'm gonna be pissed."

He rolled his eyes. "Right, Luv." Gazing back at her, he added, "Ya sure 'bout this?"

Claire nodded. "Nothing's sure in this world." She flashed him a broad smile. "Come on, Jungle boy, we're falling behind," she said wriggling out of his arms.

He pulled her back and nuzzled her. "I'm in a lotta shite, ain't I?"

Claire giggled, pulled his hat down over his eyes, and said, "Oh, yeah. But no worries, sweet as."

About the Author

Ron is a practicing architect living in upstate New York. An avid hiker and photographer, he has traveled to Nepal, New Zealand and throughout the United States, Alaska and Hawaii collecting ideas for character driven stories of romance and adventure. Other novels by Ron are:

The Lion of Khumjung, situated in the majestic Himalayas of Nepal
Loving Neil, placed on the Oregon coast and Willamette Valley
Starting Over, which takes up where Loving Neil leaves off.

All of these spellbinding stories can be found on Amazon for Kindle, and Barnes and Noble for Nook.

Connect with Ron via Facebook at R.J. Bagliere or on the World Wide Web at: www.rjbagliere.com

Manufactured by Amazon.ca
Bolton, ON